Praise for *The Memory Artists*

Winner of the Canadian Authors Association Award

Shortlisted for the Rogers Writers' Trust Fiction Prize

Shortlisted for the Sunburst Award

Shortlisted for the Hugh MacLennan Prize for Fiction

Shortlisted for the WordsWorthy Award

"Combines smartness with wisdom... Almost absurdly inventive."
—David Mitchell, author of *Cloud Atlas*,
in *The Daily Telegraph* Books of the Year review (U.K.)

"*The Memory Artists* is wonderful. Rich and humane, a repository of culture worth remembering, and a moving elaboration on the simple truth that we should do good for others."
—Colin McAdam, author of *Some Great Thing*

"A model of inventiveness."
—*Times Literary Supplement* (U.K.)

"All the hallmarks of [Moore's] fiction are here. They include an ability to create engaging characters, and a fine balance of warmth, insight and eviscerating humour."
—*The Independent* (U.K.)

"Ingenious... mesmerizing... reading it is like immersing oneself in a warm bath of words and ideas. There are many rich nuggets buried in *The Memory Artists*."
—*The Gazette* (Montreal)

"A journey of fleeting moments and repetitive scenes, juxtaposing various shades of recollection with a dance of words... *The Memory Artists* is a marvel."

—*Edmonton Journal*

"All the ingredients of an entertaining, seductive mystery... Moore repeatedly displays his ability to draw characters through subtle gestures."

—*Quill & Quire*

"Infused with the same wit, verve and zany imagination that energises *Prisoner in a Red-Rose Chain*... The sections that deal with Stella's Alzheimer's are wonderfully written and genuinely moving."

—*Literary Review of Canada*

"Complex, ambitious structure... Moore should be commended for his inventiveness."

—*The Globe and Mail* (Toronto)

"Virtuoso wit... Pythonesque (as in Monty, not lethal serpent)... crawling with tragic irony."

—*Mirror* (Montreal)

"A hilarious yet poignant book about a young genius trying to deal with his mother's Alzheimer's... Entertaining and intelligent."

—*Flare*

"Ingenious... A brainy follow-up to *Red-Rose Chain*."

—*Montreal Review of Books*

"A novel that pushes at the edges of expectations... [that] dares to be different."

—*Edmonton Journal*

"The winner of the Commonwealth Prize has again proven his talent for wry commentary... Moore's clever, complicated construction testifies to his ability and broad imagination."

—*Winnipeg Free Press*

"Dazzlingly learned... The results of Moore's novelistic experiments are the more interesting for being unpredictable."

—*Books in Canada*

"Twisted, tragicomic and extremely entertaining... *The Memory Artists* is one of those few novels that can pack humour, pathos, satire, love, friendship, hope and cynicism all in one volume... Like *Life of Pi*, *The Memory Artists* is one of those tales too fantastic to be true, yet so convincingly told that we can almost believe it. By turns puzzling, heartbreaking and laugh-out-loud funny, Jeffrey Moore's witty prose will leave the reader out of breath at the end, wondering what the hell just happened."

—*The Link* (Montreal)

"Moore's comic genius is undisputed... The oddball relationship between the son who can't forget and the mother who can't remember is fraught with hope and laughter... Ribald and compelling, the humorist is always erudite and there many hilarious sequences that left me aching for more."

—*Hour* (Montreal)

"Jeffrey Moore's characters are brilliant and infuriating. Despicable and seductive. *The Memory Artists* is one of the few contemporary novels I plan to read again."

—*The StarPhoenix* (Saskatoon)

"A metafictive puzzle box, a carefully structured collage of narrative voices... The novel is a delight... Challenging, often beautiful, and frequently inspired narrative play."

—*Straight* (Vancouver)

"Genuinely moving."

—*The Vancouver Sun*

"The story is unforgettably human... [It] leaves the reader spellbound."

—*Scotland on Sunday* (U.K.)

"It is not often that I truly cannot decide whether a tale is fact or fiction... Jeffrey Moore uses Noel's genius and synaesthesia to offer beautiful descriptions of luridly coloured (and memory dysfunctional) characters, as well as his experience of his mother's disease to portray the agony of watching a loved one's inevitable decline. He also finds time to delve into the sometimes murky world of medical research and comment on the role of medicine as an interface between science and art... Wonderfully intense."

—*The Lancet* (U.K.)

"There is a warmth and hope—even love—that infuses the relationships between the characters, all in their different ways locked in their personal prisons."

—*Morning Star* (U.K.)

"A challenging book, bristling with scientific and literary references from Feynman to Baudelaire by way of Nietzsche and Rossetti, this will not fail to make a huge impact."

—*The Good Book Guide* (U.K.)

PENGUIN CANADA

THE MEMORY ARTISTS

Born in Montreal, JEFFREY MOORE was educated at the University of Toronto and the Sorbonne. He works as a translator and lectures at the University of Montreal. He was awarded the Commonwealth Writers' Prize for his first novel, *Prisoner in a Red-Rose Chain*, which has been optioned by Valkyrie Films.

Also by Jeffrey Moore

Prisoner in a Red-Rose Chain

The Memory Artists
Jeffrey Moore

PENGUIN
CANADA

PENGUIN CANADA

Published by the Penguin Group

Penguin Group (Canada), 90 Eglinton Avenue East, Suite 700, Toronto, Ontario, Canada M4P 2Y3
(a division of Pearson Penguin Canada Inc.)

Penguin Group (USA) Inc., 375 Hudson Street, New York, New York 10014, U.S.A.
Penguin Books Ltd, 80 Strand, London WC2R 0RL, England
Penguin Ireland, 25 St Stephen's Green, Dublin 2, Ireland (a division of Penguin Books Ltd)
Penguin Group (Australia), 250 Camberwell Road, Camberwell, Victoria 3124, Australia
(a division of Pearson Australia Group Pty Ltd)
Penguin Books India Pvt Ltd, 11 Community Centre, Panchsheel Park, New Delhi – 110 017, India
Penguin Group (NZ), cnr Airborne and Rosedale Roads, Albany, Auckland 1310, New Zealand
(a division of Pearson New Zealand Ltd)
Penguin Books (South Africa) (Pty) Ltd, 24 Sturdee Avenue, Rosebank, Johannesburg 2196, South Africa

Penguin Books Ltd, Registered Offices: 80 Strand, London WC2R 0RL, England

First published in a Viking Canada hardcover by Penguin Group (Canada), a division of Pearson Penguin Canada Inc., 2004
Published in this edition, 2005

1 2 3 4 5 6 7 8 9 10 (WEB)

Canada Council **Conseil des Arts**
for the Arts **du Canada**

We acknowledge the support of the Canada Council for the Arts which last
year invested $21.7 million in writing and publishing throughout Canada.

Nous remercions de son soutien le Conseil des Arts du Canada, qui a investi
21,7 millions de dollars l'an dernier dans les lettres et l'édition à travers le Canada.

Conseil des arts
et des lettres
Québec

ISBN 0-14-301749-7

Library and Archives Canada Cataloguing in Publication data available upon request

British Library Cataloguing in Publication data available

Visit the author's website at **www.jeffreymoore.org**
Visit the Penguin Group (Canada) website at **www.penguin.ca**

To the memory of my parents,
and to Marlène

The Memory Artists

May memory restore again and again
The smallest color of the smallest day:
Time is the school in which we learn,
Time is the fire in which we burn ...

—Delmore Schwartz

Foreword

What follows is a true story. For over twenty years I studied a fascinating individual, a hypermnesic synaesthete referred to as "NB" in my numerous monographs and handbooks. Near the end of our relationship, in the winter/spring of 2002, NB and his mother (SB) came into contact with three participants (NXB, SD, JJY) in memory experiments I was conducting or overseeing. This contact proved serendipitous, the pharmacological equivalent of throwing five volatile compounds into a crucible and coming up with a miracle drug.

The professional writer-translator assigned to recount their story has combined "dramatic reconstructions" with interviews, laboratory notes and diary entries. These records have not been altered, even when unflattering to me personally; in the interests of science, and as a matter of historical record, I have considered it my duty to disguise nothing and suppress nothing. Because post-postmodernism is not my "bag" (my slang may not be current) and English not my "strong suit" (my mother tongues are French and German), I have made only minor revisions to the prose, excising weak or superfluous passages when sure that excision would improve, and bolstering the text with brief endnotes (keep a bookmark in page 299!).

And now the obvious question. Why *another* book on this scientific odyssey, at least the third in the past year? Everyone knows that a ground-breaking discovery in the field of memory was made under my enlightened auspices. Everyone knows that for this I was awarded a prestigious Scandinavian prize. Mere hours after my return from Europe, however, controversy began to swirl like fumes from a poisonous gas. Blinded, it would appear, by the demonry of a mythomaniacal "whistle-blower," three American newspapers, in serpentine fashion, have accused me of taking credit for a discovery I did not make—and of professional conduct tantamount to murder.

Now semi-retired, my glory days behind me, I wish neither to tarnish NB's reputation (in his way, the young man was a genius) nor burnish my own. Before sinking, however, into that black pit of forgetfulness, the final amnesia, I wish to set the record straight—for my wife, for my daughter, and for the history of medicine.

ÉMILE VORTA, M.Litt., MD, PhD
Neuropsychologist and Professor Emeritus
Department of Experimental Psychology, University of Quebec
Editor-in-Chief, Éditions Memento Vivere
writeaprisoner.com

Chapter 1
"NB"

Most people want to learn how to remember more; for Noel Burun, the big task, the most burdensome, was to learn how to forget. Not only the painful things in life, which we all want wiped away, but things in general. For whenever Noel heard a voice or read a word, multicoloured shapes would form inside his head that served as markers or maps, helping him to recollect, in the minutest detail, an emotion, a mood, a tone of voice, the words themselves—of events that happened up to three decades ago.

Back in 1978, for example, when they came to tell him his father was dead, this is what lit up Noel's nine-year-old brain:

A dry and crumbly voice like kitty litter ... [turning into] a pockmarked strip of tarnished brass, which tapered swordlike, seemed to disappear, then reappeared as a blood-red pendulum. It began to sway, in brighter and brighter reds, blindingly, and then a change, another voice, a spongy yolk-yellow blob with throbbing burnt-rose rings. A louder, higher voice interrupted, a cruciform shape, cranberry at its nave, the lightness fading from the centre outwards so that the edges appeared pearl white. Another voice, brassy and belching like a bass trombone, and a streak of lightning, jagged-edged and barium yellow, split the sky of my brain in two. Slowly, the serrations melted away, the yellow disintegrating into pulsating steel, and it felt like a dagger had pierced my spine. Then the gravelly voice again from the man in front of me, the tarnished brass and then ... silence, against a backdrop of Etch-A-Sketch grey. The "dead mood," I used to call it, the lull before things returned to normal. I opened my eyes: my mother was speaking, her throat strangling each syllable. A black-suited man from Adventa Pharmaceuticals was trying to comfort her, while two moustachioed men in navy blue stared at me ...[1]

Especially when he was younger and didn't know how to stop them, these images could explode like endlessly exploding fireworks, triggering more and more colour patterns and memory clusters, carrying him so far adrift, so far into the back alleys of his universe that he had trouble following even the simplest conversation. Unless it was passive communication, like watching television, Noel needed to *absorb* a person's voice, experience the distinct colours and shapes, before he could decipher the words themselves.

Not surprisingly, everyone thought Noel was off his head, and that was fine with him. His mother loved him, his father loved him, and because of the colours in his head he was able to miss more school than all his classmates combined. The images, moreover, had a practical purpose: although I've got little else going for me, Noel often thought, I've got a fantastic memory. Which sometimes comes in handy.

When he did go to school his classmates taunted him mercilessly ("It would've been better," one of them confided, "if you'd never been born"), but eventually they got used to his vacant spells and fog. "Commander Noel" was on one of his "spacewalks." His teachers, especially at first, would react with annoyance or sarcasm: "Is this, ahem, one of your convenient periods of mental unemployment, my dear Burun?" And everyone would laugh. When he told them, in private, about the colliding colours, they immediately suspected drug abuse: it sounded very much like LSD or mescaline or some newfangled hallucinogen. Was this a matter for the authorities? And so the rumours spread. The brains and dweebs avoided him, whereas people like Radar Nénon, the school's first acid-popping punk, took a sudden liking to him. He'd finally found someone who saw stranger things than he did.

"Schizophrenics have abnormal colour perceptions," one teacher told him, while another said that "It's got to be aphasia or autism, one or the other." The school nurse, a chronically irate Welsh widow, had another explanation: "You've got a definite defect, son. Deprived of oxygen in the womb perhaps—or dropped headfirst off the delivery table." But it was none of the above, as he soon found out from a friend of his father's, a renowned Montreal neurologist named Émile Vorta.

"Congratulations," said the doctor with unaccountable good cheer, in French, after a mind-deadening battery of perception and memory tests. "You're one in twenty thousand. You're blessed—although sometimes you may feel cursed—with a complex sensitivity known as *synaesthesia*."[2]

Why is he so happy? Noel wondered, as the doctor shook his little hand. Because he can experiment on me like one of his chimpanzees?[3]

"You're the first male synaesthete I've met. Now, I want you to do something that will help us both a great deal. I want you to keep a diary. Do you know what a diary is?"

"Yes, I already keep one."

"A diary is a book in which you write down things that happened to you during the day. Or the events of your past. Or in your dreams—"

"Once I dreamt I was walking through this gigantic crossword puzzle—"

"Or the colours and shapes you see in your head when people talk to you. And I'd like to see it at the end of every month. Do you understand?"

"Sometimes when people talk I wish I had a decoder ring—"

"Does anyone else in your family have anything like ... what you have?"

Noel paused. "Why, is there a genetic component associated with this condition, Doctor?"

Dr. Vorta paused. There is more to this child than meets the eye. Seven years old! "As a matter of fact there is ... as you say, a genetic component associated with this condition."

"Well, my mom's mom had some strange things in her head like me. Dad thought it was her brandy pudding. She made it triple-strength and one time I—"

"Very interesting. Yes, it's most often passed on through the female side."

"She was a witch. A good witch."

"Was she really?"

"We got tons of letters from her from Scotland—with magic spells inside—except we can't find them. When we moved we lost them. I met her once."

"Did you really?"

"I pushed her rocking chair when nobody was sitting in it and she said that's bad luck, ghosts come and sit in it."

"You don't say? Well, we'll have lots of time to talk about all that. I think we'll be spending a lot of time together. Would you like that?"

"Not really. She had two different shoes on—because she broke in her shoes one at a time, Mom said. And her tongue was black, from chewing charcoal biscuits—to stop her from farting, Dad said."

To Noel's father, in the waiting room, Dr. Vorta ended his excited diagnosis with, "Congratulations, Henry. Your son's in good company, very good company indeed. Liszt, Rimsky-Korsakov and Scriabin all had synaesthesia, and so did Baudelaire, Rimbaud and Proust!"[4]

A man of thwarted artistic ambitions, Mr. Burun beamed at the news. "You forgot Nabokov," he added.

"And the odd Nobel prize-winning scientist!"[5]

"Émile, this calls for a drink."

Like complicitous schoolboys the two couldn't stop grinning, or pumping each other's hand, as though this were the greatest, the most promising thing on earth. Noel wasn't smiling at all.

❦

"What is the highest form of art?" Mr. Burun asked his son the following evening, after dinner. "What is the *ne plus ultra*, the zenith of creative endeavour?" He would always talk this way to his son, even when he was in the crib. No baby talk. Not good for the child's cerebral development.

"Jack of hearts, jack of clubs," was the reply. "Two of clubs, two of spades. Ten of hearts … four of diamonds. Your turn."

"Noel, I've asked you a question. What do you think the highest form of art is?"

Noel looked up from the cards and slowly scrutinised each object in the room, as if the answer could be found in one of them. His gaze rested on their Zenith television console, whose portals were now locked, as they often were. "TV?" he replied.

His father shook his head. "No, TV's in the dungeon. There's no art form below that. Because of it children no longer read. We must all curse its Faustian inventor, Vladimir Zworykin."

If he had understood this, Noel would have violently disagreed. He looked at the walls, at the stereo cabinet. "Painting?" he suggested. "Or maybe music?"

"They're up there, but they don't have the most important thing. What do you think the most important thing is? When communicating something."

Noel knew the answer to this one. "Words."

"Exactly. So what combines words, images and music?"

"Cartoons?"

"True. What else?"

"Movies?"

"What else?"

Noel paused, closed his eyes. "Poems?"

"Dead on. At the top of the heap is poetry, at least as it used to be written. Nothing else goes as far, nothing goes as deep in the blood and soul. Shakespeare surpasses Beethoven because he had sound *and* meaning. Always remember that as you get older. Poetry is in the empyrean, TV is in the pit."

Noel nodded. "Poetry is in the empyrean, TV is in the pit," he whispered to himself, remembering the words, not understanding the sentence. "It's your turn," he said.

But his father's mind was not on the game. "Scientists can talk about human nature, but only poets can free those feelings we keep in the pent heart."

"Your turn, Dad."

They were sitting cross-legged on the brown shag rug of their living room in Montreal's Mile End, midway through the child's game of "Remembrance." You may know it: fifty-two cards are spread face down; you turn up two cards at random, put them in your pile if they match, turn them back down if they don't. And remember where they were for next time. It was Noel's very first card game, learned—and mastered—when he was three. He never tired of it.

"Queen of spades," said his father, turning over one of the cards. He scanned the sea of pirate ships, with black ensigns and blazing cannon. One of them he overturned. "Shite. I mean shoot. Nine of hearts."

"Nine of hearts," Noel repeated, coolly turning over the same card. "And nine of diamonds ..."

While observing his son, Mr. Burun pulled hard on a meerschaum pipe with a sultan-head bowl, which he had bought in Turkey when younger and happier. "The mother of the Muses was the goddess of Memory," he said, pursuing his theme, and he might as well have been speaking in Turkish.

"Four of hearts and ... four of clubs. Jack of diamonds, jack of spades ..."

"Mnemosyne was her name. The goddess of Memory."

"Nine of spades, nine of clubs ..." Nim-*oss*-enee, the mother of the muses, the goddess of Memory, Noel repeated to himself, depositing the words in his electron vault, the combination encrypted in colours and shapes. Where's all this heading? he wondered. "What's a muse?" he asked, because he knew his father liked questions.

"A muse is something ... someone who inspires you, in art, a guiding spirit. In Greek mythology there were nine of them, a band of lovely

7

sisters." Mr. Burun looked up to the ceiling, closed his eyes. "'He is happy whom the Muses love,' says Hesiod. 'For though a man has sorrow and grief in his soul, yet when the servant of the Muses sings, at once he forgets his dark thoughts and remembers not his troubles.'"

Silence gathered as Noel stared. "Are you on something, Dad?"

His father opened his eyes, set his pipe down in the ashtray. "So why was the goddess of Memory linked with artistic creation, you may well ask."

No, I wasn't going to ask that, thought Noel. Let's play.

"Because for the Greeks creativity wasn't associated with the idea of producing something new—as it is today. The artist built upon, or reworked, the great intellectual and cultural achievements of the past. So a great memory, you see, was considered a key part of creative activity— it gave the artist more material to draw upon, as well as a richer, more complex intellect. When James Joyce said 'I invented nothing, but I forgot nothing either,' I think he was referring to exactly this sort of thing."

Noel glanced at the bowl of his father's pipe. Hydrous magnesium silicate, he recalled, $H_4Mg_2Si_3O_{10}$. "Ace of diamonds," he said. "King of spades."

"Ah, a rare lapse from the memory artist. Ace of diamonds ... ace of spades. Eight of diamonds ... damn it, the king of hearts—the self-killing king, the suicide sovereign. Look, Noel, how he stabs himself in the side of his head."

"Eight of diamonds, eight of hearts." *The suicide sovereign?* "Five of hearts, five of clubs ..." There were now only a dozen cards left and Noel matched them all.

"Well done, Noel, I'm proud of you. You've got the memory of your late grandmother. Now *she* would've given you a run for your money. You're very lucky, lad—with a brain like yours, you'll go far."

Mrs. Burun entered the room, hugging herself as if she were cold, and Noel launched himself into her arms. "I won, Mother! I'm like Nana when she was late and I'm going to go far!"

"Yes you are, Noel dear." His mother smiled. "You're my little genius, aren't you, you're my ..."

He could listen to his mom's voice forever, and his dad's too. They didn't confuse him like everyone else's; they didn't scramble his brainwaves. Years later, he was never able to understand why people complained about their parents. He always assumed everyone had parents like his: perfect and beautiful in every way.

"We were talking about the importance of poetry," his father explained, while tapping his pipe against a swan-shaped ashtray on which Noel had affixed a New York Islanders decal. "In this secular world, this spiritually dead world, poets are all we have left. Remember that, Noel. And remember you have an illustrious ancestor—a Burun from way back."

"Do you know what an ancestor is, Noel?" his mother asked while stroking his hair. He felt euphoric whenever his mother stroked his hair. As she spoke he saw blades of burnt-orange grass swaying gently in magenta mist.

"Noel, did you hear me? Is your colour-wheel spinning?"

"Yes, Mother, I ... What did you say?"

"I asked if you knew what an ancestor was?"

"It's someone who lived before you. I mean, in your family."

"That's right," said his father. "And do you know who your great ancestor was?"

"Well," his mother began, "we don't know for certain that—"

"We've got the charts, the trees to prove it. A long line of melancholics, suicides, arsonists, incestuous paedophiles ..."

"Who's my ancestor?" Noel asked.

His father set down his pipe and paused for dramatic effect. "George Gordon. The Sixth Baron Byron of Rochdale."

Noel nodded, mulled this over. He looked at his smiling father for a cue or clue, and then at his smiling mother. "But our last name is Burun."

"Burun is the ancient Scottish form of Byron," his mother explained. "Ralph de Burun, who may be a distant relation of your father's, is mentioned in Domesday."

Noel repeated the names slowly to himself, noting the coloured shapes of the letters. His mother was a history teacher, so she knew what she was talking about. "But who ... who was he?"

His father smiled. "Lord Byron? Merely the greatest poet of the nineteenth century."

"Well, perhaps one of the greatest," said his mother. "Certainly the handsomest—as handsome as you, Noel dear. With the same lovely chestnut curls and steel blue eyes."

"Takes after his mother on that count," said Mr. Burun as he walked over to a library wall with three divided bookcases, devoted to history, poetry and chemistry respectively. "Thank God." He stepped upon a metal stool and from the middle case pulled out a slender, fawn-coloured volume. On the soft leather cover, *The Romantic Poets* was emblazoned in gold. "This was your grandmother's, and *her* mother's, published in Edinburgh in 1873. Take a look inside. It's illustrated."

Neither parent was surprised to hear Noel recite all twenty poems by Byron at the breakfast table the next day, without the book, mispronouncing scores of words between mouthfuls of Count Chocula. This sort of thing had happened before, lots of times, the first when Noel was five, when he had become so wrapped up in his Children's Treasury edition of *The Arabian Nights* that his mother threatened to take it away from him, worried he was spending too much time with it, "obsessing" over it, stubbornly refusing to read anything else. Terrified of losing his favourite book, which was almost his entire life at this point, Noel decided to stay up all night and memorise its fifty-two pages.

How did he do it? Noel had two methods, one involving "photographs" of coloured letters, the other involving "maps," which is the one he used here. As he explained later to Dr. Vorta, he "delivered the words like newspapers" in mental rows or sequences, along actual pathways—indoors and out—that he pictured in his mind:

It's like you're taking a walk inside your head, like in a dream. You see yourself going on a trip, right? And you drop the words or sometimes big chunks of words at different spots. Like down the hall you come to a vent, right? So you put some words down the vent and then you come under a picture, so you put some words there, and then you come to the door, or the stairs or maybe a room. And you might go into the room. Like if it's a living room, you put stuff under chairs, tables, lamps, or if it's the kitchen you put words in the fridge or the oven or down the toaster ... Or you could use the attic or crawlspace too, or you could go outside, on the sidewalk, or through fields or parks or parking lots, or gardens, and you could put words at certain trees or flowers, or down manholes, or at traffic lights or stores or churches ... Every memory trip is different. And you just dump a bit here and a bit there and for some reason everything is clear, like a paper route when you just remember the houses, you don't look at the numbers anymore ... And at the end it's always the same—I'm lying on my old bed in Babylon, or my new bed in Montreal, with Farquhar beside me—he's a King Charles spaniel.[6]

This explains how, that morning at the breakfast table, Noel was able to recite the Byron poems in reverse order too; he had only to start his walk from the end (".innocent is love whose heart ... like beauty in walks She").

After an article appeared in *Psychology Today*, stories by the dozen began appearing in newspapers and magazines.[7] The phone began to ring as well. Everyone, it appeared, wanted a demonstration, a carnival show from Memory Boy. A researcher from the Johnny Carson Show, a woman named Laura Pratte, offered airfare and accommodation to Noel and his parents for a week in Burbank, California. A man from Princeton, a jittery classics professor, offered to pay Noel to appear at a plagiarism hearing at the university to corroborate his "photographic memory." A detective sergeant from the Montreal Drug Squad asked if Noel could help in a case involving a wire tap of twins, only one of whom was guilty. A chess instructor from Chomedy offered to turn Noel into a grandmaster. And the late Manfredo Mastromonaco, on behalf of The Desert Inn in Las Vegas, offered Noel's parents $5,000 a week for an eight-week summer run on stage with a magician (Manfredo himself). "I'll turn your son into a memory bank!" Manfredo shouted into the line, more than once, hacking with cancerous laughter. It was a lot of money at the time.

But neither Noel nor his parents were interested in this sort of thing. Noel could memorise almost anything the doctors and journalists threw at him. He could recall a list of fifty random words in almost any language after only a few seconds of deliberation; he could recite the value of pi to a hundred places; he could memorise a deck of shuffled playing cards in under sixty seconds, eighteen decks in an hour, a 100-digit number after hearing it once at speed, a 500-digit number in an hour.[8] He could do all these things, but he didn't want to. He'd do poetry if asked, but nobody asked. Everything else bored or pained him, giving him a pulverising headache. "Why only poetry?" Dr. Vorta and his apprentices would ask, speculating that the sounds or rhythms acted as mnemonic aids. "Because poetry is the *zenith* of creativity," Noel replied. "Nothing goes as deep in the blood and soul. Don't ever forget that."

As he grew older Noel discovered tricks that would help "switch off" the synaesthetic engine: classical music (especially Liszt, Scriabin and Rimsky-Korsakov) would sometimes clear his mind or slow its activity; nibbling on zesty vegetables, like bitterroot or cherry pepper or betel nut, would often do the trick; fierce concentration would work too, albeit at the cost of a migraine that could last up to two days. And in the nineties, when he went on a series of antidepressants, Zoloft and Paxil among them, the coloured-hearing wasn't as intense.

Despite these and other stopgaps and counteragents, it was difficult for Noel to take any course, or hold onto any job, that involved interacting with others. If it weren't for a certain saviour in his life—someone who guided him, wrote letters of recommendation, hired him as a lab assistant, treated him as a son—Noel may have ended up in an asylum. This saviour was Dr. Émile Vorta.

Chapter 2
"NXB"

Norval Xavier Blaquière dreamed only two dreams. The first
played back, with assorted detours and deviations, something
that actually happened, in 1978. He was in his parents' bedroom
in the seventh arrondissement of Paris, hiding behind velvet curtains,
planning to spring out at a carefully chosen moment. With both hands
he clutched a broadsword made of tinfoil, like one he'd seen in *Astérix le
Gaulois*. Maman, he knew, would be mad at him for not being in bed,
and for wasting rolls of foil, but Papa would get the joke. Papa would
laugh and start chasing him around the room.

His father was about to leave on a business trip; he had already said
goodbye to his son and was now saying goodbye, ever so tenderly, to his
wife. When she suddenly melted into tears, Norval was so surprised that
he forgot to spring out of the curtains and prevent his father, at sword
point, from leaving. He had never seen his mother cry.

Spellbound, Norval watched his mother sob as his father walked out of
the room. Was he going away forever? Was that a tear running down
Papa's cheek? After the door closed behind him, Norval watched his
mother primp in the mirror for a few seconds, then walk to a window
overlooking a courtyard. She flicked the light switch on and off, waited a
few moments, then smiled at the sounds of a key turning in the back door
below. It's Papa! Norval thought. He's coming back! They're playing a
game! When he walks in the room I will jump out from behind the
curtains and say the line from the movie that will make him laugh! He
listened to the sound of footsteps climbing the stairs.

And then watched, in bewilderment, as a man with a black shirt and
suit entered the bedroom. A gangster? His mother ran to him, threw
herself into his arms and kissed him all over while ... unbuttoning his
shirt! He was an older man with a paunch and white tufts of hair on

13

his back. Snorting like a bull, he ripped off his mother's diaphanous night-gown. As they wrestled on the marriage bed, Norval tiptoed out of the room unseen and crawled back into bed. He put his face deep into his pillow, which got wetter and wetter. When he finally raised his head, gasping for breath, he remembered that he had left his sword behind the curtains.

Twenty-four years later in Montreal, Norval awoke with the repugnant mental image of a hairy back, enlarged as if under a microscope: a wasteland of gnarled and niggardly grey trees, filth-encrusted furrows, sewerish sweat and mountainous moles. He groggily opened his eyes and saw, directly in front of him, more hair: blonde female pubic hair. Further down, inches from his groin, were ears riddled with ornamental buckshot, and a nose run through with a trio of silver rings.

But this wasn't the strangest part of the tableau. Standing menacingly before him, in a frozen caricature of an angry man, was ... an angry man. With a Fu Manchu moustache, a spindly plume of hair sprouting out the back of his head, and unibrowed eyes narrowed into angry slits. A jealous boyfriend? Before Norval could inquire, the man said something in impenetrable *joual*, with the intonation of a death curse, before clomping out of the room with Harley boots.

Norval smiled. With diamond-cutter caution he then extracted himself from the woman's limbs and rooted around for his clothes amidst overflowing ashtrays, guttered candles, scattered pills, powders and dead bottles of wine. One by one he located his bone-white cotton boxers, heraldic-crested socks, alabaster linen shirt with Byron collar, taupe suede trousers, black nappa ankle boots, digital camera and journal. He looked at himself in the mirror, seemingly in approval, brushed back his long wavy chestnut locks. What's her name again? Some New-Age creation like Rhapsody or Revery or Radiance? It started with an *r*; otherwise he wouldn't be here.

Leaving a snoring Rhapsody or Revery or Radiance on the bed, Norval went out in quest of coffee and cigarettes. On the freshly ploughed sidewalks he had a spring in his step, a pleasant awareness of his tasteful attire, above-average height and flabless abdomen. At a café called Metaforia, while gulping down espressos, he remembered the woman's name. From his bag he pulled out a book bound in dove-grey Nigerian goatskin, with *Rover's Diary* on the cover and alphabetical tabs on the side. On the "R" page, he wrote:

R Rainbaux. A self-described "biker-bitch." Physically unimpeachable, but can never remember who came first, the Greeks or the Egyptians. Owing to a number of crippling intoxicants, I can't remember much else. And in the night that bloody dream agai

He laid down his silver pencil-pen because the lead had snapped, lit another Gauloise, then flipped backwards:

Q Quincy. The quiet sort, endearingly shy but a tad prim—the kind that never go to the toilet without turning on the tap. The kind that would take love very seriously ...

P Paola. A force of nature, a Sicilian volcano with lava in her veins. Velvety black eyes, raging raven hair, and a body to breed gladiators. One night not enough, but must play by the rules ...

O Odile. Six feet tall, obscenely healthy, but she had her breasts done. Women, write this down: small is fine, drooping is fine, SILICONE REVOLTS US ALL. When we want balloons we'll go to the circus.

N Niagara. (Her parents honeymooned at the Falls.) One of those salon-tanned women who try to look jet-setting and sexy with a pumpkin-coloured face ...

M Marietta. A shortish fortyish Mensa-intelligent Afro-Portuguese fuckstress furiosa who scratched and screamed as I tongued from sole to crown ...

L Laurie. Shorn pubic hair is bad enough in porn mags, but in real life? Women, stop this, now. All you're doing is fuelling some child pornographer's fantasies. AND PLEASE, FOR CHRIST'S SAKE: no shaven thunderbolts, hearts, arrows, exclamation points, X marks the spot or team logos. Rings, ball bearings and dangling chin-up bars should also be banished. As should buttockless underwear that cleaves to the crack ...

A green-haired waitress interrupted his reading. Leaning over the table, she slid the bill underneath his cup, along with something else: the restaurant's business card. Under the waitress's blouse, Norval remarked, was nothing but the waitress.

"You're Norval Blaquière," she said, lisping with a tongue ring. "The actor thlash writer. You were amathing in *Rimbaud in London*. And I read your book—twithe. Tho romantic! And tho thad ... God, how I cried over that book!"

Norval calmly shifted his gaze toward the card, which bore a hand-written message in red.

"You're probably asked this all the time," she continued, with slumbrous eyes and *th*'s for all sibilants, "but did you get a lot of rejections for *Unmotivated Steps*?"

"No."

"You had a hit right off the bat?"

"I started at the top and worked my way down."

"I was also wondering if ... well, you're probably asked this all the time, but I was wondering if you have any advice for aspiring writers?"

Norval squinted at the antic red letters, as if written wrong-handedly. "Yes, don't become one."

"You wouldn't recommend it?"

"There are too many already, too many welfartists walking around calling themselves writers and artists who actually do fuck-all, besides filling out grant applications."

The waitress laughed, pushed the hair back out of her eyes. "But seriously, what's the best way to get published these days? Any advice?"

"Yes. Don't recount your dreams, don't puke up your diary, don't write anything before age thirty."

"Really? That's not what my creative writing teacher said."

"That's why he's teaching."

"And didn't you write your novel in your twenties?"

"Learn from my mistake." Norval looked up from the card and gazed at her piercingly, as he gazed at every woman. "A rare Z. Pity it's not your turn."

"I'm sorry?"

"You'll be up ..." he paused to calculate, " ... in a couple of months. I *will* call, Zoé, depend on it." He drew a mint twenty from his billfold.

"But I wasn't—"

"Now if you'll excuse me ..."

On the sidewalk, or rather the gentrified cobbles of a pedestrian walkway, Norval examined the pedestrians: an assortment of touro-trash, fashion lemmings and inadvertent comedians. Some of the women, he judged, had made wearable purchases. None of the men had.

What were they *thinking* when they stepped into those clothes? What did they *see* in the mirror? There is no reason for the nineties, which will go down in fashion history as the buffoon decade, to be dragged into the zeroes. A baseball cap, worn frontward or backward, knocks fifty points off your IQ. A bucket hat? Seventy-five. Pants with the crotch at knee-level, revealing the cleft of your arse, making you walk like a penguin? A hundred. These articles are perhaps acceptable for four-year-olds, or circus chimps, but adult men?

"Excuse me," he said, "what would you keep in a pocket on your *calf*? And do you not realise that by storing toilet paper and yesterday's lunch on your thigh, your limbs assume the girth of oak trees? And what about you? Yes, you. Why is your entire family wearing track suits? Is Montreal hosting a family Olympics? And you, with the canary balloon pants and Martian green headband. You will *never* get laid in an outfit like that."

A cell phone trilled. "Shut that fucking thing off. You are too young to have a phone. You have nothing of importance to say to anyone. Yap yap yap. Generation Y: the dunderhead generation, the hundred-channel generation, basking in a state of know-nothingism. Men have fought wars, gone to their graves, so that you imbeciles can walk on treadmills and twiddle with joysticks. No one wants to hear you prattle in a public place, no one wants to hear your phone ring with a jaunty refrain. 'Devil's Haircut'? Beethoven's *Fifth*? Cute. Now go to jail."

Yes, he thought, *jail*. There should be a Ministry of Aesthetics and roving couth-squads. Instead of metal detectors or sniffer dogs, there'd be bad-taste detectors, special laser beams or spectrographs. If the alarm sounded, you'd be placed in a detention facility until appropriate clothes were found and fines levied. You'd be jailed for repeat offences. Three strikes and you're out. Not capitally punished necessarily, but you'd be locked away for a long time, out of public sight. Antarctica, say, or Neptune. You'd take courses in aesthetics while doing time.

Excuse me, sir? You heard the alarm. Yes, it's obvious you were in a hurry today. Name please? Thank you, I'll just run that through my palmtop ... Right, it seems you've got a lengthy record: reckless co-ordination, sensory assault, gaudily harm ... This one will be for stupidity. Yes, I'm afraid those trousers look inane. Did you look in the mirror today? An orange prison jumpsuit would've looked better. It's the fashion? I'm afraid that's another fine—for herdism. Now don't let me catch you on the street again in this outfit. Try to think for yourself. Eat salmon oil, which they say is good for the brain. Study yourself carefully in the mirror before going out, think very hard, and if you can't come up with anything inoffensive, stay in your apartment. Which probably looks as bad as you do. Order out for food. Call the Ministry and someone will come and advise ..."

The interior monologue stopped when Norval entered the Experimental Psych Building and saw someone standing by the elevator. Someone whose attire he approved of. He quickened his step. The elevator doors opened, the woman got in. Norval's brisk walk turned into a dash. He made a lunge for the car, like a deft fencing manoeuvre, inserting his hand between the doors as they were an inch from closing.

Chapter 3

"SD"

With an aching that began in her toes and ended in her skull, as if metal doors were closing and re-closing on her temples, Samira Darwish climbed up the black marble steps of the U of Q Experimental Psychology & Chemistry Building. She hesitated before pushing the revolving door, and hesitated again before entering the elevator, whose doors were wide open. She pressed nine and the doors closed. Almost. Some imbecile stuck his hand in to prevent them.

As the man entered she looked down at the floor, determined to ignore him. But when she darted a glance his way, something happened. A mesmeric field of some sort inside the car. She literally could not take her eyes off him. He seemed to be of another, higher race: sable curls in wild profusion swept back from a high brow above dark liquid, brooding eyes; a steel-buttoned black-and-silver greatcoat of irreproachable fit; narrow-flare slacks of grey-brown suede; black ankle boots of the supplest leather. A kind of nineteenth-century Parisian elegance ... as he knows all too well, judging by the look of princely conceit smeared all over his face.

Not exactly a stunner, thought Norval, but not below average either. He stared right back at her, deep into her dark eyes. Fey and dream-ridden eyes, as though she'd just bid farewell to Galahad or Lancelot ... He looked closer. No, more like Gilgamesh or Sindbad. "Middle Eastern, am I right?"

Samira had a roller-coaster sensation inside her stomach, as if the elevator cables were stretching like rubber and about to launch them into space. "Very good."

"I see we're both going to the ninth floor. You're seeing Dr. Vorta?"

She shook her head. "Dr. Rhéaume."

"You're one of her students?"

Samira grabbed onto the handrail for support. "Yes. But that's not why I'm seeing her." Why did I add that last bit? she wondered as the elevator stopped and the doors opened.

With a lordly flourish, Norval invited her to exit. "What's your name, by the way?"

From the hall she watched the doors rumble shut. "Must I tell you?"

"Yes. Your first name. Is it ... Zubaydah? Gulbeyaz? Nefertiti?"

Samira half-smiled, shook her head after each name.

"Scheherazade?"

Her smile widened. "This could go on forever. It's Samira."

"Beginning with an s?"

Samira looked ceilingward. "Uh, yes, Samira begins with an s."

"Perfect. S is what I require. Come. I've a few things to attend to with Dr. Vorta, to whom I'll introduce you. Then we're going for lunch. No, this is the right way—the open door on the left."

As they approached it Samira glimpsed a fluted wooden pedestal on a grey filing cabinet, which supported a plastic human head divided into numbered sections. Two men stood on either side of it, as if engaging it in conversation. Amidst a faint smell of carbolic acid and monkey stool.

"Look, there's old man Vorta now—the one with the vulturine face. My name's Norval Blaquière, by the way. You may have heard of me."

Hours later, she wasn't sure how many, Samira was horizontal, high atop a loft in the Old Port, on a miraculously soft and silk-sheeted bed. She looked up through a skylight at a torn web of clouds, sideways at the frost-blue ribbon of the Saint Lawrence, and down at what looked like an art gallery from another century.

Rows of paintings adorned the walls, late nineteenth-century paintings in a decor that combined Regency and debased Gothic with elements of pure fancy. An archery target was suspended from the ceiling at one end of the immense living room, while an extravagant candle chandelier, the biggest Samira had ever seen, hung from the other. There was a curving staircase with wrought-iron balustrade, a fireplace with a Gothic slate mantel, wainscotted walls of fog-grey, and herringbone floors of Brazilian mahogany. In the corner farthest from her was a moonstone-blue staircase that went nowhere. It just stopped, as in a Surrealist dreamscape, four or five feet from the ceiling.

"Norval?" Samira called out. "Norval?" Her prince had abandoned her. "Why did I go to lunch with him?" she asked herself, while watching a ceiling fan, inlaid with mother-of-pearl, spin languorously. "Because I was starving. Fine. But why did I come back to his place?"

She closed her eyes and tried to replay things on the dark screen of her eyelids. Today was no problem. She remembered everything: meeting Norval in the elevator, then Dr. Vorta and ... this guy who looked like Norval's brother. Noel? Who just stood and gawked, without saying a word ... She remembered descending in the elevator with this same man, then waiting for Norval in a sushi restaurant across the street; she remembered arriving at his place and asking if she could go to sleep. But why was she so sleepy? Because Dr. Vorta had given her something—a sedative? Yes, today was clear—today she remembered everything. It was last week she had trouble with. She was at a party of some sort, at a shooting-gallery or squat in Mile End that belonged to a friend of a friend's ... No, it wasn't *that* party, it was another one, in Villeray, something to do with school. But then things went black and murky and monstrous, like Loch Ness.

Where's my knapsack? She opened her eyes and saw it lying beside her on a ledge, under a telescope tripod. She opened it, checked the contents, then pulled out a diary. Looking for a clue, she flipped through its pages. Nothing. No entries since the party. She now wrote:

Memoirs of an amnesiac. January (or maybe December). I was at a party in Villeray, and then suddenly I wasn't. Things went dark & turning & I woke up with a hole in my brain & vomit in my boot. Then Dr. Ravenscroft was there, and Dr. Rhéaume, who drove me to the police. And then home. And told me to come to see her on

Here Samira put her pen down because it had run dry. She rummaged in her bag for another, unsuccessfully, then looked from side to side. Recessed into the wall, just above the bed frame, were three small drawers, painted the same colour as the wall, barely visible. She pried open the first with her fingernails and found what looked like lenses—telescope and camera lenses.

The second contained thick beige writing paper, a postcard of a church with a sketched portrait on the back, a small jewellery box and ... a gold-nibbed fountain pen. She glanced sideward and rearward, lest by some infernal magic Norval could see her, before taking the pen out. And then the postcard. And then the jewellery case.

Again she looked in all directions before opening the case, whose miniature golden key was in the lock. Inside was a silver ring, a three-part gimbal ring. Closed, the clasped hands formed a traditional friendship ring; opened, the hidden inner ring revealed two hearts, along with an engraved inscription:

Nor,
Love always,
Terry

Terry? Is Norval gay? She examined the sketch on the postcard:

She restored each item, carefully, trusting her memory for their exact positions. Still burning with curiosity, not to mention guilt, she quickly pried open the third drawer. And closed it just as quickly. You don't want to go there, she said to herself. She counted to three and then reopened it: Rakehell condoms, black silk rope and a Zorro mask. And a vial of ... white powder. With only a black "K" on the label. She re-closed the drawer.

Pen in hand, she began flipping through the pages of her diary, to a section called "MEN, or MISTAKES I have made," and added, in royal purple ink:

Norval. Met two strange men in the Psych elevator today, within minutes of each other—one on the way up, one on the way down. They had a strange resemblance, as if they were brothers. One, cute but possibly a strayed lunatic, uttered barely a word; the other, absurdly good-looking, talked the entire time. I couldn't take my eyes off him. Who <u>was</u> he? A decadently dandified baron on his way home from the opera? A brooding count with a bloodstained past? Certainly a smug bastard, with a <u>martial</u> tone that could freeze nitrogen—and a strong, virile, almost animal beauty which was, quite simply, <u>irresistible</u>. The type that entangle me in their sticky little webs, that draw me crashwards. Is that exquisitely ravaged face my fate, I wonder? <u>Why</u> am I so predictable? <u>Why</u> do I always go for beautiful brutes and bastards? Every society, I once read, must be wary of the unattached male, especially the attractive one, for he is universally the cause of countless social ills

She set down Norval's fountain pen and leafed backwards:

Claude. Maybe it's me. Maybe I'm just attracted to borderline lunatics. I meet them wherever I go—bars , bookstores, parties, movies, museums. Yet whether they're young or old, rich or poor, the scenario is always the same: After we "get involved," they go blitzoid on me. Sometimes this takes the form of them smacking me around. Other times it's screaming about how I won't "commit." Both of these things happened today. So I've reached a decision—I'm taking the veil. A vow of chastity. That's it, it's over. No more sex, no more relationships ...

Pietro. Sat beside me on the train—in a completely empty car. Forty-five minutes with a pawing Pithecanthropus bog-man with merging eyebrows and barf breath ...

Nick. Why do men do this? He started by slobbering all over me, his spinning tongue car-washing my face. He ended by chomping on my clitoris. I screamed, and the moron thought I was climaxing ...

Max. A tad effeminate, not usually my style, but a nice face, nice skin. And besides, I was <u>very</u> drunk. We quickly, much too quickly, arrived at the moment of truth, the nervy moment in every one-night stand: the unveiling. Peewee or panther—what's it going to be? Max was not a peewee, Max was not a panther. Max was a she.

Howard. Yet another man on a quest for permanent youth, fiercely resisting responsibilities of adulthood, living in his parents' basement. One of those no-life "adultescents" who, when they aren't playing with their video toys, are playing with themselves.

Jérome. A blind date. After which I severed my relationship with the matchmaker. Forever. First thing I noticed was his expensive Armani suit and strange dominating attitude, as though he'd crushed thousands in real estate deals. Next thing I noticed was his pony tail. Men, write this down: what this says is pimp, pornmaker or disturbed offender. After listening politely to twenty minutes of self-hero worship, I edgewised that I was going to the bathroom. "You're going the wrong way, girl," he said. "No I'm not, boy," I said and walked to my bathroom at home.

Samira flipped back to her latest entry, Norval, and wrote:

Muslims believe that 2 angels sit on our shoulders, one tallying our good deeds, the other our bad. The good deeds are called hasanna—the gifts we give others without thinking about the cost or benefit to ourselves. Now, although I'm a lapsed Muslim, it's time for some hasanna. I will <u>not</u> make love with Norval, even though I'm overpoweringly attracted to him. I've got my reasons. First and foremost, because of his 'Alpha Bet' hit list, which he was stupid enough to tell me about. It reminds me of the emperor in The 1001 Nights who vows to marry a woman every day and have her executed the next morning. But not only am I going to resist Norval, but somehow I'm going to get him to stop this foul enterprise, an insult to all women …

On the other hand, maybe if we make love he'll like it so much that he'll want to do it again—which will be against the rules and his Alpha Bet will be off. Yes, maybe it's my <u>duty</u> to make love with him. My good deed.

One last thing. What <u>is</u> that white powder? I had a dreadful feeling when I saw it, I hope it's not what I think it is. This whole place is starting to give me the creeps—especially the paintings on the walls—gloomy and depraved and fetishistic. God, now I wonder if he's going to kill me. What's in that vial? I can't get it out of my mind. K … Am I paranoid? Not surprising, after what happened. But what happened? Attempted date-rape? It's all a thick bloody fog, I <u>can't remember</u>. Should I try hypnosis? In the métro this morning, I picked up a soiled Maclean's magazine with footprints and read an article on Wayne Gretzky's father. Apparently when he woke up in a hospital bed after a stroke ten years ago, he couldn't remember a thing. Like the names and faces of his wife and five children—or their achievements, including those of Wayne, the greatest hockey player in history. Today, everything from the mid-seventies to the mid-nineties, he admits, "doesn't exist". Is this what's happening to me, on a smaller scale? That the last week of my life doesn't exist? Or am I just

A musical sound came from one of the partitioned rooms. The sound of a phone with a melodic phrase, a funeral dirge, then a muffled voice with no discernible words.

Chapter 4
Noel & Norval

"I know you've been calling me for the last twenty-four hours," said Norval into his cell phone, calmly. "I'm perfectly aware of that. You left *six* messages."

"Can we meet?" said Noel. "I have something to tell you. It's about ... well, the woman in the elevator. I mean the woman you introduced me to, in Dr. Vorta's office ..."

"What about her?" said Norval, distractedly. He was sitting at his desk, a pillar-and-claw library table inlaid with satinwood. After examining his image in a dressing-glass, and straightening the collar of a soft-blue cotton-gauze shirt, he returned his attention to the screen of an azurine laptop.

"Do you realise who she is? You'll never guess in a million years."

Norval pressed a translucent key. "Astonish me."

"I recognised her voice images. The funny thing is I actually saw her once before, I mean in person, in New York. She was coming out of a hotel. We never spoke, but she smiled at me as she got in a taxi. The next time I saw her was on the screen. She's an actress!"

"No she's not."

"She was in Zappavigna's *The Bride and Three Bridegrooms*. You remember? Her name is ..."

"Samira."

"Heliodora Locke. Do you remember in the opening credits, it said 'And Introducing Heliodora—'"

"Her name, I repeat, is Samira. She's an *S*—otherwise she wouldn't be here. She's a woman of the East—and not an actress."

"I never expected to see her again, at least not in person, so you can imagine my surprise when I saw her in Dr. Vorta's office. And ... well, in bad shape."

26

"Noel, I want you to focus very hard on what I'm saying. I've been speaking to you and you've not been listening."

"I think we should probably help her ... I mean, she's obviously in some sort of trouble—"

"Not any more. Come over and meet her."

"Meet who?"

"Samira."

"Samira?" Here Noel paused to visualise the colour of her voice. And eyes! How would you describe that mix, that merger as rare as radium?

"Noel, stop the colour-wheel. I'm talking to you."

"Sorry, I ... It's because of the actress, her eyes, her voice—"

"Noel, listen to me. She is *not* an actress. Do you understand what I'm saying?"

Noel took a deep breath, refocused, let his friend's words sink in. Why do I keep *doing* this? he asked himself. Getting carried away like this, putting the cart before the horse ... The strange thing is that the two are a match, their sound colours match. Perfectly. What are the odds on that? Mind you, I've made mistakes before. I've made one again. No wonder I've got no friends. Well, one. "I know that, Nor, I was just ... pulling your leg. Of course she's not the famous actress. How could she be, here in Montreal? But she ... sort of looks like her. I mean, a bit."

"She *does* look like her, now that I think of it. Like her homely sister. An honest mistake."

"Thanks, but I wouldn't say that she—"

"It's Tuesday, Noel. Shall we meet outside the theatre?"

"I thought you ... had a guest."

Norval folded down the top of his computer. Noel could hear his footsteps as he walked into another room. "I'll see if she's conscious. Let's see ... Samira? Sam? No, doesn't look like it."

"But how did she ... end up at your place?"

"Because she's an *S*."

Noel closed his eyes. "Shit."

"She had a power-outage. At a party. Someone drugged her ass."

"Oh God ... are you serious? When? With what?"

"She doesn't remember a thing. Special K, I think."

"Shit. So the cops referred her to Vorta?"

"No, I did. She had an appointment with Rhéaume. But I recommended Vorta."

27

Noel was thinking of Samira, about how terrible she looked. That would certainly explain it. Norval's commanding voice, like a judo-chop, cut the air before his eyes. He played back the tape in his head. "You *recommended* Vorta? I thought you couldn't stand him."

"I can't, but I owe him a favour."

Noel nodded. "For all the free drugs?"

"No, because I cuckolded the poor sod.⁹ See you at four. Don't be late."

❦

Outside the theatre, Norval was crushing an Arrow cigarette beneath his heel when he saw Noel approaching on a skidding, side-slipping bicycle. A woman's bicycle, and old, with a shredded wicker carrier. He watched Noel tether it to a No Parking sign, gave an economical nod of recognition, then ignored his friend's outstretched hand.

"Noel, are you aware of the season? One does not cycle in snow."

"I'm ... well, trying to save money."

"Ah yes, the scrimping Scot, who lives in posh Outremont, must pinch his pennies."

"No, it's just that—"

"Let's go in. I have balls of ice. Two below."

Inside the theatre, where the once-plush seats were unupholstered and unsteady and the majority unoccupied, Norval nodded towards two aisle seats.

"Have you got any sleep in the past week, Noel?" he asked as they sat down. "You look ready for burial. Like you have a disease that should be named after you."

"It's just ... you know, a touch of insomnia and—"

"You have the dark circles and paleness one gets in the terminal stages of haemophilia."

"No, I'm fine, really quite ... fine."

"We're early," said Norval, eyeing his pocket watch. "I think I'll go back out for a smoke."

"How is ... Samira?"

Norval tossed his spent match onto the floor and took a long haul. "See for yourself, tomorrow night. She meets the criteria."

"For what? Seduction?"

"For Vorta's amnesia study."

28

"So the police *did* send her ..." He stopped speaking because no one was listening; Norval was already halfway up the aisle.

Noel rummaged in his coat pocket, withdrew his mother's pager and set it to "vibrate." He leaned back, gazed at the theatre's gold-sequined roof and papier-mâché Ionic pillars, letting his mind run every which way.

A yellowish voice invaded his thoughts. "Are you smoking?" asked a man with a glabrous body and scalp, twice, but Noel saw only pullulating worms the colour of burnt butter. Negative words, judging by his shaking head and disapproving finger. The man continued down the aisle, his great pate flashing as he walked in and out of the theatre's spotlights. When he sat down Noel's attention was drawn to the theatre's crimson curtains, which were slowly beginning to part.

Over the past year or so, these "Tuesday Matinée Classics" had become a ritual, or near-ritual. The two men first met at this very theatre, in fact, and Noel was now sitting in the very same seat. Antonioni's *Zabriskie Point* had been playing, he recalled, with Daria Halprin and Mark Frechette and Harrison Ford and ... well, he could name the entire cast— he could still see the credits. There were only three people in the audience, one of them asleep. An ice-storm was about to occur outside.

"Piece of crap, that," was the first thing Norval had said, in French, after the movie ended. They were riding up an escalator and Norval had turned around, from his higher vantage, to say this.

The colours in Noel's head distracted him—but not overwhelmingly, as most new voices did. It was almost a cross between his father's voice and his grandmother's. Glimmering, seesawing lattices of emerald green and Tyrian purple. Very pleasant, very familiar.

"I said that was a piece of crap," Norval repeated, this time in English.

Noel concentrated on the stranger's face. Very familiar as well. He'd seen the man twice before, coming out of Dr. Vorta's lab. A man of acid and steel. "Uh, yes, I agree. Piece of crap. I ... I could hear you snoring."

When they reached the top of the moving stairs they paused, unawkwardly staring at each other in silence, neither of them in any hurry to part. It was not a wary, mutual sizing-up; it was more bewilderment at how much they resembled each other. Like standing before a mirror almost. Their hair was exactly the same length and shade of rich auburn, and it curled over their temples in exactly the same way. They had the same straight nose, the same cleft chin, the same full lips, the same blue-grey eyes that stared intently from pale, almost feminine faces. Their expressions, though, were

29

quite different: Norval exuded confidence and cleverness, Noel diffidence and dimness. And Norval, at six foot one, was taller than Noel by three inches, and slimmer, and more athletic-looking—a strong swimmer and archer, he was flat of belly and broad of shoulder. Noel, round of belly and sloping of shoulder, could get portly if he didn't starve himself, and his athleticism was restricted to moving chessmen and the pages of books. Norval spoke somewhat prosily, with sententious precision; Noel spoke in trailing sentences, in lurching stops-and-starts. And although they were the same age, thirty-three, Norval looked forty-three. His face was marked by the ravages of cigarettes, chemicals and coronary nutrition, which seemed only to increase his attractiveness to women; Noel was a vigilant vitaminiser who abused no substance whatsoever, which seemed to decrease his attractiveness to women. He had made love to a total of two women in his life and loved each monogamously, undyingly; Norval had made love to over two hundred, detachedly, including his two half-sisters.

It was this reputation as a sexual conquistador that led to the performance-art project he was now two-thirds of the way through: *The Alpha Bet*. It wasn't Norval's idea; it arose from the brain of a colleague at the U of Q, a drunken erotologist named Antoine Blorenge. The terms: Norval had to seduce an alphabet's worth of women, in A to Z order according to Christian name, within a six-month span. Twenty-six women in twenty-six weeks. The proof: "artistic" photographs of the women at his place or theirs, digitally dated, and Norval's word of honour that a sex act of some sort had occurred, unpurchased. The stakes: if he succeeded, Norval would receive a $26,000 bursary from the Federal Arts Council. Dr. Blorenge happened to be head of the jury that year. If he failed, Norval would have to teach Sunday School at the university's interfaith chapel for twenty-six weeks, while refraining from sex of any kind, including the self-assisted variety, for the same duration. Again, word of honour. Many sins had been committed in Norval's elastic theology, but going back on his word was not one of them. The only hitch so far: Dr. Édith Dallaire, Head of Women's Studies, had somehow gotten wind of the project.

Noel's brain, meanwhile, had been taken over by a mantric inner voice: *Samira Samira* ... How could he *not* think of her? He'd been in love with her for years, in his fantasy world, and now he'd met her. And now she was endangered, alphabetically endangered! He would have to do something to prevent this ... anti-art, this lettricide ...

Breaking in on these thoughts was the anti-artist himself, holding a foot-long Toblerone in one hand and a burning cigarette butt in the other. He took one last Herculean drag, inhaling the fumes of the filter, before ashing it against the chair in front of him.

"No smoking in the theatre!" the same hairless man shouted, from several rows down.

"Shut up, you fat fuck!" was Norval's arch reply. He then sat down, slouching in his seat, knees up. He reached into his pocket for a small tin of aspirin, which Noel suspected contained something else.

For at least a quarter minute, his temperature rising, Noel glared at his friend. Norval slowly turned his head. "And you would be gaping at ... what, exactly?"

"Have you ever thought about ..." The siege of *The Alpha Bet* was the subject Noel wanted to broach, but he'd already expressed his views on it, quite plainly. He'd also tried to explain that he had a terrible feeling about it—a premonition of danger, of disaster—but Norval wouldn't listen. Norval scorned presentiment and superstition. Now, however, there was a new element in the equation: Samira Darwish. Was she part of the premonition? "Have you ever thought about ..." *Ending this mad enterprise* is what Noel wanted to say, but still the words wouldn't come out. All he could express was childish anger, bravado. "What is there, Nor, except for mindless whoring, that I can't do better than you?"

Unfazed by its tone, Norval pondered the question to the count of two. "First, with this bar, I can hit that bald shitwagon sitting six rows down; second, I can swim across the Saint Lawrence River at its broadest point; and third, I can give you one hell of a good thrashing."

Noel nodded. He couldn't deny any of this, or summon a return thrust of any kind.

"Right," said Norval. "So tell me what's going on in this dungeon laboratory you've been going on about. Transforming lead into gold? Uranium into plutonium?"

Noel was upset. And when he got upset words confused him, bled into other letters from other times. So it wasn't surprising when the symbols for lead and gold, both the chemical and alchemical (Pb, Au; ♄ , ☉), leeched into his brain, followed by the opening line from *Miss Julie* ("Miss Julie's mad again tonight—absolutely mad!") since Strindberg, he'd read the night before, was interested in alchemy. With a concentration that hurt, he attempted first to decode Norval's words, and then to formulate a clever retort. "No, I ... I'm not transforming lead into gold."

"But you *are* up to something. The black arts? Frankenscience?"

I had an obscure feeling that all was not over, that Frankenstein would still commit some signal crime, which by its enormity should almost efface the recollection of the past ... To freeze the scrolling lines, Noel reached into his pocket for some Hot Rock candies, tipped his head back and emptied the bag into his mouth. "No, I ... I'm working on something for you," he said as the friable pebbles foamed and frothed on his tongue. "A cure for your sex addiction."

Norval raised an eyebrow, at both the candy and the remark. "A cure? Shouldn't you be trying to self-infect? When was the last time you made love to a woman? Or boy or goat or whatever titillates you Scots."

Noel didn't have to think. He knew the exact date, exact hour. He waited for his saliva to calm. "Norval, for the seventeenth time, my *parents* are Scottish, not me, OK? Can you remember that? It's not that difficult."

"You rotten wee scunner, what are you girnin at noo? No need to raise a stushie."

Noel closed his eyes, determined not to encourage this with even the faintest of smiles. The accent, he had to admit, was pitch-perfect.

"So answer my question," said Norval.

"Which question?"

"When was the last time you made love?"

"I ... am not going to answer that."

"Quick, what's the name of that colour?" Norval pointed to the screen, on which the theatre's giant logo had just appeared. "The perimeter."

"Amaranth."

"Amaranth?"

"Yes."

"I thought that was an imaginary flower, an undying flower."

"It is. It's also a chemical dye."

"Formula?"

Noel sighed. "$Na_3C_{20}H_{11}N_2O_{10}$."

"Principal commercial use?"

"A dye for pharmaceuticals. Banned in North America, but not in Europe."

Norval nodded, rubbed his chin. He couldn't decide whether Noel was a genius or someone who'd soon be jumping off Champlain Bridge. "Amaranth. Doesn't Keats or Shelley use that somewhere?"

"Endymion. '*The spirit culls unfaded amaranth, when wild it strays through the old garden-ground of boyish days—*'"

"OK, OK. Now shut up and watch the film ..."

But Noel wasn't listening. The letters of *amaranth* were strobing inside his brain, along with piggybacking words, phrases and paragraphs from distant times. It was like a mad librarian's slide show and he decided to let it run. First came Aesop—each sentence helically cascading into the next, like slinky toys—which his mother had read to him when he was five:

The Rose and the Amaranth

Rose and Amaranth blossomed side by side in a garden, and the Amaranth said to her neighbour, "How I envy your beauty and sweet scent! No wonder you're such a favourite with everyone." But the Rose replied with a shade of sadness in her voice, "Ah, my dear friend, I live but for a brief season: if no cruel hand pluck me from my stem, my petals soon wither and fall, and then I die. But your flowers never fade, even if they are cut; for they are undying."
Greatness carries its own penalties.

Next came soft and rubbery words from *Don Quixote*, which he'd read in bed on the night of his fourteenth birthday:

blond young maidens, none of whom seemed to be under fourteen or over eighteen, all clad in green, with their locks partly braided, partly flowing loose, but all of such bright gold as to vie with the sunbeams, and over them they wore garlands of jessamine, roses, honeysuckle, and amaranth ...

Noel opened his eyes, looked sideways at Norval, then forward at the cream-coloured subtitles of the Bergman film, which quickly dissolved into copper-coloured lines, imbricated like shingles, from *Pinocchio*. He was in his buffalo-wallpapered bedroom in 1973, wearing his favourite pair of clown-covered pyjamas, listening to his mother's voice:

The little donkey Pinocchio made his appearance in the middle of the circus. He had a new bridle of polished leather with brass buckles and studs, and two white camellias in his ears. His mane was divided and curled, and each curl was tied with bows of coloured ribbon. He had a girth of gold and silver round his body, and his tail was plaited with amaranth ...

Last, in a riverine double line, oscillating like a polygraph needle, came lambent sapphire letters from Noel's most treasured book, *The Arabian Nights*:

> She stopped at a fruiterer's shop and bought Shami apples and Osmani quinces and Omani peaches, and cucumbers of Nile growth, and Egyptian limes and Sultani oranges and citrons, and she stopped at an apothecary's shop for tinctures of Aleppine jasmine and myrtle berry, oil of privet and camomile, blood-red anemone and pomegranate bloom, eglantine and amaranth . . .

Minutes passed before the colour forms faded, the dead mood passed, and the black-and-white film images impinged on his brain.[10] He'd seen *Wild Strawberries* before so wouldn't have to ask Norval about the opening. And after the movie he might even describe these passages to Norval, who would understand and not criticise. Although everything else was fair game, he never made fun of his synaesthesia, never angered at his lapses of concentration. Why? Because he himself was trying to see this kind of thing—in experiments with Dr. Vorta. And because he knew Baudelaire and Rimbaud—Poe and Nabokov too—and thought his friend might one day become as great.

When the film ended and the house lights went up, Noel readjusted the setting on his pager, slipped it back into his jacket's inner pocket.

"What was that?" asked Norval. "A gun?"

Noel began to pull his jacket over a sleeveless T-shirt, his face crimsoning. "No, it's a ... beeper."

This gave Norval pause. "And that?" He pointed towards a tattoo on his friend's upper arm. "Very nineties. Let's have a look."

Reluctantly, Noel pulled his arm out of the sleeve, revealing a black bull's head with silver horns between two red flags with black staves. The words hold fast, in vermilion, arched over top. "McCleod crest."

"Your mother's clan?" said Norval.

Noel hesitated. Out of a fear of being called a mommy's boy? He was used to that by now; it didn't bother him a bit. He'd never thought about cutting the apron strings; they were never too tight. But some things are private. And he was tired of hearing that bloody Scottish twaddle every time his mother's name came up. But maybe he'll resist the urge just this once, to amaze me ... "Yes."

"Ay, yer daft aboot her, yer right radge. Och weel ..."

Nimbus clouds had gathered outside—noctilucent plumbago and Mars-violet nimbostrati, Noel remarked—as Norval was about to hail a cab. But at the last second, as one came sharking to a halt, he changed his mind, waving it on its way. From the pocket of his greatcoat he extracted a fresh pack of Mohawk Arrows. Plain, heavies.

"How is it," he said, piercing the cellophane with his thumbnail, "that I have not received a single invitation to your Outremont manor? We've known each other, what, six months?"

"We met at the theatre on the sixth of March, 2001. So that would make it ten months, one week, one day. Do you remember, it was just before rain, an ice-storm as it turned out ..."

"I have no recollection of the weather."

"... and we saw *Zabriskie Point*—"

"Or the film. The question is, why have I never been allowed into your house? I have waited at your door like a dunce, I have rung your ding-dong bell, but not once have I been admitted. What are you hiding? A crystal meth lab in the cellar? A lunatic mother, chained in the attic?"

Noel winced. "Not exactly, no."

Norval paused to light his cigarette. "Is it true what they say?" His words sent a vapour trail into Noel's nostrils.

"What do they say?" said Noel, sputtering, flapping his hand.

"That your mother's beautiful, extraordinarily well preserved for a woman of ..."

"Fifty-six."

"Fifty-six. And that she has a passing resemblance—nay, a striking resemblance—to Catherine Deneuve. Or is it Charlotte Rampling?"

"Maybe a bit of both."

"What's her name again?"

"Mrs. Burun."

"Her first name."

"Stella."

Norval nodded, ruminating. "I've also heard that the reason you've never had a girlfriend is that you're blindly, unnaturally in love with the woman."

Noel smiled bleakly. "Who's been telling you all this?" Surely not Dr. Vorta ...

"In the last week, how often have you seen her with her clothes off?"

Noel sighed. "Often enough."

"Brilliant. I knew it. I *knew* there was some dark ..."

Here Noel tuned out. Samira had crept back into his brain. There was something irresistible about her. Her voice, for example. A good sign! Low and rich, a trifle husky, it caused indigo diamonds with blue-tinged halos, like the rings of Saturn, to revolve inside his head ... And her incredible eyes, twinkling with irony, the colour of ... what would you call it? The human eye, he knew better than most, can distinguish some ten million colours, so there obviously aren't names for all of them. Nor in his own lexicon of two thousand colours was there a name for that shade. It was a complex hybrid: Roman umber certainly, but with lurking black opal and smoky topaz and a tinge of ...

"Noel, I seem to be talking to myself here."

"Amaranth!"

"Yes, but we've moved on from that subject."

"Sorry, what's the new subject?"

Norval sighed. He had a theory, which he now repeated, that the only woman Noel would ever be able to make love to would be someone very close, someone he had known for a *very* long time, someone he trusted with his life, someone whose voice didn't vandalize his thoughts.

" ... to conclude," said Norval, "in this house from which I am barred, are you acting upon Oedipal impulses? Are you sharing an incestuous bed? Are you in diabolical love with your mother?"

Amor matris, subjective and objective genitive: mother's love for her child, and child's love for mother. "Well, on some nights we do end up sharing a bed ... And I do love her, more than anyone else in the world. Don't you yours?"

"Leave my mother out of it. She's a sack of excrement. Answer the question."

"I'm suspicious about why you're asking it. Are you yourself, by any chance, hiding some dark secret? A homoerotic adventure? Sex with a minor? Sex with a student? An incestuous relationship of your own?"

"Homoerotic adventure? At boarding school every form of transgressive sex was openly indulged, from mutual masturbation and circle jerks to sadomasochism and gang sodomy. Sex with a minor? Every boy of good looks, myself included, had a female name and was recognised as a public prostitute. Sex with a student? In the last five years, I've not got through a single semester without bedding fewer than three students. Incest? My father remarried, had two girls. Before either had reached their teens, I'd slept with them both. For Claire, the eldest, it was the first—and last—orgasm of her life. She married a book critic."

Noel laughed. "You're making all this up, it sounds too ... too Byronic to be true."

A new cigarette appeared magically between Norval's fingers, which he lit with its predecessor. "I shit you not. The point is that *you*, not I, are hiding something."

Noel sighed, bit his lip. "I'm not really hiding ... I mean, the thing is ... I suppose I should have ... well, explained things a long time ago. I'll tell you what. Why don't you come back to the house and see for yourself?"

"A Highland welcome at last. Grr-and. I'm dying to see the ... the sink of iniquity and *mère fatale*. Not to mention the alchemist's den. In which I suspect you've been doing a bit of designing, synthesising—"

"I have, actually. But as for the house, I should warn you that—"

"Put that thing in the trunk of a cab." He nodded towards Noel's mother's bike, which had collapsed against its pole, front wheel upturned and handlebars askew. "En route, I'll tell you more about the latest member of *The Alpha Bet*."

Noel's expression darkened. "Did you take advantage of her?"

"What was that expression? Something from your mother's era, I believe?"

"Did you have sex with Samira?"

Norval inhaled nearly a third of his Arrow and sent a volcanic cloud of smoke and vapour up towards a crippled maple, its limbs scarred or shorn by ice-storms. "Hardly. When we arrived at the loft she was practically sleepwalking. In fact, we should probably stop there on our way, see if she's sentient. Do you mind if she tags along?"

I couldn't possibly have them over, thought Noel, I'll make a complete stooge of myself ... "No, I don't mind at all if she, Samira, tags along. But on second thought, it might be better if we ... if we met at my place a bit later. In a couple hours or so. I've got some things to ... take care of."

Norval eyed his friend suspiciously. "When I ring your bell you'd better answer it. And don't even think about disturbing any of the sordid evidence."

"See you in a couple hours?"

"Taxi!" was the reply.

Chapter 5
"SB"

W hen Noel arrived home he turned off his pager connected to the alarm, punched in letters on the digital lock, unfastened dead bolts. From the inside, the door had been disguised not to look like a door, blending seamlessly with the wall. He had forty-five seconds to deactivate the alarm, which was halfway down the hall.

"Mother! Everything all right?" He pushed buttons on the alarm, and was about to run upstairs to her bedroom when he heard a noise from the family room.

"Is that you, dear?" his mother replied with a mild Scots burr. "Dinner's almost ready!"

"Be right there, Mom." He expelled a sigh of relief and made his way to the end of the hall, under the new fire alarm, past the new fire extinguisher case, towards the new bathroom. He was already sweating: every time he entered the house he felt like he was on a long baker's shovel, slipping into the oven. He looked at the thermostat, turned it down to 80. A red nightlight below it was still shining; he stooped to flick it off. Shouldn't waste electricity, we're bleeding money by the bucket.

On the bathroom door was a large sketch, with the identifying word TOILET. Inside, next to the item in question, were aluminum handrails and knurled grab bars. The handrails were anchored into studs and not drywall, as the manufacturer suggested. Noel eyed the bright yellow padded toilet seat, whose lid had been removed. On the floor was a broken seat-raiser with arms, awaiting repairs. On the wall beside the toilet were instructions:

1. Lift up skirt/pull down pants, etc.
2. Sit down on yellow seat.

3. Relax.
4. Wait for egress.
5. Use toilet paper. ↓
6. Push green flushing lever. →

Noel followed the instructions to the letter, including using the pink toilet paper and pressing the lever with a FLUSH decal on it. He stood up and looked in the mirror, on which another sign had been pasted:

1. Take toothbrush. ↓
2. Put paste on brush. →
3. Brush your top teeth. ↑
4. Brush your lower teeth. ↓
5. Rinse mouth with water. ↓

Noel washed his hands, walked out of the bathroom and down the hall. Along the way, he looked for signs that everything was all right.

"Hi Mom, how are things?"

"Not so good."

"But ... what are you doing?"

Books were scattered over the rush matting of the family room, and one bookcase had capsized. His mother was sitting cross-legged on a Persian carpet, two open books on her lap. "I can never remember where we keep it," she said.

"Keep what?"

"You know."

"The money?"

His mother nodded.

"Mom, we don't hide our money anymore. I did it as a kid, remember? Because you did it as a kid."

"It's in one of these books but I can't remember which one. My entire fortune."

"No, it's not—"

"Yes it is, I just never told you."

"Mom, we don't have a fortune. Not anymore. What little money we do have is kept in a bank. Would you like to go and make a withdrawal? Would you like me to go?"

"It was him."

"Him who?"

"Our neighbour. Fred."

"Fred? Mr. Pickett? In Babylon? The president of the Long Island Parrot Society?"

"He stole our money. I never liked him."

"Mom, Mr. Pickett died in 1988. I think I know where the money is. Do you remember? I used to keep it in the *Oxford English Dictionary*. In the 'LOOK—MOUKE' volume. Because 'mouke' used to mean 'money'. I'll tell you what. You keep looking and I'll check the dictionary, OK?"

Noel walked over to the twenty-volume set, opened up the appropriate volume and, after making sure he wasn't being watched, took out his wallet, removed a wad of cash, stuffed it between the pages.

"Mom, I've found it! You were right!" He handed the volume to his mother, who smiled as she extracted the money and clutched it to her breast.

"I want to go to the bank," she said. "Now. And put this in my account."

"Good idea. But do you want me to do it for you? I'm going there anyway."

She counted the money and handed half to her son.

"Why don't you watch TV until I get back?" said Noel.

"I can't."

"You can't? Is the set broken?"

"Yes."

Noel walked over and pushed in a plastic square. The box warmed to life. "No, it's not, Mom. Look."

"The shows are different now. They're ... broken. I can't understand what's going on. It's all too much nowadays. The world goes too fast. And too far. What did your father call it?"

Here we go again, thought Noel. "Call what?"

"You know."

"No, I don't."

"Yes you do. You're just hiding it from me. As usual."

"I am not hiding anything."

"Yes you are."

"'Poetry is in the empyrean, TV in the pit'?"

"Not that one."

"'A TV is the Devil's workshop'?"

"No. You know ... I can never remember the name for anything in English. I can't think of the *English* for the thing. For anything."

"What is it in French?"

"I can't remember."

"I'll be right back, Mom, just going to the bank. Don't let anyone in while I'm gone. Do you promise?"

"I know what's going on. Don't think I don't."

"Nothing's going on, Mom."

"You don't really want me here. I know money's tight. You don't have to draw me a map."

After relocking the door, but not resetting the alarm or taking his pager, Noel walked four blocks to Prince de Tyr, a Lebanese slow-food on rue Laurier. While waiting to place his order he perspired prolifically under his down parka. I should've set the digital lock too, he said to himself, and reset the alarm, and taken ... *Le numéro deux, s'il vous plaît. Je reviens tout de suite.*

Through discoloured snow and honking traffic, Noel made his way to and from a florist's across the street—barely, as a black SUV the size of a destroyer nearly ripped off his ear with its wing mirror. Stop signs for Montrealers are mere suggestions, he reflected inside the restaurant while massaging his right temple. He then worried about his mother for forty-five minutes to Arabic music.

On the way back he invented omens. If the light ahead stayed green, his mother would get better, if he saw a black car, she wouldn't ... When he awkwardly opened the front door, his arms full of food and flowers, he sensed something different inside the house, something untoward. For he had seen a black car, and the light had changed to red.

"Mom! I'm back, I've got food! Phoenician food!"

"In here, dear!"

Noel walked into the living room. "I got menu number two, your favourite! Falalfel, baba ghanoush, stuffed vine leaves ..."

He stopped when he saw someone official-looking, wearing glasses on a silver chain and giant clip-on earrings, sitting on the chair across from his mother. She had a clipboard on her lap and a body that flirted with immenseness. Oh no, not another salesperson. How the hell did she get in?

The woman introduced herself, her voice infecting Noel's brain with bending otter-brown rectangles, which opened and closed like an accordion. Instead of returning her greeting, he turned on the stereo, slipped a silver disc into a tray: Scriabin's *Poem of Ecstasy*. He then walked to the kitchen, set the food and flowers on the counter, opened the fridge and took out a jalapeño pepper.

"I'm sorry," he said when he returned. "I was a bit distracted, Miss ..."

"Mrs. Holtzberger. From Home Care."

Weathering a tear-gas attack of perfume, Noel introduced himself. "I'm Noel, Mrs. Burun's son." He took a large bite out of the pepper, halving it, before shaking her hand. "How did you get in, Mrs. Holtzberger, if you don't mind my asking?"

"Well, I ... your mother opened the door."

"Right."

The woman eyed the remains of the vegetable. "I've come to interview your mother to see if she qualifies."

"Qualifies?"

"For assistance. For a day nurse. Two or three days a week to help your mom."

"Right." It was he himself who had filled out the application, six months before. To replace a nurse they couldn't afford.

"I'm also here to check up on various reports that have been forwarded to our department—"

Noel tried to fight through the sound of Mrs. Holtzberger's rectangles, as well as the image of her snow-and-rose complexion and stop-sign-red lipstick that went well beyond the boundaries of her mouth. What was she saying? Complaints from the neighbours? They're chronic complainers. Yes, I know she's been wandering but that's all in the past. Yes, she has one now, she has a Medic Alert bracelet ... I *know* she's not wearing it now. We'll find it, it's here somewhere. The house is a mess? A bit of an exaggeration, that. But she doesn't *want* to live anywhere else. She wants to live at home, with me. Plus she's getting better, she really is. Yes, I understand perfectly ...

"So if you don't mind I'll just begin the MMSE?"

Noel stooped to turn off Scriabin's muted trombones. "She's had several examinations already, Mrs. Holtzberger. In fact, her doctor is a world-famous neurologist. Émile Vorta—you may have heard of him."

"It won't take long. Nothing to worry about. Is that all right, Mrs. Burun? And may I call you Stella?"

Mrs. Burun's lips were pursed tightly, as if she were on the brink of helpless laughter. She was recalling that time in Spain—was it Spain?—

when Noel had tricked her into laughing for a photograph by doing a demented ballet leap. What's it called? When you cross your legs back and forth ...

"Perhaps you'd like to leave us for a few minutes, Mr. Burun?"

"No, I'll ... stay if you don't mind." Noel walked toward the front window.

"Very well. Mrs. Burun, my first question is this: What is the year? Mrs. Burun? Can you tell me what year it is?"

Was it Spain or ... that other country? Mrs. Burun saw dark weathered bricks in a zigzag pattern, and long arcades. Turin? *"Entrechat,"* she murmured, smiling.

"I'm sorry? Mrs. Burun? Can you tell me what year it is?"

Mrs. Burun gazed straight ahead. Who *is* this woman? She appears to be waiting for me to say something ...

"The year, Stella. Do you know what year it is?"

"The year? Oh, dear me. I would say ... nineteen ... we're in the nineties but I ..."

Mrs. Holtzberger wrote something down with a stubby pencil. "And what is the season?"

"Fall?"

Looking out the window, Noel sighed deeply. Through the frosted pane, black trees against the banking clouds swam before his eyes.

"What is the month?"

"October?"

"And the date?"

"Sunday?"

"Where are we? What country?"

"I don't ... Canada?"

"What city?"

"Aberdeen?"

"What she means is that she was born in Aberdeen," said Noel. "The question was confusing."

"Thank you, Mr. Burun, for the ... supplementary information. But I'm afraid this test is for your mother only. Now, Mrs. Burun, what is the name of your street? Mrs. Burun?"

"Coppertree Lane?"

"I think she means that we *used* to live there," said Noel. "In Babylon, Long Island. Where Rodney Dangerfield was—"

"And what room of the house are we in now, Mrs. Burun?"

"The dining room?"

Noel put his hands on the window sill, for support. He looked up at the dark winter sky and a freezing wind swept through him. She's taking all the latest prescription drugs, he thought. State-of-the-goddamn-art. *Why* aren't they working? Why is *nothing* working?

"I'm now going to give you three words to remember. And then I want you to repeat them to me. All right? Are you ready? Here are the three words: cucumber, lamp, nickel. Can you repeat those to me, Mrs. Burun? Cucumber, lamp, nickel."

Stella screwed up her face in concentration. "Cucumber, lamp ... I forget the rest. I'm terribly sorry. I'm not myself today, you see ..."

"That's all right, dear, you're doing fine. I now have a rather tricky task for you. I want you to start from one hundred and count backwards, subtracting seven each time."

A long silence unspun as the kitchen faucet dripped with a dead beat, like a clock marking off time, like a drum beating a dirge. Images of Europe returned. A funeral in ... that city full of water. With blackly ribboned boats, or whatever they're called, and someone beating a drum. She had thought of her husband as the sound grew louder, as the coffin floated by ...

"Mrs. Burun?"

"Mrs. Holtzberger," said Noel. "*I* can't even bloody well count backwards by multiples of seven—"

"Mrs. Burun? Can you count backwards from one hundred, subtracting seven each time? No? OK, we'll move on. Can you spell the word *radar* backwards? No? Can you recall the three words I asked you to remember earlier on?" Mrs. Holtzberger glanced at a watch that was embedded in the flesh of her wrist. "No? Do you enjoy life, Mrs. Burun?"

"Can't say I do."

"How do you feel about life?"

"I can't say that I feel anything at all." She wore a look of infinite sadness, resignation.

"She's not been well the past couple of days," said Noel. "Really. She's got ... the flu. A virulent avian strain. For that reason I'm going to have to ask you to come back and do this test another—"

"Mr. Burun, a repeat may be requested if the subject is overly anxious or upset but according to my guidelines—"

"We appreciate you coming, Mrs. Holtzberger. But I'm afraid my mother needs to rest right now ..."

"Then I'll just have to submit these incomplete test results," she said animatedly, rolls of flesh shifting and wobbling on her neck. "Which may adversely affect your request for day help. And there's another matter to be discussed. In private, if you don't mind?"

"I've no secrets from my mother."

"Very well. I have received reports, more than one, that your mother has been wandering around the neighbourhood, knocking on windows."

"I ... know of no such incidents."

"Are you aware of an incident involving your mother's cat?"

"Which ... incident are you referring to?"

"Before you arrived, your mother explained that your neighbour killed her cat, maliciously."

"He killed Morven," said Stella.

Morven died of a tumour in 1991, Noel recalled. "That's ... correct," he said.

"She also claimed your neighbour drowned Morven's kittens in his hot tub."

Noel sighed. "Alas."

"And that he then suffocated the mother by locking it inside a suitcase."

"I can show you the case," said Noel. "With teeth and claw marks. I can get it if you like."

Mrs. Holtzberger rolled her eyes. "That won't be necessary, Mr. Burun. But you will be hearing from us *very* soon. No, I'll see myself out."

꙳

A bad day, Noel said to himself as he put his mother to bed. Big deal, nothing to it—we all have bad days. Things will be better tomorrow ...

Mrs. Burun blinked rapidly to quell tears, sensing she'd done something wrong, sensing she'd let her son down. "What's wrong with me, Noel dear? I feel like something's wrong but I don't know what it is."

He had heard this before, many times, yet he could barely stop himself from collapsing into tears. It was simply heartbreaking. "Don't worry, Mom." He smiled bravely. "Tomorrow's another day. We're in the twenty-first century—things are bound to get better. We'll have a riot tomorrow, you wait and see. Oh, I almost forgot. I've got a surprise for you."

45

Mrs. Burun stopped crying, distracted by these words like a small child. In the cheval glass beside the bed Noel could see her reflection. He crossed the room and brought back a bouquet of flowers.

"Look what I got for you, Mom. Amaranth."

His mother's eyes sparkled as she smelled the flowers and caressed their petals.

"Remember when you read me 'The Rose and the Amaranth'? From Aesop? The undying flower? No? Doesn't matter. It was eons ago." Into a juice glass he poured out a frog-green liquid from an unlabelled amber bottle. "Take a bit more of this, Mom. It should help." And hopefully without side-effects. "I've got some new ideas, new tricks up my sleeve, you wait and see." He watched his mother drink. "Oh, I almost forgot, something unbelievable happened. You'll never guess who I met. Are you ready? Heliodora Locke. In Montreal of all places!"

His mother gazed at him vacantly.

"Heliodora Locke!" he shouted, unnecessarily, as if sheer volume would jog her memory. "You know, *The Bride and Three Bridegrooms*! You remember, Mom ..."

Mrs. Burun had a look of fear on her face as her son encouraged her with broad facial expressions and charade-like gestures. "Remember? We *loved* that movie. It's one of our favourites. Heliodora Locke, the girl with kaleidoscope eyes. Remember you used to tease me about being in love with ... never mind." Noel smiled, tried to hide his frustration. "That's OK, Mom. Don't worry about it. It's not important. Couldn't be less important, in fact ..."

His mother's expression gradually changed. "She found three men on the seashore. Shipwrecked. They were all unconscious."

Noel's features froze, his breathing stopped.

"She nursed them back to health, and they all fell in love with her."

Noel stared at his mother, incredulously. And then launched himself into her arms, laughing, rocking back and forth on the bed. "Yes, Mom, that's right. I *knew* you'd remember! This is good news, *very* good news." Vorta's drugs are kicking in, he said to himself. I *knew* this would be the right batch!

His mother began to stroke his hair, as she used to. And then out of the blue she said, "Your father ... had a passion for family trees. But what you didn't know, what I never told you, was that he was easily taken in. Despite his ... brilliance."

Noel tried to stop his heart from pounding, shocked at this new lucidity. "You mean ... Byron's really not my ancestor?"

His mother merely smiled. "Poets are the unacknowledged legislators of the world, your father used to say."

Why did she remember that line? Noel wondered. Because of the amaranth?[11] His brain began to generate rows of coloured letters but with effort he shut the generator down. "I ... I never heard him say that, Mom."

"Your father was unhappy with the acknowledged legislators."

Noel desperately wanted to hear more—she had never talked of his father's unhappiness in this way—but his mother's mind leapt abruptly to another subject. "I've got some stuff for Émile," she said. "Can you take it to him, dear? You can read it if you like."

Before he could reply, in the blink of an eye she fell asleep. For a moment he thought of waking her, of extending these precious moments, but he didn't have the heart. She'd suffered from insomnia for weeks. So he ever so gently lifted her fingers from his hair, and kissed her on the forehead. On tiptoes he then crept towards her blue Olivetti Lettera (a gift from her husband that a computer would never replace) and picked up a sheaf of papers beside a well-thumbed thesaurus. There was a half-finished page still in the typewriter, barely readable. Must change the ribbon, he thought. Taking one last peek at his mother, Noel switched off the light, closed the door. In the hall, after selecting a key from a ring, he locked the door from the outside—his mother's jailer!—as emotions rose to fill his throat and flood his eyes.

A sound from below distracted him. Someone was ringing the door-bell, piercingly and long, while pounding maniacally on the door. A picture quivered on the foyer wall. The cacophony of clangs and bangs continued for several minutes before a dead silence redescended on the house. At the top of the stairs he sat down and began to read his mother's pages.

Chapter 6
Stella's Diary (I)

Like one, that on a lonesome road
Doth walk in fear and dread,
And having once turned round walks on
And turns no more his head;
Because he knows a frightful fiend
Doth close behind him tread.

— Coleridge, "The Rime of the Ancient Mariner"

Friday, 9 February 2001. A huge day, in the hugely negative sense. According to the doctor I have 'mild cognitive impairment'. That doesn't sound too bad at first, but let me put it another way: I'm in the first stage of ... Alzheimer's Disease. The very names of certain diseases bring dread and AD is one of them. It's a death sentence. A long and slow one.

Émile asked me to keep this journal while I still have 'self-insight' -- i.e. the ability to recognise what's happening to me. Later on, because of the deterioration in the cells in my temporal lobe, where insights are formed apparently, I won't be able to do this. 'Don't forget to keep it every day,' he told me.

Fine, I still have insight, but that's more a curse than a blessing. Because I know the future and the future is this:

I can't remember the term for it, which is why I drew it (I used to draw better).

Or if it's not like being under the sword, it's like the Ancient Mariner, but I can't remember why. And I don't want to bother poor Noel again. ~~I used to draw better than this.~~

The sword of Damocles! (I just asked Noel.)

Thank God for Noel. And yet even with Noel here, life can be so terribly lonely. I don't see my old colleagues any more. Or my friends. Because keeping up my end of the conversation can be a real battle sometimes. Too often I can't remember the last thing said. I can remember rocking Noel in his crib thirty-two years ago, I can remember my husband proposing to me thirty-five years ago, but often I can't remember what was said thirty-five seconds ago.

I seem forever on the verge of remembrance, like trying to recall a dream, when you get the faintest of glimpses before the whole thing evaporates.

And it's so frustrating when I explain what's wrong with me. No one really understands. My lapses, I mean. My friends say things like 'We all forget things, Stella. We all lose our train of thought. It's normal in this age of PIN numbers and passwords. There's really nothing wrong with you.' And I just nod, instead of saying 'No no, that's not it, that's not it at all. It's more than that, you see.'

~~Émile says I have 'mild cognitive impairment'.~~ In conversations, just when you think of something relevant or clever or amusing to say, you forget some pertinent detail. And you lose your confidence. Or you're afraid you've asked the same question and they're tired of repeating themselves. And often you repeat something not because you've forgotten it, but because you can't remember whether you said it or merely thought it.

Sometimes you just want to find a place to hide, a place to cry. What does an elephant do when its time has come? It walks alone into the jungle. Sometimes that's what I feel like doing, assuming I could ever find a jungle.

~~Mild cognitive impairment, which is what I have, is the first sign of Alzheimer's.~~ I'm in a no-woman's land, in a strange place where I'm no longer the self-assured and knowledgeable person I once was. A history teacher, for God's sake!

But I'm not mad yet either -- I can still think, I can still reason. What annoys me is the way Émile is starting to bypass me, giving all the details about my case, and all the eye contact, to my son. It's infuriating. I'm going to say something to him next time. If I remember. I'd better write it on my hand.

13 February 2001. Fugaces labuntur anni.[12] How in heaven did I remember that, from my distant schooldays? I want to go back so badly, back to Aberdeen. I remember things that happened to me there better than things that happened here two weeks ago! Will Noel go with me, I wonder?

God, how I miss the things I used to have, the little things we take for granted. To be able to make small talk, to joke, to remember people's names, to read a book or watch a movie without getting lost. To walk or drive without getting lost!

I can't find my car keys, which has happened lots of times before, of course, but this time it feels different. This time I don't think it's a case of misplacing them, of not remembering where I left them. This time I have a feeling they've been stolen.

If Noel took them away, I must have really got lost, really gone far astray ... The mother who used to wonder where her son was now has a son who wonders where his mother is.

15 February. I wake up and my brain doesn't seem to be wired right. I feel like looking in the Yellow Pages for a good electrician, one who knows what he's doing, who won't throw up his hands at the mess. 'I can rewire it if you like, Mrs. Burun,' he'd probably say, 'or you can just wait for the fire.' And then I start to panic, and get more muddled, and then pull the covers back over me and go back to sleep.

18 February. Noel and I were going through a box of mementos today and he showed me a card he made me years ago for Mother's Day. It used the letters of MOTHER to make a poem or rhyme. I can't find it now and I can't remember what it said, but it was lovely. I've spent the past few hours, with pencil and eraser, writing an updated version. Here it is:

50

M is for the miseries of Menopause,
O is for the road to Oblivion,
T is for the Tailspin of ageing,
H is for the feeling of Helplessness,
E is for the feeling of Emptiness,
R is for my Rage over losing my Role of M O T H E R.

20 February. 'The future is not something I'm dying to get
to,' I remember Noel saying when he was six or seven (and I
laughed, seeing the dark humour). Now, I feel the opposite:
the future is not something I'm in any hurry to get to. The
future is not what it used to be.

The buy-out I signed allowed me to teach part time, which
I've wanted for years, but I now know I'll never be able to do
that. I feel like I've spent my life climbing the rungs of a
slide.

22 February. Alzheimerland is a foreign country. Time
doesn't move the same way here, calendars are fuzzy, the days
and months shuffled like cards in a deck. And space is
different too -- the land seems to wobble, the signposts
shift. You stumble through mud or sand, through mines and
traps. And it's hard to talk to people here, to speak their
language. It's so hard to get used to -- it's not like where I
grew up.

Did you ever walk into a room and forget why you went in?
Entering the FORGETTERY, I used to call it. Or was it my
husband who called it that? Anyway, we used to laugh but
now I don't find it so funny -- because that's how we
Alzheimerians spend our waking hours.

26 February. Is Alois Alzheimer spinning in his grave, I
wonder, remembered only for a disease of forgetting? Do many
Germans have this last name? Or has it died out, like Hitler's?

2 March. Someone came over today. I don't know who it was,
although the face looked so familiar. I tried to pretend, but
I don't think I fooled anybody.

It leaves me angry and frustrated. And I'm afraid I take

out my frustration and anger on poor Noel. What would I do without him? I'd be in a padded cell, that's where I'd be.

~~My plan was to go back to teaching, part time,~~

I can see myself ending up in a nursing home, and the idea kills me (Freudian slip, I meant to say 'fills me') with pain and sadness. I don't want to go. I pray my brain will hold out a little longer, until I'm dead ...

9 March. Everything inside so hollow, so grey and dry. My brain leaking memory and hope. So grey! I'm underwater, it feels like, in dark and blurry waters. Perhaps like those my husband saw, before he died.

13 March. Three days have gone by. I know this only because I saw the date on the newspaper (the only line I read these days). Three more days, cancelled days, gone without a trace. A trio of blank squares cut out of the calendar.

15 March. I'm watching too much television. That's all I seem to do these days. I like shows like ~~Who Wants to be a Millionaire~~ Jeopardy, even though Noel can't stand it. He thinks the questions are too easy. I used to agree with him, but now I'm starting to find that I can't even answer the early questions. The answers just don't come! There's another quiz show I like but I can't remember its name.

18 March. I came to sit here because I wanted to write something important but I can't remember what it was. I've been sitting here for an hour or two with a mind that feels like cake batter, looking down at the white letters on the keys, or up at ringed calendar days and not knowing why they're ringed ...

Just remembered -- after watching some stupid quiz show on TV. It's about this newspaper article I cut out. (I'm trying to read as much as I can, because Noel said it's good for the brain, but I find TV easier and it's probably too late now anyway.) In any case, I have it beside me now. It's from The Gazette.

Mercy killer commits suicide

A man who pleaded guilty to suffocating his mother in what he claimed was a mercy killing has killed himself while out on day parole.

Noel Burun, 32, pleaded guilty to manslaughter in the death of his mother, Stella Burun, who suffered from Alzheimer's disease. He admitted placing a plastic bag over her head while the two were staying at the Château Frontenac in Quebec City on September 6, 2000.

Burun, sentenced to five years, was known to have attempted suicide twice after killing his mother.

On March 16, the National Parole Board granted Burun day parole, to be spent in a halfway house. He was also serving part of his sentence at the Philippe Pinel Institute, a Quebec government psychiatric hospital. A report issued by the board indicated Burun had difficulty in dealing with his mother's death, experiencing 'severe depression and recurrent nightmares'.

I don't know why I typed this out. And why did I substitute Noel's name, and my own? What does that mean? Am I seeing the future? Should I phone ... what's his name, the doctor? Émile? Should I tell Noel what I've done? Now I'm getting worried. I'm starting to panic. Am I losing my mind? I'd better go to bed.

23 March. I looked all day for my car keys. Then Noel said he'd prefer that I not drive any more. So I became furious and stormed outside in my housecoat to see if the keys were in the ... whatever it's called. So I went outside and the doors were all locked and then I couldn't remember what I was looking for. And then I saw my licence plate and laughed. 'Je me souviens,' it says.[13]

The ignition. (Thank you, Noel.)

May? This is so hard to write. The typing part is OK, I still have most of my dexterity and finger-memory, but I have to keep looking in the dictionary for certain words and for the spelling and then I forget which word I'm looking for!

Alzheimer's is like when they switched to metric. When everything you'd known for years suddenly got mixed up. The numbers weren't the same, they didn't mean the same thing. You didn't really know how much things cost, or what the temperature was, or how far it was to the next town.

Or it's like when we came to America, when we switched from driving on the left side. Oh, you get used to it, eventually, but I'm in that place before you get used to it.

June? I've made a decision. If I can't make sense while talking, I just won't talk.

July? ~~I think I lost my car keys~~ Awful really the way I've let this place slide. But the hedges are clipped. Maybe I do better when I'm not quite all there. I wake up from a nap, look out my window ... and the hedges are clipped. Somebody must have done it. It had to be me, I guess. Who else?
I must get my eyes checked. Or change this ribbon. Things are starting to fade.

I must get my eyes checked. Or change this ribbon. Things are starting to fade

Thurs. (or Sunday?) Haven't the foggiest notion where I am or why. I woke up this morning and I was here in this place. They tell me it's my home, but I find that hard to believe. I know I wasn't here yesterday. A young lad came to the door. Or a lass, it's hard to tell these days. Maybe not young. With a brush. They're always coming and going. I don't like all the hurly-burly, it's so ... I don't know the word. And she doesn't know how to make tea. I told her so. I will not tolerate bags, nasty things. And she doesn't hot the pot! I think I'll go out for tea. I can't find the keys to my car. Why are these drawers open? Who opened them? A robber? Are

54

my keys in here? I have lots of socks in here. Must put some
in the suitcase. What time does the train leave again? I
would like to take this photograph too. He looks familiar. I
don't remember putting this poppy in here. Why would
someone have done that? This is not my toothbrush anyway. I
think it belongs to those people who were here. I'll take it
downstairs and give it to them. That woman who came to the
door. I thanked her for coming and told her I was not well
but she doesn't leave. She doesn't have any right to be here
after I've asked her politely to leave. This is still my home.
She says I have to talk to my son. Fine, give me the phone and
I'll call him now. When the bank answers I'll ask them how
much money I have in my account. I will need money for the
trip. But first I will eat this food on a tray. Is it for me? No.
I'll just go down and make some of those ... well, those round
things. Why is my sleeve all wet? I wonder what time the
train leaves. My head is all upset. It's all padded and
woolly. Noises make me that way. Or give me pains and the
colour grey. I used to be smooth and white inside, but now
I'm all grey. My son (sometimes I'm not even sure he is my
son) keeps telling me I'm getting better but I wonder. He
keeps telling me he's getting closer. Closer to what? I can't
remember anyone's name. Or face. I know my son. But who is
everyone else? Why is she here, with the soap? What's that
screechy noise? Did I light something? What's the number to
call?

XXXX. I asked Noel the days of the week and he was a
complete idiot. Not those days! The other days! Yes, what
your father called them. Well, whoever! Type them for me.

But now where did I put that blasted paper? Everything
seems to

Ok here

Moanday. I.. dshhe

Tearsday. Did not

55

Wailsday. Cant seem to

Thumpsday

Frightday

Shatterday. Will never unerstan

The quick brown fox the quck b the qu umps ove)
  Tththequickbrow thththtfojeovthethethethethetlleghe
jdlpeop Yje wuivk noten ogc mumpd obrt yhr slxy
foh.peppe;dlgkeopop0e2848u9hvndk,gjfkfkfkfkfkfkfkfkfe
oeoeoeoeodla;;p;kkpojk.Lfldjgfjlgjlerjte
ioogfdghoioihnhnorgfnogdfonfdgongldsj888888888888888888
888888888888888888888888888888888888888888888888888888
888888888888888888888888888888888888888888888888888888
888888888888888888888888888888888888888888888888888888

Chapter 7
Noel's Diary (I)

A lily lasts a week or two,
~~A month or two for roses~~ A rose gets smashed in bad weather.
But like a mother's love,
The amaranth lasts forever.

— Noel Burun, age 8

December 8, 2000. After a day at the library, went over to Mom's for a late dinner, a "European" dinner as she calls it. I set the table, lit two candles, poured a Riesling with a Gothic castle on its label while Mom brought out two plates of swordfish amandine, mashed potatoes and glazed carrots. This looks exquisite, I said. But after my first bite I realised the swordfish was cold, not far from frozen. I'll just warm everything up in the micro, Mom said. Won't be a tick. While glancing at a New York Times she had placed beside me (one more act of thoughtfulness in a constellation of such acts), I waited. And waited. I could hear clicking sounds in the kitchen. Everything OK, Mom? I shouted. Well, not really, she answered. I entered the kitchen. Mom, flustered, was fiddling with the dials on the dishwasher. I can never remember how these blasted things work, she said. I walked over to see what the problem was. I pulled down the dishwasher door and saw a strange sight: on the top tray were two plates of swordfish amandine, mashed potatoes and glazed carrots. Dripping wet. I opened my mouth in surprise, but quickly closed it. I stood there, frozen, not knowing what to do or say. What would be appropriate here? I took a deep breath. "These machines are a pain in the ass, aren't they, Mom. I can never get the bloody things to work either. Why don't you ... sit back down, relax, read the paper, let me look after it?" Mom smiled lifelessly before walking back to the dining room. After draining the dishes, and then nuking them, I returned with two steaming-hot plates. I made jokes to distract her, childhood puns that had always cracked her up before, but not this time. This time she stared at me in silence, knife and fork squeezed in her hands.

After toying with her food, and taking a sip or two of wine, she said she wasn't hungry.

December 27. Mom and I were finishing off a turkey and the dregs of decade-old Drambuie when she started talking about a buyout on her teacher's contract, an early retirement package, and why she was determined to take it. I hardly needed an explanation—after 25 years she'd been gutted by teacher's burnout, and by mother's burnout after 30 years of worrying about me. I asked her if she was still going to do her volunteer work and she said yes, she felt an affinity with the elderly, even more so now because she was one of them. You're still young, I said, with the beauty and brains of a woman twenty years younger. She waved the compliment away with her hand. And how about your night classes? I went on. Are you going to continue with them? Is there room on your walls for more diplomas? This time there was no waving hand, no acknowledgement of any kind. Which diplomas? she finally asked. What do you mean, which diplomas? Your Art History diplomas! More silence as my mother gently rubbed, between her thumb and forefinger, the embossed handle of a knife. In your office, I said. I haven't the foggiest idea what you're talking about, she said. Come on, Mom, quit fooling around. Do you want me to show you one? Do you want me to get one? Mom shook her head, fear beginning to seep into her eyes. She laid down her knife. No, that's all right, she said.

February 2, 2001. The first doctor told her she was fine. But the memory lapses and confusion continued, so I took her to see an expert, Dr. Vorta. He did some urine samples, blood samples, X-rays, CAT scans. A student-technician put her head inside a PET scan machine that traced radioactive sugar as it moved through her brain, showing how vigorously the various parts were used. I watched the monitors while Dr. Vorta pointed out what the colours of the images signified: pirate-blue for the skull casing, blood-red for the cerebral lobes, plum-purple for the tracer. Next he put her in a modified PET scanner of his own invention, which lights up the mess that Alzheimer makes with radioactive dyes: the errant gummy proteins (beta amyloid) that gum up the works. His technician then did a series of word-recall tests, asking her to repeat strings of three or four unrelated words—blue, Chevrolet, turnip, Syrian. Then she was asked to multiply 6 by 12, name the first Canadian prime minister, the current prime minister ... She was doing really well and I was beginning to think she didn't have any problems. At the end of the test, however, which took about ten minutes, she was asked to recall some of the

58

unrelated words. She couldn't remember any of them. Not even after getting clues (e.g. that one was a vegetable, another a car, etc.). Not one single one.

February 11, 2001. Today we got the news. A discernible shrinking of the hippocampus, where short-term memories are stored. And evidence of amyloid plaque. Based on that and the word tests, Mom has "mild cognitive impairment," or "premature senile dementia." Early-onset AD, in other words. What's the prognosis? I asked Dr. Vorta, well out of Mom's earshot. She has a chronic invalidating condition, he replied after a pause. Unless a cure is discovered soon, Noel, your mother will be dead in five years.

February 21. There's nothing more I can do. I can't be expected to look after her. I've got my own life, my own apartment, it's near the library, it's cheap and took ages to find. I can't just get up and leave. I have a lease. And besides, I'm not qualified to look after her. She'll be better off with people who know what they're doing. I'll stay with her this week. And then I'm afraid I'll have to put her name on a waiting list somewhere.

March 1. Sublet my apartment. Moved in this afternoon with Mom. She's happier, and so am I.

March 4. Tonight we went to the Dragon Rouge in Chinatown, which Mom really enjoyed, smiling at the waiter and saying "please" and "thank you" in Cantonese, and laughing as she twirled her chopsticks like a baton (we'd had a litre of rice wine). But when I laid down my credit card at the end of the meal she got angry, accusing me of spending all her money. She then made a solemn vow: she was getting her own place because "It's just not working out."

March 6. Nothing good to report. Mom has spent much of the past week confused, bursting into tears, forgetting the way to friends' houses, forgetting whether we drove on the left or right side "in this country," obsessively mourning her husband and deceased childhood pets.

What dark road are we travelling down? She's only 56, for God sake. Will she end up like Claude Jutras?[14]

March 7. Went to a matinée film today and when I got home Mom was furious with me for leaving her alone "for days." I met this strangely magnetic man there, someone I'd seen twice before, on the 9th floor of the

59

Psych Building. His name's Norval (I don't know his last name) and he reminds me of … myself. A much improved version. Unless it was my imagination—and it probably was, given my anti-talent for making friends— we seemed to hit it off. I'll probably never see him again.

March 11. All day long Mom's been playing songs from the sixties—over and over like a child. (She was 14 when the sixties began.) Over the past few years, for each of her birthdays, I've given her CDs to replace her scratched vinyl. I have also given her headphones, to no avail. I am now listening to a song I have heard approximately nine hundred times. Based on the number of repetitions, here is Mom's Top Ten 60s Hit Parade (not including the Beatles, which is another list):

1. Love Is All Around—The Troggs
2. A World Without Love—Peter & Gordon
3. I Only Want to Be with You—Dusty Springfield
4. Don't Throw Your Love Away—The Searchers
5. Silhouettes—Herman's Hermits
6. Catch the Wind—Donovan
7. Paint It Black—Rolling Stones
8. Bad To Me—Billy J. Kramer & the Dakotas
9. Wishin' and Hopin'—Dusty Springfield
10. As Tears Go By—Marianne Faithful

March 13. Even though Mom pleaded with me, hysterically, not to go, I went for another Tuesday matinée today. She eventually calmed down and gave her permission. Norval was there, smoking outside, when I arrived. I was really happy to see him, and he seemed happy to see me. We sat together, at his insistence, and I didn't feel awkward at all, even though he's miles above me in so many ways. He's an incredible character—I still can't believe what he did after the movie was over. As we were walking down Avenue du Parc and discussing the opening scene of Spellbound, he did something … how would I describe it? As unexpected as you can get. A few yards ahead of us, on the sidewalk, this woman's dog … answers the call of nature. Right in the middle of the sidewalk. And the woman doesn't pick up. She and dog just calmly move on. When we arrive at the scene a few seconds later, Norval stops, takes out a white handkerchief, stoops … and carefully wraps up a rather large turd. I thought he was going to run after the woman but no. He just continues on, calmly, not saying a word. I'm dumbstruck. So we're now approaching the

Banque Nationale where there's this surly adolescent beggar, a permanent fixture who opens the door for people using the cash machine. As we pass by, he sticks out his cap and says to Norval in French, "Hey, I recognise you, I held the door for you a couple hours ago. Come on you cheap fucking dildo, I'm hungry!"

"Really?" says Norval. "Well, it's your lucky day. Here you go, enjoy. Steaming fresh."

"Ah! Merci, monsieur, merci beaucoup!"

"Any time. And there's more where that came from."

March 14. Just reread that last entry. I was wondering if it was one of those you-had-to-be-there anecdotes so I told it to Mom this morning. She didn't crack a smile. So I told it again, with a slightly different angle and emphasis, and she laughed, hard and long. But not as hard and long as I did when it had happened: a sustained belly laugh that left me hurting and gasping, the kind you get, if you're lucky, when you're young, and almost never when you're old.

March 20. Mom's been up and down—good days and bad, good seconds and bad. Her mind is like a malfunctioning TV—sometimes the colours are off, the picture blizzardous, the horizontal or vertical slipping. Sometimes, after a good shake, things come in loud and clear—or dead-silent and blank.

March 21. Spring equinox. Dr. Vorta wasn't at the lab this morning—he had a press conference about some award—so I asked Dr. Ravenscroft about a hormone therapy regimen, an estrogen plus progestin combination, which seems to be all the rage for post-menopausal women. He said that brain scans hint it improves blood flow to parts of the brain important for learning and memory. And that longitudinal studies suggest women who use hormone replacement have about half the usual risk of Alzheimer's. Later in the day, when I repeated all this to Dr. Vorta, he replied, "Noel, Charles Ravenscroft is a simpleton. We will <u>never</u> use hormone therapy for any type of memory disorder. Every single claim for its benefits has come down like a house of cards. My own studies suggest it doubles the risk of dementia. The results will be published next month."

March 23. Learned today that Mom has been accepting offers from telemarketers and phone salesmen. One of them, "Ray," sold her something called an X-TERPA, a "miracle machine that measures electromagnetic energy flows and blockages via electrodes in your skin, then alters those flows to cure all ailments, including cancer and brain disorders." With taxes and handling charges, she paid just under fifteen hundred dollars for it.

March 25. Mom received yet another delivery today, the third this week, and I was beginning to wonder if she was having an affair with the Fed-Ex man. This box she hid, unopened, until just before going to bed. After I read her a Somerset Maugham story ("Mr. Know-All"), she whispered in my ear that there was a parcel behind the curtains, or in the closet, and that I could open it if I liked. It was not behind the curtains. Or in the closet. I finally found it under her bed, beside an "Australian Hunter's Lamp." I opened the new package, clumsily, and under styrofoam pellets and polystyrene bubble wrap I discovered a black pistol, like a science-fiction ray-gun. According to the enclosed pamphlet it was a "Gamma Gun that activates the quarks and superstrings that kill the parasites that cause cancer and other diseases, including Parkingson [sic] and Alzheimer." According to the enclosed invoice, she got it at a special discount price of 5 easy payments of $99.

March 26. This morning, after gently knocking on and then opening Mom's door, I noticed she was looking at images on the Internet. I was pleased—I'd set it up weeks before and it was the first time I'd seen her using it. But after shamelessly creeping up behind her and looking over her shoulder, I discovered that she's been corresponding with a gentleman named Alex H. from Hartford, Connecticut. Today Alex sent her a full frontal of himself, complete with oiled breasts like a wrestler, nipple rings and shorn pubic hair. Not a happy combination. In return he asked for a j-peg of her in a similar pose, and a Fed-Ex box with her "pantie-hoze" inside. After dinner, while Mom was taking a bath, I changed her e-mail address.

March 27. Mom has taken to circling dates on her calendar and writing things on her skin. Her left hand is covered with blue reminders: across the palm and up and down all five fingers. And these sad words across her wrist: "I am Stella Burun."

March 28. At bedtime Mom and I paged through an album of photographs—including a priceless one of her in hysterics—of a trip we took to Italy in '89. One of the great things about travelling in Europe with Mom, among many great things, was that she knew almost everything about each country's history. All the rulers, battles, scandals, intrigues, etc. I could listen to her for

62

hours. And so could others. At the Palazzo Diamanti in Ferrara, a group of New Zealanders followed us around from room to room, hanging on her every word as she talked about the Borgias for close to an hour.

Now she walks from room to room carrying a bucket or broom, whose purpose she's already forgotten.

March 29. This afternoon, as I was finishing up some work for Dr. Vorta, Mom decided she wanted to go to Mount Royal Cemetery to place gladioli on Dad's grave. "Won't be a tick," she said. When it finally registered what she was doing, I went running outside in my slippers. But the car was already half way down the street. Oh well, I said to myself, it's only a five-minute drive. She was gone for four and a half hours. The whole time I told myself there was a perfectly rational explanation for her being away so long (a friend of hers lives near the cemetery, for example—maybe the two had just stepped out when I called) but I was tortured with worry—and about to call the police—when I saw her pull up the drive. She couldn't remember where the cemetery was, she explained, so she turned around and—eventually, after driving onto a ferry which took her to an Indian reservation—found her way home.

March 30. Today Mom took a computer driving assessment test with Danielle, one of Dr. Vorta's assistants. She had to respond to various driving tasks and situations by touching the screen or pushing a button. Those who score in the top third, Danielle explained, are considered competent to drive; those in the middle have to take the test again; those in the bottom third should "get the hell off the road."

"Madame Burun," said Danielle when the test was over, "I want to emphasise that this evaluation does not reflect upon your intelligence, only on your ability to continue driving. Do you understand?"

Mom nodded. She placed in the bottom third.

March 31. Took Mom's keys away. Painfully hard, on both of us. But I wouldn't back down, even when tears as thick as glycerine beaded and fell from her eyes. Because I'm afraid she'll forget the difference between red and green.

April 3. Tonight we watched one of Mom's favourite shows, Jeopardy, which I suspect she always wanted to go on. She was certainly as good as any champion I'd ever seen. But ten years ago, when I encouraged her to audition, she said it was a silly show made ludicrous by having to put your answers in the form of a question. It made no sense, I remember her saying, to ask the question "Who is Abraham Lincoln?" to match the answer "He was assassinated on Good Friday." Tonight, in any event, halfway through the show, more tears came, a regular occurrence these days. I knew why she was crying but asked her why anyway. "Because," she answered convulsively, "I don't ... I can't ... not a single ..."

And yet after dinner she was quite cheerful. We played cards, children's games like Crazy Eights, until well after midnight. We got on a laughing jag at one point and couldn't stop—we were shaking with laughter, crying with laughter. About nothing really.

April 4. Mom seems very fond of her new Australian Hunter's Lamp, which she shines while roaming through the house in the middle of the night. She's also starting to look in on me, while I'm sleeping, shining the 200-watt beam in my eyes like an interrogation lamp.

April 5. Bath time still looms up as a major project for me, almost like scaling Everest. If I don't start the bath and practically rip her clothes off, Mom simply won't take one. So I phoned Health Care and arranged for a Bath Lady to come in twice a week, on Tuesday and Friday. Maybe she'll also sort out Mom's closet and make sure she changes her clothes. And scrub the ink off her hand.

April 6. Dad's birthday. Would he be alive today if he had taken one of the tricyclic or SSRI antidepressants like Prozac, which came out after his death? The question's been haunting me for years. I know from sorting out his free samples that he must have taken phenelzine sulphate and tranylcypromine, which are real horror shows.

April 8. At bedtime Mom said, "Tell me a story, Noel dear. Tell me about my life." So I told her about the time she and I went camping in Algonquin Park in '85, when I was sixteen, and a cinnamon-coloured black bear came to our tent. As I shone a quivering flashlight at the bear, it calmly sifted through two garbage bags, sniffed at our tent as we held our breath, then nonchalantly left. We didn't sleep for the rest of the night. When the sun came up, Mom discovered that the bear had taken something hanging from a tree branch: her bathing suit. She'd laughed and laughed at the time, perhaps picturing the bear in a bikini ... But tonight she merely smiled at the story, which clearly didn't register, then informed me it wasn't proper for us to be living together. I told her it was fine, that we were mother and son. "No, my son's name is Noel." I told her that I was Noel; she asked for proof. I showed her my birth certificate. She said that proved nothing.

April 13. My mother's French seems to have disappeared. She used to be fluent and now she speaks English when people speak French to her (including Dr. Vorta). And she used to watch Ultimatum, the French version of Who Wants to Be a Millionaire, but now she just gets angry. Tonight she told me to "Turn off that gibberish. What country are we living in? Gibberia?"

Had my recurring dream last night, the one in black-and-white, where I run along the squares of a mammoth crossword puzzle, looking for clues and numbers that aren't there. So I run blind, and the squares turn into deserted alleyways, and the alleys turn into a labyrinth with towering hedges, except there's no exit and I know there's no exit but I keep running anyway, looking for signs, getting more and more lost and tired and terrified ... But last night, for the first time, I thought I spotted a light in the distance—the exit?—but when I opened my eyes I saw it was the ray of my mother's hunter's lamp.

April 14. Mom has a rash of some kind on her left inner thigh, which she claims is from the "chemicals" I've been spraying her with. She then added that I was treating her like "some sort of weed." I'll have to get the Bath Lady (who Mom calls the Wife of Bath because she's had several husbands) to have a closer look.

The Bath Lady—the Home Health Nurse I guess I should call her, a Portuguese woman named Sancha Ribeiro—has this breathy amber voice which is kind of nice. She's also very warm, touching me on the arm with her multi-ringed hand when she talks. She wears next to nothing in the house— summer clothes, beach clothes—I guess because it's so hot in the house.

April 16. "Alzheimer's is the disease that kills two people"—that line is still haunting me. It's from Iris Murdoch. Tonight Mom and I watched a video about her last days with her husband. I'd planned on watching it alone, and tried to in my bedroom, but Mom came in around midnight with

*her trusty power-lamp and asked me to rewind it. "When are we leaving?"
was Murdoch's repeatedly asked question. Mom's is very similar: "What
time does the train leave?"*

*April 17. Mom wandered all night long. At 3 a.m. I found her at the front
door in her nightgown and yoga shoes, with a purse around her neck and
plastic bags stuffed with photos and underclothes. "What time does the
train leave?" she asked. Not sure what train she's referring to. After my
father died, we used to go back to Long Island every few weeks to visit
friends and relatives. But when she was a young woman she also used to
take a train from Aberdeen to Edinburgh, almost every weekend, to see her
boyfriend (my father). In any case, I managed to get her back to bed
without too much fuss.*

*April 19. Looked through a stash of old letters of my mom's, some of which
I read to her. Now, after midnight, with Mom sleeping, I'm feeling awful,
thinking of all the letters Mom wrote to me after I moved out, travelled, then
got my own apartment. I threw them all out, once after laughing with a friend
at the banal summaries of her day. But that's all life is! The everyday details
that accrue to form a life. The problems with the vacuum cleaner, a plant that
died, a pet that strayed, making gifts for friends ... How I wish I had kept those
letters, each one brimming with love and thoughtfulness. Or committed them
to memory instead of some poem or story or chemical formula! I seldom
finished the letters, I shudder to admit, let alone replied to them. And along
with every letter she would enclose newspaper articles ("Thought you'd enjoy
this," she'd write on a yellow Post-it, "Thinking of you when I read this ...").
How I wish I had those letters and articles now! How I wish I could hold them
to my heart, thank her from the bottom of my heart for thinking of me when
no one else was.*

*April 21. At breakfast, over a pot of her favourite tea (Yorkshire Gold),
Mom said she was worried about "the mountain." Which mountain,
Mom? "You know very well which one." Mount Royal? "Yes, it's going to
erupt, I heard it on the radio." Your radio is broken, I pointed out. "I'm
worried about you, not me—I hope I die in it, fall in the ... whatever it's
called." The crater? "Yes, the crater." She then said when the time comes,
to please end it for her, quickly. "Noel, if you really love me, do it. Push me
in. Do you promise?"*

April 24. When I got back from the library, the minute the Bath Lady left, Mom bombarded me with questions: "When are we going back to our other house, and stop renting this one?" *You own this one.* "How much did we pay for it?" *A lot.* "How many bedrooms does it have?" *Seven.* "Where did we get the money for it?" *From selling your mom's house in Aberdeen.* "When is that lady going to move out?" *Which lady?* "How much rent do we pay?" *None, you own it.* "Where did we get the money for it?" *From Dad's insurance and selling your mom's house in Aberdeen.* "When the lady moves out will she take the clock and the microwave?" *Which lady?* "Where does that door go to?" *To the basement. Any more questions, Mom?* "Yes. Where are my car keys?" *Any others?* "What time does the train leave?"

May 2. My matinée day with Norval (*Tati's Jour de Fête*). Mom freaked when I told her the Bath Lady would be staying with her all afternoon. "I hate that sexpot and I hate this Norval creature!"

In the audience was someone who works for Dr. Vorta, an eccentric gentleman named Jean-Jacques Yelle ("JJ"). When Norval saw him he ducked down in his chair, but too late—JJ spotted us both and came bounding over to sit beside us. A white candy cigarette was hanging out his mouth and he was wearing pink socks. He's a really nice guy, smiles a lot, but I sometimes have trouble with his voice, which has the cracking quality of an adolescent. When the film started Norval told him to go back to his seat.

After the movie I discovered that Norval is an absolutely merciless judge of his mother. Most of the people I know, in fact, complain about their parents— the way I complained about my mom when I was a teenager. But the fact is, without any bias at all, she ~~was~~ is one of the most beautiful women in the world, inside and out. The most selfless person I've ever met. Do women like her still exist today or is that a thing of the past?

May 8. We watched a video this afternoon: *House of Mirth.* Mom had told me that she wanted a "matinée—like you have with your boyfriend, whatever his name is. Be careful of him, by the way, because he carries a knife." She's never met Norval (and never will). She then told me that my cousin Rita got married and that we should have gone to the wedding "at St. Rose's." Three times she told me this, and three times I agreed with her, although I don't have a cousin named Rita. And St. Rose's is not a church, but a building not far from where we used to live in Long Island, on Route

67

110 in Farmingdale. It's derelict now, its windows smashed and roof long gone. It used to be a home for wayward girls.

May 11. Had another all-nighter. First at 2:15 and then at 4:30 Mom woke me with her trusty lamp. How is it that she loses everything but her bloody Australian Hunter's Lamp? When I shouted at her, ordered her back to bed, she said, "This is not working out. You're impossible to live with." She stormed off and slammed her bedroom door. I tossed and turned for half an hour, then went to her bedroom, where I got her another blanket, as she seemed to be shivering. I said I was sorry, but she just stared silently at me, her face empty of expression, looking like a waxwork model of herself.

May 19. Tonight I made tuna tartare with roast tomatoes, which I didn't think was all that bad. But at the end of the meal Mom said she couldn't "understand why this place keeps serving this junk. Hard as a rock. You could've soled your boots with it."

May 24. Mom didn't get up until 4:40 in the afternoon. Three times I tried to wake her, but no go. When she finally did get up she claimed it was my fault she slept so late. "I sleep a lot better when you're not here playing your bloody music," she said. I replied that I only play classical music (which she used to like) and never when she's sleeping. She looked at me and said, "I sleep a lot better when you're not here playing your bloody music."

May 29. Mom was in a foul mood today, again. Among other things, she accused me of "ripping off" her stuff, including her shower cap. She then concluded a long and scattered tirade by saying that I should "fire the bloody postman for not bringing the bloody post every day."

June 12. Been trying to stay out of the sphere of Mom's anger the last few days, without much success. Dead tired all day, worse than usual, could barely move. Seem to have forgotten how to sleep. On a video I got from the Canadian Alzheimer's Association, a woman said that when she was taking care of her husband she didn't sleep for three years.

June 15. Mom wandered again tonight, turning on lights in room after room. Wearing a poppy on her nightgown. In June.

June 21. Summer solstice, longest day of the year. Found almost $3000 in Mom's drawer, in twenty-dollar bills. When I redeposited it at the bank, the teller told me that last year Mom had been going to the bank every day to make withdrawals. When I asked the teller why she didn't report it, she said she did, to the manager, who reported it to her brother-in-law in New York. Also found an envelope containing forty-eight Super 7 lottery tickets, which I just finished checking out on the Internet. Won 10 dollars and 2 free tickets.

July 2. The burglar alarm woke me up last night, at midnight. I jumped out of bed and scrambled downstairs in my boxers. Before I could shut the alarm off, there was loud knocking at the front door. I didn't know what to do, with the alarm still going, so I turned the outside light on, looked out the window and saw ... Mom, elegantly dressed in a pin-stripe business suit. I let her in and then shut the alarm off. By then the Étoile Security people were calling to see if everything was OK. I was shaking when I told the guy what had happened— and almost couldn't remember our password! After I hung up Mom explained that she was on her way to school and had come back because she'd forgotten her notes.

July 15. Mom is now registered with the Alzheimer's Wanderers Program, and wears an ID chain.

August 20. Been busy renovating. I changed the dead bolts on the front door and the kitchen door to double key locks. I also papered over the doors. And made lots of other changes around the house. Dr. Vorta gave me some ideas, the Bath Lady gave me others. But I'm too tired to write about it.

August 22. Dr. Vorta gave me a list of ways of keeping Mom active, mentally and physically, and more changes that should be made in the house itself. As for treatment, he says there are essentially 4 drugs to treat Alzheimer's. And they're not terribly effective—at best, they mitigate symptoms. I've already tried two: Exelon (rivastigmine) and Reminyl (galantamine, first derived from the bulbs of snowdrops and narcissi). Both modulate the neurotransmitter acetylcholine. But neither stops the progression of the disease, and there are side-effects: nausea and vomiting, stomach cramps and headaches, diarrhoea, dizziness, fatigue, insomnia, loss of appetite ...

September 21. Autumn equinox. Been trying two new anti-aging neuro drugs over the past few days (neither available in Canada—thank you, Dr. Vorta!). One is Centrophenoxine (Lucidril), a carboxyl-linked dimer (two molecules linked to a C=O group by a –O– connection) of p-chloro-phenoxyacetic acid and DMAE (DiMethylAminoEthanol). The other is Hydergine (Ergoloid Mesylates), a mixture of alkaloids that come from a fungus (ergot) that grows on rye. One of them seems to be working, in any case, because first at dinner and then at bedtime, Mom was astonishingly clear.

"What poem shall I read tonight?" Noel asked his mother. She had been particularly lucid that night, especially at the dinner table, going on at length about one of her favourite books, *The Golden Bough*. She was now in bed, ready for her bedtime story.

"I don't want a poem tonight," she said. "I want to hear about the Struldbrugs. Because I think I'm turning into one."

"The Struldbrugs?" Noel repeated, in amazement. Even his own brain took some time to retrieve this name. "From *Gulliver's Travels*?"

"Where else?"

His mother used to read this novel to him, at Noel's insistence, almost every night for six months, from May 14 to November 11, 1977. As much as the book, he loved the colours of his mother's voice and the ambrosial scent of her skin: lily-of-the-valley with a whisper of lime.

"You're not turning into a Struldbrug, Mom. They're immortal."

"They're old and demented, you mean. Can you tell me the story, Noel dear?"

"I'm not sure I can remember it all. I may have to get the book, although I haven't seen it in a while. It may be in the attic."

"It's from the Voyage to Luggnagg."

"Is it?"

"Are you losing your memory, Noel?"

"No, I just … I'll give it a shot. It's murky, though. And there might be a few bits missing:

The Struldbrugs commonly acted like mortals, till about thirty years old, after which by degrees they grew melancholy and dejected. When they came to fourscore years, they had not only all the follies and

70

infirmities of other old men, but many more which arose from the dreadful prospect of never dying. They were not only opinionative, peevish, covetous, morose, vain, talkative, but uncapable of friendship, and dead to all natural affection. Envy and impotent desires are their prevailing passions ...

They have no remembrance of anything but what they learned and observed in their youth and middle age, and even that is very imperfect. And for the truth or particulars of any fact, it is safer to depend on common traditions than upon their best recollections. The least miserable among them appear to be those who turn to dotage, and entirely lose their memories; these meet with more pity and assistance, because they want many bad qualities which abound in others.

As soon as they have completed the term of eighty years, they are looked on as dead in law; their heirs immediately succeed to their estates, only a small pittance is reserved for their support ... "

Noel opened his eyes as the words became garbled, like portions of a video erased or recorded over. "Here it gets blurred, Mom. Then it goes:

At ninety they lose their teeth and hair, they have at that age no distinction of taste, but eat and drink whatever they can get, without relish or appetite ... In talking they forget the common appellation of things, and the names of persons, even of those who are their nearest friends and relations. For the same reason they never can amuse themselves with reading, because their memory will not serve to carry them from the beginning of a sentence to the end; and by this defect they are deprived of the only entertainment whereof they might otherwise be capable.

The language of this country being always upon the flux, the Struldbrugs of one age do not understand those of another, neither are they able after two hundred years to hold any conversation with their neighbours the mortals; and thus they lie under the disadvantage of living like foreigners in their own country ..."

Noel stopped when he realised he'd lost his audience. He bent towards his sleeping mother's face—so pale, so lifeless—as if to hear some last word. Swift's days ended in memory-crippled dementia he recalled as he drew closer, felt her breath mingle with his.

October 4. Tonight we watched a documentary on actor Christopher Reeve and his battle to recover from his spine injury. Mom said she hoped with all her heart that he was still around when they found a cure. "Do you think they'll find a cure?" she asked, wiping a tear from her cheek. "I'll never know what happened to him, because I'll be dead before him. Or have lost my mind." "Mom," I replied, with my arm round her shoulder, "you'll both be cured—I know it, I have a gut feeling. I bet you'll both be cured in the same year! That's my prediction. You can beat this, don't give up. Use Superman as inspiration." (Superman! The TV actor became an alcoholic and put a bullet in his head; the movie actor became a quadriplegic after falling off a horse.)

October 15. I've asked the Bath Lady to come in four days instead of two and she agreed. This will give me more time for myself, but just about exhaust what's left of our savings. I'll deal with it later.

October 31. Hallowe'en. In the afternoon, Mom and I cleaned. As I vacuumed she dusted furiously, really getting into it. She then got out the broom and began riding it like a witch, which made us both laugh. Five minutes later she was slouched in a chair in an unlit room, morosely watching TV, switching from one game show to another.

November 2. We're running out of money. Prescription drugs are supposed to be free after out-of-pocket expenses of $68.50 a month. But for some reason (either a computer error or Mom forgot to pay the annual premium) they've cut us off from the plan. Aricept alone costs $158.50 a month. Now wondering if I should ask Dr. Vorta for a loan. Or Norval?

November 3. Had to let the Bath Lady go, which wasn't pleasant.

November 11. Today Mom was shivering all day; I had to crank up the heat even higher. It felt like Calcutta. Anxious to know why Mom is sleeping 18 hours a day. Death practice? Which drug is responsible?

November 17. Five minutes ago, instead of me reading Mom a nighttime poem, she had one for me (shockingly):

There was a young lady from France
Who hopped on a freight train by chance
The fireman fucked her
As did the conductor
While the brakeman shat in his pants.

*For a second or two I thought a new neurological disorder was rearing its head:
Tourette's or something. She added, whispering behind her hand, that she'd
heard it from her childhood friend "Rita."*

*November 22. The dryer broke this afternoon, so I began hanging Mom's
things up on a makeshift clothes line in the basement. She appeared behind me
and nearly gave me a coronary. She was very upset. She said I had stolen all
her underclothes and was now washing them so as to give them to my
girlfriend. I continued to hang up her clothes, including a white bra. "Who are
you referring to, Mom? Which girlfriend would that be?" "Don't you dare ask
me the W questions!" she screamed. "Don't ever ask me who, which, when or ...
where. You're only trying to confuse me! You've been trying to confuse me for
fifty goddamn years!"*

*Five minutes ago, when I went to say goodnight, Mom was posing before
her full-length mirror, semi-dressed with her brush in her hand, standing like a
statue. I asked her what she was doing. She said she was waiting for me to
brush her hair.*

*December 18. This morning Mom received a postcard from Bermuda from
Aunt Helen and Uncle Phil, with a postscript for me that said, "Keep up the good
work, Noel. Really wish we could be there to give you a hand. Merry Christmas."*

*December 21. Winter solstice. I always think of my grandmother as the
seasons turn over, since she was the one who taught me about such things. Not
only about the tilt of the earth, but how the seasons correspond to the four
ages of man: spring lasts until 19, summer from 20 to 39, fall from 40 to 59,
winter ever after. She also told me that each new season must be ushered in
with a good stiff drink. Or drug.*

*December 24–25. Mom slept through Christmas eve and almost all of
Christmas day. She was feeling "down" and didn't feel like celebrating or*

opening gifts. To get her in the mood I put on The Twelve Days of Christmas, *but she told me to turn it off after three French hens.*

Placed half-consumed cookies and milk by the fireplace, hoping Mom would laugh (she didn't seem to notice), and then tried to make shortbread. Followed her recipe <u>to the letter</u>, *but the dough was friable and wouldn't cohere, and it just expanded and melted, spilling over into the oven. When Mom saw me cleaning up it was the closest she got to a smile all day.*

December 26. Was listening to A Child's Christmas in Wales *on headphones when a sound that didn't belong made me jump. The fire alarm. At 4:10 a.m. I leapt down the stairs, where clouds of brown smoke were filling up the kitchen. On the stove, eggs had boiled black in the pan. And Mom asleep in her chair.*

Don't know how much longer I can carry on. I think I've reached the end, I'm incurably tired but can't sleep, I'm starting to drink my Mom's sherry by the bottle, Dr. Vorta's drugs aren't working, we've almost run out of money, Mom's going to burn the house down …

I thought I could make her happy by coming home, but clearly haven't. Maybe a nursing home would be better. I phoned Uncle Phil, who returned from Bermuda today, left a message. And a long e-mail.

December 27. Uncle Phil and Aunt Helen both e-mailed back, apologising for not being able to come up for a visit. They could put Mom on a waiting list at a home in Long Island if I liked. "A very good one," said Aunt Helen. "Oyster Bay Manor, it's called. Let me know."

As I was changing the battery on the fire alarm, Uncle Phil phoned, saying that he had found a bed at the Babylon Beach House on Yacht Club Road. But it had to be filled this week. The cost: $780 a week. I said I would think about it, then called him back and said no. (We don't have the money and I don't want to do it anyway.) I explained to him that things were getting a lot better lately.

December 28. Phoned the Beaumont Health & Rehabilitative Centre in Outremont—$98 per day—therapy and medicines extra.

December 29. Did something rash this morning. After finding the top burners on the stove glowing red and a raw roast of lamb in the oven, I called Beaumont and told them we're ready next time they have an opening. I'm running low on gas and patience. Can't do anything more for her. With regard to her memory, I'm beginning to grasp the meaning of the word "irretrievable." Time to let go. Besides, it could be six months or more before they have an opening.

At 5 on the nail they called back: they have an opening on January 2. In three days.

December 30. Mom's been agitated all day. She knows something's brewing, something cataclysmic. Ten minutes ago, at midnight, I opened her bedroom door to see if she had managed to calm down. A shaft of light crossed her sleeping form. I was about to close the door when I noticed something else, something scrawled on the tilted mirror of her dressing table. I tiptoed closer. There were two words, written in dark-red lipstick, the colour of drying blood: HELP ME.

December 31. Cancelled at Beaumont. It'll be all right, I'll find a way. For the first time in my life I feel clear. And unafraid. I know what I've got to do. At dawn I went downstairs, through the locked door, to my father.

Chapter 8
Henry & Noel Burun

By his late twenties, in Edinburgh, Noel's father was a blazingly talented chemist. By his late thirties he was head of a pharmacology department in New York, with two dozen researchers working under him. When his company, the Swiss-based conglomerate Adventa, relocated from Long Island to a Montreal suburb for tax reasons, he was asked whether he would accept a transfer, at twice the pay. He would accept the transfer, he said, but at half the pay—as a drug rep. The company's chief executive officer laughed, then recommended a psychiatrist, then threw up his hands. And thus Henry Burun ended up not combining chemicals for the betterment of the world, not devising new drugs to cure its maladies, but rather ... selling them. A travelling pharmaceutical salesman. What does your father do? they'd ask Noel at school. My father sells drugs. And everyone would laugh.

At first Henry liked the new job, travelling from town to town in lower Quebec and upper New England, but eventually it ground him down trying to see doctors and pharmacists who had little time to see him. When he was granted his five minutes, he told the truth about the drugs—which ones were hyped, which ones had failed clinical trials, which ones had withdrawal problems or crippling side-effects. He was an abysmal salesman and he knew it. Which is why he drifted from company to company, let go in turn by Adventa, Pfizer, Merck Frosst and NovaPharm. So why didn't he go back to the research lab, which would have rolled out the red carpet? Because he couldn't take the *stress*, the responsibility for others, the pressure of producing the next Big Drug as patents for older ones were expiring and making shareholders nervous. The pressure to fudge clinical trials, to downplay side-effects. It was this pressure, along with sixty-hour work weeks, that gave him his longest nervous collapse ever, a dark six-month depression that nearly drove him to hanging himself from a beam in the basement. At least the salesman's job allowed him to be *alone* most of the time, watching the world through a car window, numbing himself with the latest tranquillisers and anti-depressants. With a wife and child he adored, he should have been in love with life. Instead, through some baffling process, some chemical dishar-mony, he became increasingly despondent, constantly seeking a reason to live.

"Did we kill Dad?" Noel asked his mother, after the crash was ruled vehicular suicide.

"No, Noel, we didn't! Don't ever think that!"

Suicides become vampires, the children told him at school. And suici-dal parents, according to the Welsh nurse, will have children who are suicidal. "Did the world murder Dad?"

Mrs. Burun remained silent before rising from her chair and walking out of the room. "Did Dad leave because I was bad?" Noel wondered as he heard, from the kitchen, his mother's sobs. Could there be a worse sound in the world? The living room walls suddenly appeared to be streaked; he realized he too was crying. His mother's sobs, and father's death, filled him with a bone-deep sadness he would feel, on and off, for the rest of his life. He would never ask these questions again, shutting them up with triple locks inside himself.

When Henry Burun returned from his sales trips, his son would be on the lookout, either from the front porch or, in winter, from behind the closed curtains of the living room, his nose pressed against the frost-covered pane. At the first sign of the silver-blue Chevy Impala or sunfire-red Pontiac Laurentian, he would explode out the door and down the walkway, once barefoot in snow, and his father would set down his bag and lift him high in the air, twirling him round, making him squeal with laughter.

Inside, he would follow his father's trail of pipe fumes around the house, irresistibly, like a child of Hamelin. He was waiting for his father to give him his briefcase so he could do "the sorting." Inside the worn Gladstone bag were pharmaceutical advertisements by the pound, blotters with pictures of internal organs and magical names of curatives, business cards from doctors and pharmacists, stacks of his own cards with the logo of his company (which, like the company car, would change almost every year); but the best thing by far were the samples, which usually came in blister-pack booklets. He would put them into piles: analgesics, heart medications, muscle relaxants, tranquillisers, antidepressants (usually empty, seals torn), vitamin pills, energy boosters ... The complex medicinal smells never left him; they could be summoned years later by the drug name itself. Noel was not quite sure why this "sorting" had to be done, but he could do it happily for hours, memorising formulas, ingredients, dosages ...

Sometimes in summer, on rural routes in Quebec and New England, Noel would wait with his father in doctors' and veterinarians' offices in towns like Lacolle and Bury, Killington and Brattleboro, Ossipee and Rindge. Other times, with the car doors locked and radio on, he would memorise baseball stats on cards that his father had bought to help him pass the time. It didn't matter how long it took—Noel would wait forever. When his father returned he would quiz Noel on batting averages and RBIs and ERAs. Baseball is a mathematician's dream, his father told him, and a poet's too. Or it used to be. "Like every other sport, it's now a venal business circling the drain."

There were other quizzes too as they drove, an attempt by Mr. Burun to get his son to memorise worthwhile things. Famous quotations, for example, or the names of the classical compositions as they came up on the radio, or the gods and goddesses of ancient Greece, or the meaning of obscure words (especially ones that would make him laugh, like *callipygian* or *steatopygic* or *merkin*), or the names of two hundred phobias, including three of his father's: kakorrphiaphobia (fear of failure), hypegiaphobia (responsibility) and lyssophobia (madness).

"By the way, Dad," Noel said after a Greek goddess quiz, "I've decided what I want to be when I grow up. I want to be like you. I want the same job as you."

His father was working at his Comoy's pipe, tamping down the black Latakia with his middle finger and testing its draw by sucking loudly on it. "Not a good choice, lad. If you want to work with drugs, work in a lab, work in research. It's more creative. I couldn't do it, but maybe you can."

The next day Noel wrote Santa for a chemistry set. In June. Nothing else was on the list, just a chemistry set. If he could have a chemistry set Noel promised to be good until he retired. It was the most magical thing he could imagine and he had trouble sleeping for the next six months.

With the first light of Christmas Day, after lying awake all night, Noel raced downstairs, barely noticing Santa's half-eaten cookies on the mantel or the stocking his mother had made for him, crammed to bursting point. His eyes were directed elsewhere, and they spotted it immediately. Under the tree, unwrapped, was a shiny radium-white metal box with hinges and a clasp, and THE A.C. GILBERT CO. embossed in red across the top. His heart was dancing in his breast, a joyful rumba, as he raised the lid. "Open sesame," he whispered.

Inside, embedded in styrofoam, were rows of cubic jars with red and white labels that proclaimed their contents in bold black capitals: NICKEL AMMONIUM SULPHATE (an elegant triple-barrelled name!), TANNIC ACID (dangerous sounding), PHENOLPHTHALEIN (which his father admitted to sprinkling on his chemistry teacher's sandwiches to cause diarrhoea), MAGNESIUM CARBONATE, COBALT CHLORIDE, POTASSIUM NITRATE (the same chemical, his father explained, administered in army barracks and monasteries to prevent "hard-ons," something Noel had not yet felt), SODIUM SILICATE, ZINC OXIDE, AMMONIUM CHLORIDE (the famous Sal Ammoniac of the Arabian alchemists!), COPPER SULPHATE, MANGANESE DIOXIDE, POTASSIUM PERMANGANATE, CHROME ALUM, COCHINEAL (a red dye, his father explained, obtained from the crushed bodies of female cochineal insects), and the two most boring-sounding chemicals in the whole world: BORAX and LOGWOOD.

Over the next month or so, Mr. Burun set up a laboratory in the basement for his son, in a locked room his mother once called "the black dungeon," her husband's refuge when his moods swung low and dark. There he showed Noel mercury (a slippery, magical substance that seemed to defy physical laws), phosphorus (which burst into fire if exposed to air), potassium (which burst into fire if exposed to water), magnesium (which would burn *under* water), the "Acids" (the noble triumvirate of nitric, sulphuric and hydrochloric, "to be treated with respect"). He showed Noel how to make invisible ink, which would appear only when the paper was held over a flame; he showed him how to make a slow-burning fuse, and gunpowder (five parts potassium nitrate, one part sulphur, one part charcoal), and a burnt-orange pyramid with potassium dichromate which, after you lit it, would writhe up like a charmed snake.

In the first of a series of lectures, brief preludes to the experiments, his father spoke about the direct ancestor of chemistry: alchemy. And the most famous alchemist of all, Paracelsus the Great,[15] who was searching for the one prime element from which all the other elements derived: *alkahest.*

Alkahest, alkahest ... Noel repeated to himself, over and over like a chant from *The Arabian Nights*. "What's that?" he finally asked.

"This substance—if ever it were found—would be the philosophers' stone of medicine, a cure for every human disease."

"I want to find it!" said Noel. "We can work together on it, Dad, in our lab! We can discover it!"

"You must be very careful down here, Noel, especially when I'm away. Get to know all the properties of every chemical you own, or are able to make. Is that clear? If you make a compound that's poisonous or explosive, you put the skull-and-crossbones label on it immediately. Do you promise? Noel, are you listening to me?"

"If I promise, can we make laughing gas and nitroglycerine?"

"Noel ..."

"I promise. Cross my heart, hope to die."

In another lecture—the final one as it turned out—his father talked about art. "In some ways," he explained, "chemistry can be seen as a marriage of science and art, an earth poetry, a sensory kaleidoscope of smells, tastes, colours, textures. Painters and sculptors have been drawn to it, and musicians in particular. Sir Edward Elgar dabbled in chemistry and Aleksandr Borodin *was* a chemist. He used to scribble musical notes all over the laboratory walls, absent-mindedly, while conducting his experiments. And then there were poet-chemists like Humphry Davy, who discovered sodium and potassium. His notebooks were filled with chemical experiments jumbled together with new lines of poems. He and Coleridge even planned to set up a laboratory together! And there's Primo Levi, of course, who regarded chemistry as an art of weighing and separating, just like writing."

In the basement laboratory Noel found the serenity and solitary happiness that he found nowhere else, except in books. When his father was away on business, Noel spent hours in the lab, in hookeydom, with Borodin's *Polovtsian Dances* or Elgar's *Pomp and Circumstance* playing on a portable record player as he dreamed about discovering things. He would gaze at the rows of chemicals on one side, and rows of books on the other—including *The Life of Philippus Theophrastus Bombast of Hohenheim, Known by the Name of Paracelsus* ...

Noel began to learn the formula of every chemical he owned, every one he had made or ever could make. He memorised, photographically, every element of the periodic table pinned to the wall: their position on the chart and all their properties. He had only to say or see the letters of the element and its square would pop up. Take krypton. In Noel's hippocampus the sound and letters formed a fibrous cinnamon teardrop shape, which stored the following properties: noble gas; symbol Kr; atomic number 36; atomic weight 83.80; cubic, face-centred crystal; gas at 20°C; electronic configuration $[Ar]3d^{10}4s^2p^6$. Or take lithium (as Noel would later): alkali metal; symbol Li; atomic number 3; atomic weight 6.941; cubic, body-centred crystal; solid at 20°C; electronic configuration $[He]2s^1$ ...

In some of his reveries, sitting back in his father's swivel chair, Noel would play games of chemical chess, with pieces cast in metal. The white and black pawns were usually Lead and Tin; the castles Iron and Chromium; the knights Mercury and Palladium; bishops Barium and Arsenic; queens Gold and Platinum; kings Silver and Titanium. "Who would win," he asked his father, "in a fight between Lead and Mercury? Or Barium and Palladium? Or Gold and Silver? Which one's more powerful? Who would destroy who, in a battle?"

Mr. Burun laughed. "Well, mercury would certainly eat up tin or lead. For the others, I guess you'd have to compare their densities. Gold, for example, is one of the heaviest metals, much heavier than silver. But it's also the most malleable and ductile."

"What ... does that mean?"

"It's the softest."

"What's the hardest?"

"Well, the two densest substances in the world are iridium and osmium."

Noel's eyes opened wide. From then on, his queens became Iridium and Osmium.

One fall day in 1979, on the third Monday of September, Noel sprinted home from school. There was something he was dying to check out: nitrogen iodide crystals, "explosive on concussion," were drying on a blotter. He and his father, with the help of *Smith's College Chemistry*, had spent the previous evening trying to make them. Did they get it right? he wondered. His father had warned him not to go near it until he got back from his trip, but Noel couldn't wait.

He pushed his way through the torn screen door, ignored his mother's greeting, leapt down the stairs three at a time. Would it work? Would it actually *work*?

Breathless, heart rate rocketing, he took a metal rod and "tickled" the raisin-black precipitate. Nothing. Was it a dud? Not yet dry? He tried again, with a little more force ...

The result was an ear-splitting explosion and thick, reddish-purple clouds that expanded as if in slow motion, filling the room. Mrs. Burun, from upstairs in the kitchen, let out a scream before scrambling down the stairs. Panic-stricken, she pushed open the door and tried to see through the dense purple clouds. "Noel! Noel dear! Where are you? Are you all right?" She heard a faint noise on the other side of the room. Flapping at the air with both hands, she groped her way towards the sound. "Noel?" Her voice quivering, she strained to catch a glimpse of her son, fearing the worst. "Noel? Where are you? *Please* answer me, dear ..."

"I'm over here, Mom. I'm cool, everything's cool."

Noel was sitting on the floor, his clothes and face blackened with smoke as in a Disney cartoon. He put his hand to his forehead and felt a warm patch of blood. When his mother finally reached him, he had a grin on his face. "I just need a styptic drug, Mom, a haemostatic agent. A bit of ammonium aluminium sulphate. Or maybe some tincture of iodine. Top shelf. I made them for situations just like this."

His mother put her arms around him, squeezed him with all her might while faintly sobbing. She then examined his face and saw that his eyebrows had been blown off. "Whatever it is you did, *don't* do it again! No more explosives. If you don't promise, I'm going to make your father get rid of this lab forever. Toss everything into the trash bin. Do you understand? Noel, I'm talking to you!"

Noel promised, but he had his fingers crossed, and his toes crossed for good measure. And he wasn't really sorry; his only regret about the explosion was that he couldn't tell his father what had happened, about their success in making *Nitrogen Iodide*. For Henry Burun had left that morning on a two-week business trip: the first week in upstate New York, the second visiting his brother in Long Island. So Noel wrote his father a letter, care of Uncle Phil:

Dear Dad,
   You'll never guess what happened. We did it!! It worked, just like you said it would. Dad, we made the NH_3NI_3. I tickled the precipitate just like you said, with the brass rod, and a huge bang went off in my ~~left~~ right ear. It's still ringing! There were humongous reddish-purple clouds and a funny smell like chalk dust and sulphur and iodine. All three blotters went off! There are holes all over the blotters! The time is now 7:30 and my ears have been ringing since 12:30! It's driving me nuts! My face was all black too and I have no eyebrows! Mom was really mad but she

cooled down a bit. I didn't tell her about our surprise for her. I finished painting the lab walls white like you said and it looks pretty cool. I miss you, Dad.

Your son, Noel

Noel's letter arrived but his father never read it. For around the time Noel was tickling the nitrogen iodide crystals, his father was in a water-filled quarry south of Lake Placid, in his Pontiac, slowly sinking to the bottom.

After another all-nighter, as the sun rose for the first time in 2002, Noel was sitting at his usual position atop the staircase, head bowed. He had been playing back these and other memories for almost an hour. He opened his eyes and stared down at the door leading to the basement. The wood had been wallpapered over and the doorknob removed. That door led to another door, which he had avoided opening for years. He stood up. It's time, he said, to open it.

The lab was still there, its flasks and test tubes shadowed in dust, its walls shaggy with cobwebs. On the table were rubber gloves, a small pair handshaking a larger pair, and on a door hook were two yellowing lab coats, a child's resting on the back of an adult's. His father's brown leather medical bag, an heirloom from *his* father, was sitting on the floor, locked.

Noel had ranted and raved whenever his mother tried to throw anything out, so she eventually locked the door and left things more or less as they were. But he himself had never been able to enter the room; the pain went through him like a spear.

He examined the labels on the chemical jars, which he and his father had brushed with hot liquid paraffin. With a pale pink J-cloth he affectionately dusted off each bottle, turning them round in his hand, holding them up to the light. In the laundry room he filled up a yellow plastic pail with steaming hot water, threw in some Clorox and Cheer, put on his father's black rubber gloves. With three different brushes he scrubbed test tubes, beakers and Florence flasks; pipettes, funnels and Erlenmeyer flasks; graduated cylinders and eyedroppers; pinch-cocks, crucible tongs and rubber stoppers ... He cleaned his Bunsen burner and retort stands and clamps with acetone, and his laminated Periodic Table with Windex. He put order back into drawers, swept the floor. He removed cobwebs from the walls, and dust from the top of books. He saw three scuttling spiders but, as his father would have wanted, left each in peace.

It's time to do something more, something more serious, he said to himself. Beyond plying his mother with brain nutrients and memory boosters, or blendering up cocktails with over-the-counter drugs. The prescription medicines, like rivastigmine and galantamine, weren't doing much—apart from giving her nausea, insomnia and nightmares. *Unless a cure is discovered soon, your mother will be dead in five years* ... Yes, it's time to do something more. If he couldn't get the newest drugs because they were unapproved or unaffordable, he would simply make them himself ... Well, maybe not simply. "With my memory, I'll restore hers," he whispered to himself. "I *will* save her." With his head bent and eyes closed, he clutched the battered wood desk with both hands.

When he opened his eyes he saw the robin's-egg blue of the cement floor beneath the table. The paint was faded and peeling and poxed by chemical spills. As he was trying, impossibly, to remember which caustic compounds had caused which stains, he was distracted by the sight of his father's leather bag. He reached down for it, ran his finger through a layer of dust. And then tried the lock, which yielded with a minimum of fiddling.

Inside was a tiny red three-ring binder, with My Experiments written on the cover. He opened it to the first page:

Exp. # 1
Pour a little Citric Acid solution (lemon juice) in a glass. Stick the point of a toothpick in the juice. Write a secret invisible message with the juice. Heat the message (with an iron). It should appear brown.

Exp. # 2
Take red cabbage pickled in Acetic Acid (vinegar) and add some ammonium hydroxide (Clorox). The juice will go all through all sorts of colours, from red to all kinds of purple colours, to turquoise and blue and then green.

Exp. # 3
Hold a red rose over burning Sulphur so that the SO_2 bleaches it white. Dip into water and the colour is miraculously restored!

There were other notebooks as well, in zip-locked bags. His dad's diaries? With his vision blurring, Noel pulled out three identical binders, all black, one with the insignia of the first drug company his father had worked for in Scotland: Meridian. The most recent one, dated two months before he died, had these entries on its last page:

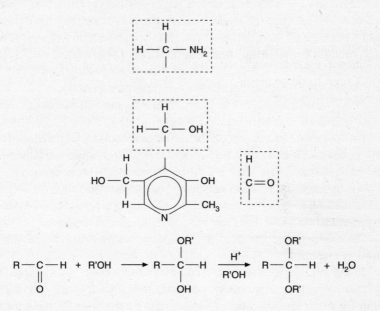

In bed, several hours later, Noel leafed through each of them. The first summarised three years of work on a process that someone had patented a few days before his father had applied for a patent. The second outlined three more years of work on a drug for Parkinson's—a blockbuster, as it turned out—that only his company profited from. And the third dealt with his attempts to create drugs that would both reduce the swelling of certain cerebral cells in dementia patients, and eliminate abnormal inclusions called Pick bodies. Tucked inside were a sheaf of letters to and from the U.S. Submission & Patent Office, along with a page from a spiral notepad, the ink of its scrawled message weeping freely:

A. Borodin's work on aldehydes
B. Beauty is the lodestar—a cure must be beautiful

The following day, after some faxing and photocopying, Noel went to see Dr. Vorta. For some advice, and some under-the-counter drugs.

"*Einen Moment, bitte,*" said the doctor, while pressing buttons on a spectrophotometer.

"Did you get my fax? Can you get them for me?"

After glancing at his Swiss watch, which rivalled Greenwich in exactitude, Dr. Vorta noted the readout on the display. "Noel, they'll put me in jail if I get you all those drugs on your list. Just be patient, will you? Have you brought your journal? And your mother's? *Danke schön.*"

"*Bitte sehr.*"

"Now if you'll excuse me, I have a very interesting patient—"

"Look what I found. Some of my father's notes. On aldehydes. And Pick bodies. He may have been on to something big."

Dr. Vorta froze for two seconds before turning round, his eyes trained on the notebook. He had a cataract in one of them. "You found your father's ... Right, leave it with me." He took the book from Noel's hand, opened it up. "Your father was a brilliant neuropharmacologist, Noel. But remember, near the end, your father was not ... a well man." He perused the bleeding letters. "I'll take a look, but these are probably just mad ravings ..."

After wincing at that last phrase, Noel slumped out of the office, mutely and meekly.

In ten minutes he returned. "I can't wait any longer!" he screamed at Dr. Vorta, barging in on his synaesthesia tests with a young patient. "I can't wait for the approval of new drugs, I can't wait for the clinical trials! My mother is dying! Don't you understand that? I can't be patient, I'm looking at infinity. This is not supposed to happen at her age. Soon she'll forget who I am. Then she'll forget to eat, to swallow, to breathe. She's fifty-six and she's sinking into a black freaking pit! She's no longer the same person—she's not a person at all! You're her doctor and you've done nothing. The only thing you've ever done is write about her and put her in 'promising' drug experiments. But you put her in the *placebo* group! You wasted a year of her life!" Noel punctuated this last phrase by picking up a laurel-wreathed bust of Wagner and smashing it on the floor, which caused macaque monkeys in hidden cages to scurry and scream. He then began sweeping things off the doctor's desk, looking for his father's notes. "And don't you *ever* call my father mad, do you hear me?"

"Noel, do *not* touch anything on that desk. I'm warning you, you little ..." He picked up the phone. "*Madame Prévert? W4. Oui, c'est ça ...*"

"And if this is a Farnsworth Musell test, what was that girl doing with her top off?"

Dr. Vorta, after hanging up the phone and nervously stroking his chemically whitened beard, closed the curtain and informed his patient the test was over. He then instructed Noel to get out of his office and stay out, that if he ever came back there'd be a straitjacket and van waiting for him.[16]

Chapter 9
Norval & Samira

Norval Blaquière lived in a converted millinery factory on rue de la Commune in Old Montreal, which he had turned into a kind of nineteenth-century salon. There were framed reproductions of Thomas Cooper Gotch's *Death the Bride*, with a woman in a field of poppies; Henry A. Payne's *The Enchanted Sea*, with drowned and drowning women; Rochegrosse's *Les Derniers jours de Babylone*; Félicien Rops' vampish *Woman on a Rocking Horse*. Others reflected Norval's penchant for long-haired women: Millais' liquid-locked *Ophelia*; Stanhope's orange-haired prostitute in *Thoughts of the Past*; Henner's *La Lectrice*, in which a naked Mary Magdalene reads from a book encircled by her flame-red curls; Waterhouse's *La Belle Dame sans Merci*, the Keats heroine who holds a knight captive in her long tresses.

"Why do you have these morbid pictures of women all over the place?" Samira asked, on her third day at the loft. "And what is it about women's hair? A fetish?"

"Long and loosened tresses are a symbol of a woman reverting to a state of nature. Like an animal's mane ..."

"Oh, please ..."

" ... It was a powerful symbol in the nineteenth century—in a period of hats and chignons. Today, of course, hairdressers butcher and plastify women's hair, which I'll never understand. It should be a wilderness. Worse is shorn underarms and montes pubis. I trust you've not dared ..."

"Is that a picture of Astérix over there? With the sword? Why would you—"

"Never mind." Norval banished the question with a wave of the hand.

"And who's that guy in the photograph next to it, sitting on your bed? It's the only picture of a man in the whole place, apart from Astérix. Is that you?"

"No, it's ... Noel."

"Noel?"

"Yes."

"Is Noel ... never mind."

"Is he what? A crypto-homo? Am I?"

"Is Noel related to you?"

"Not even distantly."

"You're almost like twins."

Norval sighed. "So we've been told. Which may be one of the reasons we clicked. The doppelgänger phenomenon, the search for the invisible twin, the demystification of narcissism ..."

Why does he speak like he's lecturing? Samira wondered. "And the presage of imminent death?" And why am I sounding like the brown-nosed student?

"That too. Like matter and its double, anti-matter. You shake hands and you're annihilated."

Samira smiled, then thought of a novel she'd been forced to read at school, and a line in an essay that got a checkmark in the margin. "Is your friendship like the one between Max and Emil in Hesse's *Demian*? A bond that frees a person from other bonds and leads into a new dimension?"

"No."

"Right. So is Noel your double, or your opposite? You're different in so many ways."

"He's left-handed, I'm right."

"Noel seems, well, anal retentive, whereas you seem ..."

"Anal explosive."

"And you two move so differently—"

"Especially when he's nervous. He gets so spasmodic you start looking for the strings. Remember when he met you?"

"Yes, but ... why did that make him nervous?"

"Because he thought you were an actress he's in love with."

Samira nodded slowly, lost in a maze of thoughts. "The poor actress, to look like me."

"Well, it's true you look like hell, but when healthy I imagine you look almost average."

"Such flattery."

"Perhaps I did get carried away."

"You don't like women, do you."

"Generally, I hold them in medium esteem."

"And men?"

"Much lower."

"You're a misanthrope, in other words."

"How can anyone not be? The human species, the evolution of the human species, was all a colossal mistake. Darwin must have realised that. Humans and chimps evolved from a common ancestor around six million years ago—we share 98.7 per cent of the same genes. But the genes in *our* brain somehow evolved differently, giving us greater brain power. So what have we done with this brain power? We've used it for the pursuit of narcissism, to prove that we're the only living things that matter in this world."

"But you're ... never mind." You're quite a narcissist yourself, she was about to say.

"And this evolution, this development of the brain, has not gone well. In fact it's been botched—the glitches, bugs, cross-wirings in the brain have given us things like depression, schizophrenia, Alzheimer's ..."

"And misanthropy?"

"Yes."

"So what should we do? What can humans do with all this bad wiring? Should we dumb down, go back to living like chimps?"

"That's already happening."

"Think of all the great individuals, the geniuses in the world, the great scientific advances—"

"Modern civilisation no longer produces great individuals, geniuses. Instead of forests with giant trees, we get scraggly saplings with roots no deeper than a thimble. If you doubt that, watch any awards show."

"How about John Lennon or Kurt Cobain or Marie Curie or Krzysztof Kieślowski or—"

"We're on the same path as the dinosaurs. Nature will have its revenge, and the sooner the better. The world is obscenely overpopulated. What we need, what Noel should concoct in his laboratory, is a pathogen that would destroy half the world's population overnight."

"Only half? So as to save a race you detest?"

Norval arched an eyebrow. "OK, all. And I shouldn't say *nature* will have its revenge. Nothingness will have its revenge—a rogue black hole with the weight of ten million suns will take things back to that ... that not-anything state that preceded the big bang."

"You don't say. And have there ever been ... exceptions to your general dislike of humanity? Noel, presumably?"

Norval took a drag from his Arrow. "Correct."

"Does he teach Symbolist lit as well? Is that where you met him? At school?"

"No. But I pulled strings to get him in. He lasted one course."

What is my role in this conversation? Samira asked herself. Prompter? "Why did he last only one course?"

"He had trouble understanding the students' questions."

"Does he have ... qualifications, a degree?"

"No, but he was accepted at MIT as a teenager by getting unheard-of marks in the entrance exams. And he was *asked* to attend McGill by the Dean of Sciences."

"But he didn't graduate."

"No."

"So what do you two ... share?"

"The relief of being wordlessly understood. A companion mind."

"I mean, he seems so taciturn and unsure of himself and, I don't know, unhappy, whereas you seem—"

"He's a Scot. Ipso facto, not of a sanguine nature. Like his father he's got the black choler, the humour of despair. When he's down he thinks the period will never end, when he's up he thinks it will shortly end."

"Are you sure he's OK? I mean, he looks ..."

"He needs a bit of sleep, that's all."

" ... crushed, depressed, heading towards a crash. He's got that dark look on his face. I've seen the symptoms before. He seems so ... grave. In the three times I've seen him at the lab he's not smiled once. Does he ever laugh? Does he have a sense of humour, is he witty?"

"Noel couldn't concoct something amusing to say given a month's notice."

"Is he ... all there? Mentally, I mean?"

"Noel Burun? Are you kidding? Do you know his pedigree? Related on one side to Lord Byron himself, and on the other to a long line of Scots physicians. Noel's superhuman, he can visualise things with painterly awareness, summon things you or I would never be able to summon given a hundred lifetimes, things never seen in the wildest visions of a witches' Sabbath. Don't be fooled by Noel—he has the mind and imagination of a master artist, or master scientist. He's a fluke of fucking nature, a psychomnemonic wonder, with almost unhuman eidetic powers."

"I thought you said there weren't any geniuses left."

"He's the last. You should bear his children."

Samira laughed. "So does he belong to any, you know, organisations, like Mensa or ..."

"Mensa? You've *got* to be kidding. A self-congratulating club of wankers who don't have the intelligence not to be a member. Games of three-dimensional Scrabble and a cup of Ovaltine—Noel's beyond that crap. He's in another dimension."

"What did you mean by 'eidetic powers'?"

"A photographic memory, preternaturally vivid and persistent. With self-generating links and catalytic images that spawn other memories, right back to his suckling hours. He's a *hypermnesiac*—he doesn't forget a goddamn thing. He's like Proust, like Proust squared. He's got a million megabytes of memory, a million emotions and sensations and images and God knows what else to draw on.[17] He's not there yet, but he'll be a great writer one day, greater than Proust. Or perhaps a visionary artist-poet like Rossetti or Blake. Mark my words."

"I never know when you're joking. Are you now?"

"Never felt less inclined to. What's the most important material for an artist?"

"According to Proust? Memories?"

"Infancy. Which most of us forget entirely. When a young child sees, for the first time, a rainbow in the mist of a crashing wave, a *trompe l'oeil* wheel turning backwards, a 'ghostly galleon' behind clouds, *that* is when a great poem or great painting or great symphony is born. On a subconscious level, naturally. So it becomes a question of finding, of recapturing that pure moment of pure sensation, that ..."

"So what's stopping—"

"... that vividness and anarchy of an infant's vision. What I'm referring to is the *infinity* of childhood."

"The essence of innocence itself."

"When an infant sees the world he doesn't fear it, he *marvels* at it. When he's older it just fills him with anxiety, dread. Why? Because of death, an awareness of death. But Noel can still summon that primordial vision, those prelapsarian colours—if he sets his mind to it. It's all there, intact, in Noel's mental kitchen. If he breaks the shackles, he could be another Rousseau,[18] for Christ's sake."

"Rousseau? Great. The man who put all five of his children into foundling hospitals."

"Or Baudelaire, who thought that genius was no more than childhood recaptured at will, with an adult's means to express it."

"Would another analogy be the music of our youth? Which we never forget? Because it's the only music that ever really reached us, touched our soul? I mean, old people *never* listen to new music, they reject it all, they return perpetually to the music of their innocent, impressionable youth. Lullabies, children's songs, teenage music. Is that the sort of thing we're talking about?"

Norval stubbed out his cigarette. "No."

Samira nodded. "Right. So what are the 'shackles' you mentioned? What's stopping Noel from being a great artist?"

"A weak motor and broken rudder. And like every failure he spends an hour worrying for every minute doing. But he'll get there eventually."

"What does he worry about?"

"You name it. He worried the first time he had shit stains in his diapers. He then ground his teeth in his sleep so savagely it took three orthodontists to fix them. Now he worries about his weight. And his mind. Just like Byron, who had two fears, of getting fat and going mad—and who was sometimes both."[19]

Samira fell into a thoughtful silence. "Noel seems too ... sensitive, too melancholic, to be able to ..."

"Melancholy's good for art. Look at Proust. He wrote *À la recherche du temps perdu* while lying in bed, in a chronic state of depression."

"... to be able to deal with life. He seems monstrously sad—I think he's the saddest man I've ever seen. Even the word 'sad' seems inadequate. There's something broken in him, something completely shattered, crushed."

"As most geniuses are. They see the flaws, the deadly disorder in the machine."

"I have this feeling that if someone close to him dies, or if he's rejected by a woman—"

"He's been rejected by women all his life. At first they find him cute and put up with his tongue-tied confusion and mind of many colours, but soon find him unmanageably weird. 'Rigid, mechanical and emotionally dissociated' is how Vorta describes him in a file I ... came across."

"Really? That's not what I would've thought. I thought he'd be ... well, oversensitive emotionally, dangerously oversensitive. Someone who would never get over, never forget a death or a rejection."

"Forget? Noel can't forget anything, can't block out anything. His memories haunt him forever. One of the things he can't stop reliving, in lurid detail, is his father's suicide."

"Oh, God …"

"His wife was having an affair with Vorta. He found out, drove his car into a water-filled quarry."

"Are you serious? Is that what happened?"

"It's possible. Anyway, don't think Noel's problem is a woman or a broken heart. Oh, no. Noel never goes out with women."

Samira paused. "He prefers men?"

"There may be the odd scuff mark on the closet door. But what I meant was that he doesn't go out with women because he already has one. He's already in love with a woman."

Samira nodded reflectively, but said nothing.

"I might as well tell you," said Norval. "The news will be out soon enough. Noel's been living with a dark secret for years, ever since his father drowned himself. It involves a Scotswoman of fabulous wealth and Deneuvean beauty."

"What? What are you talking about?"

"A perverse passion—with a Greek precedent."

"Not *Oedipus Rex* …"

"And a French precedent as well. After his father died, Baudelaire and his mother lived together in what he admitted was a 'period of passionate love,' a 'verdant paradise' in which she was 'solely and completely' his own. It's a bit like that for Noel and his mother."

"Are you making all this up?"

"About Baudelaire? Absolutely not."

"About Noel."

"Shall we get started?"

"Started?"

"On *The Alpha Bet.*"

At the breakfast table the following afternoon Samira asked, "Are you ever going to ask any questions about me? Like who I am, for example?"

Norval didn't look up from his mail, which included the *Nillennium Club Newsletter*. "Wasn't on today's planner, no."

Samira repressed a smile. "You're incorrigible, mad. Not to mention a son of a bitch."

"You must know my mother." Norval folded up the newsletter, emptied his third cup of espresso, then stood.

"You must have some redeeming qualities," said Samira.

"No, none whatsoever."

"What does Noel see in you?"

"Ask him. Listen, I'm off to the Schubert. Be back by four."

"The Schubert? The *Piscine* Schubert?" How out of character, she thought. "You swim?"

"Daily. It's a dress rehearsal."

"A dress rehearsal? For what, a play?"

"Death. I plan to end my days in water."

"You're not serious."

"I've heard there's a clarity of memory that drowning people have. Which might relate to our first immersion—in amniotic fluid or the shock of baptism ... not something you Arabs would ever feel, I suppose. Anyway, as you're drowning it seems there's this detonation of memories, crystal-clear memories from the first plunge to the last."

Samira shook her head. "I still can't figure out when you're kidding and when you're not." Or quoting from one of your lectures. "Isn't air the final resting place of the soul?"

"We're more water than air—it's our origin and destination."

"You write fiction, don't you? I saw a book on the shelf with your name on it. A novel?"

"Some have called it that."

"What's it about? What ... kind of novel is it?"

"Well, I felt that Joyce didn't go far enough in *Finnegans Wake*. That he held back. This was an attempt to take it one step further."

"Very funny. You're French, right? From France?"

"Right."

"Then why do you sound like some depraved British ... viscount or something?"

"The depravity comes naturally, the accent from a string of indifferent British public schools. Where I was sent—or rather exiled—by my whore of a mother."

"Why do you say she ... Why did she send you to England?"

Norval sighed as he pulled out his watch, opened the lid. "Because she wanted me out of the way. Because I'd been pestering her for years to let me go there. Because my favourite authors at the time were Baudelaire and Rimbaud. I knew that Baudelaire had learned English as a young boy, and went on to translate Poe, and that Rimbaud had lived in London as a teenager, where he wrote his best stuff. So if I had to be exiled, if I had

95

to go to boarding school, England was where I wanted to go. It all made sense—in my convoluted logic of youth. My mother, in any case, was happy to send me there. With my father's money, of course."

"But why would your mother ... why would she want to 'exile' you?"

"Because she wanted to fornicate in private, without having to lock me inside my room for hours. Because our shouting matches were upsetting the neighbours. Because she thought I was going to poison her."

"Were you?"

"I toyed with the idea."

Samira looked deeply into Norval's eyes, trying to determine whether they mirrored truth or falsehood. She couldn't decide. "So ... tell me more about her, about your mother. Is she—"

"My mother? My mother is a sack of excrement." Norval lit up another cigarette. "A lustful she-ass." He blew a stream of smoke into Samira's face. "Do you want me to bring you anything back? Any addictions to appease?"

"No, I ... I should really go ... somewhere else. I'm taking your bed."

"One of them."

"I mean, I could ... stay a bit longer."

"There's a wad of bills in my desk drawer, if you're short."

What do you expect in return? Samira wondered. "Thanks, but ..."

"Did you get one of these?" From his inside coat pocket Norval extracted a white card with florid silver letters, like a wedding script.

"What's that?"

"The 'laudanum and absinthe readings.' Yelle's party."

"Right, I forgot, at the lab ... JJ mentioned something about it."

"You going?"

"Well, I ... wasn't planning on it, no. I mean, I just met the guy and I'm not really into drugs anymore."

"No loss. I can't see him serving any real drugs. Worse, he's planning on reading poems."

"And? What's wrong with that?"

"Poems should never be read in public."

Samira frowned. "Don't be ridiculous. They're meant to·be spoken, and besides—"

"Poetry is a lonely pleasure, a solitary art. You don't want other people distracting you, you don't want others reading poetry in ways you wouldn't. The way to make poetry ridiculous and effete is to read it

96

in public. T.S. Eliot, for example, should never have recorded his poems for the world."

Samira laughed. "Or given us *Cats*."

"Authors should be read and not heard. If you doubt that, go and hear Margaret Atwood."

"Nonsense. How about Dylan Thomas's readings? Or Charles Dickens? Or Mark Twain?"

"There have been exceptions." Norval paused, eyeing Samira intently, as if he had just noticed an undervalued piece in an antique shop. "You sound like you're a student of literature."

"I believe that's almost a personal question. The first since the elevator, if I'm not mistaken."

"Do you want a job?"

"Doing what?"

"Teaching."

Samira laughed. "I've only got a general BA. A shaky one, at that."

"We'll cook up some degrees for you, along with some publications and references."

"No, I don't think I could possibly—"

"What school did you go to?"

"Cornell."

"Perfect. What was your field?"

"I didn't have one."

"What fiction do you like? What century?"

"Well, right now I'm sort of into the Female Gothic ..."

"Really? Like Anne Radcliffe? You like that sort of thing? Terrifying adventures in lonely castles?"

Samira sighed. "There's more to Anne Radcliffe than just—"

"Terrified girl flees, pursued by ghosts and lecherous monks. Caught, she then escapes, is caught again and escapes, is caught again and escapes."

Samira smiled, despite herself. "There's more to Anne Radcliffe than just—"

"That's settled, then. You'll give a couple of courses on the Gothic novel."

"But how can you just—"

"Because I've been having intercourse with the director since the day she hired me. Three years ago. Which is the only reason I've not yet been sacked. Well, maybe not the only reason. If my tenure were revoked, there'd be a revolt from the student union."

Samira rolled her raven eyes. "And why is that?"

"I give all my students an A, and no assignments."

"And sexual edification, I presume?"

"If requested."

"But what's all this got to do with—"

"Blorenge begins his sabbatical next semester. I'll tell the director I've got a kick-ass replacement. And since Blorenge will be spending his sabbatical in a detox centre, or perhaps in sex-offender therapy, it could end up being permanent."

Samira stopped to think about all this. "Sex-offender therapy?"

"The women's swim team caught him hiding in a locker, looking through the vents, in onanistic ferment. So you want the job or not?"

Samira shook her head. "No. I'm not qualified to teach literature. And besides, I've moved on."

"To what?"

"Art therapy."

"You've *got* to be kidding."

"No, I'm not."

Norval again fished out his pocket watch. "*Maasalaama.*"

"Can I ask you one more question before you leave?"

"If it's the last."

"What's that staircase for?" Samira pointed. "That one, that goes nowhere."

Norval hesitated, took a final drag from his cigarette. "Unmotivated steps."

"I'm sorry?" Wasn't that the name of his novel?

"In architecture they're known as unmotivated steps. They do nothing, they have no destination. They're a reminder."

"A reminder of what?" She looked at Norval and knew he wouldn't answer: his mind was a kingdom to him, a kingdom never invaded. "I mean, it's none of my business, you don't have to tell me ..."

Norval was already turning the doorhandle. "Glad you feel that way."

"Wait, Norval, don't go. You're not serious about ... you know, what you said before, about ending your days in water and ... all that? I mean, anytime soon?"

"Perfectly serious. After Z, I'm dead."

Chapter 10
"JJY"

The Cemetery Gatehouse was all that was left of the Yelle family fortune. Gaétan Yelle, in the latter half of the nineteenth century, had made his money manufacturing tobacconist goods, but his son Jean-Jacques was not cut out for the smokeware business and eventually sold it. After his wife died he spent most of his legacy on horses at Bluebonnets or bingo at Église St–Ambroise, although he did make one rather strange investment: along with a partner, he bought Le Cimetière Mont-Royal. He ended up selling this too, except for the gatehouse, a mock Gothic structure of wood and stone, where he lived the last twelve years of his life, a happy widower, in the company of his happy son Jean-Jacques Jr, whom everyone called JJ.

From as far back as he could remember, from the day he hit a bases-loaded triple to win a Little League championship (though some said the ball was foul), everything had been happy for JJ. There had been happiness with his father, collecting novelty gags and formula jokes, building great bonfires of leaves and found furniture, bowling at Quilles Bec every Thursday night while describing his plans to make a fortune as an inventor. There had been happiness with his mother, who taught him how to make Chinese box kites and waxed leaf scrapbooks and French-silk pie, who introduced him to Mille Bornes and nonsense verse and stilt-walking, and who reminded him daily what a cute little boy he was. In Grade 3 there'd been happiness because Mademoiselle Proulx had liked him. He hadn't applied himself, he hadn't got good grades, and he'd once painted a picture of bare-naked women bowling, but still Mademoiselle Proulx liked him. *Un bon petit garçon*, she had written on his report card.

JJ grew into a lubberly bear of a man, retaining the freckled face, orangey-red hair and teapot cheeks of his youth. As an adult, most of his time was spent trying to make money from his inventions and hobbies—

herbs and magical potions, "fun" gadgets and commercial writing—via the Internet. For his dot.com company he bought a half-dozen early-nineties computers at a bankruptcy auction, which he repaired himself and which he continued to repair as they crashed one by one.

Inside the once-opulent gatehouse, which had previously housed a gardener and his family, things tended to accrue: advertising leaflets he'd written himself, pieces of salvaged furniture and stereo equipment, stacks of natural therapy magazines, sacks of fertilizer, shoe and cereal boxes containing "special products," and a kitchen midden that was rising daily.

On the gravel path leading to the house, where crabgrass and dandelions accumulated in the summer and unploughed snow in the winter, his 1984 Dodge Aries (his birth sign) was parked. He had bought the car "for peanuts" from a New Brunswick firm called MUMMY'S YUMMY CHICKEN. On its sides, to cover up the logo and lettering, JJ spray-painted rust-coloured undercoating and affixed decals from places he had visited in the Maritime provinces and New England. To the car's roof he attached large patches of canvas and blue plastic, held down with yards of rope and bungee cord, which made it look like he was transporting something of very irregular shape. Some speculated it was a kind of travelling pup-tent or rooftop bed, which JJ with an inscrutable smile would not deny. When he crossed the border into the States he was usually asked to remove the canvas and plastic sheets, which took a good quarter hour. What the border guards eventually found was a large red-and-yellow metal chicken, which had been welded to the roof.

Although now an adult, JJ was bubbling with childlike glee on the day of his party. He had sent out *fifty* invitations. Where would he put them all? There were four kitchen chairs, a sagging sofa with urinous scent (a legacy from a family pet, an incontinent poodle), a winged armchair whose springs were gone (a legacy from his mother, who was plenteous), and five tip-up seats (a legacy from the Rialto cinema, uprooted by vandals). That should seat about, what, a baker's dozen? Of course, there's always the floor ... He examined the floor and seemed surprised at what he saw: soiled industrial carpeting that made him wince when his nose got too near it. Too many Swanson dinners and soft drinks walked into the weave. When he attempted to roll the carpet up, some of the rubber underpad adhered to the floor, while the rest crumbled into a fine powder. He decided to leave the rug where it was. A good spray with Lysol should do the trick. He was on his way to the bathroom when a crashing sound startled him. He turned round to see what it was. Upside down on the floor was *The Ice Bridge*, a J.W. Morrice forgery that had fallen from the wall. Oh no, he thought. When a picture falls it means somebody's going to die!

JJ closed his eyes, made the sign of the cross, then continued on his way towards the bathroom. After rooting around in a jungle of products beneath the sink, and pausing to toss rancid items into an already full garbage pail, he found what he was seeking: an aerosol can of lemon-scented Lysol. He pushed the nozzle. And pushed again. A few drops of liquid oozed out. What else is in here? Let's see ... a bottle of Aqua Velva with dust embedded in the oily glass, unused since his father's last shave, and a vial of Fleur de la Passion by Duverné, the preferred scent of his mother. He went back into the living room where he sprinkled each of these onto the rug.

To wash off the scents from his hands he returned to the bathroom, which was fitted with equipment that seemed to have been salvaged from a 1950s restaurant. There was a urinal, a sink with faucets of the water-saving design, a rotary dispenser filled with pink granulated powder, and a hand dryer with these instructions:

SHAKE EXCESS WATER FROM HANDS.
PUSH KNOB. STOPS AUTOMATICALLY.
RUB HANDS LIGHTLY AND RAPIDLY.
TURN LOUVRE UPWARD TO DRY FACE.

At least this is what it had once said. Some of the words had been scratched off with a coin or knife:

SHAKE
        KNOB.
    RUB   LIGHTLY AND RAPIDLY.
    TURN   UPWARD TO   FACE.

JJ chuckled as he blow-dried his hands. This *still* cracks me up, he thought. But is it a tad schoolboyish? Should I remove it, or spray-paint over it, before the guests arrive? No, it's fine for now, I'll do it tomorrow. He went to his bedroom, his hands slightly damp. A faded and threadbare patchwork quilt made by his mother was staple-gunned to the window frame, and the wallpaper—winged bear cubs with bows and arrows—was only half-installed, interrupted when his ex-girlfriend said her pregnancy was a false alarm. Film posters of his father's, including *Les Vacances de Monsieur Hulot* and *The Nutty Professor*, with yellowed Scotch-tape marks across the corners, were tacked to the wall. I'd better clean up the place, he thought. Do a complete overhaul.

With an old baby buggy, his own, JJ carted out plastic submarines, water guns, teddy bears, board games, joke books, and made a motley mound outside. He carried out items from his clothes closet, including his father's perma-press pants and naphthalene-smelling cardigans. He paused to look through a shoe box of old letters: form-letter job rejections, angry threats from collection agencies, bills from Hydro-Québec and Gaz Métropolitain, a sheaf of parking tickets, letters from lawyers acting on behalf of Mount Royal Cemetery. In a plastic case was a Rowntree Cherry Blossom box, discarded by a girl named Solange. He first saw Solange coming out of the Villa Maria School for Girls, in a pleated skirt and jacket of subdued crimson, and he had tried to glimpse her leaving school every afternoon till the end of the year, nine months in all. His love for twelve-year-old Solange was like Dante's for Beatrice. He got within twelve feet of her twice, exchanged a nod once, and thought about her for the rest of his life.

The memory faded, but only slightly, when he met his first girlfriend. She was a Greek girl he encountered at a summer camp for underprivileged kids, where they both worked as counsellors. In the same shoe box were three letters from her. "My dearest JJ," one began. "I love you more than yesterday, and less than tomorrow ..."

JJ cleared away pots of dead flowers and threw them, pots and all, onto the mound outside. He carried out piles of herbal magazines, some from the late eighties, and tossed these onto the heap as well. Tonight we'll have a bonfire, he decided. I'll greet my guests with an Eskimo bonfire! We'll roast marshmallows! A marshy-roast! No, for heaven's sake, what am I thinking? I'm turning over a new leaf, I'm no longer a child. But a marshmallow or two would be good now. He went to the cupboard and, through a window propped open by his mother's corrective wooden spoon, tossed out miscellaneous bottles and boxes, including a family-size can of petrified Quik and multi-packs of miniature cereal with the sugared ones removed. Some of the tins, covered in dust, came from dates before Best Before Dates. While eating the dregs of three plastic bags containing coconut, almonds and dried cranberries respectively, he spied a bag of marshmallows. Yes! I *knew* I had some! He reached into the bag and pulled out marshmallows as hard as golf balls. Through the window, left-handed, he threw these too onto the heap outside. "Goodbye youth!" he exclaimed. "Burn memories, burn!"

The last bus of the day, the "Widows' Shuttle," was squeezing out the gate as Norval, Samira and Noel entered Mount Royal Cemetery. The wet windows of the bus were agleam with amber, the black silhouettes inside barely visible. The driver, unaccountably, honked his horn twice as he passed in the opposite direction.

In the day's last lighted hour they walked without words, foot-high packing-snow crunching beneath them and an enormous sunset—with apocalyptic reds and purples—above them. Following Samira's lead, they paused to wipe the snow from various monuments and mausoleums, revealing memorials to Scots parentage, wealth or benevolent deeds, bravery in war or "good wives." Some of the dead, Noel remarked, came from famous sunken ships like the *Titanic* or *Lusitania*. Others, Samira discovered, were famous themselves, like Anna Harriet Leonowens, immortalised in *Anna and the King of Siam* and *The King and I*. Others were infamous, Norval pointed out, like Alexander Armstrong English, who after a career in the British army became Canada's itinerant hangman. And a vicious wife-beater.

Fifty yards along a winding road, at a fork, was a signboard whose paint had been flaking off for decades. A pale red arrow pointed towards:

LOGE DU PORTIER
GATEHOUSE
(PRIVATE)

They followed the arrow and the mood of the cemetery gradually changed. The opulence of the Victorian section, with its intimations of immortality, gave way to humbler graves of immigrant, infant, soldier, pauper. After a quarter-mile or so, at a crumbling white statue of a naked child leaning against a skull, like a baby Hamlet, the trio saw smoke gyring into the sky. They passed a NO TRESPASSING sign nailed to a tree, then an ad hoc electrical box that looked like it was wired by an Indian,[20] then a rusting boat of a car that appeared to be carrying a large boulder on its roof.

"Anyone want some of this?" asked Norval, before taking a drink, not his first of the day, from a zinc flask of rye. "You may need it." As he wiped his mouth with his hand, noises came from behind: first a dog barking, then what sounded like muffled voices. He looked back but saw no one. He took another hit before rejoining the others.

The three approached the run-down but not ruined gatehouse, the original structure of which was charming and fairy-taleish with its conical roof and twin turrets, but which a series of additions had rendered unshapely and asymmetrical, like a house drawn by a young child. They passed a tumbledown carport, which sheltered a 1950s hearse on cinder blocks, then a large maple tree whose trunk and lower limbs had been painted pale blue. A patch of snow beneath it bore two yellow j's inscribed in urine-writing. As the two men inspected the engraving, Samira pointed to a figure standing next to a smoking mound: a panda-ish man sporting one of those hats that dads wear fishing, a monstrously oversized wool sweater that had seen—on his or someone else's shoulders—better days, a dandelion scarf, fat-pants with leg pockets, and furry brown boots that looked like hooves.

When Samira smiled and waved he became animated, dropping his shovel and windmilling his arms. As they drew closer they noticed rings round his eyes, as if he had just smoked his way through a kilo of weed. His face was lined, more with laugh lines than worry wrinkles, and fringed with gelled stick-up hair, boy-band hair, and a preliminary scenario for a goatee.

"Welcome partiers!" he shouted, oversalivating. "Welcome to my crib, you're the first to arrive!" He took Samira's hand and chivalrously kissed it. He began a playful sparring with Norval, but Norval told him to stop. As he was affectionately clapping Noel on the back, a dog began to bark. Furiously this time. They all paused to listen.

"That's Merlin the Second," said JJ. "He's a stray. He warns me when people approach. Hey Nor, what dog loves to take baths?"

"I'm sorry?"

"What dog loves to take baths? A shampoodle."

"Right."

"Why did the poor dog chase his own tail? He was trying to make both ends meet. What do you get when ..."

"Please," said Norval. "Our sides can only take so much heaving."

" ... when you cross a sheepdog with a rose?"

"Let's see. A collie-flower?"

"Yes! Who can resist dog jokes, eh? Come."

They followed JJ to the door, which he opened and held for them. "Enter. Make yourselves at home. Don't worry about your boots. Have a look around."

They did as bid, stepping over the worn threshold, and were surprised at what they saw.

"Let me take your coat. If it's OK with you guys, we'll wait a few minutes for the others to arrive. Hope I have enough room for everybody!"

The visitors remained mute as they took in some of the objects in the room: a cigar-store Indian, a stuffed cat, two tennis presses and a buggy whip hanging from nine-inch nails, a set of shoetrees resting on a suction bath mat—and other accoutrements signalling mental derangement. In the background was the sound of two black-and-white televisions broadcasting in two different languages.

"Nor, every time I see you I'm like, amazed," said JJ. "You know who you look like?"

Norval said that he did.

"You look a bit like Byron! And so do you, Noel. Although Noel looks more like Émile Nelligan.[21] Samira, I meant to ask you last week. Is that a Greek name?"

"Arabic."

"Really? It is true what they say? About the jihad?"

"What do they say?"

"That a man who dies while on jihad will be able to have sexual intercourse with seventy perpetual virgins in heaven?"

Samira smiled. "Well, it's based on a verse from the Hadith, but it's a literal translation that's not ... you know, embraced by many people—"

"Arabs," said Norval, shaking his head, "were once in the vanguard of civilisation. What the hell happened?"

"You French were too," Samira countered. "What the hell happened?"

"I knew a Greek girl in school," said JJ, who seemed not to have heard this exchange. "You're as beautiful as her, I met her at summer camp when I was thirteen, she had hairy legs. I was in love with her, we were never apart as teenagers, in fact I'm still in love with her. She was the thief of my virginity. I learned how to be a hippy from her. She was a bona fide hippy, even though her parents were rich. She ran away from home and grew cabbages in a farmer's field ..."

Calm down, Samira wanted to say, you're like my mother's neurotic Chihuahua. Calm down little guy, Norval wanted to say, you've had way too many chocolate bars. Noel had no wish to say anything: like faulty reception across the stormiest of airwaves, JJ's chatter was not coming in; the blunt and boxy shapes, which gave him little trouble in the lab, were now a train wreck of tangled, dirty-white cracks, pops, bangs.

"So it didn't work out?" said Samira. "With the Greek girl?"

"No, her parents took her to Switzerland for six months in the hope she'd meet someone else."

"And did she?"

"No. But when she got back to Quebec she did. A member of Les Beaux Gars."

"A rock band?"

"Biker gang. But I have a feeling she'll come back to me. I saw her at a summer-camp reunion. She ignored me. But I'll wait as long as it takes— forever, if necessary, till the stars turn cold. I have a feeling we'll end our days together, that it'll all twist together, her fate and mine. If not, perhaps there'll be a reunion in eternity, where love stays unchanged. Be back in a jiff, I got to change out of these clothes. You can watch TV while I'm gone. The Olympics! We're kicking ass, eh? It's believer-fever, it's fandemonium!"

After JJ disappeared into his bedroom, the three guests stared at each other, slack-jawed. Norval shifted his gaze to the room's walls, papered for the third or fourth time decades before, with outlined patterns coloured in here and there with wax crayon. Noel examined oddly positioned paintings—covering cracks or holes, he assumed—which depicted the innocence of children, the benevolence of the old, the purity of lovers, the cohesion of families. Samira was drawn to the room's centrepiece: the large, weather-beaten cigar-store Indian, with a stuffed cat at its feet. The Indian, JJ revealed later, was his grandfather's and the cat his grandmother's. And the paintings were creations of his youth, he further explained, adding that he had been guided by numbers.

"This place is ... amazing!" said Samira, struggling to find the right words. "It ... smokes!"

Noel, glancing from object to object, was struggling to take it all in. There was a feeling in the house of everything coming apart at once. Norval thought he had entered a home for the crazed.

"It's ... it's like a museum!" Samira exclaimed. "Look at this!" She pointed to an old clock with a golden face showing the phases of the moon and conjunctions of the planets. "And this!" Beside the clock was an antique spyglass of tarnished brass. "And this!" Everyone looked up at a chandelier above her, originally a gasolier that had been converted to electric light in the twenties. There were still gas jets and fittings all over the house, as if JJ planned to return to gas lighting if electricity didn't catch on.

"Are we looking at a neurological deficit here?" asked Norval. "Is JJ crazed, permanently or periodically?"[22]

"Shh," Samira whispered. "He's a sweetheart. If you say one single word against him, one single sarcasm ... well, I don't know what I'll do. Or not do. I think this place is fabulous."

Norval screwed his heel into the floorboard, causing the wood to powder away. "It's seen better days," he said.

"So have you."

Norval sniffed left and right. "What is that mephitic odour?" His nose led him to the defeated carpet and sagging sofa. "Bordello perfume and ..."

"Dog piss?" Noel suggested.

"Formula?"

"K_9P."

"Shh," whispered Samira again. "Come on, you guys, behave. He might hear you. What's your problem anyway? Cleanliness is as bad as godliness. Hey, look at this." Samira nodded towards a ceiling-high bookcase made of red bricks and particle board, with uneven rows of files and books. Large green albarellos served as bookends.

Norval and Samira began examining the spines. The top rows included *Natural Alchemy, Medical Underground, Fringe Medicine, Metaphysical Medicine, Renegade Medicine, Clandestine Laboratories, Granddad's Wonderful Book of Chemistry, Holistic Approach in Ancient Medicine, Necromancy for Dumbies, Acupuncture for Dumbies, Hypnosis for Salesmen, Colour Healing, Secrets of the Chinese Herbalists* and *Laughter Therapy Is No Joke*. On the sagging middle shelves were volumes of *Frontier Science* and *Psychology Tomorrow*, piled corkscrew-wise, as well as joke anthologies, a shoebox of letters with a heart on top, a half-dozen books by Émile Vorta, and a scrapbook with the doctor's name on the cover.

"God, no spine-faking here," said Norval. "It's all shit."

"No, it's not." Samira pointed to the bottom shelf, which included works by Saint-Exupéry, Jules Verne, Alexandre Dumas, Antoine Galland, Ulrich Boner[23] and John Creasey.

At the opposite end of the room, where Noel was now foraging, were higgledy-piggledy mounds of computer and electronic equipment of modest manufacture: not IBM or Mac or Toshiba, but Capital, Cicero, Apex; not Sony, Panasonic or JVD, but Yorx, Citizen, Claretone. Two no-brand televisions, connected to automotive stereo speakers, showed two different Winter Olympic events in two different languages. One had a story about some French figure-skating judge, the other an interview with a Canadian athlete, which Noel turned up:

"So how do you feel? You must be disappointed."

"Not everyone can medal, eh? I'm happy just to be here."

"Right. But you came sixty-eighth."

"I'm here for the experience. To meet the other athletes. Watch their events now that mine's over. Just relax for the rest of the week."

"You don't feel disappointed?"

"I'm happy just to be here."

"So this is like a junket for you, a joyride?"

"I'm here for the experience. I hope to build on this for the next Olympics."

"But you're forty-three."

"I'm happy just to be here."

"Anybody else show up while I was changing?" asked JJ as he emerged from his bedroom wearing a T-shirt that said THE RIGHT CHEMISTRY, filthier than the one it replaced. "I've invited some mega-watt scientists, including Dr. Ravenscroft and Dr. Rhéaume—and of course Dr. Vorta. I'm his number-one fan, eh? I keep a scrapbook on him. And you know what? He's the one responsible for us meeting in the first place!"

"Think we could have a glass of that red?" Norval nodded towards the table.

"I haven't done the dishes for a while."

"I'll drink it out of the bottle."

"Will a paper cup do?"

"Fine."

"Or plastic?"

"Goatskin, anything."

"Would you like some wine, Samira? How about you, Noel?"

"Noel is a temperance expert," said Norval. "I'll have his glass. Didn't you mention something about absinthe and/or laudanum in your invitation?"

"I'm saving that for later. I'll just pour Noel a taste. Here you go, Noel, Sam. I'd like to propose a toast to the world's greatest scientist, Dr. Émile Vorta!"

They clinked plastic cups, with the exception of Norval, who was already pouring himself another.

"Today is a magic day," said JJ, wiping his wet chin with his T-shirt. "In five minutes we'll be experiencing something that won't happen again in our lifetime."

To anyone else, the stretch of silence that followed might have been seen as disturbing indifference. Not to JJ. "Yup, a magic moment is about to occur ..."

"Really?" said Samira, like an actress suddenly remembering her lines. "What won't happen in our lifetime?"

"At two minutes past eight, the clock will read in perfect symmetry. It will say 20:02, 20/02, 2002. It's only happened twice before in history and will only happen one other time, in 2112. It's a thing of mathematical beauty—and a palindrome! And that's why we're meeting tonight, that's why we're inaugurating our club tonight, at this time! It's a palindromic moment!"

They all clinked cups again with the exception of Norval, who was blankly watching an interview with a British ski-jumper. His attention was diverted to three pump-like contraptions standing beside the television. He picked up one of them. "Uh, JJ?"

"Yes? You'd like to know what those are for?"

"I would, actually. But first I'd like to point out that today is the second of February."

"That's correct."

"Your 'palindromic moment' will not occur until the twentieth."

With a worried look, JJ began writing in the air with his pointer finger. "Oh my God! You're right. I'm a blithering idiot!"

"*Maleesh*," Samira said comfortingly, her hand on his shoulder. "I got confused too. Why don't we just make tonight a kind of ... dry run, test flight. We'll hold the official inauguration on the twentieth."

"Yes!" said JJ. "What a great—"

"You were going to tell me what these are," said Norval, still clutching one of the pumps.

"Well, the one you got in your hand is an inside-out sherlock, that one there's a purple flamer, and the other's a standup double mushroom side lock."

Norval nodded. "Penis enlargers?"

"Bongs. Hand-blown soft-glass pipes. Using the X-Tractor, the ultimate cold water extraction system."

Norval examined them further. "So I presume you have something interesting to fill them with? Is that what's in those boxes over there?" He nodded towards a recess in the room, a kind of alcove.

"Not exactly. Come, everyone, I'll show you."

The three followed JJ to his special storeroom, the size of a walk-in closet, which contained an assortment of boxes stacked raggedly to the ceiling: Payless shoe boxes, Roi-Tan cigar boxes, Lucky Charms cereal boxes, perhaps fifty in all, most of them spray-painted and covered with magic marker hieroglyphs.

"Are you a shoe salesman?" Samira asked.

JJ laughed, a high-pitched yodel. "These boxes aren't filled with shoes. Or cereal or cigars, for that matter. They're special kits. Filled with ... well, special things. This one's called Top Dog. Canine steroids—you know, for frisbee championships? This one's for nervous dogs: Doggie Paxil and K-9 Quaaludes. This one's an appetite suppressant for dogs, this one contains a dog whistle and transponder so humans can hear it, this one contains funeral eye caps and hypno-coins, this one post-divorce pills, this one placebo Viagra ..."

Samira laughed, then quickly covered her mouth with her hand. "What's in this one, with the skull and crossbones?"

"Anthrax. Re-engineered. The bacterium's been disabled to make it harmless, except to certain cancer cells. And this one contains black hellebore, or Christmas rose, also a poison."

"But ...why do you have poisons?"

"I got a deal off the Internet for the whole lot. E-bay. Roaming the Net is my hobby. I'm an internaut."

"And that one?" Samira pointed higher up, to a pea-green box with saffron stars.

"Which one? Oh, that's The Wedge. You got your wedge, your foam, your fill bottle, gloves, temp strip, hose clamp, swab."

"But what is it?"

JJ took the box down, opened it up. "Well ... I'm a bit embarrassed to say in female company."

"Don't be."

"You place the wedge between your butt cheeks. I can demonstrate if you like."

Samira paused, finding the image in her head rather alarming. "Not ... necessary. But what's it for?"

"It's a pass-the-piss-test," said Norval, by the entrance, still turning one of the bongs over in his hands.

"Exactly," said JJ. "It allows you to pass someone else's water—clean and at the correct temperature. Here's another one, the Whizzinator 3000, which is synthetic. Comes with a very realistic prosthetic virile member, in lifelike skin tones—black, brown, Latino, tan, white. Uses only the best synthetic urine on the market. No batteries, no wires, no metal to set off alarms. It comes with organic heat pads to maintain body temperature."

Samira nodded. "You sell them to athletes, I imagine?"

"Yeah, in fact a Canadian athlete who's now in Salt Lake City bought three. A biathlete by the name of ... but wait, I shouldn't be telling you any of this! It's also for anyone who might have trouble passing an employer's test."

"Right." Samira lifted the lid of an electric-blue box at eye-level. "And this one is ...?"

"A scrotal infusion kit."

"I'm not sure I want to know more."

"You got your wax, your catheter, saline solution, intravenous bag. Everything you need. Well, not *you*."

"Need for what?"

"Scrotal inflation. You dip your scrotum in hot wax several times to relax it, inject a catheter into both sides of the testicles and fill them with a dripping saline solution from an intravenous bag. You can go up to two litres if you want. That'll give you three days of monster balls—expanding anywhere from fifteen to twenty-two inches in circumference—before the solution is absorbed into the system and things get back to normal. It's perfectly safe."

"But ... *why?*"

"Some gentlemen like the warm heavy feeling when they're all puffed up. And deflation is good too, because there's a constant tugging on the scrotum. So they say—I've never tried it. Plus it looks hot, it looks awesome."

"What's this sack of powder for?" asked Norval, from a kneeling position, his nose stuck in the bag as if he were about to snort it.

"Just add water and stir. Got that from a lab in Delaware. It's listed on my website. Very popular among university students."

"You smoke it or snort it?"

"Neither. It's fake excrement. You can smear it anywhere. It's very lifelike. But completely harmless, of course."

"I know I'm repeating myself," said Samira, laughing, "but ..."

"What's it for? Frat parties, revenge on teachers, parents, enemies. You name it. It's *very* big in New Hampshire. But most of this stuff is from a former life, from my misspent youth—I've left it all behind. I'm about to toss most of it onto the bonfire. I'm now into CAM. I'm a CAM artist."

"You're a cam-artist," said Norval.

"Exactly."

"And that would be ...?"

"Complementary and alternative medicine—everything from medita-tion, acupuncture and herbalism to chelation, colonics and leech therapy. This, for example, is a colonic irrigation kit. You run this tube through your rectum in order to cleanse the intestines with warm water. This one's an iri-dology kit. You diagnose illness by studying the iris of the eye. And this last one is for Hopi ear candling—you insert a burning candle in the ear canal to remove impurities from the brain and sinuses. And these three are for aromatherapy, this one colour therapy, this one for acupressure, this one's Bach flowers, and these three contain the Schuessler Tissue Salts."

"Bach flowers?" said Samira.

"Oh, I forgot one. This one here's for magnet therapy, based on the belief that blood circulation can be improved by mounting magnets at various points on the body."

"Haven't all these procedures, without exception, been debunked as useless or dangerous?" said Norval. "And hasn't the FDA banned the importation of ear candles?"

"Well, I ..."

"I think," said Samira, "that its proponents are practising religion or philosophy as much as science, isn't that right, JJ?"

"Yes, that's very true. The testing data on CAM suggest that there's another dimension to human life and healing that's not material. A lot of traditional drugs—like Prozac, for example—have been found, in study after study, to be no better than placebos. So something else is going on, in another dimension."

"Herbal cures haven't received much attention from pharmaceutical companies," said Samira, as the three made their way back into the living room. "Have they, JJ?"

"If they can't patent 'em, Big Pharma won't touch 'em. Take Taheebo tea. It's been around since Christ was a carpenter. Everyone knows it could eliminate cancer. So what's the drug industry's reaction? Not interested. Taheebo can't be patented. It's the bark of a tree! God made it! Pfizer and Merck can't patent it!"

Samira picked up a cookie from a plastic bowl next to the cigar-store Indian and put it in her mouth. "Oh ... what the ... These taste like dog bis-cuits. No, these *are* dog biscuits."

"I keep them for Merlin, and other strays. They're herbal—made with stone mint, fennel seeds and tincture of stavesacre. A nice canine mouth detergent."

"They aren't too bad, actually," said Samira, while crunching. "Would you like to try one, Noel?" she said, articulating each word, as if he were a child with learning disabilities.

"Hey Sam," said JJ, "which animal keeps the best time?"

"I give up."

"A watch dog. You hear that one, Nor? A watch dog."

"Side-splitting."

"You've got some great books here," said Samira, smiling. "Are you a writer yourself?"

"Yes, as a matter of fact. I started off in the entertainment industry. I used to write film teasers and taglines. After taking a creative writing course at a prestigious non-accredited university. I've worked on lots of films."

"Really?" said Samira. "Which ones?"

"Well, the latest one hasn't been released yet. There's some legal snags. It's called *Lord of the Rings: The Assistant Editor's Cut*. I worked in the field for years. Freelance, like. I wrote some stuff for Sony—you know, fake reviews? And I'm the one who came up with the tagline 'A film about blank blank and other blanks.' It was me who started all that. And now I'm thinking of suing the companies that stole it. A film about blank blank and other blanks. That was me."

Norval shook his head, not knowing or caring what JJ was talking about. As far as he was concerned, all conversational value had been squeezed out of the fact that JJ once worked in the entertainment industry. "So how about we start stuffing these bongs ..."

"I've got an article about it, from the *Hartford Courant*." JJ reached for a knob and yanked repeatedly at a blocked drawer. He pulled at a crumpled newspaper, which ripped as he extracted it. "Listen, all these are mine: 'A film about husbands, wives, children and other natural disasters.' 'A film about life, love, airplanes and other bumpy rides.' 'A film about work, marriage and other forms of combat ...'"

"We get the idea," said Norval.

"'A film about friends, families and other vicious animals.' 'A film about kidnappings, car thefts and other rituals of dating.' All those were mine. You may have heard them. And then everybody started to steal the formula. Like *High Fidelity*: 'A comedy about fear of commitment, hating your job, falling in love and other pop favourites.' Which is way lame. And *Panic*: 'A story of family lust, murder and other mid-life crises.' And ..."

"Yes, fine," said Norval.

"*Wag the Dog*: 'A comedy about truth, justice and other special effects.' You see now why I want to sue?"

"Yes," said Norval. "Got anything else in that drawer, preferably illegal—"

"I also worked in the music business. I thought up misspelled words. In fact, I'm the one who got that whole thing going. It's huge now, eh?"

"What ... exactly do you mean?" said Samira. "Like Led Zeppelin or Def Leppard or Limp Bizkit ..."

"I'm the one who extended it to songs. You know, like 'Majuk Karpit' and 'Toolz4Luv' and 'Sk8er Boi.' That really took off. Musicians *love* misspelled words. It's rebellious. Then I moved on to an ad agency. I wrote tons of slogans. Here's one I did for Funds-o-Rama in Vermont. Are you ready? 'Don't just invest. Upvest.' That was mine. 'Don't just invest. Upvest.'"

Norval looked vacantly at him. "And that would mean ... what, exactly?"

"I'm not sure. Everyone liked it, though. They ended up selling it to another company for big bucks."

Norval nodded. "How about 'Up your Assets'?"

"Here's another one: 'It's not a fridge. It's an ideology.' That was mine. 'It's not a fridge. It's an ideology.'"

"That was big, was it?" said Norval.

"No, they never used it. I also did that vitamin-pill equation? That was a classic, eh. You know, number of pills plus x. That was mine."

"Which ... what are we talking about now?" said Samira.

"Well, you don't get 100 pills anymore, do you. You get 90 + 10 free. You don't get 50 pills. You get—"

"Forty plus ten."

"Correct. It was me who started that. And then I quit the ad agency to write a novel. I got a hundred and forty-three rejections. Which I believe is a record. I sent the file to Guinness—you know, for publicity?—but they said they didn't have that category. And weren't planning to.[24] I did get a nibble from the biggest publishing company on the Falkland Islands. Anyway, I ended up paying for the publication myself, at least a bank loan did, worth every penny too. The Laurentian Bank's still after me." For some reason JJ here erupted in a loud belly laugh, not the irritating kind but the infectious. He walked over to the bookshelf and got down on his hands and knees. Squeezed under the bottom shelf was an entire row of hard-cover books, of uniform colour—dun—with nothing on the spines. He extracted one of them. "Here, take a look."

"What's it about?" said Samira.

"Lost love united. Getting a second chance. It's not a novel of traditional form. It has no plot—it's symphonic in design. I composed it in eight weeks at white heat. It didn't get great reviews, but I tried to put a positive spin on things. That's what my mom used to tell me. Look for the silver lining. I Fed-Exed a copy to Oprah."

Apart from his eyes, which were rolling reflexively, Norval was keeping his natural sarcasm and vehemence in check. Not because he cared about hurting JJ's feelings—the man was shatterproof—but because he was too easy a target: he'd been wearing a self-hung "Kick Me" sign for years. It was like ridiculing Sir Andrew Lloyd Webber or Sir Elton John. Besides, Norval had something else on his mind: the promise of ecstatic herbs. Feigning interest, he picked up one of the books and read the back cover:

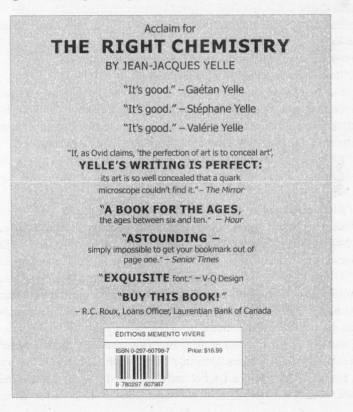

Acclaim for

THE RIGHT CHEMISTRY

BY JEAN-JACQUES YELLE

"It's good." – Gaétan Yelle

"It's good." – Stéphane Yelle

"It's good." – Valérie Yelle

"If, as Ovid claims, 'the perfection of art is to conceal art',
YELLE'S WRITING IS PERFECT:
its art is so well concealed that a quark
microscope couldn't find it." – *The Mirror*

"A BOOK FOR THE AGES,
the ages between six and ten." – *Hour*

"ASTOUNDING —
simply impossible to get your bookmark out of
page one." – *Senior Times*

"EXQUISITE font." – V-Q Design

"BUY THIS BOOK!"
– R.C. Roux, Loans Officer, Laurentian Bank of Canada

ÉDITIONS MEMENTO VIVERE

ISBN 0-297-60798-7   Price: $16.99

9 780297 607987

"This is a joke, right?" said Norval.

"It's PR parody—and self-parody. It's postmodernism squared. And those are real quotes—I didn't make them up!"

"It ... it works," said Samira, tentatively. "I like it."

"I learned lots of things in my creative writing course. Like how you should use similes whenever you can. Because critics and jury members like them. I've got thousands: '... like a vine clinging to a dead tree,' '... like being shaven by a drunken barber,' '... like broken kites in an attic ...'"

"OK," said Norval, "we get the—"

"'... like an idle race car,' '... like an asterisk for a missing footnote,' '... like birds entering the mouths of crocodiles and cleaning their teeth,' et cetera, et cetera. I've got them all on floppies, in alphabetical order. I just have to find the bits that go before."

So far, Noel had not understood everything. Not only because of his aural visions, but because Samira's presence made him dumbstruck, his lips numb and stuck. Whenever her eyes—those midnight eyes of the East!—gleamed into his he could feel his legs soften and melt like a cheap candle. Inside he was a mess too, his ears taking pictures his mind couldn't develop. He mimed attention.

"But you know what? The book flopping was the best thing that ever happened to me. Because I know now that I'm no writer. But I had to give it a shot, you know what I mean? I still do it as a hobby. But now I've found something I really enjoy. That I'm good at. And can make money at."

"I'm afraid to ask," said Norval, "what that might be."

"CAM."

"Right."

"But I seem to be fielding all the questions!" said JJ. "What are *you* guys up to these days? Who wants to start? Put up your hand."

"Norval," said Samira, "why don't you tell JJ about your latest project. Your performance art."

"Why don't *you*?" said Norval.

"All right. Norval has set himself the challenge, the considerable artistic challenge, of making love to twenty-six women in twenty-six weeks. In alphabetical order."

"Get out of town!" said JJ. "You scurvy knave! Hey, I might be able to get you a condom sponsor. How far have you got? On target?"

"Ahead of schedule, actually," said Norval. "I started in the middle of last semester, so I just went through my student lists."

JJ nodded. "But isn't that against ... regulations? And ethics?"

"That's the point. The guiding theme of French Symbolism is that objectivity, particularly in morals, is a sham. Morality is devised by human beings with no ground or sanction in reason or nature."

"But aren't morals there to prevent people from hurting each other, hurting themselves, or to prevent us from falling—"

"No one was ever hurt by a fall—it's the halt at the end that does all the damage. In fact, since the invention of sky-diving and bungee and BASE-jumping, free-falling has become a sport, a kind of suicide practice, where you can savour the aesthetics of descent. Metaphorically, that's what I'm doing."

JJ scratched his head. "I guess that makes sense. Don't get me wrong. I'd love to take on the alphabet project myself, but it'd take me a bit longer than twenty-six weeks. In fact, unless I paid for it, I don't think twenty-six years would be enough. I've never been much of a horndog, a babe magnet. But isn't anyone, you know, protesting? Isn't the word getting around?"

"Yeah, some asshole informed the Head of Women's Studies."[25]

"Oh dear. But ... why alphabetical? Why so many?"

"Because," said Samira, "it's worth twenty-six grand. And because he's like one of those characters in Greek mythology—half goat."

"The alphabetical order allows me to explain to my collaborators," said Norval, "after they fall in love or clamour for an encore, that it was a limited run, a one-night-only performance. It gets me off the hook, in other words."

"And because of his sex addiction," said Samira, "Sir Thunderpants would be doing this kind of thing anyway. Might as well get paid for it."[26]

"You're a sex addict?" asked JJ, staring at Norval with his eyes grown big.

"It started out recreational, ended habitual."

JJ let out a yodel-like guffaw. "Lots of fish in the sea, eh? Can't settle on one?"

Norval took another gulp of wine. "Are you familiar with Baudelaire's *flâneur*?"

"Uh, no, not really."

"It's someone who wanders through the city seeking deliverance from the miseries of the self—first through drink, then sexual depravity—in search of an elusive ideal: perfect love. But because people are not naturally loving and monogamous, but essentially self-seeking and unfaithful, this quest will never be ... successful. So he goes from woman to woman, affair to affair, ever questing, never finding."

How brilliantly phrased, thought JJ. A true poet. "So you're a man with a mission." He gazed at Norval humbly, reverentially, as though he were his manservant or page.

"More like a dog with an erection than a man with a mission," said Samira. "I've never heard such bullshit."

"All right," said Norval, "here's another explanation. There are two pleasures in life: food and fornication. In that order. All the rest is rat-ass futility."

"What are you going to do with the money?" asked JJ. "Buy food?"

"None of your business."

"I respect that," said JJ.

Noel lifted his nose from a bookmarked page of *The Count of Monte Cristo*. "He's giving it to the WWF," he said quietly, prodded by Norval's rudeness to betray a secret. The three turned to look at him. Glower, in Norval's case.

"He's giving twenty-six g's," said JJ, scratching his head, "to the *World Wrestling Federation*?"

Noel squatted, returned the book to the shelf. "No, the World Wildlife Fund."

"All right!" JJ exclaimed. "Nor, you da man! Yeah, baby!"

"It was either that," said Norval, "or the Canadian Centre for Misanthropy."

JJ blew loudly through his mouth, his cheeks full like a gopher's. "So how far have you got? What letter are you on?"

Norval paused before answering, slowly extracting an Arrow cigarette from its sheath. Noel held his breath, braced himself for the answer. But seconds ticked away and no answer came. A hissing sound broke the silence as the red phosphorus of a match ignited, a safety match that must have been JJ's.

"I think you said you were on *S*," Samira said finally. "Did you not?"

Norval regarded her coldly, blew smoke in her direction. "Yes, *S* is next."

JJ waited thirty minutes for other guests to arrive—none did—before announcing the name of his new club: The Alchemical Poets of Persia Society.

"I just made that up now," said JJ. "On the spot. I was going to call it 'The Alchemical Troubadours,' but then I found out Sam was from Persia. Plus troubadours are men, aren't they?" Here JJ paused to click keys on a computer. "And here's how we're going to fund our new club. Check it out, it's on the screen now!"

"I know the founder and CEO of the company!" said JJ. "Personally!"

"You know the founder and CEO," said Norval. "Personally."

"Yes! He's an old school buddy!"

"Do you really mean that?" said Norval. "You have no idea how this news fills my cup. The skies are suddenly opening—"

"Norval, isn't your performance project posted on the Web?" said Samira, with searing eyes and tone. "I'm sure JJ would like to see it."

119

Norval said he was just as sure JJ would not.

"Au contraire!" said JJ. "Is it the Fed site? Hold on, it's in My Favourites. Right. So I punch Lit? Then ... Funded Projects?" As JJ squinted at the screen he began to resemble a schoolboy, tongue protruding as he frowned in concentration. "Then ... 'A' for Alphabet?"

"In two words," said Samira, looking over his shoulder.

"Let's see ... here's something called *The Acrorats*, an 'ephemeral *in situ* water-ballet proposal to fill a barge with rats, then set it on fire to watch them dive off ...' OK, got it!" said JJ. "*Voilà!*"

Project title:	***THE ALPHA BET***
Artist:	Norval Blaquière
Genre:	performance /ephemeral art
Duration:	26 weeks
Synopsis:	In an erotological tradition extending from Apuleius to *The Thousand and One Nights*, from Boccaccio to Byron and Baudelaire, this abecedarian series of intromittent acts heuristically deconstructs the teleological codes of courtship and monogamy, the illusory Modernist pursuit of objective truths by linear paths, and the mythological ideal of Romantic love promulgated in such decentred phenomena as cyber-matchmakers, the unstable sign-referent engine of which is calibrated to confuse the simulations with the simulacra of pursuit and seduction.

FUNDING APPROVED ✓ **($26,000)**

"Jesus Chrysler!" said JJ. "That's awesome! Although I have no clue what it means. Except for the bottom line. Way to go, Nor—"

"JJ, the moment has come. The chemical phase of the evening. Now, or I'm fucking off."

"Motion seconded. The tribe has spoken. Follow me, guys."

In what may have once been the dining room, JJ kicked aside a carpet and opened up a hatch door. The faint sounds of an old French song could be heard as the three guests followed JJ down a wooden ladder with rungs missing. Although less than six feet high, the basement was surprisingly spacious. It was also extremely bright—there were six 1,500-watt growlights—and extremely hot. Exhaust fans spun, sucking air through charcoal filters, while a series of ducts vented air out the side.

"Exquisite," said Norval, bending over, examining some dozen plants in two-gallon buckets, between four and six feet tall, not far from harvest. "I don't think I've ever seen plants like these. What kind of system are you using?"

"Ebb-and-flow, phototron. A heat pump that keeps the room a hair under eighty-five degrees. A generator—over there by the wall—in case of power failure. Or nosy parkers checking the meters."

"What's with the Trenet?" said Norval.

"Grow music. Beautiful, eh?" They paused to listen to a French song from the forties. "*Que reste-il de nos amours / Que reste-il de ces beaux jours ...*"

"The plants *love* Charles Trenet," said JJ. "They really respond." For some reason he smiled at Noel, who was smiling himself, enjoying both the sounds and odours. Not to mention the news regarding *S*.

"Why does it have to be so hot?" said Samira, wiping her temple.

"The trick is to get the flowering tips of the female plants to produce as much resin as possible, which the leaves and flowers excrete as protection from the sun—growlights, in this case."

"What are these beauties?" asked Norval, pointing to the two tallest plants.

"This one's called Love-in-Idleness. Steamy spicy fumes, exquisite after-bloom. Safe, short-acting, non-addictive. This one's called Yelle-berry, named after its creator. Made from plants my grandfather found—plants of a species never determined by science, never seen before, never seen since."

"This club," said Norval, mouth-wateringly, "is getting better all the time."

"But aren't you afraid of the cops, JJ?" Samira asked.

"Why?"

"Well ... because, you know, it's illegal."

"What's illegal?"

"Growing ... marijuana or jimsonweed or whatever this is."

JJ laughed. "This is not marijuana or jimsonweed. These are organic alternative mood elevators, imported rare and exotic herbs. Completely legal."

Norval closed his eyes, hoping that when he opened them, JJ, the room, the club would have disappeared. He opened his eyes. "JJ, you have taken all three of us down here, into this confuckulated dungeon shit-hole, to show us *legal* plants? You can *not* be fucking serious. If they're legal, how can they be any fucking good?"

"You'd be surprised," said JJ, unruffled. His baby face creased and dimpled. "No, it's not the cops I'm afraid of, Sam. But I am afraid of someone else."

"Who? Bikers? Hells?"

JJ nodded, with a slightly worried look. "And the Rock Machine. The first thing growers learn is this simple rule—do not mess with either gang!"

"And have you? Messed with either gang?"

"Yeah, I've sold marijuana substitute to both gangs. They found out I had a grow op—they track you down through the hydroponic supply shops, which they run—and paid me a visit. A knock 'n' talk. When you get a knock 'n' talk from these guys it's way more serious than the Mounties showing up on your doorstep. They give you two choices. One, work for them. They protect you, tell you when and how much to grow and the price they'll pay for grade-A bud, and that you better not screw it up. Or two, you give them your lights, bud, money and whatever else they want. Obviously, you can't go to the cops. But if you're stupid enough to, they set fire to your farm."

"And have you had a ... 'knock 'n' talk'?" asked Samira.

"Yeah. The next day I found Merlin hanging from a tree. My dog. I've tried to explain my herbs are legal and not cannabis or poppy or jimson-weed or 'shroom. But they keep coming back and threatening me. I've thought of growing the illegal stuff but decided against it, being of a lawful disposition. Plus my mom and dad wouldn't have approved. Treat your body like a temple is what I say. Most of my stuff is good for you, body and soul. Here, take a look at this batch—they're all 'up-lifting.' Fijian Kava Kava, Caliban Root, Byronic Heroine, Baby Hawaiian Woodrose, Syrian Rue, Equatorial Guinean Iboga, Japanese White Heliotrope ..."

The magic of these words held Samira like a spell, and Norval like a bad dream. This is so wrong, he thought, on so many levels ... Noel's mind was spinning like a blender, crushing and mixing and whipping up fruit-coloured forms. JJ's last two words, "White Heliotrope," triggered lines from a poem he associated with his first love. A retinal circus of images, sensations, emotions ...

"Colouring?" said Norval, seeing his friend's fluttering lids. "Noel?"

Noel rubbed his eyes with thumb and forefinger. "Uh ... it's nothing really ..."

"Tell me."

"Just a ... poem. 'White Heliotrope.'"[27]

"White Heliotrope? You want to start with that?" said JJ, missing one bus but boarding another. "A smooth customer, that one. A blend of black haw, cramp bark and morning glory seeds. Rolled with wood betony and laced with oil of heliotrope."

Here JJ opened a salesman's attaché, with rows of small plastic display cases. "For our second choice, we'll choose between Northern Laudanum and Absinthe MHGF."

"Absinthe?" said Norval, sceptically. "I'm afraid to ask what those letters stand for."

A smile of delight split JJ's face in half. "Absinthe Makes the Heart Go Fonder."

"I'm going home," said Norval.

For Norval, slumped on the sofa with his coat on, things could not have gone more wrong without loss of life. Was JJ a punishment, he wondered, for all the sins he'd committed? "You sure this crap is mind-altering?" he asked, while looking at his watch.

"Judge for yourself," said JJ. "So what's our second choice going to be?"

"Why don't we toss everything into a blender," said Norval, "pour in a quart of vodka?"

"Why don't we start with the Heliotrope and move on to the Absinthe—a mix of poppy seed, Monk's pepper, dog's mercury and a legal derivative of wormwood. A bit like E—but better for you. And then to top things off, I'll roll you a bone of my signature strain, the Yelleberry. Shall we start?"

"I'll pass," said Samira. "Drugs don't ... I mean, they can make me paranoid, more than I already am. How about you, Noel? Noel?"

"Pass."

"Are you sure?" said JJ, while rolling three joints the size of toilet paper rolls. "This is primo stuff. The Yelleberry's so resin-laden we'll have to roll loose-logs, or else we won't be able to draw through the goop. It may be best done through this." From under the sofa, JJ produced a gas mask, circa First World War. "You'll being seeing things, imagining things you never saw or imagined before." He lit one with his father's Zippo and offered it to Noel.

"I hallucinate enough as it is," said Noel, shaking his head.

"The only side-effect with this first one, for some people at least, is a bit of stuttering," JJ explained. "But for some reason only on the letter *m*. And because the paper's dipped in deglycerinised liquorice, it may change the pitch of your voice. It's never happened to me, mind you. For me, when I'm ripped on this stuff, I don't say 'yes,' I say 'yesh.' And I don't say 'no,' I say 'noo'."

Norval, after removing his coat, had fired up a pair of cigars over the fireplace and was about to inhale both through the customised Cartman gas mask. He lifted up the mask. "You say either, ripped or not, and you're out of the club."

"I don't think you should do that much," JJ warned.

Norval inhaled nearly half of each roll before slumping back onto the sofa, gas mask still over his face.

"Norval?" said Samira, smiling. "Are you all right?" When there was no response, her smile disappeared. "Nor?" Norval groped at his mask but couldn't get it off. Samira reached over to help, prying it off.

Norval gazed at each member of the club with a spasmodic grin and bloodshot eyes. The heliotrope and wormwood, especially together, were almost immeasurably potent. "I *love* this club," he slurred in a high-pitched voice. "I love everybody. Especially you, JJ."

"Hey, I love you too man—"

"Can I come back to-m-morrow?"

Norval, for the next half-hour, spoke in falsetto French about childhood games he played in Paris, a pet bunny named Mitsou, a sword made of tinfoil and, moving clockwise, his love for each person in the room. He then went to the bathroom, where everyone thought he was going to throw up.

Instead, he reappeared with a smile on his face. He had draped a stole of pink toilet paper round his shoulders and was beginning to perform fencing manoeuvres with a plunger. Abruptly, he then sat on the floor in a lotus position, insisted they were all in heaven, and fell asleep.

"He maxed out," said JJ. "I warned him. Moderation is the best policy."

Noel was feeling good from breathing in the ambient fumes. His mind was colourless and clear, his confidence at a high level. "Norval is a foe of moderation," he said proudly, while gazing at his best friend. "A champion of excess. Which is one of the things I envy about him."

Samira nodded. "I agree. The road of excess, as they say, leads to the palace of wisdom." She had changed her mind, sampling two different blends. She too was feeling euphoric and shockingly clear-headed. She smiled at Noel, who suddenly looked extraordinarily handsome. She closed her eyes and was drifting off when a troubling sound infiltrated her brain. A voice from that night, the black-out night ...

As JJ spoke to no one in particular, Noel's gaze shifted from object to object in the smoke-filled room: from the brass bongs, like ancient oriental hookahs, to the rows of scented candles (bergamot and myrrh?), to the cigar-store Indian and stuffed cat. He glanced at Samira, who seemed in the midst of a blissful dream. He inhaled the mix of perfumes and mystic smoke, closed his eyes and watched the room transform itself into a grotto, its objects into beautiful statues. It was like a page from *The Count of Monte Cristo*, when Aladdin smokes hashish offered by Sinbad and the statues suddenly advance with *smiles of love, their throats bare, hair flowing like waves, holding him in a torturing grasp, delighting his senses as with a voluptuous kiss* ...

Noel opened his eyes. His body felt soft and pliable, like Plasticine. And the carpet in front of him seemed to be moving, the cigar-store Indian advancing towards him—but now as an Indian princess, flanked by a cat-eyed maidservant! He rubbed his eyes, turned towards Samira, who was reclining on the divan like a beautiful houri. She was made of marble but her sensuous lips were pink, like the inside of a seashell ... As JJ continued to speak, in a tongue that sounded like Arabic, Noel reclosed his eyes and re-entered the grotto. *Lips of stone turned to flame, breasts of ice became like heated lava, so that to Aladdin, yielding for the first time to the sway of the drug, love was a sorrow and voluptuousness a torture, as burning mouths were pressed to his thirsty lips ... His senses yielded and he sank back breathless and exhausted beneath the kisses of these marble goddesses* ...

Noel half-opened his eyes and watched Samira's lips move ... Was she seeing the same things? Were they on the same page? He looked to his right. The Indian princess had retransformed into the cigar-store Indian. And the feline maidservant? Noel was searching for her when a loud boxy voice distracted him.

"So that's my idea!" said JJ excitedly. "We all write down our favourite poems of all time. A Hit Parade. And we'll all—"

"How about a Shit Parade?" said Norval, adding a lunatic gunshot of a laugh. He then went entirely inert, regarding Samira with glazed immovable eyes, like the stuffed cat.

"We'll each use a pen with different coloured ink and then—"

JJ's sentence was never finished. First came the sound of a dog barking and then, from the back of the house, a crashing sound, the sound of splintering glass. Something metallic, with hissing smoke, came scuttling down the hall.

Samira let out a scream, a blood-red explosion in Noel's head. "Fire! Over there! Look!" She sprang from the couch and pointed towards the bathroom, towards black smoke shooting out from under the door.

"Jesus Chrysler!" His eyes abulge, JJ dashed into the kitchen, grabbed a fire extinguisher. Another canister came hurtling down the hall. But this time nothing happened—no explosion, no fire. Noel and Samira watched it to the count of five heartbeats, not knowing what to do. Another smashing sound, another window breaking ...

"Let's get outta here!" Noel shook Norval by the shoulders. "Nor!"

Samira and JJ were now scrambling for the front door. "Where's your phone?" Samira shouted.

JJ's face was contorted with fear. "It's ... dead. My battery—" He dropped the fire extinguisher with a loud clang.

"Do you have a hose?" Samira shouted. "A garden hose!"

Norval, finally roused from his delirium, exploded into laughter as he watched JJ scurry out the door. The smoke from the bathroom was now getting thicker. Samira was waving her hands about, fighting through it, towards the kitchen faucets. Noel grabbed Norval, who was cackling hysterically, and dragged him by the arm towards the door. He took three coats off the rack. "Put one on! Give one to JJ!" Noel pushed Norval out the door then raced back into the kitchen. "Sam! Get a hose through that window! Tell JJ! And don't come back in. Here, take this!"

Samira caught the coat in her arms. "You come too, Noel!" she cried, with fearfully roused eyes, before darting out the door.

Noel was trying to get the fire extinguisher to work when he heard JJ's voice through the bathroom window. "My letters! Noel! The box with the heart! And my scrapbook! Do you remem—" The wooden Indian toppled onto the floor, split in two, each half bursting into flames. It blocked the front exit. Was there another way out? The smoke was getting thicker.

Noel stumbled towards the sofa, coughing and rubbing his eyes. He reached down blindly until his hand felt the gas mask. He put it on and groped towards the bookcase. He grabbed two items, trusting his visual memory, before heading into a hallway, towards the back of the house. He opened the first door on the right. JJ's bedroom?

"Noel!" Samira screamed, a muffled sound in his ears. "Noel! Are you all right!" Water came bursting into the bathroom. Along with a hail of snowballs. "Noel!" she cried, her voice dripping with fear. She spun round to look for Norval. The last time she looked he'd been sitting in a snow bank, smiling stupidly, wearing two coats. "Norval!" she cried, hoping he would do something, go for help ... "Norval!"

But Norval was no longer sitting in snow. He was in the back yard, peering through JJ's bedroom window. A human form appeared in the semi-darkness, with a giant insect's head. Noel was struggling to open the window. But it wouldn't budge.

Norval looked left, right, behind him. He clawed the snow out of a wheel barrow with his bare hands, picked it up and heaved it at the window. It came bouncing back at him. He heaved it again. Same result, except this time the glass cracked, in a jagged slant across the bottom. "Noel!" he thundered. Long seconds passed before he saw a foot kicking at the cracked window pane, at the anti-theft window that JJ had nailed shut. Black smoke began to curl up from the crack. Norval pounded at the window until his fists were red with blood.

Samira arrived as Noel's head and shoulders were protruding from the shattered window. "They'll be cut to pieces!" she muttered, as Norval dislodged a jagged shard of glass with his bare hand, grabbed Noel by the underarms and pulled, and pulled again, until he lost his footing and tumbled backwards into a flowerbed of snow. Still wearing his gas mask, Noel squeezed out of the window, this time with Samira's help, and fell into Norval's outstretched arms.

Huffing and puffing, JJ came zig-zagging over with double handfuls of snow and ice-coated, frou-frouing fat-pants. But before he reached his friends the lights inside the house flickered and fizzed, then dipped and died. In the darkness he lost his footing, not far from where Norval had lost his. He went down hard, in a belly-landing on a frozen puddle. The first thing he saw when he lifted his chin, on moonlit snow splattered with blood, was a scrapbook and a box of love letters.

Chapter 11
Noel & JJ

imsky-Korsakov's *Scheherazade* was starting as Noel placed a fake log on the fire. Lounging in Mr. Burun's La-Z-Boy, wearing a burgundy bathrobe that was risibly undersized, JJ observed him while cracking nuts and sipping camomile tea.

"Hey Noel, why did Handel get rid of his chickens? Because they kept saying 'Bach, Bach, Bach'."

For the last hour JJ had been trying to laugh, to self-treat with joke-therapy, to counteract an urge to cry. He put his sock feet on the ottoman, pointed them towards the fire, wiggled his wet toes.

"I wish I could say, 'And then the alarm clock rang—it had all been a dream!' Oh well, that's the way the mop flops, I guess. No sense being a droopy drawers. Thanks for letting me stay here, Noel. But it'll just be for one night. Cross my heart. I'll go back home tomorrow—it's really not that bad. I'll have the place shipshape in no time."

By now JJ's voice was back to normal inside Noel's head; the boxy shapes and crayola colours were no longer a train wreck of collapsing rectangles but rather children's shiny stackable blocks. "JJ, you can stay here as long as you want. Your place is uninhabitable."

"Really just the one room. Or two."

Images of the bathroom paraded before Noel's eyes. All that was left were the exoskeletal remains of the bathtub, hand dryer and urinal. In an inch of water. "There's smoke and water damage everywhere. And your bedroom window's smashed, which means the place will be freezing." He pictured the orange garbage bag that Samira had stapled to the window frame.

JJ cracked another walnut. "I love your nuts, Noel."

Noel remained silent, wondering if this was more joke therapy.

"I've been racking my brains," JJ continued, scratching his copper hair with the nutcracker. "I still can't figure out who would've done it. Did you hear Nor's theory?"

"Yeah."

"He said it was the Head of Women's Studies, who was out to get him."

"I think that was a joke."

"Oh."

"You're sure you've got no enemies?"

JJ paused to reflect for three or four seconds, which for him was a lot. "Well, the cemetery's been trying to get rid of me for years. But they've got lawyers working on that. Arson's hardly their style."

"You don't think it was bikers?"

JJ slurped his camomile tea. "It's possible, I guess."

"Is that why you wouldn't let us call the police? Or fire department?"

"Well, I've got a few electrical ... illegalities, and some stuff the cops would hassle me about, even though it's legal. Which reminds me—I lost some of my best kits in the fire. And flood. Along with my journal for Dr. Vorta."

Noel's photographic memory conjured up scores of red magic-marker letters scrawled like hieroglyphs on the boxes. "So what else went up in smoke? What were those flashes and strange smells from the bathroom? What was that from?"

"Cheese."

"Cheese? You keep cheese in your bathroom?"

"Cheese powder, which explodes in those aluminum packets. I had a carton of Kraft Dinner. Six dozen boxes. E-bay auction. Got a wicked deal. Ten cents a box."

Noel was trying to hide a smile, but when JJ began to giggle, Noel exploded, laughing for longer than he had in months.

"They should put a flammable warning on that stuff," said JJ.

"You lose anything else? I mean, more valuable than macaroni and cheese?"

"My journal. Did I mention that? I used to keep it right beside the toilet, where I do my best thinking. Oh well. Thanks again, by the way, for rescuing my letters—and my scrapbook. You're a hero. I don't know how you remembered where they were. They would've gone up for sure."

"Could it have been a prank of some sort? I mean, kids are always hanging out there at night. Vandalising, desecrating tombs."

JJ pointed to an object on the floor. "I doubt it—that thing looks pretty serious. A customised device. What did you say it was?"

"Formulated mercury, at least in one of them." Noel picked up one of the two arson weapons, a 37 mm Ferret barricade-penetrating projectile. "It's a tear gas shell that was altered, filled with some flammable liquid, I'm not sure what. I'll find out tomorrow." With a kitchen knife he began prying open the other device, a film canister, which for some reason had not gone off. Inside was a half-sheet of paper smudged with black:

http://www.phylliskiller.ca

ok this is a cool little bomb that you can make in 5 minuts ok this is what you need 1.black "powder" 2. 1 film canister 3. firework fuse 3.gasoilne 4. a rubberband small one 5. a plastic sandwithch bag and now what to do take the film canister and the black powder fill the canister just a little you only need to melt the bag. Poke a hole in the side of the film canister make sure the fuse is in the black powder. Now take the bag and the fule and put the fule in it not to much just enough to fill the canister up so after you filled the bad a enough tie the corner off with the rubber band then cut the rest of the baggy off put the end witht the fule in the film canister and your done now go out some where that is wide open so you I get caute by the dam cops put the canister on the ground and light the fuse and run when the black powder lights and the bag melts a big fireball will go up

"Shall we analyse the powder in your lab?" said JJ.

"Tomorrow, first thing?"

"I've heard a lot about it."

"From ...?"

"Norval."

"He's never seen it."

"Can we take a gander?"

Noel tried to arrest a yawn. "I'm dead tired, JJ. And you must be too. After all we've been through. And it's late ... after two."

"It's early in China."

"I'll show you your room."

"You're the boss. You sure your mom won't mind me staying?"

Noel rose from his chair. "She'll be a bit confused at first. I should really wake her up and introduce you, so she doesn't think you're a burglar or rapist or something. But she hasn't been sleeping that well. Just keep your door locked. She ... well, she sometimes wanders a bit, goes from room to room, looking for things. With a ... lamp."

He nodded. "The lady with a lamp." Still lounging in his chair, he began looking around the room, at the digital locks, camouflaged door handles, large-print signs. At the cobwebs and clutter. "I noticed in the bathroom ... some signs and things. Your mom has ... fairly serious problems, right?"

"Well, I wouldn't say ... I mean, she has a few, you know, minor memory lapses." Noel sat back down. "To tell you the truth, JJ, they're major. But she's getting better all the time, she really is. I'm working on ... solutions."

"Good for you, Noel, don't give up. Because it's still there, eh? Like a computer, her memory's there somewhere—it never disappears, you just need a good technician to restore the data. Unerase, undelete."

Noel nodded bleakly. "I hope you're right."

"It might be too late for a whole new cerebral hard drive, but you're never too old for a simple upgrade." JJ took a Kleenex from his pocket, then a wad of gum from his mouth, put one inside the other. "So you two are quite a pair. How ironic, eh?"

"The irony, I assure you—"

"Your mom's overdrawn at the memory bank, while you're a millionaire."

Noel winced at the metaphor.

"So you've got to find a way," JJ extended, "of transferring some of your capital."

Noel sighed. "I had the same idea."

"I've got a terrible memory. A memory like a ... What's the expression again?"

"Like a sieve? Or goldfish?"

"Yeah, like a sieve."

Mine's like a hermetically sealed jar, thought Noel, a radioactive-waste container.

JJ slurped down the last of his tea. "A guy goes to a doctor. 'I think I'm losing my short-term memory,' he says. 'Really?' says the doctor. 'Just how long have you had this problem?' The guy looks at the doctor. 'What problem?'"

"Right, I've heard—"

"I've got a memory like a sieve, you've got a memory like an elephant."

"Well ... I think that's a myth. Elephants don't really have great memories."

"They don't? You sure? Which animal has the best memory?"

"The sea lion. It seems they never forget."[28]

JJ paused, recalling the time he went to MarineLand in Niagara Falls with his parents, when he burst into tears while watching a sea lion balance a ball on its nose. His mother thought he was frightened and tried to pull him away by the hand, which made him resist and wail even louder, hysterically. But it had nothing to do with fright; it was simply too much beauty to bear, too much joy, and something had to give. "It's not Alzheimer's, is it Noel? Please don't tell me your mother has Alzheimer's."

"I'm afraid she does."

"Oh my God. I'm so sorry, Noel, I ... That must be so hard—on both of you. To see your mom change before your eyes."

"Yeah, she ... she's not the same person."

JJ put his hand to his cheek, like a bad actor. "Like in *Total Recall*. You remember?"

Noel said that he did.

"The psychic mutant baby, covered with slimy mucus? Who asks Arnold Schwarzenegger what he wants? *The same thing everybody wants*, says Arnold. *To remember*."

"I recall the scene." And those aren't the right words.

"*Why?* says the mutant. *To return to who I was*, says Arnold."

"Right." JJ's German accent, thought Noel, sounded oddly Jamaican.

"So you said your mom's getting better, becoming more herself?"

"Well, she got a bit of lucidity last night. She remembered something important—and fairly complex. I'd given her something new in the morning."

"What'd you give her?"

"Oh, you know, the brain-booster-of-the-month. A real witch's brew."

"That you made yourself? Really? What'd you put in it?"

Noel shut his eyes. "Choline bitartrate, dimethylglycine, dimethylamino-ethanol, phosphatidyl choline, phosphatidyl serine, acetyl-L-carnitine, L-phenylalanine, alphalipoic acid, dehydroepiandrosterone, theobromine. Plus compounds of boron, manganese, zinc, copper, silicon—the standard brain-power elements."

"Hmm. No herbs?"

"A bit of black bryony, that's it."

JJ squinted, made a steeple with his fingers. "Black bryony. European yam, am I right? To improve blood circulation in the brain?"

"Right."

"So it worked?"

"Seemed to. I mean, to some extent. Except she's been peeing from morning to night."

"Right. Next batch, take out the bryony, replace it with a bit of brahmi and butcher's broom. They do the same thing. Increase blood flow in the brain. But no side-effects."

Noel nodded. "Brahmi, butcher's broom. OK."

"Even better is *qian ceng ta*, also known as Hyperzine A. It's a Chinese herbal extract that balances abnormal chemistry. And restores acetyl ... whatever."

"Acetylcholine."

"Right. I can get everything off the Net, cheap. Couriered the next day or it's free. And don't forget balm and sage, which are colisterine inhibitors."

"Cholinesterase."

"Right. And in your next brew, throw in some milk thistle extract. Very good for the old grey matter. Oh, and a pinch of yerba maté, which fights ageing and wakes up the mind. Round it all off with a bit of gingko biloba and you're sailing. Keep your mom in fine fettle."

Noel laughed. "OK."

"I mean, you've tried inorganics, right? They've not worked, so let's go natural."

"But some of them *have* worked. It's just that some of the compounds have killer side-effects ..."

"Like peeing."

"Worse than that."

"Anal leakage? Premature evacuation?"

"And nausea, cramps, vomiting. And the new ones I want aren't approved yet—like Memantine, which is only available in Europe—or else need special equipment to make, or the ingredients are ridiculously expensive—"

"I might be able to help you out there. Have you tried tincture of rosemary? I once tried rosemary, puffer powder and salmon oil before a memory test and got a perfect score. And once Dr. Vorta gave me some ..."[29]

But Noel was distracted. When he was tired his mind could wander badly; a single word could propel him into another time, into the back pages of his youth. With the word *rosemary*, Noel's cortex lit up like a Christmas tree. After mad Ophelia ("There's rosemary, that's for remembrance") came *The Three Musketeers*:

On the following morning, at five o'clock, d'Artagnan arose, and, descending to the kitchen without help, asked for some oil, wine and

rosemary, among other ingredients, the list of which has not come down to us. With his mother's recipe in his hand, he composed a balsam with which he anointed his numerous wounds ...

Then *Don Quixote*:

Sancho did as he bade him, but one of the goatherds, seeing the wound, told him not to be uneasy, as he would apply a remedy with which it would be soon healed; and gathering some leaves of **rosemary**, of which there was a great quantity there, he chewed them and mixed them with a little salt ...

And finally Jules Verne's *The Mysterious Island*:

Herbert gathered several shoots of the basil, balm, betony, and **rosemary**, which possess different medicinal properties, some pectoral, astringent, febrifuge, others anti-spasmodic, or anti-rheumatic ...

A muffled voice, as if heard through glass, penetrated Noel's dead zone: JJ's voice, his boxy wax-crayon colours.

"Earth to Noel, come in please. Earth to Noel ..."

Noel shook his head, as if surfacing from a dive. "Sorry, JJ, I was just ..." He had not lost sight of the topic, but could see it only dimly through the semi-transparent pages. "... thinking about rosemary."

"According to a study in England, it's supposed to increase alertness and long-term memory by fifteen per cent. Does she use lavender? In her hand soap or bath oil or anything else?"

With a few dry sprigs of rosemary and lavender stuck here and there between the leaves ... Noel was off again, this time with Charles Lamb, but the scrolling words were suddenly frozen by JJ, who pinched him on the side of the neck, hard. Noel, startled, rubbed his neck. What was going on? The pinch had a sobering, clarifying effect. "Yeah, I ... I'm with you. We were talking about ... lavender. It's one of my mom's favourite scents. In the summer the backyard's full of it."

"Get rid of it. Torch it. Lavender oil slows the brain and impairs memory. It's good for diaper rash, that's about it."

Where do you get all this information? Noel wondered, as he continued rubbing his neck. Is it reliable? And what the hell did you just do to me? "Where do you get all this information? And what was that ... pinch all about?"

"All my knowledge comes from the Web. I once surfed for seventy-two hours straight. Which I believe is a record. It's totally addictive, eh? It's like what Norval said about sex. 'It started off recreational, ended habitual.' I love that line. That guy's amazing, eh?"

"Yes, he is. But the neck pinch. What was that all about?"

"Upper thunder point."

"Acupuncture?"

JJ nodded. "*Shanshangdien*. It's used on stroke victims and people who drift in and out of consciousness. I learned about it from this Net sage from Shanghai. You know what we could also try? Some liquid Vitara. The 'Viagra for her.' I can get it in bulk, cheap, I'm talking drums of the stuff. It should give her a bit of clarity. A bit of friskiness too. Hey! You know what also might be worth a shot? Ricin. You know it?"

"Yes. It's a protein extracted from the castor bean."

"Shall we try it?"

"No. It's twice as deadly as cobra venom, with no known antidote."

"Exactly."

"So the idea is to get rid of my mom's Alzheimer's by killing her?"

"It *would* kill her—if she took enough of it. The trick is to give a minuscule amount, a microscopic amount. Just enough to shock her cerebellum, get her brain cells dancing again."

"I don't think so."

"We could try puffer fish."

"*Fugu?* That's one of Norval's favourites."

"Shall we get some?"

"No, it has the most lethal skin, intestines, liver and gonads in the world."

"The Japanese are nuts about it."

"It kills hundreds of them every year. Tetrodotoxin. It's what Haitian sorcerers use to zombify their victims."

"Here's the kicker. The right amount—a minuscule amount—can kick-start the whole nervous system. It's already being used to treat terminal cancer patients and heroin addicts! And it's being researched— right here in Montreal—for other diseases!"

"Like Alzheimer's?"

"Well, not that I know of. Shall I get some puffer guts at the sushi place on Saint Lawrence?"

Noel shook his head. "No."

"Good decision. Speaking of Saint Lawrence, there's a new oxygen bar—have you seen it? Beside the place that does microdermabrasion and laser hair removal? It's got three flavours of O_2. Passion fruit, grapefruit and ... I can't remember the third. Shall we take your mom there for a fill-up? Pump some good old O_2 into the upper storey?"

"No."

"I've got another idea. Distaval. They're coming up with radical new—"

"Distaval? You mean thalidomide? Are you out of your mind?"

"I know that's what Norval thinks."

"No, I'm sorry ... I didn't mean ... I meant it rhetorically. And Norval doesn't think that either."

"He said that I wasn't overfurnished in the brain department. That I'm as dumb as a box of rocks."

No, what he actually said, Noel recalled, was that you have moments of spasmodic illumination, like a bulb that's gone loose in its socket. And that I am to push him down a long flight of highly polished stairs if he ever becomes like you. "No, JJ, he doesn't ... think that, he just, you know, he's like that with everybody. Take everything he says with a grain of salt. A drum of salt."

"I overheard him at the party. While I was changing he asked if I was 'crazed'. But you know what? I don't give a beaver's dam."

"Well, first of all, he was quite drunk, and second—"

"It doesn't matter, I don't mind, it's the brain God gave me. I've never complained. But I'm not as dumb as he thinks, it's just that sometimes I get overexcited and my brain overheats and everything bundles together and sounds stupid."

"I know the feeling."

"You do?"

"Perfectly."

"I think that Norval judges people only by their brains, their intellectual powers. If there's no logic, no learning, he just ... ridicules. But there are two kinds of intelligence, my mom used to say—that of the brain, and that of the heart. And I think the second kind is the most important. Don't you?"

"Yes."

"The best people I've met have something Norval doesn't have: intelligence of the heart. Kindness, generosity, tolerance, acceptance of weakness. *L'intelligence du coeur*—that's what Mom called it. And that's what you have, Noel. You have both kinds, in fact."

"Well, thanks, but I'm not sure that—"

"You do, trust me."

Noel fidgeted, never good at fielding compliments; he hadn't had much practice. "You do too, JJ. In fact, I was wondering if ... well, if I could use your intelligence, if you'd like to help me out, go into a kind of partnership. I need someone like you—a Web magician, herbal alchemist, inventor."

JJ's face shone, taking on a shade of peach. "Really? Anytime, Noel. You can count on me, I'm your man."

"I'll pay you—"

"You can pay me never. You're my friend, like a blood brother. And you rescued my scrapbook and love letters. You're a hero in my book. You risked your life. I'll never forget that."

"Well, thanks, but I ... I hardly ..."

"You did. Now can we see your lab?"

Noel sighed. He was afraid they'd be up all night if he agreed. "Tomorrow? Aren't you ... exhausted after a day like this?"

"I only need four hours. I'm usually too excited to sleep. I need less sleep than Edison. Did you know that according to a recent study, those that sleep less than the sacred eight actually live longer?"

"I didn't know that. I guess I'm going to live a long time."

"Hey Noel, why did the man run around his bed?"

Noel paused. "Uh, let me see. Because he wanted to catch up on his sleep?"

"Yes! You heard that one? Shall we take a gander at the lab now?"

"Tomorrow?"

"Do you think we can make some stink bombs or laughing gas or cannon crackers?"

Noel laughed, remembering the days with his father when they made all three. "Why not?"

"You know, now that I think of it, we should ask Sam for her help too."

"Samira? She's an actress ... I mean she's an expert in literature, isn't she?"

"She's a woman. She'll know what to do. She'll know how to help your mom."

"Well, fine, I'm sure she ... could be very helpful. But I doubt if she'd—"

"Is Sam fly or what? Is she slammin'?"

Noel paused, wondering whether he'd misheard. What language was that? "I'm sorry?"

"Sam. Is she hot or what? Is she not swoonworthy?"

"Oh. Yes, I ... I suppose she is. Swoonworthy."

"Don't tell her I said this, Noel, but I think she's got a crush on you. Just a hunch I got ..."

To Noel the word "crush" was like a blast from a stun gun, or the tremor of an earthquake. He was stupended. Impossible, he thought, JJ's got things *totally* backwards. But what if. Yes, *what if* ...

"Can I ask you a question, Noel? Why does your mom have such a huge house?" JJ scrutinised his new best friend, his facial transformations. "Noel? You with me? Noel?" He was headed for another upper thunder point, but Noel saw it coming.

"Sorry, I ..." Noel struggled to tear his thoughts from Samira. "The house ... it's a long story." Impossible, I couldn't have heard him right ... "My dad ... he's the one who wanted it. He used to drive by it all the time. And then my mom inherited some money and they decided they wanted a big house. 'To fill it up with children,' Mom said. But it didn't work out that way. And then after my father died she wanted to 'fill it up with orphans.' But it was too late. The adoption agencies were looking for couples. Plus she was into her forties by then."

"That's very kind, very generous of her. She must be a sweetheart—like *my* mom. And like Samira—she told me she wants to adopt because she doesn't think she can have kids of her own."

"Really? She said that? When, tonight?"

JJ put his hand over his mouth. "I don't think I was supposed to tell anybody."

"Don't worry, I—"

"But didn't I see a 'For Sale' sign outside? You guys moving?"

"Yeah, we ... we can't make the payments, the remortgage payments."

"Oh bummage. But you guys must be rolling, you live in Outremont! These ceilings must be eighteen feet high!"

"Well, we *were* ... rolling, kind of, after my grandmother died. But the money's long gone. Med school was expensive and then ... renovations, and now the memory potions I'm making, and the new lab equipment. Plus my mom lost some of it on ... well, bad investments, shall we say, and we had lots of debts before that. Because of me. I've been a lifelong drain—"

"Take the sign down."

"I'm sorry?"

"You want to stay here?"

"Yes, but—"

"Take the sign down. We'll find a way. I'm great at finding money, plus I'll move in for a few days, if it's OK with you and your mom. And pay rent. And sell off some of my kits ..."

"No, really, JJ, that's *absolutely* not necessary ... I mean you can move in for a while, as long as you want, but I can't expect ... Where are you going?"

JJ was heading for the door. "How do you open this thing?"

"A then Z. Twice."

"Got it. First, the sign comes down. Then we go down and check out your lab."

JJ stayed the next fifty-two days. Gradually, Noel began to spend less and less time with his mother—only an hour or two a day for meals—and more and more time in the lab. He also saw less of Norval; they took turns cancelling their weekly matinée. As for Samira, he saw her once leaving the Psych building, but she barely acknowledged him. So much for the "crush," thought Noel.

Most days Noel would work from late morning to 4 a.m., which included trips to McGill's Health Sciences Library, memorising JJ's natural therapy books (the sections relating to the brain), and working and consulting with Dr. Vorta. At least four hours a day he would have company downstairs: labouring on a rickety bridge table with his recon-ditioned computers, JJ now shared Noel's equipment, patiently preparing his homeopathic elixirs and admixtures, grey-matter elevators and memory escalators.

Like his mother, JJ related things more than once, not out of forgetful-ness but out of a child's excitement at reliving, at sharing, cherished moments of the past. This never bothered Noel.

JJ also liked to whistle. At first Noel found his meandering strains—usually "Yellow Bird" or improvisational and keyless variations—distracting, but after a while he found it oddly comforting. He also got used to his habit of playing tunes on his teeth with a pencil, and of slurping *every* liquid, including herbal teas, through a straw. Nor did Noel mind when JJ urinated in the laundry-room sink, rising on his toes, glancing furtively this way and that. None of this bothered Noel because he was starting to make progress, real progress, and JJ seemed to be a part of that.

What he did mind was JJ's grunts as he listened, on his headphones, to his mother's *Hits from the Sixties* box set. Without Noel knowing it, JJ repeated three in particular, over and over, perhaps for luck: "Do You Believe in Magic?", "Love Potion #9" and "Magic Carpet Ride." Also for luck, with Noel *very* much knowing it, JJ wore his bubblegum-pink socks in the lab, day after day.

After four and a half weeks of toil and quest, on the first Sunday in March, Noel got a flash of inspiration, a glimmer of supranormal insight. He was at Mount Royal Cemetery, watching cloud-shadows sweep across the fields, when a rustling sound distracted him, a squirrel or bird perhaps, foraging in graveyard grass. He turned and saw a shaft of sunlight illuminating, ever so briefly, the chiselled letters of his father's headstone. Back home, he scrambled up to the attic for books from his childhood, then flew down the stairs like a five-year-old at Christmas. For the rest of the day he worked in the basement, alone.

Around nine, JJ came down with a tray of sandwiches. "Your mom made these for you. You must be famished."

With a magnifying glass Noel was examining prismatic beads and globules frothing inside an Erlenmeyer. He replied with a grunt.

"Hey Noel. Two travellers are crossing a desert. What would they live on if their food ran out?"

"Just a sec."

"They'd live on the sandwiches there."

Satisfied with the colour change in the emulsion, Noel lowered the flame beneath it with fingers blackened by chemicals. He replaced the magnifying glass in its sheath, copied some entries into a notebook.

"They'd live on the *sand which is there*," JJ repeated.

Noel looked up from his notebook. "Is that tuna? Good, I could use some brain food. I'm trying to make a leap here ..." Of imagination, he nearly added. He felt it as though it were a new sense, arriving late, like wisdom teeth.

"What are you up to?"

Noel nodded towards the flask. "Pyridoxal phosphate."

"Cool." JJ leaned over and examined the billowing liquid. "What's that?"

"It's ... well, involved in the synthesis of two neurotransmitters—serotonin and norepinephrine. There's something about it in my dad's notes."

"*Very* cool. Everything on track?"

"I think so. How about you, JJ? How are things going?"

"Rollin'. All four tyres pumped." He grinned, gleamed.

JJ was always gleaming—his very blood must be high-gloss, a special glaze or lacquer. Which protected him from things like loneliness or boredom or depression, which allowed him to go through life with a smile on his face, to see life as a treasure hunt and the world as Aladdin's cave. "Do things *ever* go badly for you, JJ?" said Noel, between mouthfuls of white tuna. "Are you *ever* unhappy?"

The question made JJ shrug. "I guess I'm hardwired for happiness. Every day there's something new and magical in life. Although I have to admit I'd go back to my childhood in a second. The past is safe ..." JJ let the sentence trail. "I remember one time after a baseball game—"

"You were carried on your teammates' shoulders, I know. But as an adult do you *never* get sad or depressed? What about ... I don't know, after losing family members or ... friends?"

"Well, I was sad when *papa* met his Maker in '97, and when Jesus welcomed *maman* to heaven in '91, and when my girlfriend dumped me in '86. Of course I miss them. But I'm grateful for the time I spent with them. You see, no one can take that happiness away from me. It's mine, for ever and ever. I still have that love, inside me. I carry it around wherever I go. It lives on in memory."

Noel nodded, swallowed. "And those three times are the *only* times you've been unhappy?"

"There's been other times. But heh! If you want the rainbow, you gotta put up with the rain. Under the snow lies summer, remember. If everything was perfect, we'd appreciate nothing." JJ poked one of his nostrils with his finger, causing Noel to look away. "When life zigs, zag!"

Noel smiled, his mind drifting to something Norval had said about JJ, about his "fatal penchant for potted wisdom." But this was not a bad quality, Noel decided, and certainly not fatal. JJ lived his life by adages such as these, and they were worth living by. In a state of abstraction Noel gazed at his guest's attire: a fire-engine-red bathrobe with a toothbrush sticking out of one pocket, a cell phone out of the other.

"Do I look fat in this?" said JJ.

"No ... not at all, I was just—"

"I know. I took one of your toothbrushes. Your new purple one, I hope you don't mind. But you've got so many ... I mean, it's none of my business, but why do you have so many? Do you sell them?"

Those with small heads are fourteen times more likely to develop AD, Noel recalled as he gazed at JJ's huge head ... He pushed pause, rewound an inner audio tape. Why so many toothbrushes? For Noel and synaesthetes like him, the answer was obvious. Because each day's a different colour. Monday, for example, is dirty yellow, like smoker's fingers; Tuesday a shade of orangey red, like paprika; Wednesday the rich blue of a Phillips' Milk of Magnesia bottle; Thursday ...

"Earth to Noel, come in please, Earth to Noel ..."

Noel watched his friend's lips move for two or three seconds. "Sorry, I ... I guess I just like variety—it's one of the things that stops me from going mad. Or madder."

"I hear you. Variety's the condiment of existence, eh?"

Noel eyed JJ's bathrobe again; the sash was slowly loosening its grip round his waist. "Listen, I should let you go ..."

"Yeah, I have to shake a tower."

"You have to ... take a shower."

"And then I have to fake a moan call."

"You have to ... make a phone call."

JJ exploded into laughter. "I've got tons of them. Do you want to hear more?"

"Another time?"

"Time? Time wounds all heels."

"Right."

"Your mom loves these. They slay her. Laughter's good therapy, eh? Especially in Montreal. It massages the vital organs, it's a form of internal jogging. Neurobics. He who laughs, lasts."

Noel's forehead puckered. "Especially in Montreal? Because of ... what? The Just For Laughs Festival?"

"No. What's the city's most famous street?"

"Saint Lawrence Boulevard?"

"What river's the city on?"

"The Saint Lawrence."

"And who was Saint Lawrence?"

"Uh ... a martyr of some sort?"

"The saint of laughter. He died laughing. In the third century. While he was being roasted to death on a gridiron, he asked to be turned over, saying that he was underdone on the other side. Now *that's* a sense of humour, that's laughter therapy at its finest."

Here JJ's cell went off. He paused to read a text message.

"Great. It's in. An extract from red-wine fermentation called ANOX. It's from Switzerland. It's for your mom. A source of red-wine polyphenols, which have a much bigger effect than either red wine or red wine powder on the inhibition of platelet aggregation *in vitro*."

Noel nodded as he rolled these words over in his head. "JJ, you're a quick learner. Very quick. Thanks. We'll certainly try it. How much do I owe you?"

"Nada. A guy owed me a favour. No hay problema."

"But I'll pay—"

"Oh, before I forget. I've been doing some experimenting—on myself. So far so good. You want a clear, razor-sharp brain for your research? Don't pleasure yourself in the morning or afternoon or evening. If you have to do it—and I'm not saying you do, I'm just advising you based on my research—do it only late at night, just before going to sleep. Otherwise, it saps your strength, fogs your brain. It's the curse of Onan."

"Good night, JJ."

Chapter 12
Noel & Samira (I)

When Noel checked on his mother that night he found her in her nightgown and tennis shoes, packing her bags. There were two grey Samsonite suitcases on the bed, and she was now sitting on a third, trying to get it to close. She turned to look at her son, her face scarlet from exertion. "I know money's tight," she said. "I know I'm a burden."

A red horeshoe began to pulsate inside Noel's brain: the PET scan image of his mother's shrinking hippocampus. "Let me help you with that bag. They can be a real bugger sometimes." One step forward, two steps back. Why is *nothing* bloody working?

"They don't work ... like they used to."

After removing a pair of winter boots and two umbrellas, he closed the case and snapped it shut. "Who said money was tight, Mom? That's the first I've heard of it."

"Him. That man."

"JJ?"

His mother shrugged.

"If he did, he's mistaken. We're rolling. Here, shall I put these ... in a better spot? Ready for the morning?"

His mother stared straight ahead, worry creasing her forehead, as Noel pulled each piece of luggage off the bed and placed them by the door. The sheets, he noticed, were coiled and mangled, as though she had been wrestling with some powerful force. Her husband? The feel of the empty half of the bed, he knew, still tortured her. Alzheimer's hadn't changed that.

"How about a bedtime story, Mom? Or a game of cards?"

His mother's expression softened. She raised the twisted sheets, slipped under them, tennis shoes and all. "A story."

144

Near the end of Wilde's "The Nightingale and the Rose" his mother's eyes began to flutter and close. She would always awaken if he paused at this critical point, so he carried on to the end. He then watched her slide deeper and deeper into sleep, that dry-run for death, feeling in turn worried, spent, scared.

Noel was asleep himself, slouched in his mother's armchair, when he thought he heard someone knocking—softly, unsurely—at the front door. JJ? No, JJ was asleep upstairs. He could hear his donkey-snore through the floor boards. What time is it? One thirty? In the mists of sleep he rose from the chair and crossed the room, to the dotted Swiss curtains of the front window. He drew them back and saw a night coloured yellow by street lamps and mounds of snow built by snow-ploughs. On the driveway, parked at an odd angle, was JJ's humpbacked car, which a midnight blizzard had painted white. At the end of the street he glimpsed the beacon of a taxi as it fishtailed around a corner. He craned his neck to see the caller at the door, but saw only a knapsack and the arm of a coat, a soldierly charcoal-and-black coat of the kind worn by ... Norval. He returned to his mother's side, pulled a woollen blanket up to her chin, glanced in her oval mirror. I look horrible, he thought, a geriatric version of myself. He edged towards the door, gently closed it behind him. He took off his shoes and began to creep down the stairs.

What in God's name is Norval doing here? At one-thirty in the morning. Should I let him in? Mom, JJ and Norval—*not* a good mix. Noel punched in letters, unbolted the front door, peered outside.

It was Norval's coat all right, but Norval wasn't inside it. It cloaked a smaller figure, a woman's figure. She was sitting on the front step, on a large courier bag, with a canvas knapsack beside her.

"*Salaam.*"

It was only one word but he recognised the colours immediately. He gave a gasp and his heart began to rev—at one hundred, one fifty ...

"Sorry, Noel. I know it's late. I was passing by, I saw a light ... JJ said you worked late ..."

... two hundred beats a minute.

"Can I come in?"

Noel nodded, mechanically, like a bobble-head doll.

145

"Sorry for the intrusion, Noel, it's not like me. I've got a few ... problems, temporary problems ..."

Noel inhaled deeply, willing himself to calm down. Had he learned nothing from Norval? He took in another lungful of frozen air before closing the door behind them. "Can I ... take your coat?"

Samira hesitated before slowly unbuttoning it. "JJ told me everything. About your mom, I mean. I'll help you guys out if you think I can. Sorry I took so long to tell you that, I've been ... busy."

In gentlemanly fashion, he helped her off with Norval's coat, while discreetly observing what this revealed: a cropped fawn-coloured jacket, short jean-skirt, dark brown tights. He opened the closet door, clanged around nervously for a hanger. "I ... I'm sure you can help, and I'll pay you of course. I mean if you have the time."

"I'll make the time. But that's not ... exactly why I'm here. Although I did want to tell you that—I *will* help out if I can, I swear." She looked directly into Noel's eyes after he had closed the closet door.

"I believe you," he said. The light in her eyes remained fine as pearl, but she was clearly distressed, underslept.

"Did I get you out of bed, Noel? I'm really sorry ..."

"I wasn't in bed."

"I feel *so* stupid, this is *so* embarrassing. The thing is, to make a long story short ... I've had a really heavy load of courses and lots of expenses and I ... well, couldn't pay my rent. So I was kicked out, evicted. So I went to stay with this guy, this friend, but then his girlfriend, well she sort of ... kicked me out. Tonight. In a jealous fit. At like, midnight. But I've got money coming in, a student loan, and Vorta owes me a bit and ... JJ said you had a big house and ... I mean, I could go to my mom's now but ... well, I was wondering if, just temporarily ..."

"I'll show you your room."

In a room down the hall from his mother's, Noel was carrying in fresh bedsheets when Samira emerged from the bathroom, an Arctic white towel wrapped around her, as in a Doris Day movie. "I took a whore's bath, hope you don't mind. I'll go back tomorrow for the rest of my stuff. Like all my clothes. Do you have something I could wear to bed? It's silly, I know, but I don't feel comfortable ... sleeping naked."

Noel glanced at Samira's square neckline for a discreet microsecond, then at the skirt and tights she clutched in her hand. "Yes ... of course, I don't sleep naked either. Though I probably should, I'm so incredibly hot. I mean the house is ... incredibly. The temperature ... I'll get you something." He remained rooted to the spot, staring at the floor, visualising the patterns—plaid, pinstripes, fleur-de-lis—on his three pairs of pyjamas. Which ones would be most suitable? He darted out of the room as fast as Mercury, as if delay could be fatal.

Samira, when he returned, was stroking away creases from the bottom sheet, leaning over the bed, still covered by the towel but only just. Noel looked at the ground and other unresponsive objects. Samira hadn't heard him enter. When she saw him she straightened her torso and towel, eyed the tartan pyjamas. No, I meant a T-shirt, she was about to say. "Thanks, Noel. That's perfect. Listen, this is just for one night, OK? I really don't want to cause any problems for you ... and your mom." She took the pyjamas, opened Noel's closet door and stepped behind it. As she was putting on Noel's top she began to think about what she had seen in the bathroom. Not only the signs on the wall, but its general condition. It was a shambles, it hadn't been cleaned in weeks. Like the rest of the house.

Noel stood awkwardly by the door, wondering whether he should still be there.

"Is your mother ... here?" Samira asked, peering round the closet door.

Noel nodded. "She's sleeping down the hall."

"She won't mind if I stay? Just until I find a place ..." Samira stepped out from behind the closet door, holding the towel and pyjama bottoms. "Your mom's getting worse, isn't she. In the bathroom I noticed ..."

Noel could not believe what was happening, that Heliodora Locke was standing before him, dressed only in his pyjama top. Was it a mirage, a product of stress or sleep deprivation? A creation of some *jinnī*, formed in an instant and destined as quickly to dissolve?[30] Had he been slipped one of his mother's neuro-drugs or Norval's hallucinogens? He closed his eyes and saw the opening scene from Zappavigna's *The Bride and Three Bridegrooms*. A cor anglais playing merrily in the background ...

"Noel?"

Water racing up sand, her beautiful voice, an orchestra of hues ...

"Noel, are you all right? Noel?"

He opened his eyes, one at a time, and seemed startled by what he saw. "Sorry, I was just ... spacewalking, a bad habit of mine, I really have to cut down. We were talking about ..."

"I asked if your mother was getting worse. The bathroom ..."

"Right." He shook the film footage out of his head, replaced it with the signs in the bathroom, the handiwork of the Bath Lady. "I'm not the one who put those signs up. They're really not needed. Or all the other crap either. My mom's getting better all the time, she really is. JJ and I are ... working on things."

"I'm just going to get under the covers. Why don't you sit down?"

Noel looked around for a chair. When he realised there wasn't one, he sat down at the foot of the bed, tentatively, placing a very tiny portion of his rear end on the edge of the frame.

Samira smiled, then looked deep into his eyes, a habit of hers. "You've been looking after her all by yourself, haven't you. For how long? Months, years? Which explains why ... which explains why you look so terrible."

"Thanks."

"No, I meant why you look so ... tired. It must be incredibly hard on you. Are you getting enough sleep?"

"Of course I am. Well, maybe not always ... sometimes it's hard to get my eight hours."

"Eight? You look like you've been getting two."

"No no, I'm fine, really, sleep like a top. It's just that JJ and I have been really busy the last few days. And when you get close to something, you get excited, and sometimes adrenalin keeps you up all night. I'm fine, really. I don't need much sleep." I'll sleep when I'm dead.

"You should take care of yourself too, you know. Not just your mother. Give yourself a break."

Noel nodded. "You sound like the Bath Lady."

"The who?"

"The ... the day nurse who comes in. Sancha."

"Well, you should listen to her. You have to take time out for yourself, you know."

There's no time out, Noel thought, even when I'm in bed. Either my brain is still in the lab or my mother is burning a light into my eyes. "I try."

A lowboy beside the bed caught Samira's attention, a fine piece but spotted and scarred. She reached over and traced a line in the dust on its walnut surface. "Don't you have any relatives who can help out?"

"Not in Montreal. But my uncle in New York has promised to help."

"How exactly?"

"Well, he ... he didn't really say."

"Can't you hire somebody?"

"We have the Bath Lady, who comes in twice a week. We can't afford anyone else."

"But ... Norval said you were rich. And this house, it's a palace. Or was."

"We used to be ... comfortable."

"What happened?"

Noel heaved a long sigh. He had never been able to tell anyone—including his relatives and best friend—what had really happened, the gory details. It would've been a filial betrayal.

"You don't have to answer that. It's none of my business."

He looked deep into her eyes, boldly, for the first time ever. She stared right back. He barely knew her, but it didn't matter. "What happened? Everything just seemed to ... unravel, fall to pieces, when Mom took early retirement. Not right away. But after a few weeks of idleness—recuperating, I should say—she started acting a bit ... strange. Out of character."

"What do you mean? Like forgetting things?"

Noel paused. "She began giving all her money away. Or most of it. Writing out cheques to childhood friends, distant acquaintances, dubious charities ... even beggars on the street. Not to mention every canvasser that phoned or knocked on the door. She fell for the usual tele-marketing scams, about winning a Tahitian holiday or helping to free some political prisoner in Chad ... It was very uncharacteristic of her. She used to have a radar for that kind of thing."

"And that was when she began to have her ... memory problems?"

"Right."

"Couldn't you have tried to get her into a part-time ... help centre or whatever they're called? Something subsidised?"

Noel nodded, relieved to be able to skip some of the details. "Adult day-care. I did. A place called Sun Valley Assisted Living. I planned to drive her there and back every day. The first time she was waiting for me on the porch with all her luggage. Like she was going to stay there for the rest of her life. What she couldn't fit into her suitcases, she'd stuffed into plastic bags and pillowcases. 'Please don't make me go there,' she said to me, so softly I could barely hear her. 'Couldn't I stay here with you, dear? Just a bit longer? I'll try to be better.'"

"Oh my God. So what'd you do?"

"I grabbed her bags, took them back upstairs, told her she could stay with me forever."

Except for JJ's snoring, the house was still until dawn. In her troubled state, Samira decided to take the sleeping pills that Noel offered, two crude blue pills that looked home-made. She slept blissfully. Noel had taken the same pills, but tossed and turned until someone with a light entered his room.

"There's a man downstairs," his mother said in his ear, her voice and hunter's lamp quivering. "A big man with red hair. I caught him red-handed, making bacon and ... those round things. Shall we call the police?"

Noel squinted at her shaking hands, one almost entirely covered with blue-ink reminders, like tattoos. "No, Mom. He's a friend of mine, you've already met him, he's staying here."

"He's got a knife."

"I'm sure he's just—"

Here a head poked through the door, a head with orange stick-up hair. "Morning, people. I thought I heard some voices. Morning, Mrs. B."

"You put quite a scare into my mother, JJ. She thought you were coming after us with the carving knife."

"Now Noel, I did not say that. I only said—"

"That's all right, Mrs. B. Entirely my fault. I'm the intruder. Takes some getting used to. Are you hungry? Feel like a good old-fashioned *petit déjeuner québécois?*"

Mrs. Burun shook her head. Who *is* this man? "No, I ... I'm not really hungry."

"I found another album of photographs, in with the recipe books. I was wondering if you'd take me through it. If you have time, that is."

Mrs. Burun's aspect changed, as if she'd just recognised a childhood friend who had come over to play. "The album ... in the kitchen? With the recipe books?"

"That's the one."

"Some of those pictures are quite dear to me. They were taken by my mother, you see."

"Were they, now? I noticed a picture on the cover. A beautiful girl with curly blonde hair. By the seaside."

"Why, that's ... me."

"No!"

"Let's go down, shall we?" said Mrs. Burun excitedly. "Take a look? Did you manage to find everything in the kitchen ..." Here she paused, trying

150

to remember the gentleman's name. She *should* know it, he's been around here long enough ... How many days, now?

"Not everything," said JJ. "I've been looking high and low for the tea strainer. I said to myself, JJ, you must be blind!"

"I can't find it either! I think somebody must have stolen it!" She turned to look at her son.

Noel was now sitting up in bed, bleary-eyed. "I know where it is, I'll just get dressed and—"

"You stay in bed," said JJ. "We'll manage. I'll bring your breakfast up later. In the meantime, get some sleep. Your mother and I have some things to do, don't we, Mrs. B?"

"Why, yes, I suppose we do ... JJ."

After a long shoving-match with insomnia, his regular nocturnal visitor, Noel found himself onstage, a snow-blindingly white spotlight boring into his eyes. He put his hand up as a shield and squinted out at the audience. On one side he could make out, just barely, his mother's face, and on the other, Norval's. The spotlight shifted to something approaching from offstage: a chryselephantine horse-drawn carriage, spattered with mud. Inside was a bare-shouldered woman wearing a jewelled crown that sparkled with colours he had never seen before, colours not derived from the primaries. With great fanfare, a tuxedoed man with a microphone asked Noel to name the person inside the carriage. As it rattled closer, dark shadows fell across the woman's face, but he recognised her anyway, because she was speaking. The meaning of her words did not register. "Time's almost up," said the quiz-master, who began to look like Dr. Vorta. Even though a correct response was worth thousands of dollars, Noel decided not to answer the question. "I don't know who it is. I've never seen her before." It was Heliodora Locke, the actress. He gazed at her as she passed, but she did not return his gaze. Her lustrous eyes were directed elsewhere, toward ... Norval? As the carriage disappeared from view he could hear the rhythmic sound of a drumbeat—or was it horse's hooves? Rat-a-tat-tat rat-a-tat-tat ...

"Noel?"

He unglued his eyelids, listened. It was the sound of someone rapping on his door. "Mom, is that you?"

"Can I come in?" The door slowly opened. "Sorry, Noel, but I thought it was time to wake you. And there's a call for you."

Noel squinted into the semi-darkness. The jigsaw pieces of his dream lay scattered on the floor, which a beam of light from the hallway vaporized. "Is that ...? What are you ... right." His heart began to churn. "Come in. Are you OK? Is my mother OK?"

"Everyone's fine."

"I've just been ... what time is it?"

On Noel's writing desk Samira set down a covered stainless-steel platter, on top of which a portable phone was balanced. "Eight, eight-thirty."

"In the morning?"

"No, at night."

He sat up. "You're not serious. That's impossible ... My God, twelve hours? Why didn't someone wake me?"

"Because you needed the sleep."

"I haven't slept that long since ... age two." He stroked his cheek: stubble, almost a beard. He felt like Rip Van Winkle. "Is my mother all right?"

"She's fine, Noel, we spent the day together. But there's a call for you." She handed Noel the receiver, whose red battery light was flashing. "It's Norval."

Noel rubbed his eyes, shook out cobwebs. "Can you ... tell him I'll call him back?"

"Can he call you back, Nor? No? Tell him what? OK, fine. Ciao."

"What did he say?"

"He said fuck you very much, and that he can't make tomorrow's 'classic mat'? Does that make any sense?"

"Yes. Is my mom OK?"

"Noel, your mother's fine, relax. You've got other people—employees—working for you now."

"I do? Oh, right. And how about you? Everything OK? Accommodations satisfactory?"

"Couldn't be better. Can I turn this on?" She nodded towards his bed lamp.

Noel yawned widely, like a lion. "Yes, go ahead. I can't believe I—"

"Are you hungry? No, don't get up." She watched Noel out of the corner of her eye, amused. "Do you always sleep with your clothes on?"

"No, I ... I must've been really tired." He leaned back against the head-board and stretched his arms, while surreptitiously smelling his armpits.

"Move over." Samira set the platter on the side of the bed then dramatically opened the lid: poached eggs, home fries, sausages, grilled tomatoes, two crumpets, orange juice and a Dresden blue pot of tea, its spout chipped in a way that had been familiar to him for years. "Your mom said you like breakfast at night sometimes. I wish I could say I made it for you."

"JJ?"

"Your mom."

"Really? Fantastic. She hasn't done that in ... a while." He examined the items on the platter. Everything was done the way he liked—the finest of membranes on the yolk, a well-done crispness to the potatoes ... His mother used to remember things like that. She remembered everything about him, it seemed. Even as a child, it touched him that she bothered. "Where is she now?"

"Playing Crazy Eights with JJ. While playing songs from the sixties— and singing all the words."

Noel smiled, then began a sentence he couldn't finish. He started another. "I ... really ... you know, appreciate—"

"Eat."

As Noel salted and peppered, Samira pulled the stringed tea bags from the pot and poured out two cups. Noel paused, his eyes at a level coinciding with her centre of gravity. He speared a cherry tomato and popped it into his mouth. A morsel of potato followed, then another, then half a glass of orange juice, then another tomato. With his mouth full he said, "Want some?"

"Don't talk with your mouth full."

"Right."

"Have you always been so close to your mom?"

Noel swallowed, then emptied his glass of orange juice. He was feeling good. Like a castaway he felt exhilarated talking to someone. "No, I was an idiot in my teens. Like most adolescents I 'rebelled'—except how can you rebel against someone who devoted her life to you? In my twenties I wasn't much better. Selfish and stupid. But I woke up. Just like that, mysteriously, like a voice telling me to return. The prodigal son. She never once reproached me either."

"'How like a serpent's tooth to have a thankless child.' *King Lear*?"

How *sharper than* a serpent's tooth ... "Right. Act one, scene four."

"No line number?"

"Around nine hundred, I think."

Samira laughed. "That's ... phenomenal. I've heard a lot about you, Noel. All good. So tell me what you do for Dr. Vorta. Do you use your memory in ... whatever you do?"

Noel took two quick gulps of tea. "I just help him out with his research. And certain memory experiments. Part time. Whenever I can. He's very understanding, very flexible."

"That's good, since you already have a full-time job. Your mom. So is that what you took ... I mean, what did you study at school?"

"Chemistry, biology, poetry, art history, music. A hodgepodge that led nowhere. I worked as assistant editor of a poetry magazine that couldn't pay me. Then, out of the blue, Dr. Vorta got me a summer job with Pfizer—as a lab technician. He personally recommended me, even though I had no qualifications. Then he helped me get into McGill, and eventually hired me as a research assistant."

"You studied medicine?"

Noel nodded before swallowing. "For two years. Then I got interested in experimental chemistry, pharmacokinetics, pharmacodynamics, that kind of thing. I guess because of my dad."

"Did you graduate?" She watched Noel shake his head, his mouth full again. Has he eaten in the last week? "It wasn't up your alley?"

Noel swallowed, broke the yolk on his second egg with his fork. "No, I liked it, I found it quite easy. It's just memorisation, really. And as for lectures and interacting with my fellow students and stuff, I'd learn to control my ... You see, I didn't start university until I was in my late twenties, and by that time I'd learned to control, more or less, my problems. Inside my head. But I ... you know, had other problems."

"Such as?"

"Well ... Mom started having *her* problems, the ones inside *her* head, and I couldn't really do both, deal with both. So I quit school and moved in with her. I have no regrets, mind you—none whatsoever. It was no great sacrifice. I wouldn't have made much of a doctor anyway. Or pharmacologist or neuropathologist or whatever."

"I think you would have. It's never too late."

Noel took a sip of his Scottish Breakfast Tea. He was feeling better than he had in months. And the words, uncharacteristically, flowed. "My father always wanted me to be one. A writer or doctor or preferably both. He liked to remind me how many great writers were also doctors, or were first drawn to medicine. He had great respect for people like that, and for the Renaissance ideal of excelling at both science and art."

"Which authors were drawn to medicine?"

"Maugham, Chekhov, Joyce, Keats, Smollett, Goldsmith, Céline, Hoffmann, Duhamel, Campion ... I could go on and on."

Samira laughed. "Do. I'm curious."

"Oliver Wendell Holmes, A.J. Cronin, Arthur Schnitzler, Aldous Huxley, Ethan Canin, Walter Percy, Robert Bridges, Leonid Tsypkin, Sihan Seyhi, Nérée Beauchemin, Moacyr Scliar, John McCrae, Josephine Bell, James Bridie, Fernando Namora, Alfred Döblin, Georg Büchner, C. Louis Leipoldt, Heinrich Stilling, Lenrie Peters, Guimarães Rosa, Yusuf Idris, Dannie Abse, Hans Carossa, Francesco Redi, F.R. Kreutzwald, Jacques Grevin, Enrique Gonzalez Martinez, Saul Tchernichowsky, Justinus Kerner, Gottfried Benn, T'ao Hung-ching, Firishtah, Nahmanides, Nicander, Empedocles and scores of other Greeks and Romans ... The list goes on and on."

Samira burst out laughing. "You forgot an Iraqi."

"Mazloom?"

"Very good."

"My father always regretted not being among them, so I suppose that's why he encouraged me to try."

"Norval mentioned that your father ... died when you were young?"

"Yeah, he drowned himself when I was nine." When I was 3,639 days old, Noel nearly specified. "I've often thought of doing the same."

Just like Norval! "You're not serious, are you?"

"Yes."

"So what's stopped you?"

"My mother."

"Thank God for mothers. So do you know what your father ... what prompted him or ..."

Noel's features, until now stoical, revealed pain. "It's a mystery. A dark curtain that falls from nowhere. I sometimes get it myself. I don't think I'll ever understand it, not entirely. All I know is that he used to have these heavy, oppressive dark periods. 'The black dragon paying me a visit,' he once said. Sometimes for days on end he'd hole up in his office in the basement. But the curtain would always lift, the dragon would move on ...[31] Sometimes I think that being a gifted scientist wasn't enough for him, that he wanted other things, more spiritual things. He wanted to be a gifted artist as much as a gifted scientist. A Leonardo or Raleigh or Primo Levi. He wanted so badly—and failed so badly in his view—to be a Renaissance man."

"Didn't Levi commit suicide too?"

"Yes."

Noel became conscious that Samira was staring at him. She was sitting at the foot of the bed, her tilted head against the wall, watching him through half-closed eyes, like a painter looking at a canvas. He wanted to reach out and touch her black hair, blacker than the raven wings of midnight, as Poe would say.

There's a suggestion of Norval in his face, Samira thought, but it's like a bronze sculpture copied in wood, or a melody sung slightly out of key ... How cruel, she thought, to think like that. It would be so much better, in fact, to be in love with him, not Norval. So much easier. "Does it bother you when people say you look like Norval?"

Noel sighed. "I used to be sensitive about it. It was always that I looked like him, of course, that I was a pale imitation of him—which is only natural, I suppose, since he was the famous one, the more attractive one ..."

"What does your mother say about the resemblance? Doesn't she think he could almost be her son?"

Noel slowly emptied his cup of tea. "She's never met him."

"No? Why not?"

Noel paused, examining the faint rings inside his tea-stained mug. "Sometimes I wonder if, subconsciously, I didn't want her to see a better-looking version of me. Or if I didn't want to share her with him. But I don't think that's it entirely. I suppose I didn't want him to make fun of the way my mother and I got along, our intimacy, the fact that we're each other's best friend."

"Why would he make fun of that?"

"Because he despises his mother. Unnaturally, psychotically. He'd never understand our closeness, and besides, I just didn't want to explain ... you know, everything, her illness. I kept putting it off, in any case."

"Putting off introducing them?"

"Yeah. For some reason I didn't want him to see all that. He's come over a few times—but I just couldn't open the door."

Samira remained silent as Noel finished his last crumpet, her gaze resting on various objects in the room.

As in Norval's loft, the walls were covered with peculiar images. There was Kandinsky's *Blauer Ritter*, Hockney's illustrations for *Six Fairy Tales of the Brothers Grimm*, a sepia image of Solomon Shereshevski,[32] a multi-coloured drawing of Iris, the rainbow goddess, and a large poster of the Nine Muses, with their names and domains written beneath them: CALLIOPE, Muse of Epic Poetry (holding a writing tablet); CLIO, Muse of History (holding a water clock); ERATO, Muse of Lyric and Love Poetry (playing a lyre); EUTERPE, Muse of Music (playing a flute); MELPOMENE, Muse of Tragedy (wearing a tragic mask); POLYMNIA, Muse of Sacred Poetry (a pensive look on her face); TERPSICHORE, Muse of Dancing and Choral Song (dancing and holding a lyre); THALIA, Muse of Comedy (wearing a comic mask); URANIA, Muse of Astronomy (holding a globe).

Samira sat with her legs ajar, her black skirt draped between them as she examined each figure in wordless absorption. In the frame of an oval mirror, she then spotted a wedding picture, presumably of Noel's parents, as well as a Polaroid of Norval, with longer hair, standing regally before the red curtain of a theatre. Her heart trampolined. "Norval looks like a decadent prince in that photo," she said trying to hide a tremor in her voice. "He's not an aristocrat or something, is he? He certainly acts the part."

"Yes, a certain majesty is assumed." Noel set the silver platter on the floor. "But in fact he does have some blue blood in him. The de Blaquières were minor and poverty-stricken Norman nobility who arrived in Quebec in the eighteenth century. A violent, dissolute and pathologically irascible bunch—at least, so he tells me."

"But he was born in France."

"His father studied in France in the sixties, where he met his wife, returned to Quebec, then eventually became head of an engineering firm in Paris."

"And his mother? What's she like? Have you met her?"

"No. In Norval's words, she's a vulgar, nether-class *banlieusarde*, given to hysteria and lovers. Which he's never forgiven her for—that and the fact that she spends most of her time at a nudist resort and votes for Le Pen."

"But that's not enough to *hate* her, surely?"

"She cheated on his father when Norval was a little boy. So he feels betrayed, neglected—especially when a parade of men, one after the other, began to fill up the house."

Samira nodded, bit her lip, began to think of something else. *Dissolute, pathologically violent?* Is that what he said? Which may explain ... She watched the beside clock blink greenly from 8:59 to 9:00. "Do you know what 'K' is?"

"K?"

"I found a vial of it ... somewhere, and I want to know what it is. Could it be potassium? It's a white powder."

"Well, potassium is silver-white. But it's explosively reactive—it oxidises when exposed to air and reacts violently with water, so it's always stored under a liquid that it doesn't ... you know, react with. What kind of vial was it in?"

"Is there anything else it could be?"

"Well ... lots of things. I don't know. Where'd you find it?"

"Uh, well ... in an alleyway."

"In an alleyway? In that case, it could be ketamine, which is quite popular these days. It's also known as Special K, Kit Kat ..."

"Which is ...?"

"An anaesthetic. Veterinary and medical."

Samira looked puzzled. "Oh, maybe that's what it is."

"At lower doses it has dissociative and psychedelic effects—it's used to produce the 'near-death experience.'"

"Really?" Oh, I get it now. It's one of Norval's hallucinogens.

"It's usually combined with rohypnol. It's a date-rape drug."

Samira's jaw sagged. So I was right about that man. He's worse than the populations of Sodom and Gomorrah combined. "Oh shit. You're not serious. So Norval's a date rapist."

"Norval? What's Norval got to do with—"

"And maybe I was next."

"*Next*? Oh no, I think you've got the wrong—"

"I found it in a drawer beside his bed! Maybe that's how he gets through his freaking alphabet! Hold on, I'll be right back."

"Look at this," said Samira, minutes later. She set down the vial on Noel's bed table, hard.

"Really, Sam, I don't think—"

"I knew there was something ... satanic about him. The party I went to a few weeks ago ... somehow Norval is behind all that. It wasn't just a coincidence he stepped into that elevator."

"But ... that doesn't make any sense. It's not his style. He doesn't need drugs to seduce women."

"And at JJ's party, that line about 'excess and the palace of wisdom'— I think I heard it as I was being drugged. Or when I came to. Maybe it was Norval who said it—it's something he would say, isn't it?"

"Well ... possibly." He has said it before, Norval recalled. More than once. He picked up the vial, which he recognised as one of Dr. Vorta's, and held it up to the light. "And that's all you remember? Was it Norval's voice?"

"I ... I'm not sure."

Noel unscrewed the vial, inserted his baby finger. He looked closely at the colourless crystals before putting them lightly against his tongue.

"Special K?" Samira asked.

Coloured *C*'s and *H*'s and the numbers two and three began to bounce inside Noel's head like lottery balls. "Chloral hydrate."

"What does it do? Make women unconscious, comatose?"

"It's a sedative. And hypnotic."

"I *knew* it!"

"It's being used in one of Dr. Vorta's studies. He thinks that it may be the future for treating certain types of brain cancer."

"Brain cancer? I don't get it. Why would Norval keep a bottle of ... He doesn't have cancer, surely to God?"

"Not that I know of."

Oh hell. She remembered his words about ending his days in water. *After Z, I'm dead* ... She looked again at the Polaroid of him in the frame of the oval mirror. "But why was it ... next to his bed? And why does it say 'K' on the label?"

"*Klor ortanca*. It comes from a lab in Istanbul. I'm pretty sure he just uses it for insomnia."

Samira nodded slowly, her face strained.

"I wouldn't worry about him. It's also sold on the street as an aphrodisiac. It's big in France." Maybe his mother told him about it, Noel silently conjectured.

"Oh. Maybe that's it. It's none of my business anyway. Sorry, I ... I shouldn't have jumped to conclusions. And, well, mistrusted a friend of yours."

"I've made worse mistakes."[33]

In the silence that gathered Noel could hear his own heart beating. Chloral hydrate was a nightmare. In severe overdose, death occurs within five to ten hours. He'd have to tell Dr. Vorta about this ... theft. He looked at Samira's face. It's obvious she's in love with him. Or is she? Why don't I simply ask? He cleared his throat and cursed his own cowardice. It was a perfectly easy thing to say. It would be over quickly, like a dentist's hypodermic. "Are you in love with him, Sam?" he finally asked, in a near-whisper. "With Nor?"

"No!" she replied, with a quickness and force that surprised them both. "Not at all, I mean I'm ... I don't know, physically attracted and ... intrigued or something, like being on the edge of the cliff and this voice is telling me to jump off ... I've done that kind of thing before in my life, but it's something I'm trying to ... put behind me."

"It's really none of my business ..."

"But it is. I mean, I want it to be. I'm pretty mixed up about him, I can't figure him out at all, and thought maybe you could help ... clarify things."

"I wish I could, believe me. But he's a mystery to me too. He just won't talk about himself, about personal things. His past is full of blanks and gaps. 'Don't expect me to tickle your idle curiosity,' he once told me."

"Do you think he was ever in love? With someone who dumped him, or died? Do you think he's capable of love?"

"I don't know, I really don't."

Samira thought of the ring she had discovered. "Does he ... could he, well, prefer men? Sexually, I mean?"

"That would surprise me. But you never know. Byron had male lovers—which for Norval may be a seal of approval."

"Every heard of Terry?"

"No, who's Terry?"

"He's just ... a name I saw somewhere."

"Where?"

This was not something Samira wished to divulge. "I'd be surprised if Norval was ever in love, with anyone—male or female. It seems no one's good enough for him, everyone's inferior—intellectually, socially. And he's a misogynist par excellence."

"He dislikes both sexes."

"He's the most prejudiced person I've ever met. Like some old fogey."

Noel paused to think. "Yeah, in some ways Norval *is* fogeyish—old at heart, prematurely conservative. He can't stand the new generation— their consumer products and diction and garish clothes and brand names. But he hates the older generations too, the Establishment, especially law firms and drug companies."

"He's your best friend, right?" said Samira.

Noel opened the door of his bed table, a converted apothecary chest with Hermes' staff carved in high relief on the sliding door. He pulled out a bottle and stoneware goblet. "He's my only friend."

"Why is he such a ... sack-artist, a midnight plowboy? You don't believe that Baudelaire crap, do you?"

"No, that's all a snow-job, government-grantism. He's got this theory ..." Noel paused, as if confused by the objects in his hands. "Would you like some port? It's my mom's, it helps me sleep—or used to."

"Thanks."

Noel poured. "Hope you don't mind, this isn't the right glass and I only have one. I'll get another—"

"Don't bother. We'll share it." She took a sip and handed back the cup. "You were saying ...?"

Noel hesitated before turning the goblet to where Samira's lips had touched it. He closed his eyes and drank. Footage of Heliodora Locke began to appear ...

"... about Norval's theory?"

Noel shook his head and his neck crackled. "Right, he ..." He felt his face reddening as he groped for the thread. "... he thinks that sensation ... that the great object of life, or sole object of life, is sensation, what Byron calls the 'craving void,' which drives us to things like gambling and war and travel and sex. Especially sex. That the sex instinct dominates all human thought and activity, that it's the chief source of energy. Or only source."

"A sexistentialist."

Noel smiled. "Exactly. Sometimes I think he's turned into one of the writers on his syllabus—some Decadent from the 1890s.[34] He's convinced that civilisation is in a state of terminal decline ..."

"Hard to disagree ..."

"... and that faith in any kind of progress is futile—there is simply no better world to come. So he's decided that life itself must become a kind of artwork—an exercise in style—because there is nothing else it can be."

"So instead of rebelling, like the Romantics did, he's chosen apathy and cynicism."

"And hedonism. The only way he can re-fire his spirit, or so he says, is through new sensations—more and more dangerous sensations. What Baudelaire calls the artificial paradises of the imagination. Drug-induced hallucination, calculated perversity ..."

"Alphabetical perversity?"

Noel's smile shaded into a grimace as he wondered what letter Norval was on. "'Harmless perversity,' he calls it."

Samira was turning the bottle to read its label: Quinta do Noval 1994. "*Harmless?* Come on, *The Alpha Bet* does damage. It's manipulative, exploitive, deceitful ..."

Then why are you in love with him? Noel wondered as the list of adjectives grew.

"... callous, mercenary, chauvinist ... So why does he do it? Why does he *treat* women this way? And why *so many*? Revenge? Because his mother betrayed his father he's decided to fuck over as many women as possible? Or because he was so shattered by that betrayal—by the loss of his mother, really—that he's been looking for a substitute in the arms of every woman who crosses his path?"

Noel paused to think this through. "All that's possible. I really don't know. I've sometimes thought that losing himself in sex is a distraction."

"A distraction from what?"

"Failure, self-doubt. An inferiority complex."

"You've *got* to be kidding. Norval? You mean a *superiority* complex, don't you?"

"The two usually go hand in hand."

Here Samira paused, recalling his remark about the stairs that went nowhere. A *reminder*, he called it. "So that's why Norval is so prejudiced? Because what he hates in others he sees in himself? But wait, that can't be it. Can't be failure and self-doubt. Didn't he have all kinds of success with his novel? And that film?"

"True, but for him mass appeal is a sign of failure. And besides, that was over a decade ago. He hasn't done anything since."

"Is that why he's so bitter? Why he drinks so much? Because his glory days are behind him?"

"Hardly. He willingly got out of the business."

"Did he have any other offers, film offers?"

"Lots. Withnail in *Withnail and I*. Jaques in *As You Like It* ..."

"And what about his novel? Was Bess modelled on anyone? Someone from his own life? Did he live in Nottinghamshire?"

"He's always maintained she's pure invention. But I 'hae ma doots,' as my mother would say, I hae ma doots. He actually did live in Nottinghamshire, where I think he met his one true love. I think the answer, the key to Norval, is in that book. Have you read it?"

"Yeah, it was in his bookcase, spine turned back to front. I couldn't put it down. I think it's absolutely brilliant. That notion of turning back the clock, trying to recapture something lost—it made me cry my eyes out. And his romantic scenes ... they're so beautiful! And so out of character—I can't believe he wrote that book."

Noel refilled, handed the goblet to Samira. "I can."

"Well, you know him better than I do. So is that where he got his money? I mean, his place is ... amazing. And he spends like a sultan."

"He also wrote two songs, believe it or not. In the early nineties. He had a burst of creative energy, producing one masterpiece, or minor masterpiece, in every genre he tried. And then just stopped creating entirely."

"He wrote *songs*? Good God. Anything I might know?"

"'Jardin de supplices'? It got some airplay in France and Spain."

"Never heard of it. So he made lots of money off that?"

"No, not from his version. But it appeared on a Céline Dion album."

"Are you serious? Christ! Born under a lucky star or what ... What was the other song?"

"'Dream Door.'"

"*Dream Door*? By The Extinction Bazaar? *Norval* wrote that? You can't be serious! I was a teenager when I heard that song! I bought the album because of that song! But ... that doesn't make sense. It's a ballad, it's romantic. He couldn't have written that song!"

"Don't tell him I told you, whatever you do. He can't stand hearing it. The other day we heard it at the theatre and he almost went into convulsions."

"But why did he ... give it all up? He just topped out, apexed? Lost his muse?"

"I can think of a number of possibilities. Well, three."

"Which are ...?"

Noel rotated the cup, took a long sip. "First, it's not easy seeing things clearly through a haze of drink and drugs."

"Others have done it. What's the second?"

"That his muse was a single memory. His songs and novel really only deal with one thing—loss."

"And an attempt to regain what was lost."

"Right. But once he had written about that one dominant memory, there was nothing else left, nowhere else to go."

"What's the third possibility?"

"Well, when Norval was younger he thought art would fill the vacuum, the void opened up by the ... the decay of religion. That the world's problems could be healed, or alleviated, by art—that 'great undogmatised church,' he called it. But now, when he looks around at today's art, music, film, he's lost hope of that ever happening. He says today's art is all about vanity and ego. That celebrity matters more than truth; hype and popularity more than merit."

"Hard to disagree there. The entertainment industry—it's a freaking cesspool."

Noel eyed Samira closely. You would know, he thought. "And he says that egalitarianism is to blame. Or unionism. When you pay plumbers and postmen and athletes that kind of money, you're going to get films and books and TV shows directed at them, designed to take that money away."

Samira smiled as she studied the floorboards, as if following the path of some insect.

Noel hesitated. "Didn't something like that happen to you too?"

Samira raised her head, the smile dying in her eyes. "Something like what? What do you mean? I'm not a musician or writer."

"True, but you were once an actress."

"An actress? Me? What're you talking about?"

"Does the name Heliodora Locke mean anything to you?"

Samira emptied the cup, in large gulps. "Should it?"

Noel regarded her searchingly. "Yes, it should."

"And why is that?"

"Because you're her."

"My name is Samira Darwish."

Noel tried to look into her eyes, the one place you can't conceal the truth. "I'm sure it is. But you used to be an actress, right? Your stage name was Heliodora Locke?"

"Listen, I ... can we change the subject?"

"It's none of my business anyway."

Samira bit her lip. "You wouldn't have a cigarette, would you?"

"No. But I can get you some."

"Don't bother ..." That bloody film, she reflected, was made ... what? Eight years ago? Nine? At my peak, my high tide. I've aged, I'm not wearing make-up, my hair looks like shit. "How did you ... you know, recognize ..."

"Your voice colours."

Samira nodded. "Right."

"So that's why you cut off all your hair? So as not to be recognised?"

"No. Because hair down to my waist just seemed to attract men, like a red cape before a bull."

"And you don't want to attract men."

"Or bulls. I've made a vow of chastity. No, *seriously*."

Norval and Samira, thought Noel. A natural pair. Each had a moment of fame and was repelled by the stench. Each attracts and is repelled by the opposite sex. "So you have a lot in common with Norval."

"He's taken a vow of chastity?"

"No, I meant—"

"He's accomplished way more than me."

"Why'd you stop?"

"Acting or sex?"

"Acting."

"Because ... because some people are cut out for it, some aren't. I don't like seeing myself on screen, I don't like being recognised, I don't like money enough to have to deal with ... well, the cesspool, as Norval called it."

"You called it that."

"The critics, the creeps, the poseurs, the paparazzi, I just couldn't stand it. And I never really wanted it. It was just a ... fluke. It was a dark period in my life, a big black patch ..."

"Why? Because of ... getting involved with the director—Federico Zappavigna? When you were eighteen and he was forty-eight?"

"No, that was exciting. Do you read *People* magazine or something? Or *Teen People?*"

"No ... I ... was just wondering what happened to you, so I ... floated your name on the Net."

"Great. Those stupid interviews, those idiotic illustrated profiles, will haunt me forever. I'll never do another interview, never let a photographer near me as long as I live."

"Because of that nude scene on the Adriatic?"

"Which one? The one in the film or the one in the tabloids taken by that ... that Venetian snorkeller with the telephoto lens?"

"The one in the film ..."

"Well, you know what I'm talking about."

"... which was sort of integrated into the plot, I mean the character ..."

"Me lying naked in a gondola, rubbing Coppertone on my thighs? It had nothing to do with plot or character. It was more like product placement. Listen, Noel, please don't tell anyone about this, OK? I'm trying to put it all behind me. I have my reasons. Noel, will you promise?"

"Of course I will, I give you my word."

Samira looked him straight in the eye. Yes, she thought, I can trust him. "Can we change the subject now? Can I ask *you* some personal questions?"

"Within reason. But first I have to go the bathroom."

"You mean to your mom's bedroom to see if she's all right."

"Uh, well, that too."

When Noel looked in on his mother he found her sitting in the bathtub, in an inch of lukewarm water, wearing a bikini. "What time does the train leave?" she asked, more than once, while shivering. Where's the Bath Lady when I need her? Noel asked himself. And why isn't JJ looking after her?

"Find a phone," said his mother. "Call the principal. I can't remember his name. Just say 'the principal.' Tell him I won't be in today."

It took almost an hour to calm her down, another to get her into bed.

Noel pulled a chair close to her pillow, wondering which words would work this time. "Would you like to hear about ... let's see, that time in Florida, when the hurricane hit? Hurricane Emily? Do you remember? When everyone fled the island except us two? And the governor came on the radio and said 'Flee or die!'? And we ran out of food, but not alcohol, and got plastered?" Instead of smiling at the memory, his mother gazed at the ceiling with deadened eyes. "Would you like to hear a poem instead? A funny one, by Stevie Smith? No? I know which one. One of your favourites. You remember?

> *Wild nights! Wild nights!*
> *Were I with thee,*
> *Wild nights should be*
> *Our luxury!*
>
> *Futile the winds*
> *To a heart in port,*
> *Done with the compass,*
> *Done with the chart.*
>
> *Rowing in Eden!*
> *Ah! the sea!*
> *Might I but moor*
> *To-night in thee!"* [35]

With her head to one side, Mrs. Burun regarded her son with a quizzical air. "I'm feeling better now," she said softly. "Thank you, dear. I'm going to sleep now." She placed her cheek languorously against the lilac pillow. Noel leaned over and kissed her on the forehead. He turned off the bed lamp, tiptoed out of the room.

From the hallway, with blurred vision, he glimpsed a light shining palely from under a door. Samira's door. He walked to within an inch of it, but didn't knock. He'd apologise in the morning.

He continued on to his own room, where a surprising image—an optical illusion, a trick of the light?—awaited him. Sprawled out on his bed was the woman of his dreams, fast asleep, her dark hair spread out like a fan on his bone-white pillow. Her turtleneck sweater was pulled up, across the bridge of her nose, like a half-veil. He folded the bedspread over her bare legs and switched off the lamp. He then went down to his lab, where he worked until dawn.

Chapter 13

Samira & JJ

T he next day the Burun house was a hive of activity. Picture albums were out. Loose photographs were out, in motley mounds on counters and sideboards. Playing cards were out: one deck halfway through a game of Crazy Eights on the rush matting of the family room, two others on a butler's cocktail table in the dining room, paused in double solitaire. Interactive Art, including sand paintings that moved when you turned them, was waiting to be interacted with. A box of Pelican watercolours waited to be painted with. A large institutional clock now hung in the kitchen, above a bold-faced calendar, with a way of marking off the days as they passed. There was a "reality" board in the same room, with date, place and weather conditions, as well as a "Schedule of Activities" bulletin board.

After a brain-deadening day at the library, Noel thought he'd entered the wrong house, a neighbour's perhaps.

"To help her orient herself," Samira explained in the kitchen. She and JJ were wearing red-bordered name tags. "Even I had trouble with your old clock, with the Roman numerals. And as for her tiny wristwatch, well, not only do you need a magnifying glass to see it, but it has to be *wound* every day."

"She never wore it anyway," said Noel, examining the reality board.

"Because she could never find it, or couldn't read it?"

"Both, I guess." Noel looked to his left. On the English-oak table, between stacks of photographs, were bags of groceries and a case of wine. And above the case, pinned to the wall with four green pushpins, was an ink-jet list:

MEMORY FUEL

B12
Fish; Spinach; Poultry

FOLATE
Leafy Greens;
Dry Beans; Peas; Chickpeas
Tomatoes; Oranges; Beets; Soybeans
Fish; Eggs

VITAMIN E
Leafy Greens;
Sweet Potatoes; Avocados
Whole Grain

ANTIOXIDANTS
Blueberries; Pomegranates
Broccoli; Brussels sprouts; Carrots
Cocoa powder

OMEGA-3 OILS
Oily fish (such as sardine and tuna)
Walnuts; Flaxseed; Canola

"See the last item on the list?" asked JJ. "Do you know where it comes from?"

"Canola? Yeah, it's a rapeseed oil, low in erucic acid."

"It comes from 'Canada oil—low acid.' We invented it!"

Noel knew this too, but pretended not to. "Really?" he said, while continuing to absorb the various changes and additions. "So ... where'd all this stuff come from?"

"While the cat's away," said a grinning JJ, "the mice will play."

"But ... who paid for it all?"

"A mystery donor."

"Come on. Was it you?"

JJ shook his head.

"Who, then?"

"A credit card."

"I scissored my mom's credit cards."

"It wasn't your mom's."

"Whose, then?"

"We can't tell you. When Norval authorised us to use his AmEx, he asked us to shut up about it."

"I was wondering," Samira quickly interjected, "if you could put the important numbers in speed dial, and then we'll put them up on the reality board. And fill out these name badges when people come to visit her. Your mom's been working really hard today, by the way. I've been cracking the whip. Hope you don't mind."

Noel was getting confused. Information overload. *Norval* paid? "What ... kind of things? What's she been doing?"

"Let's see. I asked her to set the table, water the plants, iron two blouses, sort out the laundry ... among other things. JJ's been helping her."

"You did the laundry? But we have someone who does that. The Bath Lady."

"Oh, we were thinking of letting her go. You don't really need her anymore. You can't afford her anyway."

"No, you can't let her go. She ... doesn't cost all that much, really. Her services are ... subsidised."

Samira paused. "I've arranged your mom's clothing by colour and in a sequence—it'll make decision-making easier. She's not changing her clothes ... enough."

"Sorry, I ..."

"It's not your fault, Noel. It's the Bath Lady's. And in your mom's bathroom I've arranged her things so they're easier to use. And I've posted a bathing schedule on her calendar of daily activities."

"Wow, this is ... amazing. How did you ..."

"I got some advice from Dr. Rhéaume and Dr. Ravenscroft. And took out some library books."

"That was my idea," said JJ.

Noel nodded. "Look, all this is great, and don't think I don't appreciate it ... but I'm not sure my mom is at the stage where ... I mean, I think she's getting better and I plan on making things even more ... better. I'm working on ... JJ and I are working on ... things."

"I understand that," said Samira, "and if anything can be found to help her, I'm sure you two guys will find it. But for the time being, Noel, your mom has problems. You have to realise that. I know she's up and down, but she still has serious problems. I'm just trying to make things easier for her. And you."

"Thanks, I ... appreciate it." Noel quickly looked away from Samira's penetrating gaze. In the cabinet beside her, he noticed an unfamiliar hole. "Where's the television?"

"In the garage," said Samira. "Along with the two others."

"But ... my mom likes history programmes and quiz shows and—"

"That was my idea," said JJ. "It's the eighth annual TV-Turnoff Week. Last year six million pulled the plug. Their website lists a hundred and one suggestions for alternative activities—like baking, yoga, gardening, reading. There's a connection between obesity and TV-watching, Web-surfing and video games."

"And passive screens don't exactly help Alzheimer's," said Samira.

"OK," said Noel, nodding. "My father would've approved."

"We also went through the kitchen cupboards," said JJ. "We threw out everything that contains artificial sweeteners, including two cases of Diet Pepsi."

"But why? I'm trying to cut down on calories and ..."

"Because," said JJ, "aspartame has been linked to Alzheimer's. Monsanto has known this for years. The information is freely available on the Net. The Palm Springs Institute for Medical Research in California says it causes convulsions, blindness and loss of memory."

"That sounds like a complete load of—"

"Oh, and we took the liberty of buying a case of red wine," said JJ.

"For my mom?" asked Noel. "But didn't you just order some red-wine extract from Switzerland?"

"The ANOX? It's been held up. Anyway, a new study says the wine itself is just as good. Some chemical in it, I can't remember the name, stimulates nerve regeneration."

"Resveratrol. Researchers in Italy found that when it was added to human nerve cells growing in culture, they grew contact points."

"Contact points, exactly. And people with Alzheimer's have fewer contact points, am I right? So by having daily shots of wine you prevent, you know ..."

"Neurodegeneration. Where's my mother now, by the way?"

"Sound asleep. She had a bit too much wine. Don't worry about her, I've got my hand on the wheel. Oh, by the way, I fixed her treadmill. We're going to boil her blood for forty-five minutes every day. That's the key to alertness and longevity—boil your blood for forty-five minutes a day. That's what my grandfather used to say."

"By 'boil her blood' you mean get her heart going."

"And brain. Neurobics, I call it."

"How old was your grandfather when he died?"

"Fifty. He fell off his bike and broke his neck. Oh, and we were looking at your mom's scrapbooks. Amazing. She's got articles on your dad's work back in the eighties! And articles on you when you were a little boy! You were both famous! And Dr. Vorta is quoted in some of them! So I'm making copies for my scrapbook, if it's OK with you."

"And we found some things in the attic," said Samira. "I hope you don't mind us poking around."

"What'd you come up with?"

"These." From the kitchen table Samira picked up a sheaf of ice-blue airmail letters, with British stamps.

"My grandmother's letters! You found them! Fantastic!"

"There's magic spells inside a couple of the letters," said Samira. "Witch's spells, I mean. Good spells."

"I know, I've been looking all over for them for years! I remember some of them from when I was a kid. Where'd you find them?"

"In here." JJ held up a red-and-white chequered book, a battered and food-stained *Better Homes & Gardens*. "Flattened like leaves inside the pages. Maybe we can try some of the spells on your mom."

Noel stared at the cover of the book, remembering certain flour-thumbed pages that had made his life happier; he could now smell and taste the desserts he had helped his mother make, like Rice Krispie squares and vanilla fudge and lemon meringue pie ("*a luscious filling made with real lemon tucked under a fluffy blanket of lightly toasted meringue ...*"). "OK, I'll try anything."

"One last thing," said Samira. "Your mom is becoming more and more ... silent. As I'm sure you've noticed. So I'm going to get her painting—it'll help her to express herself. Art therapy, by an amateur like me, hope you don't mind. I've only done one semester, but I'll do my best ..."[36]

"Yes, by all means, art therapy sounds like a good idea. A *very* good idea—"

"Our next concern is you," said Samira. "Because your system's run down. Caregiver collapse. Depression, exhaustion, maybe even guilt—it's common according to Dr. Rhéaume. So JJ and I have drawn up a Top Ten list for you."

"Most of these are Sam's," said JJ. "Try to guess which two are mine." He handed Noel a piece of lined yellow paper.

1. Get enough sleep, and take time out to relax, so you can focus better on things that are important (like finding a memory cure!).

2. Eat three square meals to give you energy for things that are important (like finding a memory cure!).

3. Allow others to help, because caring for your mom is too big a job to be done by you alone.

4. Take one day at a time rather than worry about what may or may not happen in the future.

5. Structure your day because a consistent schedule makes life easier for both you and your mom.

6. Remember that your mom is not being difficult on purpose; her behaviour and emotions are being distorted by AD.

7. Have a <u>sense of humour</u> because laughter helps to put things in a more positive perspective.

8. Focus on and enjoy what your mother can still do rather than lament over what is lost.

9. Try to depend more on OTHER RELATIONSHIPS for love and support.

10. Draw upon the <u>Higher Power</u>, which is available to you.

"Take a guess—which ones are mine?" JJ repeated.

"Well ... let's see. Seven and ten?"

JJ responded with a woofy laugh. "Bingo! You know what the Higher Power is?"

"God?"

"A belief in mystery, magic and miracles. The three *ms.*"

Noel's brain filled up with acres of sunny blue sky. "Thanks for this, both of you." Tears were rising, but he coaxed them back to their source. His arms ached to hug them both, but remained lifeless at his side. He reread number 9, drawn into the vortex of capitals, desperately hoping it was a hint, a kick under the table, a coded Valentine.

Chapter 14
Noel & Samira (II)

I t was not a hint after all, Noel concluded, after scarcely seeing
Samira for the next seven days. She passed him in the hall with only
a syllable or two, walked by him in Dr. Vorta's office with barely a
nod. Not surprising, he thought. What a fool I was to expect anything
more! It's always the same. In any case, it was all a big distraction. I've got
better ways of occupying my brain.

To prove it to himself, Noel spent more and more time underground.
He ignored pleas from his mother and JJ to come up for air, just as he
ignored his Ten Commandments, which he decided were unobeyable. He
drove himself harder and harder. He would sleep in his chair, rarely using
his bed, for the mornings seemed years away from the night. Time was
the enemy, the poison.[37] And though he felt lonely, and out of joint, he
also felt he was making progress. He was sure of it. And he was losing
weight—an added benefit.

He was also starting to lose his mind, he strongly suspected one night.
For inspiration and clues, he had begun combing through a book of
mediaeval Arabian chemistry, as well as four versions of *The Thousand
and One Nights*—including Galland's translation, a charred edition
borrowed from JJ. After a day of frenzied speed-reading, thinking himself
into a stupor, he snapped the books shut. "That's it," he whispered to
himself. "I've lost it ..."

He was sitting in his father's swivel chair, staring catatonically at a
dirty-white wall that matched the interior of his head, when a percussive
sound jostled him. A rhythm he had heard before. In a dream? Rat-a-tat-
tat, rat-a-tat-tat. Softly. Then a muffled, disembodied voice. "Noel?"

Déjà vu, literally, in his mind. "Yes?" he said.

"Can I come in?"

"Yes ... of course. The door's unlocked."

"Can you open it?"

With his heart galloping, Noel sprang from his chair and yanked open the door. Samira, in a camisole and flared boot-cut pants, both black, was holding a tray against her bare midriff.

"Come in, sorry. Here, let me take that ... Sorry, Sam, I was just ... in the clouds. As usual."

"JJ made them for you. Brain food." Samira set the tray down, kissed Noel on both cheeks, giving him a gentle hug in the process.

The contact, only the fleetest touch of skin and hair, aroused Noel from his catatonia like a branding iron. "Thanks. I mean, not for the ... I mean for that too, but, you know ..." He nodded at the plate of salmon sandwiches encircled by walnuts, carrots and grape tomatoes. "I appreciate it ..." He could still feel her kiss-prints burning on his flesh. And especially the ... well, keeping my mom company."

"That's JJ's department, not mine, I have to admit. I haven't been around much these past few days. It's crunch time at school."

Noel took a breath, his first in a while. "I understand." He lifted his gaze from the tray to her face. She was radiant, a vision of beauty. The way she used to look!

"What a great lab this is! JJ gave me the grand tour the other day, I hope you don't mind."

"Not at all. You're ... welcome to come down. Anytime you want."

"Thanks." Samira looked away, at the rows of chemicals, trying to conceal her shock at how awful Noel looked. Pallor of a corpse, JJ was right. "Well, *bon appétit*. I'll let you eat in peace. And then maybe you should ... you know, take a break. I mean, after you've done what you have to do ..."

"I've finished. For the day. My mind's shot. I don't suppose ... no, never mind."

"What?"

"You ... you wouldn't like a drink, would you?"

"I'd love one."

"Really? Great. Here, sit down. No, this chair's more comfortable. I've got something that JJ distilled. A Newfoundland recipe."

Samira laughed as she sat down. "Screech? Thank God for JJ."

"Amen." Noel opened the bottom drawer of a battered wooden filing cabinet and pulled out a bottle with a skull and crossbones on the label. He filled two beakers to the halfway point, held out one to Samira.

175

"Thanks. الصحة والسعادة. Health and happiness." She clinked her beaker against his then took a sip. "Hey, that's not ... as bad as I thought it would be."

Noel laughed. And then grimaced as the rum and God knows what else burned down his chest like lava.

It was Samira's turn to laugh. "The last time we had a drink I ended up falling asleep on your bed. Which I forgot to apologise for."

"My fault entirely. I was ... away much too long."

"When you left, I think it was my turn to ask some personal questions."

"You've got a good memory." Noel took another sip, cautiously. "Fire away."

"I wanted to ask you about ..." Samira paused as she noticed the books on the table. "Is this ... *The Thousand and One Nights?*" She picked up one of the volumes and opened it. "A really old edition. Beautiful." She smiled. "So is this what you've been up to all day?"

"No, I ... just ... wanted to check something out." He took the book from her. "So what did you want to ask me about?"

She took another sip from her beaker. "About the colours in your head, your synaesthesia. I never knew it existed until I met you, or rather until Norval told me about it. I mean, I know what it is in poetry because we studied it at school. But what is it ... you know, what happens inside your brain? Do a lot of people have it?"

Noel reached for his glass. The sensations he had felt not five minutes before—numbness, fogginess, sluggishness—were all converted into their opposites. His mental horizon was clear, cloudless; he was floating in something close to pure happiness. And it wasn't only from the bathtub rum. He smiled, something he hadn't done in a while. "It depends on who you talk to. Some researchers put it at one in two thousand, others at one in twenty thousand. But we all have it—we're all synaesthetes for the first three months of our lives. But we forget this, of course. Infantile amnesia."

"Norval says you can remember your natal hour."

"Norval *would* say something like that. If it's sounds good he'll say it."

"He also predicts you'll be a great artist one day."

"He also predicts the winners of horse races. Not very well."

"Does he think you'll be a great artist because his favourite authors—Rimbaud, Baudelaire, Nabokov—all had synaesthesia?"

"Probably. But great art like that is definitely out of my league. So is mediocre art, for that matter."

176

Samira held Noel's eye for a full quarter of a minute, until he looked away. "Are there any great scientists who had it?"

"Richard Feynman, for one."

Samira laughed. "You're kidding. I just read an article on him—in a section of the paper I never read, even while listening to my mom on the phone. There was a *long* delay in the metro. A suicide jump, I think. He was into quantum mechanics, right? In the sixties?"

Noel nodded. "My father liked him because of his ... range. Because he wasn't your average boring scientist, as you probably know. He wrote on science and religion, on the role of beauty in scientific knowledge, on gambling odds. He cracked uncrackable safes, played bongo drums for a ballet ..."

"Painted a nude female bullfighter."

Noel smiled. "Right. My father once had a drink with him. In Queens."

"Are you serious? Wow, a brush with greatness. I'm just trying to remember ... Didn't he have some famous last words?"

"'I'd hate to die twice—it's so boring.'"

Samira burst out laughing. "That's it. Almost as good as Dylan Thomas's."

"Really? What were his?"

"'Seventeen whiskeys. A record, I think.'"

It was Noel's turn to laugh. "What number are *we* on?" He held up the bottle then poured.

"Three—we've a ways to go." She swivelled in her chair, put her feet up. "So I can see why your father liked Feynman. Maybe one day you'll be like him."

Noel gazed at Samira's dark brown ankle boots, at the criss-cross of laces wound through button hooks. "There's no' a snowball's chance in hell of that happening, as my mother would say."

"Great Scottish accent! Almost as good as Norval's."

"Right."

Samira traced her finger round the lip of the beaker. "You've made quite an impression on JJ. He says you're a genius."

"JJ has kind words for everybody—it takes some getting used to. But there's more to genius than having a good memory." Noel's mind began to stray, but he corralled it. "The funny thing, about Feynman I mean, is that I got some ideas about memory loss—about memory being physical particles—after looking at a Feynman diagram in my dad's notes."

"What's a Feynman diagram?"

"Well, briefly, it's a graphic method of representing the interactions of elementary particles, a way of calculating the processes that occur, for instance, between electrons and photons. One axis, for example the horizontal axis, is chosen to represent space, while the other represents time. Straight lines are used to depict fermions—particles with half-integral values of intrinsic angular momentum, or spin, and wavy lines are used for bosons—particles with integral values of spin, such as photons ..."

"This is the brief explanation, right?"

"Sorry, I ... I'm not a very good storyteller. Or teacher. I always lose people."

"No, no, it's ... it's my fault. Entirely. Go on."

"I'll get to the point. Descartes, as I'm sure you know, famously divided the world into two parts—'extended things,' i.e., the physical world, and 'thinking things,' i.e., the mind. So the brain for him has two kinds of material—mental material, in which the thought exists, and physical material, which is where the memory is stored. So ever since Descartes philosophers and scientists have debated whether the human mind will ever be knowable."

"Because if it's not physical, how can you study it?"

"Exactly. But now, the standard view of neuroscience is that when we have a new thought, or a new memory, our brain has *physically changed*. With the formation of engrams, memory-traces. So the mind doesn't exist beyond that—beyond the grey mush, the nerve spaghetti of the brain—and therefore memory is a biological process that can be manipulated like anything else. And not only can you manipulate it, you can improve it."

"With a memory pill, for example."

Noel smiled. "Precisely."

"So Descartes was wrong. But what's Feynman got to do with all this?"

"Well, we still have to understand the interaction between the mental—the thought or new memory forming—and the physical. How do the two influence each other? Descartes thought that the pineal gland—via the eyes—was the point at which the two interacted, which is ridiculous, but now scientists think that the interaction happens at the *quantum* level."

"Hence your studies of Feynman."

"Well, I'm ... not really at that level. And never will be."

"Noel, I'm sure you'll get there, and beyond. All you need is ... well, confidence. Or arrogance—the arrogance of Norval."

Noel managed a half-smile. "Yeah, I guess I could learn a few things from him."

"And JJ can show you a few things too."

"I know. He's good at re-routeing my thought patterns—at de-ingraining bad mental habits, if that's a word."

"Has he converted you to CAM? To 'neutraceuticals' instead of pharmaceuticals?"

"No. Big Pharma's bad, but the 'wellness' industry is worse. Unregulated and dishonest. Untested and unreliable. For the most part, anyway. But I'm trying to keep an open mind—it does have some things to offer. And I love JJ's enthusiasm, optimism, which rubs off."

A patch of silence followed, which neither person seemed to notice, let alone be uncomfortable with. Noel gazed up at the small basement window, like a dungeon grate, and saw snowflakes dance and cling to the glass. Each one was worth an hour of study under the microscope, his father had told him, each one a map of divinity.

"I'm trying to remember," said Samira, her words slightly slurred, "how we got on to all this."

Noel shifted his gaze. "I'm the one who got us off track. You were asking about coloured hearing."

"Right, I wanted to know if it's a good thing or a bad thing. Does it screw up your life? Would you ever want to get rid of it?"

"No, I wouldn't. Ever. I have trouble, in fact, conceiving of a world in which letters and sounds are neutral, clear, white, whatever. Sometimes I think those who don't have synaesthesia are missing out on something. Almost like being colour blind. I think all synaesthetes feel the same way. Mind you, we're not all the same—most have mild cases, which don't interfere with their everyday life, while a few have trouble functioning in society because of it, like some artists. And me."

"Did you ever try to get help? Did you ever see a psychiatrist or neurologist or—"

"Yeah, hordes of them. Dr. Vorta among them."

"Did he help?"

"He did, but his colleagues didn't. One put me on lithium carbonate, which made things worse, another tried acupuncture, which might've worked if he'd known what he was doing, another gave me nineteen electro-convulsive treatments, which almost left me brain-dead. And then they all got together and wrote articles about me."[38]

"They didn't help you to control it, or channel it ..."

"I more or less found out how to stop it on my own."

"With classical music? And certain tastes?"

"Yeah, and I've learned to put myself into a kind of trance, deliberately emptying my mind."

"Like Zen Buddhists?"

"Only if they get terrible headaches while doing it."

"Are your dreams as wild? As colourful?"

"Not at all. They're in black and white most of the time, and usually involve quiz shows or labyrinths ... And I usually wake up with this wish to be transported on my mattress back to my bedroom in Babylon ..." Noel's mind, vibrant and viatic, began to travel but he forced it to stop, pressing his hands against his temples. "In high school, in Montreal, everybody wanted me to go on this quiz show called *Reach for The Top*. But I refused and everybody was furious with me for the rest of the year, the principal most of all. Especially when our school didn't make it past the first round ..."

Samira laughed. "I remember that show. So you're still dealing with high school trauma. Still trying to find a way out of the maze."

My mind is a maze, thought Noel. With no exits but only entrances into more mazes. A Gordian knot of coils and loops and convolutions. "Maybe."

"What does Dr Vorta have to say about all that?"

"About my dreams? Nothing much. What's your ... take?"

"Well, people are always testing you, testing your memory, so that may explain the quiz shows. As for the maze, it may represent, I don't know, your trying to escape your ... problems." Samira shrugged. "I'm no expert. I know that for the Egyptians the labyrinth represented creativity, or creation. A mysterious feminine power that brings life, and then as the queen of night or queen of darkness, the sleep of death ... As you probably know."

Noel turned these words over. When you find the exit, death is waiting. You're dead on arrival. "I didn't know that."

Through a heating duct in the ceiling came a muffled sound: a gust of carolling laughter from JJ.

"Why don't you just memorise *everything*? It'd be so much fun to walk around with Shakespeare's entire works in your head, or Jane Austen's or the *Encyclopedia Britannica* or twenty different languages. No?"

"There's no room left. My brain's crammed to bursting point. And besides, my problem has always been *using* the stuff I remember, making a synthesis, something new."

"Do you remember *everything* that happens to you? Everything you read or hear?"

"No, I usually have to make an effort. Most of the stuff I've stored is from my childhood, when I tried to retain it with memory maps. Poems mostly, children's stories ... Or I else I sort of photograph it—if I concentrate the coloured letters or coloured voices will remain fixed in my mind forever ... or quite a while. A lot of the stuff wasn't hard to memorise—because I'd read certain stories or poems over and over again, or I asked my parents to read me the same stuff over and over again."

"So it's mostly just poems and children's stories?"

"I've stored lots of data about Byron, because he's an ancestor according to my dad, though not according to my mom, and also on chemistry and pharmacology. And now memory disorders. I don't really *try* to memorise anything else, it just happens. Sometimes I feel like my brain is going to burst some day, like a vacuum cleaner bag. Memory dust flying all over the place."

Samira laughed. "Time for a bag change, I guess. Or a *lobotomy?*"

Noel smiled bleakly. He'd once considered that. "As a kid I used to fantasize about finding some magical elixir to help me out, some nepenthean potion. Especially after my dad died."

"Nepenthean potion?"

"It was used to induce forgetfulness, by the ancients. It's mentioned in *The Odyssey*. And *The Faerie Queene*."

"I'll bet you know the lines."

Noel closed his eyes, perused his portable photo-library. "No, not in the *Odyssey*. Nothing's coming in."

"And *The Faerie Queene?*"

Am I too tired? Noel wondered while reclosing his eyes. The downloaded letters were misty, like breath-fog writing. "*Nepenthe ... whereby all cares forepast Are washt away quite from their memorie.*"

"How lovely. Continue. Do you mind?"

Yes, but I'll do it for you, thought Noel. He squeezed his eyes shut. The coloured letters were now cock-eyed, chaotic, an alphabet soup of images:

"I'm a bit rusty, Sam, I ... don't often do this sort of thing. Anymore. And I'm not always a hundred per cent accurate." He waited for the letters to realign themselves, concentrating until his head hurt. "Let's see:

Nepenthe is a drinck of soverayne grace,
Devized by the Gods, for to asswage
Harts grief, and bitter gall away to chace,
Which stirs up anguish and contentious rage:
Instead thereof sweet peace and quiet-age
It doth establish in the troubled mynd."

Samira was leaning forward, her gleaming eyes mesmerized. She shook her head in disbelief. "That's amazing, Noel. An amazing ... gift. So the colours or shapes of the letters, or voices, or the mental maps you draw are there ... always? Indestructible? Like an airplane's black box?"

Noel rubbed his eyes. "More like a computer with more input than it was designed to process. Slow down, freeze, crash, reboot—my life in a nutshell."

Silence gathered as Samira digested these last words. Her eyes focused on Noel's, sharply, as if she could see into his skull and was panged by what was there.

"That can't be easy," she said finally. "Especially when you store memories you'd rather get rid of. Dark and oppressive memories ..."

"Like the day I learned my father killed himself. When his boss and two cops came to the door. I replay that day, the colours and shapes, over in my brain almost every day. And some traumatic things that happened to me in school as well. But I'm hardly alone in that respect. That's what psychiatrists are for. For people who can't forget."

"Is that why people are depressed? Because they can't forget? Or have a hard time forgetting?"

"It's hard to say which came first. Are people depressed because they can't forget, can't properly process and digest things? Or is it that they can't properly process and digest because they're depressed?"

"But thinking about bad things all the time, having unwanted memories continually coming to the surface—that leads to depression. Post-traumatic stress disorder. Right? What they used to call shell shock?"

"You know as much as I do."

"I just learned that last week, in my art-therapy class. Have you ever tried to paint, by the way? As an outlet, a way of exorcising the demons of the past? Or write?"

Noel gazed up at the window again, watched the snow falling ... *the snow falling faintly through the universe and faintly falling* ... See? There I go again, he thought. I'm capable only of remembering other people's descriptions of nature, other people's expressions of emotion. I'm like Christian in *Cyrano*, who never learned the language of sentiment, who had to get someone else to express ...

"Uh, Noel?" For a second she was worried; he seemed on the verge of a seizure or something. "Noel?"

He looked at her in surprise. "Sorry, it's ... I was just ... it's something you'll have to get used to, I'm afraid. Norval says it looks like I'm nodding-off on heroin. But it's not as bad as it looks. What were you saying?"

"I asked if you've ever tried to write or paint or compose ..."

"All of the above. Lots of times. But when I finally come up with something, I realise it's something dredged from memory, recovered from ... the black box."

"But why is Norval so convinced that one day you'll—"

"Norval doesn't know what he's talking about. I belong to a certain class of people who never accomplish anything, it's as simple as that. Who try to make beautiful things, or beautiful discoveries, but can't. Every line I write conjures up other lines, better lines, from other writers. Every image I paint, or song I write, conjures up better images from better painters, better music from better composers. Every scientific 'discovery' I make has already been discovered. So I decided long ago to stop beating at doors I'll never enter."

Samira felt another tug—or stab—at the heartstrings as the seconds ticked by. It wasn't so much his words as his look of sadness. She waited until Noel lifted his gaze from the floor, which took a while.

"You can do anything, Noel, if you want it bad enough."

Desire is creation. If you could measure desire, you could foretell achievement. His father told him that. "I'm not sure that's true."

"Can't you combine the things in your memory, creatively, or use them as a base or ... I don't know, influence? I know you can. Don't ever give up."

Noel's mind raced back to a certain game of Remembrance, when his father expressed this same thing ...

"Noel? Can't you combine things, combine imagination with memory?"

"No, I can't even do that. I have trouble making new patterns, new combinations. My mind's a museum, a library—not a debating hall, not a crucible."

"Maybe you just need encouragement or someone to ..." She let her sentence trail as she watched Noel's expression cloud over, darken. "Noel?"

183

"Yes?"

"I know Norval's your best friend, but I was wondering if you had someone else to... if you had a girlfriend, or if you go out with ... you know, girls, women. I know that sounds stupid ..."

The question caught Noel off guard, and it took him a while to frame a coherent reply. "Well, I really haven't had time for women ... I've spent most of my free time in labs and libraries. And now my mom takes up most of my time. And besides, women aren't really ... never mind."

"Aren't really what? Your cup of tea?"

"No. I mean yes, they are ... my cup of tea. It's just that I can't really get close to anybody, I'm sort of blocked. I have trouble expressing ... One psychologist suggested I take ecstasy."

Samira laughed. "You're joking. What for?"

"In his words, for 'heightened emotional responsiveness, lowering of defensive barriers, openness and sense of closeness to others.'"

"Did it work?"

"No, but I continue to take it—four times a year, every equinox. Any more than that and the drug's a total waste."

"And has it helped with your relationships? With women?"

"No, women aren't really ... I seem to have this anti-talent for attracting them, the Midas touch in reverse."

"I have a similar talent—for attracting the wrong men. But you'll find someone with the right chemistry, I know it. Sometimes it's just a question of patience. And luck."

Noel closed his eyes as he spoke: "*Tendency to brood, emotional numbness, general confusion.*" He reopened his eyes. "The words of another doctor. No woman can handle that, no woman will ever take me on. Plus I'm always going overboard, head over heels, whenever I meet the woman of my dreams. It scares women off. And if I don't know the woman that well, I have to concentrate so hard that I usually end up with a horrendous migraine. Scintillating scotoma. I'm afraid I'm quite hopeless. Women generally think I'm retarded."

As I first did, thought Samira. "Scintillating scrotoma?"

"Scotoma. Migraine aura—I see this brilliantly lit image, a kind of throbbing, zigzagging line."

"And you get this when you make love?"

"Most of the time, yeah. I also get it when I meet someone ... special, for the first time. A woman, I mean."

"Did you get it with me?"

184

"Well ... yes. So now I'm into abstinence, *coitus nonexistus*. It's a lot less complicated."

"Join the club. I'm on the sexual wagon too. Be right back."

As he waited a half-dozen lines, all flattering, swirled through Noel's intoxicated brain. *You are a vision of loveliness* was one; *I find it impossible not to gaze at you with uncivil persistency* was another, which he'd heard Norval use to good effect. Norval. The great satrap with his twenty-six concubines. Wonder what letter's next for His Serene Highness ...

"You are a vision of uncivil persistency," Noel mumbled when Samira returned, holding an unlit cigarette between her fingers.

"I'm sorry?"

Noel shook his addled head. "Nothing. You ... you look lovely, Sam."

She regarded him with raised brows. "You tell one more lie, Noel, and you'll turn to stone."

Noel opened a drawer beneath the lab bench and pulled out a tarnished lighter, which he'd refuelled but never used. His hand trembled like a compass needle as he held a flame under Samira's cigarette. *Should I ask if Norval is past S? No, don't be an idiot. Relax, take a deep breath ...* He raised and closed the lighter's lid, stared at its faded insignia, a tegulated AP. His father's final employer.

"Thanks," said Samira, with a puzzled expression.

Far things felt near. "When I was young I ... no, never mind."

"What? Tell me."

He took a deep breath. "Well, you'll probably laugh but I used to dream about meeting an Arab woman like you. An Arab princess, actually. Probably because my favourite book of all time was ... well, this one here." With his cheeks afire and heart beating louder than his breathing, he nodded towards a volume of *The Thousand and One Nights*. "Do you speak Arabic?" he blurted into the vacuum of silence.

A smile played about Samira's lips. "Yeah, although I probably sound like a ten-year-old. Or younger. My parents came to Montreal as children, so we spoke mostly English at home, except when my grandfather was around. He's the one who sent me to a *madrasa* for two years, where I dutifully memorised my lessons."

"What nationality are they—your grandparents?"

"Persian—although my grandmother's people were from Egypt. Alexandrian Jews."

"*Persian?* How old are they? Or is that a euphemism for Iranian?"

Samira smiled. "They came to Montreal in the thirties—when the country was still called Persia."

Noel nodded. "And Egyptian Jews. Did you know that *The Arabian Nights* draws extensively on Jewish sources?"

"No, I'm not really up on ... either."

"In 'The Sultan and His Three Sons,' for example, and 'The Angel of Death,' and 'Alexander and the Pious Man' and ..." He stopped when he saw tears forming in Samira's eyes—from a protracted yawn. I'm literally boring her to tears, he thought. "Would you like some more of this?" He held up the bottle. "Will we get to seventeen, do you think?"

"I think I've reached my limit. But go ahead."

"No, I've reached mine too." He replaced the glass stopper in the bottle. "So you ... grew up here. You went to university in Montreal?"

"No, the States."

"Where?"

"Cornell."

"Really? That's where Nabokov taught. While writing his autobiography."[39]

"And *Lolita*."

"We used to live down there—in New York State, I mean. Long Island. I was there until the second grade. I'd love to go back one day ..." Letters and numbers began percolating inside Noel's skull: the chiselled Baskerville capitals of BABYLON ELEMENTARY SCHOOL, the pebbled black plastic 22 on his classroom door, the sinistral chalk letters of Miss Schonborn ... Noel rubbed his eyes, refocused. "Ever been there?"

"Long Island? Once. I went to see an Islanders game."

Cards began to fly from the pack, bouncing off Noel's inner walls: dog-eared cards of Mike Bossy and Denis Potvin, Bryan Trottier and Bobby Nystrom, Clark Gillies and Butch Goring ... Their stats, as in a centrifuge, began to spin and scatter. He pressed his thumb and forefinger against his eyeballs, hard. "So ... what'd you study? At Cornell."

"Well, my father had this master plan. He thought I should study marketing, so I could help expand the family business. He owned a restaurant in Lachine."

"Which one?"

"Le Tapis Magique."

"You're kidding! That restaurant by the water, near Saul Bellow's old neighbourhood? That's an institution."

"Maybe I served you."

"No, I've never been there." Noel ran his fingers up and down the skull-and-crossbones label on the bottle. "So you got your MBA?"

Samira shook her head. "I was *totally* not interested in business, so after a semester of boredom—of pain—I switched over to the arts. Without telling my father, who hated ... impractical things."

"What'd you take?"

"Impractical things. English lit, astronomy, psychology, art history. Oh, and theatre arts."

"Which is how you got the film part?"

"Not really, no. My roommate happened to see a poster on campus, some film production company looking for an 'Arabic-American teenager.'"

"So you went for an audition."

"To this day, I have no idea why. It's not something I ever wanted to do, at least not professionally. I guess I went because I had almost no money, and was tired of taking orders from the assistant manager of Wendy's. Next thing I knew I was flying to Venice."

"Where you met Stirling Trevanne."

"Yeah. Whose real name is Lionel Lifschitz. An asshole, as it turned out, like all my boyfriends, but breathtakingly handsome—as his teenage fans kept reminding me. Daily. Anyway, after the shooting I moved out of my apartment, took a bus to New York and the red-eye to LA." The vertical city to the horizontal one, she recalled thinking, a tremor of excitement running through her as she gazed on each from the sky.

"To live with him," said Noel.

Samira sighed. "Yeah. Then the film comes out—and the shit hits the fan. The film's a mega-hit, critically at least, wins awards in Venice and Berlin, Stirling loses his mind, my father has a massive coronary."

"Are you serious? Your father had a heart attack?"

"While watching the film."

"My God. And he ... Is he better now?"

"No, he died. I went back for the funeral, and my mother guilted me out the whole time, saying that I'd killed him, that the nude scene in the movie killed him. She'd walk around the house holding his shirts to her breast, weeping for hours. Especially when I was there to see it. Must be her Jewish blood. Anyway, it was a terrible time for me, I just had to get out of there. So I went back to Santa Monica."

"To Stirling."

"Yes, who was beginning to act strange."

187

"I ... I read about that, about him giving names to his furniture and kitchen appliances. After the accident. What happened exactly?"

"Well, he was a vegetarian, right? Which is fine. So was I, more or less. Except he became more and more radical, obsessive, evangelical. He'd take forever in the health-food stores, pestering the staff, peppering them with questions about the labels, the packaging materials, how and when the fruit was delivered to the store, carping about this and that, you name it. If the salesperson didn't have an answer, there'd be hell to pay. Insults, threats to have him fired ... The veins on his neck would just bulge. If the food was touching paper or Saran wrap, he wouldn't buy it. He'd comb the racks with crystals that checked the 'life force' of foods, or with Geiger counters or ray-guns that buzzed and beeped. I'm not kidding. The man was insane. He was a raw-foodist. The only thing he'd eat was fruit and vegetables—but only if they'd been picked less than fifteen minutes before he ate them. Which cut down on his choices, n'est-ce pas? And he wouldn't chop a vegetable, because it would destroy its 'etheric field.' Or eat out of pots and pans, because they were contaminated by 'fleshy vibrations.' So he nibbled on alfalfa sprouts, umeboshi plums, quinoa seeds ... He ended up looking like Gandhi after a fast. His big aspiration was to become a Breatharian."

"Which is ...?"

"People who fast and live on pure air. Anyway, if you ever confronted him about not eating he'd just say he was going through a 'purge, a cleansing process.' He'd faint from time to time—from protein deficiency, I guess. And then he had the big accident, crashing his Ferrari into a hairdressing salon, which I guess you read about."

"Is that how it happened? He passed out while driving? And how is he now?"

"No idea. When he got out of the hospital I left him for good."

"Probably wise."

"Yeah, except I've not been lucky in my choice of men since then either. Norval included."

Noel jumped, at least on the inside, but strained not to show it. "So you ... never went back to acting?"

Samira shook her head. "No, I went back to Ithaca, to school, which my film money paid for more or less, without having to go back to Wendy's."

"And did your mother ever ... you know, chill? Did she realise your father's death had nothing to do with you? Am I asking too many questions?"

"No. It's nice to get some. Especially after being with Norval. No, my mom's still blaming me, tormenting me, living in the past. The house is like a museum, a shrine—with a stopped clock marking the time my father died. An Arabic tradition, she says. And she sold the restaurant."

Noel looked down, dolefully, at the floor. "That's a shame, that's so ..." He let the sentence trail, the right word not coming. "So now you're studying psychology? I mean, art therapy?"

"Just started this year."

"Is that why you went to see Dr. Rhéaume after you were ... drugged? She's one of your teachers, right?"

"Yeah. In fact, she and her husband—Dr. Ravenscroft—were there that night. It was an Art Therapy party, a get-acquainted kind of thing."

Noel nodded. He'd been to one of those. "Charles Ravenscroft? He's her husband? I didn't know that. So what happened exactly? That's a stupid question, you can't remember."

"I really can't, I just ... blacked out. One minute I was drinking cranberry cocktails and the next I was feeling dizzy and disoriented, seeing everything in multiple images. And losing control of my movements."

"Was Dr. Rhéaume there when it happened? Did she know who could've done it, who could've spiked your drink?"

"Yeah, she and her husband were both there, just about to leave. In fact, they're the ones who drove me home. But she hasn't a clue who could've done it. She insisted I report it to the police. In fact, she took me there herself. She and Charles."

"So the police ... Dr. Vorta also did some tests, right?"

"Yeah, but only because he paid me. It was Norval's idea. Vorta took blood and urine samples and then turned on a tape recorder for some article he's writing. Then enlisted me in an amnesia study."

"It was GHB, right?"

Samira nodded.

"And were you ... never mind."

"Raped? No, thank God. Or rather thanks to Dr. Rhéaume. I was in a back bedroom, don't ask me how, and she came in—either to get her coat or say good night, I'm not sure which—and saw the guy scrambling out the window, onto a fire escape."

"Are you serious? Did she get a good look at him? Did she give the cops a description?"

"It was pitch black in the room, and it all happened so fast. And she didn't know what was going on. She may have thought I was making out with the guy."

"And you ... don't remember a thing."

"Just that one detail, about hearing that bit about 'excess and the palace of wisdom.'"

"Right." Noel saw the line from Blake. "I wonder if we should try that same blend of herbs again, see if it triggers anything more."

"No, it's probably nothing, I'm probably imagining things ..."

"I'll talk to JJ about it. Because it did some strange things to me too."

"Nothing to lose." Samira emptied her glass and stood up. "OK, time for my bath. Wow, my legs feel like rubber. Listen, Noel, are you sure it's all right if I stay here? I mean, just for a couple more days?"

"Stay as long as you want. There's lots of room. And I think the world ... I mean my mother thinks the world of you."

"Thanks, Noel. You're a sweetheart. I wish I could fall in love with a sweetheart like you, I really ..." She stopped, realising she'd said something stupid, something insulting, and not knowing how to take it back.

Noel winced. The words stung. His lips began to move: a mumble rose to a gabble, the words tripping one another, his brain out of step with his tongue.

"I'm sorry?" said Samira. "I didn't quite catch—"

An orangey orb distracted them both. JJ was peering round the door with a brattish boy's grin, as if holding a water pistol behind his back. "Hope I'm not being a budinsky ... Hey, are you guys into the shine, the giggle-water?" He held two large books under his arm, which he plunked down on the desk. After low-fiving Noel he gave Samira a long bear-hug. Overly long, it seemed to Noel.

"Have I got news for you, my friend," he said to Noel, with a wink and a wag of the head. "I found the clue—for the cure! In *The Arabian Nights*! Open sesame!" He feverishly opened the two volumes at various book-marked pages, to which there clung the faint tang of peanut butter. Each had some underlining in pencil:

Then he followed the highway leading to the neighbouring city and entering it, went to the perfumers' bazaar, where he bought of one some rarely potent <u>bhang</u> ...

Nay, more, doth she not drug every night the cup she giveth him to drink before sleeptime, and put <u>bhang</u> into it?

Now she had been drugged with <u>bhang</u>, but when she awoke she <u>remembered</u> ...

And for the rest of the remedy she made a China dish of the daintiest sweetmeats that can be made, wherein she had put <u>bhang</u> ...

Then the Caliph crowned a cup, and put therein a piece of <u>Cretan bhang</u> ... So he took it and drank it off, but hardly had it settled in his stomach when his head forewent his heels and he fell to the ground like one slain ...

"Cretan bhang!" said JJ, running his finger along the words, as if taking an impression from braille. "That's got to be it!"

Noel eyed JJ's pudgy forefinger, then his popeyed face. "But bhang is ... hashish."

"Exactly."

Noel nodded. "Thanks, JJ, but I ... I've already ruled that out as a clue."

"Right. I'll keep on looking. Oh, I almost forgot—your mom wants to see you. Sorry for barging in like this, eh?"

"No problem." Noel glanced at Samira, first at her beaming face, then downwards, at the fingers of her left hand. They were entwined with JJ's. He closed his eyes. *No, this cannot be happening* ... He heard voices and knew they were for him, but he heard them as a drowning man hears people on the shore. With a rigid grin and red face he stood there half blind, half deaf, watching their mouths move, filled with a desire to run fast and far.

Chapter 15
Noel's Diary (II)

January 2, 2002. On a Sunday in winter when I was not yet 5, during a game of Remembrance, I told my father about the colliding colours I had in my brain and how hard it was to escape them. He called it a "collideorscape." I liked the sound of this, and we used the code name for years. (It was from Finnegans Wake, I learned later.) I think of this now because I have begun to see my mother's mind as a kind of kaleidoscope as well: the slanted mirrors inside her are reflecting pieces of her past and present—names, faces, events, dreams—which are rotated by some mysterious hand to make new patterns, new connections: her husband's face appears with my name; our neighbour's breast cancer becomes hers; her father returns to life; a dream is confused with reality ... And then the kaleidoscope turns again, and the mirrors create yet another warped view of reality, yet another helter-skelter mosaic.

January 7. Mom walked into the lab as I was kneeling on the floor, picking up pieces of a dropped Erlenmeyer. After looking this way and that, examining all the chemicals and apparatus, she bit her lip, obviously struggling with her emotions. Mom was never one to cry a lot, but now she's doing it almost daily. But this time she kept her composure. She told me, quite sternly, that I was spending too much time in the lab, just as I did when I was a boy, just as my father used to do. She said at this rate I'd never find a girl, never get married.

At bedtime, with this in mind, I recited a poem from the 1890s by Constance Naden, to see if Mom would laugh (she didn't), and to see if she would remember reading it to me (she did):

> *I was a youth of studious mind,*
> *Fair Science my mistress kind,*

Which held me with attraction chemic;
No germs of Love attacked my heart,
Secured as by Pasteurian art
Against that fatal epidemic.

When my daily task was o'er
I dreamed of H_2SO_4
Whilst stealing through my slumbers placid
Came Iodine, with violet fumes
And Sulphur, with its yellow blooms
And whiffs of Hydrochloric Acid ...

After I told Mom the name of the poet for the second time, she said, That's right, you just told me. I guess that little madman inside my head, Al Zeimer, needed to know again.

After she fell asleep I returned to the lab, where I sat, head in hands, thinking about the little madman inside her, the turner of the kaleidoscope. Where did you come from? And why? A creaking sound, as if in answer, made me jump. In her white gossamer nightgown, Mom shimmered through the unlocked door like a ghost. She gave me a big kiss, thanked me for staying with her, said she loved me and would be lost without me. She then slipped away without another word.

January 10. I was talking to Mom tonight, repeating something she had not remembered from five minutes before, and for some reason got close to her ear to say it, as if this would make the message stick. In mid-sentence I stopped, suddenly thinking of the "memory holes" from Orwell's 1984, the slits or openings scattered throughout the rooms and corridors of all the buildings. You simply had to lift up a flap and drop an item in and it would be "whirled away on a current of warm air to enormous furnaces hidden somewhere in the recesses of the building." They were part of a scheme to control the past, to control all records and all human memories—so as to control the future. As I was speaking into Mom's ear, I began to see her memory loss as a war inside her, a dystopian war with enemy soldiers rampaging through the ventricles of her brain, committing acts of sabotage, snipping this and torching that, controlling her by erasing or distorting her memories—so as to control her future. And I realised that my mission was to annihilate these enemy soldiers—with chemical warfare, biological warfare, whatever it takes.

But do I have what it takes? The brains? The courage? For there is fear to conquer too, not of defeat—the odds are so absurdly stacked against me—or even the memory of past defeats, but of friendly fire, of killing the patient with the cure, of the death in ambush that lies in every pill.

January 12. My mother's decline can be measured in acrosses and downs. When she was well, hooked on crosswords in the Globe and Mail, she could do them by leaps and bounds, in unwavering ink capitals. Then I noticed the occasional phantom row—written in invisible ink I madly hoped—then more white squares than capitals, then an orphan word pencilled in here and there with many more around it erased, and finally nothing at all, the newspaper unopened ...

January 14. Mom's been up and down, mostly down, sinking as if from a slow leak. Over the past year, none of Vorta's "smart" drugs—and none of mine—have stopped the plunge, including:

Diphenylhydantoin (Dilantin)	DMAE (DiMethylAminoEthanol)
Lecithin/phosphatidylcholine	Nimodipine (Nimotop)
Piracetam (Nootropil)	Selegiline/l-deprenyl
Vasopressin (Diapid)	Vincamine (Oxicebral)
Vinpocetine (Cavinton)	

So will now try my own combinations, my own counterpoisons. But first I'll have to make some domestic changes—it's simply impossible to look after my mom and work in the lab at the same time.

January 16, 3:20 a.m. Thermometer in the garden wavering around 20 below. And the power has been off for almost six hours. Put a thick Mennonite quilt on Mom, lit 3 candles and read silently as she slept. A story about Ra, the Egyptian sun god who loses his memory and lives forever in a senile haze ...

January 18. Some good news, finally. A message on the answering machine from Mrs. Holtzberger from Home Care, saying that my "application for a subsidised day nurse has been approved." As for the "other issues," they have all been "ironed out at a higher level." By Dr. Vorta, as it turns out! How nice to have friends in high places. Phoned Sancha immediately to see if she was still available. She is. And seems happy to come back. She starts next week.

January 23. In my mailbox at the Psych Dept there was an invitation to a party next week from Jean-Jacques Yelle, who works for Dr. Vorta. Oddly, it's scheduled to begin at precisely "8:02." Not sure what it's all about exactly, but of course I won't go. I'm too busy, I don't know him that well, and I don't function at parties.

January 27. Am trying to get Mom to drink more coffee, instead of tea, because Dr. Vorta says there's evidence it can prevent AD.[40]

February 3. Decided to go to JJ's party after all—at Norval's command. And what an evening! JJ's like a mad apothecary—he has all kinds of magic kits and alchemical philtres and mystical herbs. Legal, apparently. He's quite a character—I thought Norval was going to smother him with a cushion at one point but I think he quite likes him. Samira, I can tell, likes him too. Speaking of Samira, what can I say? She's clever, charming, considerate, attractive. I dreamt about her all night long, I'm ashamed to admit, the same way I used to dream about Heliodora Locke ... I'm sure Sam thinks I'm an idiot and feels sorry for me. But more later. Mom's calling.

Right. Two things I didn't mention: (1) As incredible as it may sound, JJ's place was hit by an arsonist (!?). While we were all there, the four of us, under the influence of various substances. Not too much damage luckily, apart from smoke and water, although JJ's cigar-store Indian was burnt to a crisp. He's now staying with us, temporarily. JJ, not the Indian. (2) I made a discovery— Norval hasn't made love with Samira! Not yet, anyway. I'm going to do something, I have a plan involving the Bath Lady ... But more later. Mom's calling again.

5:15 a.m. A radical downturn, a Lethean fall—Mom's hit rock bottom. Wondering if she'll ever resurface.

February 8. Been working with JJ in the lab. As a partner. Because I need him, I need his kind of mind. With no disrespect intended, he's a kind of idiot savant, a celestial idealist who's playing with a different set of marbles, which is what this project requires. He lets his whims and instincts lead him. He makes the big leap, the mad leap. I'm a literalist, a rationalist, with no feel or flair or intuition. Even though I've got a great memory for facts, I miss things, obvious connections. I'm blind to the miracle.

What's more, JJ's an angel of a man—kind, trusting, non-judgemental, always looking on the bright side (regarding my mom's relapse, he said, "Sometimes a condition must worsen before bettering"). And he has a quality that means more to me than any other: loyalty. He's set up a card table and computer beside my desk, so we share a lot of equipment. He usually talks all the time or whistles, but when he starts surfing or mixing herbal concoctions he shuts up. Sometimes there'll be silence or near-silence for hours, apart from some occasional wind-breaking, or grunting if he's on his headphones, after which we work together, compare notes ... He's interested in everything I do and I'm trying to learn from him, for he's an unbiased, open-minded, knowledgeable man with a heart of Au.

February 9. JJ's started on Mom's insomnia and sundowning. I've taken her off Halderon and given her something JJ made, a frothy infusion he calls an "Earth Shake," a hot brew of German camomile, skullcap, hops, vervain and tincture of wild oats that Mom actually liked. To me it tastes like steamed hay. Last night he gave her a biochemic tissue salt (potassium phosphate, triturated until soluble). And tonight, around ten, he gave her a long massage with mandarin oil, spending five minutes on each of the following reflexology points: 3, 4, 9, 17, 20, 52. (I know the numbers but not what they signify.)

February 10. Mom slept for ten hours! Which she so badly needed. And no wandering, no lamplighting.

February 11. Tonight JJ drew a bath with aromatic marjoram oil, which Mom loved and wouldn't come out of until the water got cold. She now says she wants JJ to prepare her bath from now on, and doesn't want the Bath Lady anymore! But I want to keep Sancha because ... she starts with an S. But it's probably too late. Won't see Norval this week—he cancelled for Tuesday.

February 12. Quiet day. Nothing worth mentioning.

February 14. Inexplicably, Mom is becoming more and more silent so JJ is getting her to talk about her life through her photo albums. He seems to love imagining her past—he peppers her with questions about her childhood and then talks excitedly about his own. Yesterday he found an old tape in her bookcase, a recording my mom and I made of a "play" we'd written together called The Phantasmagorical Phantom of Firenza. We no longer have a reel-to-reel recorder to play it, so JJ went home and got his. And then actually played the damn thing. *Speak, Memorex.* Mom had written her part—a Florentine princess locked in a moated grange—and I had written mine: an occasionally invisible mediaeval knight-wizard who saves her with anachronistic weapons while using big words like "vagaries" and "vicissitudes." Mom laughed and laughed, probably because JJ was rolling on the floor.

February 17. For his first ten days here, JJ spent almost the entire time in the lab, even eating sandwiches down there, which Mom prepares for him in Saran wrap and a lunch bag, like he's going to school. He even drinks hot chocolate out of my old thermos. But now he spends most of his time upstairs—with Mom. Which is fantastic not only because she likes him a lot—she sometimes cries with laughter at his puns and cornballisms—but it gives me more time in the lab, uninterrupted and unworried.

February 18. I've taken the last two nights off. Tonight the three of us had Chinese take-out, rented *Defending Your Life* and *Withnail and I*, ate burnt popcorn and laughed uncontrollably—as we had the night before watching the same movies.

February 19. Mom got up early today, dressed herself elegantly, put on make-up, and was in a great mood all day. She looked totally refreshed—and energised, as if she were about to tango or belly dance at any second. JJ's laughter therapy is obviously kicking in.

Haven't seen Norval in a while. He's cancelled two Tuesdays in a row—and today he just didn't show up. When I phoned him he said he "forgot" we met on Tuesdays. Forgot?

Haven't seen Samira in a while either.

20:02, 20/02, 2002. The palindromic moment has just passed, without fanfare. Everyone, including JJ, seems to have forgotten about it. And about a second meeting.

February 21. Mom was wandering at night again, with her trusty lamp, so JJ prepared something new for her: a maple sugar base with extracts of pennyroyal and rock mint, combined in a decoction of California poppy, Jamaican dogwood and Madagascan periwinkle.

What's strange is that Mom takes whatever medicine JJ and I give her, unquestioningly, like a trusting child. I can only pray her trust is well placed ...

February 24. There are starting to be extraordinary variations in my mother's memory abilities. I'll have to share the information with Dr. Vorta, see what he thinks.

February 26. No matinée today. Couldn't reach Norval all week. He may be out of town. With Samira?

March 1. JJ's memory for jokes seems near-infinite. So much lightness, so much laughter inside his brain—it must be what makes him so ... the opposite of world-weary. Must ask Dr. Vorta about this.

At breakfast, between mouthfuls of Lucky Charms, he reeled off this one: "So I'm talking to this friend of mine and he goes, 'Yup, I'm colour-blind to one colour.' So I ask him what colour he's blind to, and he goes, 'I don't know, I haven't seen it yet.'"

None of his jokes, I grant, are particularly funny (except in their unfunniness or delivery), and this one is no exception. But for some reason, after laughing politely this morning, I've been thinking about it all day. Perhaps because it points to a main difference, or divide, between science and art. Our "rational" side sees the humour of the punchline because it's self-contradictory, absurd, at variance with common sense. Our "artistic" side, however, sees a vein of truth within it—regarding imaginary fears or invisible barriers—because paradox is the currency of poetry. But science has room for paradox as well, as Einstein will tell you. "Don't be in thrall of reason," my father once said, "or you'll never invent anything, never be a great scientist. The pursuit of sanity can be a form of madness too, don't forget."

More later. Mom's calling ...

March 3. Something incredible just happened. Still not sure if I dreamt it. Samira Darwish arrived! Here at the house, well after midnight, out of the blue. The incredible part is that she's now staying here. Heliodora Locke! She said just for one night but I'm hoping for one thousand and one. More later. The sun's about to rise.

March 5. Spent this afternoon, in a daze, at the Osler Library, where Dr. Vorta had reserved some "Restricted" books for me, for on-site consultation only.

Turned out to be a blind alley. Or maybe I was distracted by ... other things. Anyway, when I arrived home, a surprise awaited me. Samira and JJ had made some radical changes—improvements—to the house. Which Norval may have paid for (?!). Tried phoning him today, but no answer, not even from the answering machine. Beginning to worry.

March 6. Didn't see Samira today or yesterday (except briefly last night as JJ and I let off some fireworks for my mom, which left Sam unimpressed, underwhelmed).

TV reenthroned in the family room after I found Mom, in tears, searching for it in the garage with her hunter's lamp.

March 7. Mom had wild, shrieking nightmares last night, so JJ prepared an antidote, a Schuessler Tissue Salt: Natrum sulphorica, 12X. Thank God for JJ. I just don't have time to do this sort of thing. I'm putting in twelve hours now, both in the basement and at Ex Pysch, where Dr. Vorta's been generous with his time and facilities. What would I do without him?

This morning Mom came down and asked me if I had any extra money, just a little bit because she'd like to go shopping. She said a birthday was coming up and she had to buy a gift. Whose birthday is it, Mom? Your Uncle Phil's, she replied. And she was right.

Came up to spend the evening with Mom—JJ went back to his place to work in his hothouse—and she wanted to watch tennis all evening, because her favourite player (despite his headbands) was playing: Roger Federer.[41] *"Federer is getting better-er and better-er," she used to say. In any case, after he won, I was about to turn the TV off because the Friday night blue movie was coming on TVQ. Mom asked me if they are going to show naked men or naked women. I said both. Won't be a tick, she said, I'll just clean my glasses.*

Didn't see Samira today.

March 8. In between quiz shows, a trailer for the movie about Iris Murdoch came on and Mom said, Shh! It's about AD and I want to hear it! Clearly, Mom's getting better. But which drug is responsible? Is it the Hyperzine A, the qian ceng ta, that JJ's been slipping into Mom's tea?

March 9. Have hardly seen Samira at all. We had one great evening together, but that's about it. We pass each other in the house, but nothing more. She's usually out the entire day. At school, or with Norval?

March 10. At two in the morning, when I was sure everyone was asleep, I played my tape of Samira's movie, all the way through. I wanted to check out something. There are colours in her voice, subtle gradations, that I've never heard in real life, only on film. They're velvety and haloed with trivalent vanadium, and I realise now they occur only in her scenes with Stirling Trevanne. They're the sounds of love.

March 11. Watched another quiz show tonight—Mom and I for the first half, then joined for two minutes by ... Samira. She said I should try to be a contestant, that I'd be really good, that I could win some money to keep the house going, and that she'd be really proud of me. She then vanished for the rest of the evening.

March 12. Saw Sam again today—for a few seconds. She looked angry and barely acknowledged me. I'd gone to see Dr. Vorta to give him a copy of my lab notes, which include JJ's concoctions, and on my way out, he introduced me to a fellow synaesthete, a woman from Chicago named Kelly. (I'd seen her several months before, when I blew up in Dr. Vorta's office, but she didn't seem to remember me, or my voice, which goes to show all synaesthetes aren't alike.) Anyway, we talked for a while, laughed a lot, and that's when Samira suddenly emerged and walked right by us without saying a word.

Kelly and I went for a coffee at Café Apollinaire and started talking about American and Canadian accents. She said that Jane Mackay, the British painter, could tell the difference between the two because "the Canadian accent is more yellow." We then compared our alphabets and Arabic numerals. Like me, she assigns a sex to letters and numbers—although hers are quite different and much more detailed.[42] We agreed on the top five most frequent consonant sounds (n, t, d, s, l), but not on their colours. Or on the colours of the days of the week. We disagreed on every one (including her "Ruby Tuesday") except for Wednesday, blue. And the only letter we agreed on was O (white—nearly 50% of synaesthetes see O as white). Anyway, we had a great time. She has a laugh that shimmers, like a credit-card hologram, with bursts of mango orange and cornflower blue.

When Kelly began talking about Dr. Vorta and how much she admired him, I asked her about that time in his office, when I barged in on a spectrograph test, when I saw her half undressed. She said it was all very innocent—while waiting for him she simply decided to change out of her work clothes, because she was going blading later on with her boyfriend …

I walked her to the Champs de Mars métro and was going to ask her if he was still her boyfriend but didn't because that's an adolescent question. What is one supposed to say? Are you attached? Are your affections engaged? "Shall we go for a drink?" I almost said, but I almost say things much more often than I say them. The words just wouldn't come out, stuck to the roof of my mouth like peanut butter. "Bye," I bleated. I then decided to walk all the way home, perhaps to punish myself, which took a good hour. Five minutes in and freezing rain came down in squally gusts. I was shellacked and sopping when I arrived and Mom, just like old times, was very concerned after hearing me coughing and putting her hand against my forehead (I already had some sort of fever, before the storm). Suddenly her memory was restored as she prepared her standard cures—fizzing vitamin C, aspirin, steam inhalation (with a towel, over boiling eucalyptus leaves), chicken soup—while I, at her command, took a hot bath. "Then watch cartoons," she said. "I'll be up in a tick."

As I was closing my curtains a frostbow appeared in the sky, only the second I've seen. Exactly like a rainbow, except that it's a lustrous white. A good auspice? Before I could call out to my mother, or anyone else, it was gone.

March 14. Mom was in great spirits all day; I was quite sick. Not so much from the cold, but from tiredness, numbness. I could barely move. Mom kept asking what she could get me, did I need anything at the drugstore, did I want some chicken soup? In my bedroom, while JJ worked in the basement, we watched Who Wants to Be a Millionaire and Mom shouted out some of the answers (most of them wrong). We then watched a similar show called Tip of Your Tongue, a low-budget satellite channel knock-off. The contestant chose History as his subject, and Mom knew some of the answers, which made her happy. Five minutes before the end, Samira appeared, and watched from the doorway, in a shaft of late afternoon sunlight. She smiled at my mother, and then at me, and the next time I looked she was gone.

4:20 a.m. Can't sleep. Sam left coloured residue in my brain, like a comet trail, that's been burning into my past. Not from her voice colours, but from something she was wearing: a diaphonous off-the-shoulder blouse of the darkest brown. In the light of the sun, mingled with the colour of her flesh, it took on this deep Rembrandtesque brown, with gold leaf and Roman ochre reflections ... The colour of Coca-Cola, almost. A shade I first saw in the summer between kindergarten and first grade, when I mixed all my mom's oil colours together on the stones of our patio. And saw for the second time in the Adirondacks, north of Ticonderoga, when I was with my father on one of his sales trips. He held me on his shoulders under a waterfall as the sun lit up a frothing stream of Coca-Cola...

He drowned in waters not ten minutes away.

March 15. For the past two weeks, after visiting my father's grave, I've been thinking about a skein of "coincidences" that revolve around The Arabian Nights. I've tried to block them out—because they're unscientific, illogical, superstitious—but they've been gnawing away at me like an unkept promise. One. It finally dawned on me where my crossword puzzle/exitless maze dreamscape comes from: from the frontispiece of the Sir Richard Burton translation. How could I not have made this connection before? Two. JJ has a copy of the Galland translation, which I'd never read before. Three. Even though it's a sham, Norval mentions The Arabian Nights as an influence for his Alpha Bet. Four. Samira Darwish comes into my life. Five. At the cemetery, while gazing at my father's tombstone, I calculated the time between my mom's first suspicions of memory loss and the first signs of clear improvement: two years, 9 months. Or ... 1001 days. This is courting madness, I know. JJ's numerology and arcana have contaminated my brain. Still, if I push this one step further—and my dad, after all, said that irrational art and rational science should never be separated—perhaps number six will relate to the memory cure itself. That its ingredients, or the treasure map leading to them, will lie within the pages of The 1001 Nights.

After three tumblers of mulled wine ("plotty" my mom calls it), I recounted all this to JJ—he's the only one I could think of that wouldn't laugh—and he said YES, YES, YES!, jumping up and down and practically soiling himself. He then went to consult my Burton and Lane volumes (the ones that weren't in my room he dragged down from the attic) and began to read them on my bed, scouring them for clues. Why he has to do this in my room, on my bed, I'm not quite sure.

What I didn't tell him is that I already have a hunch about the clue, based on the fact that Norval, JJ and I are all—quite likely—in love with Samira. There's a similar triangle in "Prince Ahmed and Fairy Pari Banou," in which the Sultan's three sons—Ali, Houssain and Ahmed—are all in love with their father's ward, Princess Nouronnihar. To determine who should be the bridegroom, the sultan sends them out to find "the most extraordinary things" they can. Whoever brings back the rarest object will win the hand of the princess. So, Ali finds an ivory tube with a glass that will show any object he wishes to see. Houssain finds a magic carpet that will transport him wherever he wants to go. Ahmed finds an artificial apple, the scent of which will cure any illness. As they display their gifts, Houssain, looking through the tube, sees the princess, apparently on the point of death. They all jump on his magic carpet and are whisked to her bedroom, where Ahmed uses his magic apple to revive her ...

Now, Norval has a telescope, and he wrote about a "magic" telescope in his novel, so he's <u>Ali</u>. I'm working on a cure, so I'm <u>Ahmed</u>. Which means that JJ has to be <u>Houssain</u>. I'll have to ask him about a magic carpet ...

March 17. Just read yesterday's entry. Was I drunk? Of course I didn't ask JJ about a magic carpet. Am I losing it? No, because today I realised something: that all this toil and quest is folly, that <u>I will never succeed</u>, that my mother, like all Alzheimer patients before her, will worsen and die.

March 18. Spent all morning, afternoon and part of the evening downstairs, poring over a quartet of translations of The Arabian Nights, stopping only when I could no longer see the words. What was I doing? An undoable jigsaw, with half the pieces missing, of a fucking polar bear in a snowstorm.

I stared at the wall and emptied my mind, waiting for ... what? For a ghost to come and touch me? For Dad to whisper a clue in my ear from the beyond?

A knock on the door. Samira delivering me from madness and delusion with potent drink and her even more potent presence.

March 20. Feverish again, with burning eyes and ears and a tremor in my cheeks. I am in a bad way.

Haven't seen JJ and Sam holding hands again, or signs of trysts or anything like that. Not that I'm looking, not that it matters. I wish them well.

March 23. Spent the last three days, every second, in my basement oubliette. Even slept there, dozing off and on like a sentinel drunk at his post. I don't want to see anyone. Fever now blazing its way into my brain—at the convict hour between 4 and 5 I stepped outside, into a blizzard, hatless and bootless, in that unreal clarity that comes from a lack of sleep and sustenance, chanting "alkahest, alkahest ..."

7:09 a.m. A ray of light has pierced the gloom. I finally found the clue. It wasn't in Lane or Burton or Payne but in JJ's edition, in Galland's "The Sleeper and the Awakener":

She went quickly to a druggist's shop, and asked of him a drug often administered to men when diseased with forgetfulness. Without a word he ground up blossoms of Aleppine jasmine and Damascene nenuphar, bulbs of poet's narcissus and rootstalks of curcuma, seeds of club moss and stems of amaranth ...

March 26. Spent last three days checking out the phytochemical structures of each. Three, possibly four, may be worth a shot, particularly in combination: narcissus, which is already used in the AD palliative Galantamine; club moss (JJ's qian ceng ta or Hyperzine A); curcuma (turmeric), whose polyphenols may protect the brain from lipid peroxidation and scavenge nitric oxide-based free radicals; and amaranth, whose stems and roots contains colloidal carbohydrates similar to those in apple pectin, which eliminate toxic metals that likely contribute to dementia. A desperate, pathetic long-shot—but what the hell. When combined, at least on paper, the chemical equations line up beautifully, almost a work of art.

March 29. A sea-change in Mom's condition. She finished the crossword puzzle in the Globe and Mail—something she hasn't done in over two years. JJ said he didn't help her and I believe him. Might be on the verge of something ... Something that works almost immediately, like an intravenous drug.

March 30. A major and minor relapse. My wonder drug may not be so wonderful. Not performing as I hoped it would. Dr. Vorta extremely sceptical. "Lucid intermissions are not uncommon," he says. I've thought of something else, a simple fix, but won't say anything now because I don't want to jinx it.

April 1. Good signs the past two days. Including this morning. While reading the newspaper at breakfast, Mom told me she has totally recovered, remembers everything and is going back to teaching full-time. April Fool's, she added.

April 3. Think I've found it. A memory pill I've provisionally called Nepenthe-Amaranth-56.[43] It'll need months—years—of animal testing and development, but I will not wait. We have neither months nor years to spare.

April 5. Finally got hold of Norval. And even asked him about The Alpha Bet. On target, he said. I asked what letter he was on. "None of your business. But if you must know—the plural letter. A bit of a stumbling block, that." The plural letter! Is that possible? With a deadline in 5 weeks. Is he stalling because he's in love with Samira? I didn't ask, naturally. In any case, I've more important things to worry about.

April 6. Mom in a great mood all day, Sam in a bad. JJ as joyful as ever. More later. Still madly tinkering.

April 9. My mind feeling viscous and slow, like mucilage. No, more like the motor of a car that's been to Mexico and back—no stops, 24-hour ignition. So today took a break—for the first time in 2 months, Nor and I met for our matinée. While waiting for the film to start he made a strange confession. Indirectly. JJ, it seems, has been "pestering" him for a couple of Top Ten Lists (poetry—one in English, one in French, no particular order). He wouldn't reveal his French list, but—astonishingly—he gave me his English:

> *Rochester, "Song" ("Love a woman? You're an ass!")*
> *Larkin, "Aubade" and "The Old Fools"*
> *Lord Byron, "Don Juan" and "Darkness"*
> *Delmore Schwartz, "Calmly we walk through this April's day"*
> *Donne, "Go Catch a Falling Star" or "Woman's Constancy"*
> *MacNeice, "Sunlight on the Garden"*
> *Dante Rossetti, "Without You"*
> *Dowson, "Cynara"*

Fair enough. Except for the fact they're weren't all Decadent or Symbolist, no real surprises—except for the last two or three. Laments for dead lovers.[44] Which is what his novel is about, more or less. And there was a strange look on his face when he mentioned them, as if he were trying to confide in me. Must get to the bottom of this. But not now—have more important things to do.

April 10. Can't focus. Completely blocked. So spent the day at the McLennan library memorising passages of Arabic literature and language. Why? Because last week at the lab Samira seemed dazzled by Norval's "knowledge" of Arabic (which is three bloody phrases at most, two of them lewd). Pathetic, I know. But I had to get my head out of the dungeon anyway.

Dr. Vorta called after supper. He wants to do a "revolutionary" experiment on me, with a trans-magnetic stimulator of his own invention. It sounds a bit dangerous to me, but I trust him. He said it's to study my synaesthesia, but when I told Norval about it over the phone, he said the experiment was designed to eliminate it! Which naturally I don't want—I'm afraid my memory could go along with it.

April 15. Mom's excited—next month Norval's going to try to get on one of her favourite shows, Tip of Your Tongue. (I refused.) She can hardly wait. It's a horrible show really—amateurish sets, fake applause, a Vegas emcee with a toupée and girdle, etc. The studio's in Montreal North, in an industrial plaza. It's considered camp by university students, maybe because it comes on Friday at midnight and has the odd "X-rated" question. The top prize, in any case, is fifty grand. But no one has gone all the way yet, which is unusual for a show that's been on the air for two years. They've made the final rounds extraordinarily difficult, almost impossibly difficult. So most contestants quit while they're ahead, take the money and run. In any case, it's a bit of a long-shot for Norval even to get selected as a candidate. We're all going to cheer him on. JJ said Dr. Vorta is going to try to make it as well.

April 21. Still can't focus in the lab. Totally zoned out. Had a good week in late March but the days since have been foggy and downhill.

April 23. With the hope of unblocking, met Norval again for the matinée. For Shakespeare's birthday they were showing Brook's King Lear. The last acts always hit me hard—too sad for words—but today they were simply crushing. I tried to stop the tears, tried to hide them from Norval, but couldn't. It was these lines that got me going:

I fear I am not in my perfect mind.
Methinks I should know you, and know this man;
Yet I am doubtful; for I am mainly ignorant
What place this is; and all the skill I have
Remembers not these garments; nor I know not
Where I did lodge last night ...
Be your tears wet? Yes, faith. I pray weep not.
If you have poison for me, I will drink it ...

April 27. Finally got a kind of clarity, a view from another realm, for twenty-six hours straight. Where there were walls there are now doors. Decided not to give up on the NA-56, even if Vorta and the leagued universe are against me. Made one small addition and one small subtraction, epiphanically, like a sacred sculptor. Result: it began to take on the faintest of scents ... of green apple.

Chapter 16
Samira's Diary

February 4/02

Left Norval today. Or rather, left his loft for other accommodations ... I was a roommate in January, nothing more. We barely saw each other.

The few times we were together he ignored me, either reading or maniacally playing bow & arrows, or should I say "practising his archery." With his Turkish & Mongol bows—made by some Hungarian "master bowyer" ... Phoom, thwack, phoom, thwack ... Usually in the bull's eye, like Robin Hood. Or through an apple, like William Tell.[45]

The whole time I was in a period of chastity, and lust. Norval has this force field, this presence—like some being who's visited heaven & hell & brought back the best of both. Worst of both? It was so frustrating being around him, listening but not being listened to, at the altar of his ego. He has a knack for making anything I say sound stupid far in advance of my saying it. I felt like a bug, something that could be stepped on without notice. I was an S, for God's sake, nothing more! When I told him I wouldn't be part of his vile game, wouldn't be another name flamed, placed in the kill files, that was it. He never came on to me again. After that he just looked at me with subwayish blankness, listened to me as though he wouldn't care if I hanged myself from his candelabra.

February 5

Now living with Ted, an old (Platonic) friend from high school. He's a tech-crash victim who used to have money to burn. Already, after one day together, I think there could be problems. Among other things, he talks about mutual funds, endlessly.

I would've made love with Norval—if he'd cancelled the Bet. Because of what he said about killing himself after Z. I mean, if he's remotely serious, then I can hardly help him on his way to Z, can I ...

208

But maybe he's simply out of my class—too much intelligence, too much beauty (his body would've satisfied the standards of Michelangelo himself). And what is my class? "Almost average" in his words.

February 6

Ted beginning to stare at me, continuously. In some cultures breasts are considered something for babies to be interested in, not grown men.

February 7

I know it's stupid, self-destructive, but I just can't stop thinking about Norval, hoping—for what? Love, affection? A phone call? Why am I so bloody duncical? Isn't it only men who fall for physical beauty & are blind to everything else?

Stirling looked great, but in conversation seldom rose above the sound-bites expected of celebrities. After him I swore that actors & artists were out—they don't know who the hell they are, and make those around them feel the same way. It's all vanity & ego, they're walking & talking pathological disorders, usually in co-dependent relationships with a therapist or mother or ex-girlfriend. And now I'm being sucked back into all that … Am I one of those who get as much excitement from looming disasters as others from looming success?

Does Norval have anything else besides beauty? Yes. He can be shockingly funny, sharp-witted. (But so much thought & so little feeling! Wit is the salt of conversation, as they say, not the food.) And although he hates humans, he loves animals. His dream, he said, is to go on an African safari and shoot elephant poachers.

February 13

Things getting to the up-to-here point with Ted. And especially with his bubble-head girlfriend "Galaxy." But don't know where else to go. Almost no money left. Thank God for Dr. Vorta.

February 20

JJ's magic "palindrome" day. Everyone seems to have forgotten about it—& about the club's second meeting—& I didn't do any reminding. Norval wouldn't have come anyway—plus our clubhouse is out of commission. I miss those guys, I really do, but doubt I'll ever see them again, socially at least.

February 21

When Ted isn't talking about pork futures or telling mind-numbing golf stories, he's coming on to me. Plus his girlfriend & I don't exactly see eye to eye. She's giving me little hints that she wants me out—like last night, when she screamed at me to leave her boyfriend alone (?!), and this morning when she suggested I'd be "much happier" somewhere else.

February 22

Ran into JJ in the Ex-Psych elevator! Really happy to see him. He was bringing Vorta a coffee & doughnut. (I thought JJ was a research assistant, but it looks like he's a gopher, a gruntworker) Anyway, he set the tray down on the floor, gave me a huge hug & then asked me something very strange—to "help out" Noel & his mother, who has some sort of memory problem. He couldn't remember Noel's phone number but he wrote down his address for me. I didn't know what to say as I took it, just said I'd think about it. I mean, what can I do to help? I know almost nothing about these things.

March 3

Galaxy went ballistic last night—she thinks I'm sleeping with Ted. Because she counted condoms & didn't get the figure she was expecting . (I didn't tell her that Ted's sleeping with someone else.) Anyway, she ended up throwing all my stuff onto the street—some of it, anyway. At one in the morning! Into a bloody snowbank!! I managed, by some miracle, to flag a cab & was on my way to my mom's, rooting around for loose change in my purse, when I came across Noel's address. Destiny? Unlikely, but I decided to go to his place anyway, then & there, unannounced— ridiculously late at night, in a snowstorm! Plus it was a cheaper cab ride. If I see a light on, I said to myself, I'll stop. I saw a light on.

My embarrassment needle was off the scale at first, but I calmed down and Noel & I ended up talking for hours. Really for the first time. He's a very strange man—and fascinating. I can see why Norval likes him so much. He's gentlemanly & courteous in an old-fashioned way & a really kind soul, very warm & gentle, the kind of man I adore but am not attracted to—it's a disease, I think, a genetic impairment that will probably ruin my life.

Noel's life seems to be on hold while he looks after his mother. Although he's got a great memory, he seems to have forgotten about himself.

It was so weird talking to Noel about everything—about my "former life." But I had to, because he dropped a bombshell! He guessed my secret!! From my "voice colours." But I asked him not to tell anyone & for some reason I know he won't.

What I didn't tell him about was the abortion. Which may have been the real reason Stirling lost his mind. And for my mother to hate me. It's a black zone that's off limits to everyone. Maybe because it brings on this awful gut feeling, this nightmarish warning from a crystal ball: THAT I'LL NEVER GET PREGNANT AGAIN.

Sterling once told me I wasn't good for men. That I was like a contagion, a retrovirus that gets into them & makes them sick . . .

March 5

While Noel was at the library, I spent all day with JJ, shopping & cleaning up the house & making adjustments that will make it easier for Stella to function—some of the things I've learned in class and from Dr. Vorta. Anyway, we laughed all day, about totally silly things. JJ's like joy medicine. Despite having a few . . . idiosyncrasies, shall we say. For example, he's a compulsive butt-clencher—clench-release-clench-release, hundreds of times a day— walking down the hall, making lunch, talking to Mrs. Burun. It's hard to look at anything else. You find yourself counting, tapping your toes and, if you're not careful, squeezing right along with him.

March 7

Got to see Noel interact with his mom today. From a distance, kind of eaves-dropping. I could learn a few things from him—he's patient, attentive, warm . . . Every night, according to JJ, he reads to her, every night he fills in gaps in her forgotten life. Last night, at her request, he & JJ made these incredible fireworks & set them off in the back yard. His mother watched them like a little girl, totally spellbound. (JJ was like a little boy, literally jumping up & down.) It's so nice seeing Noel & his mom together, the way they smile, touch, communicate without words. Wouldn't mind having that kind of relationship with my mother. With anyone.

Better stop here, starting to sound like Pollyanna.

March 8

Things are working out well. School is good, living here is good. Haven't seen much of Mrs. Burun because I've been at school or the library—making up for missed classes! Haven't seen Noel either, who's down in the cellar most of the time. My only regret is that I'm not helping his mother very much, as I promised to do . . .

March 10

I suspect—no, I know—that Noel has feelings for me. And I hardly needed my woman's intuition to figure that one out. I better be careful—he's the last person I want to hurt.

Would that be remotely possible? A relationship with Noel? No, simply not in the cards, ever. (1) I'm besotted by his best friend. (2) He's "unmanageably weird," as Nor says, with too many problems—I have more than enough of my own, thank you very much. (3) I don't need any more men in co-dependent relationships with their mothers. (4) I'm not attracted to "nice guys," unfortunately, never have been & never will be. (5) I'm not good enough for him—I'm hardly the saint he thinks I am.

March 11

I think JJ's good for Noel, seeing things that Noel is sometimes blind to—like the guy who sees all the engineers futzing with a broken machine and realizes that no one has thought to plug it in. Today they were down in the lab all day, so I ended up spending the entire time with Noel's mom. She's a wonderful woman, very elegant & refined & beautiful—especially after I did her hair & helped her select some things to wear! Diane Von Furstenberg & Kate Spade classics. She looked fabulous! Fifty-six going on thirty-six. I learned quite a bit about her from going through her albums & books. She's an historian—or was—and even wrote bios on Hypatia of Alexandria & Ada Byron, Countess Lovelace (which I've borrowed, because I hadn't heard of either one).

March 12

Haven't seen Noel in a while. It's like he's avoiding me, or angry with me. For not doing enough around the house? Maybe he's just not interested in me, in the way I thought he was. Or maybe he's just too busy, too obsessed with his work downstairs. Or maybe he's got a new girlfriend. Or maybe I'm paranoid ...

March 13

That new girlfriend may be the "Bath Lady". A merry divorcée with flamenco-red lipstick, plunging neckline & huge, seemingly inflatable breasts, which she practically engulfs him with every time they hug/meet. She's been coming on to him for months, according to his mom. They seem to have a certain intimacy ... I've found notes she's written—pointless Post-Its regarding his mom with X's or hearts at the end. Not that it's any of my business, but I don't think she's right for Noel, and I don't think she should get her (long & painted) claws into him. It may be my imagination, but she seems to be treating the house as if it will one day be hers. In any case, with JJ & I here, she's really no longer needed. And it's not like they can afford her.

For the second time, I walked by as Noel & his mom were watching some quiz show on TV, and wanted to join them. But from the way they looked at me, I felt like an intruder, disrupting their privacy.

Spent a great evening with Noel down in the lab, drinking some volcanic brew that JJ concocted & chatting about everything under the sun. Including some of the things Noel has had to endure in life—the "personality disorders" that got him certified as "disabled" when he was sixteen. Like a fear of leaving his house on his own, of being in the presence of others, which could hit him like "blinding sunlight." But he's worked on his problems—with medications, therapy & mind-over-matter—& now he's more or less OK. Except for worrying about his mom and not eating or sleeping.

When our evening ended, after JJ dropped in, Noel glanced down & saw JJ & I holding hands. Which JJ does all the time, even with Mrs. B, like a little boy instinctively grabbing his mother's hand. Still, it was awkward & I felt like taking my hand away. But I didn't. Maybe because I wanted to get a reaction from Noel. Was there one? No. None whatsoever.

Suddenly I'm quite happy, believe it or not. I'm learning a lot, enjoying my art therapy courses, staying rent-free in a beautiful room with a view of the mountain & cemetery ... and I think I'm in love with three men! Has that ever happened in history?

Haven't seen Noel in days. He's back to locking himself away downstairs, rarely coming up for air. And with JJ spending more time with Mrs. B, I'm starting to get a bit lonely. I just don't feel like seeing my loopy friends anymore, my bar-hopping, pill-popping rutting friends in ruts. (The only difference between a rut & a grave, says Norval, is the depth.) God love 'em, but it's like I've turned the page on all that. I've wasted <u>way</u> too much time & money on drugs—& I'm even starting to blame myself for that date-rape attempt. Because when I arrived at the party I was already blitzed on various illegal substances, which left me wide open. Dr. Rhéaume said that line of thinking is "backwards & counterproductive."

Took a stab at phoning Norval—had all the numbers punched in but hung up before it rang. Then hit my mom's speed dial. She seemed happy to hear from me, and even happier to answer questions about recipes from the restaurant. I'm going to see her on the weekend—her suggestion, believe it or not.

Sunday dinner with Mom went fairly well, all things considered. No screaming, at least. We even talked like friends for a change—not exactly like we used to, but it's a start. On my way out the door, out of the blue, she hit me with an Arab proverb: "Never marry a man who dislikes his mother. He will end up disliking you."

Got sick today. A groggy kind of nauseous exhaustion. Maybe from school or from something Dr. Vorta gave me for one of his studies … Noel & JJ were darlings the whole time. They both came up with "meals on wheels" & when I started to feel better they read poems or stories to me—Noel off the top of his head (a tale from The Arabian Nights about a sultan & his three sons), and JJ childhood poems from battered old books—nonsense poems which made me laugh, mostly out of seeing him in hysterics, wiping tears from his face.

JJ is a dream. He just gave me a kit, a get-well present that must have cost a fortune. I was jumping up & down & hugging him in my bedroom when Noel walked by. But before we could show it to him, he ran right down to the basement!

Anyway, when I offered to pay for it, JJ said Dr. Vorta owed him a favour—and gave it to him for nothing!! It's called a Neuro-Art Therapy Kit. It comes in a big binder which converts to an easel. Which I just opened up. There's a 12-pack of pastels & a CD with exercises for Memory & Attention, there's computer games & therapeutic drawing exercises for improving "traumatic brain injury, stroke, learning problems, sensory integration, Alzheimer's dementia, memory problems, visual spatial problems and sensory difficulties." What a sweetheart JJ is! Must remember to ask him to marry me.

JJ says he's developing a "revolutionary" new kind of cigarette, a healthy replacement for tobacco. But not to tell Noel.

Got a visit today at the lab from … guess who? The alpha male, the über-cool dandy lion of the boulevards, for whom the belles toil—Monsieur Blaquière.

Surprise, surprise. He didn't say anything terribly nasty. In fact, he said he heard I was sick and asked if I was feeling better. I tried to remain as nonchalant as he was, which was hard because my mind was as steady as a drunkard's piss-line and my heart was doing backward somersaults and I ended up spilling Maxwell House all over my chest. But then, after he left, I was surprised at how I felt—I was actually relieved that he was gone!!

April 12

Incredibly, miraculously, Mrs. B seems back to normal! Like the magician's assistant who enters the casket and comes out the other side, transformed. She's smiling & joking & her short-term memory is back!! Most of the time, anyway. Everyone has played a role, says Noel, but warns there's still a long way to go.

The only problem now is ... Noel. He looks like he's been rolling around in a dingy dryer for weeks. His hands and clothes are stained with chemicals and he's haggard and gaunt, with bags under his eyes like bruises. As far as I can tell, he's stopped eating, except for soda biscuits—though I once caught him gorging and gobbling everything in the fridge like a famished dog. He's heading for a major crash, I'm almost sure. What's strange, eerie, is that with the lost pounds he's starting to look more and more like... Norval.

April 13

Noel seems in much better spirits. He's spending less time in the lab, & going out more. I wonder where? He could be seeing that American girl I saw him talking to at the lab, the synaesthete with the heart-shaped neckline. They laughed like hyenas together. And she kept flipping her hair back & letting her skirt hike up when she sat down. Or maybe he's out with the Bath Lady. Who the hell cares?

April 14

Art therapy classes going well. Getting straight A-minuses. After years of aimlessness, of turnstiling through bars and no-future jobs, I think I've finally found something I want to do! Am now using Mrs. B as a guinea pig. She's done six paintings so far & they're all superb! She's really talented & should have her own exhibition one day. If I had any initiative or willpower, which I don't, I'd try to arrange it. Is it possible that her memory disorder has made her more creative? In a great guest lecture last week, Dr. Vorta mentioned that this kind of thing—creative outbursts—was possible, that FTD (frontotemporal dementia) can have this effect. That damage to one side of the brain (the left) may liberate the other side. Or something like that.

215

Speaking of Vorta (who's getting a tad frisky, shall we say, in our lab sessions), I asked Stella about him, trying to find out if there was any truth to what Norval said, about Vorta having an affair with her, about him causing her husband's suicide. But she had nothing bad to say about him at all. On the contrary. She said he was a close friend of her husband's, practically a guardian angel to her son, a brilliant scientist, etc, etc. I should've let it go at that. But in my prying way I actually came out & asked her, point blank, if she had an affair with him. She laughed. And then said, with a wink: "Oh, he was after me all right. A very persistent man." While your husband was alive? I asked. "No, except for a bit of harmless flirting, it started long after that. But he stopped, very suddenly." Stella stopped here herself, which was probably a cue for me to mind my own business. Why did he stop? I asked. Stella paused, bit her lip. "Well, he came over to the house one evening, on some absurd man-like pretext, & handed me an envelope, which he insisted I open then & there. Which I did, feeling quite anxious, even frightened. Inside was a letter full of stiff, scientific-sounding phrases & a poem he composed himself ... It was a love letter. And, well, that was the end of that." Again Stella gave me a look, a discreet look that said "I've gone far enough." And? I said. Why was that the end of that? Stella again hesitated, looking me in the eye for several seconds, perhaps wondering if she could trust me. "I guess because, no matter how hard I tried, I just couldn't stop laughing ... "[46]

April 16

Am starting to like the Bath Lady. A lot. Feel <u>terrible</u> for ever wanting to get her fired.

April 17

Beautiful sunny day. A real spring day. Sat out front listening to Arcade Fire and The Dears, over and over like a preteen. On Noel's discman. JJ went back to his place & returned with a bag of equipment: knee pads, elbow pads, helmets. I thought he was going to invite me out but no such luck. He & Stella laughed like maniacs as they put it all on, to the sounds of Avril Lavigne's "Sk8er Boi" on JJ's ghetto blaster. Then they went out blading! I watched them from the living-room window, as they careened madly through puddles & slush holding hands & collapsing into each other's arms.

The Bath Lady—Sancha, I should say—arrived as I was watching them & I asked her if she'd seen Noel around. She said no. She then said, out of the blue, that I should marry him (!?)

April 21

Semester over. Exams over. Fingers crossed.

April 22

Made couscous today—spent all day on it—& ended up eating it alone. JJ & Mrs. B went to a play at the Centaur and Noel, while timing something with a stop-watch downstairs, nerved on coffee & eyes blackly circled, said he wasn't hungry. "Food dulls the senses," he mumbled cyborgly, "and slows the mind."

So after a few riveting games of solitaire, I took Mrs. B's bicycle out & rode blindly round the neighbourhood like a backward six-year-old, arriving home in darkness, my clothes soaked in sweat.

April 23

Pelting rain outside, the wind playing some old instrument, like a crumhorn or sackbut or something, on the loose drainpipes. Shakespeare's birthday today, maybe that's why. I was going to ask Noel out to celebrate, but he zipped past me on his way out to his sacred "matinée" with Nor. (Naturally, he would never think of inviting me.) He mumbled something about "finding out Nor's secret", whatever that means.

While JJ & Stella were downstairs, roller-blading up & down the halls to Steppenwolf's "Magic Carpet Ride," I was lying on Noel's bed—don't ask me why—when I got a flash, a memory flash! About what happened that night I was slipped the GHB. I was at a party all right, but not when I woke up. I was in a _lab_ (!?!)

Chapter 17
Noel & Norval (II)

After *King Lear*, at a bistro across from the theatre, Noel sat at a table heaped with skeletal remains: chicken bones and mussel shells, potato skins and baguette heels, on and off the plate, a-swim in beer, wine, coffee, ketchup. On a saucer a forgotten cigarette was smoking itself. As he was sheepishly trying to draw the waitress's attention to all this, someone approached the table. A busboy? No, a nondescript man with a laptop, who seemed to know Dr. Vorta. He spoke slowly and clearly, as if he knew all about Noel's coloured hearing, repeating things twice and three times. His pansy-purple voice stretched and unstretched like a trampoline, sprinkling gunpowder green on the higher notes.

After two or three minutes of one-way conversation, Noel spotted Norval coming out of the men's room. From the opposite direction came a large man in Stygian black leather, who planted himself in Norval's path. He had a spindly ponytail, unibrows, and a drooping moustache like a seal. An angry seal.

"You're not going to move, I take it," he heard Norval say.

"I never make way for assholes," said the man in slithery squid-brown tentacles.

"No? I always do," said Norval, stepping aside, allowing the man to pass.

The gentleman with the laptop, when he saw Norval heading his way, gathered up his things and fled, as if Vikings had landed.

Norval watched the man turn tail. "Who *is* that guy, anyway? That ponce with the laptop and billowy trousers. Of the kind worn by pan-talooned palace eunuchs. He's been pestering me for weeks." After a quick glance at the table, he summoned a waitress twenty yards away with a kingly head-jerk.

"He's a ... ghostwriter, an as-told-to-ist. His name's Geoff something. He's doing something for Memento Vivere."

"Volta's vanity press? What's he doing? A hagiography for its editor-in-chief?"

As the unsmiling waitress cleared the table, deftly emptying things into a bucket, Noel glanced at the gentleman in question. He was sitting at a table half-hidden by a pillar, pushing buttons on a tiny machine. "He ... well, he asked me to keep it quiet."

"He's not doing that product-placement novel is he? For Vorta? In which everyone sits around drinking Maxwell House coffee?"

"I don't think so."

"Vorta's memoirs?"

"Something like that."

"Memoirs," said Norval, shaking his head. "The favourite genre of people who never had a memorable thought."

"Come on, Nor. There are lots of—"

"Has-beens with imaginations so barren they can't write fiction. And memories so barren they can't write the truth.

Noel again glanced over his shoulder. And got a better look at the machine the man was fiddling with: a mini-CD-R recorder.

"His fees must be as paltry as his writing skills," said Norval, "if he's working for that dwarfish quack."[47]

"Why has he been 'pestering' you?"

"He wants permission, for some reason, to publish a chapter of my novel. Which he'll never get. He was also harassing Sam last week. I think he's in love with her."

Noel furrowed his brow. "It was JJ who got him the job. After Vorta fired two other writers."

"For telling the truth? So this hack hiding behind the pillar is a last resort?"[48]

Here a woman, an underdressed platinum-haired woman with breasts padded to videogame dimensions, stopped at the table. When Norval rose, as if to embrace her, she began poking a finger into his chest, her voice rising from twenty to seventy decibels. As her anger grew her words became less and less comprehensible, almost a foreign tongue. She began to sob and moan as her body heaved. Norval observed her, with shocking unflappability. "Be back in a second," he said as he escorted the hysterical woman outside.

Noel watched the two through the window, as in a pantomime, as Norval evidently sorted things out. The woman was no longer crying; she was kissing his fingers. Noel shook his head. If she knew what acts those hands had committed, she might think twice before lifting them to her lips. She was now walking away—calmly, even contentedly by the way she glanced back at him. Why do women bother? Surely it's not a turn-on, surely the truism is not true: that women, and beautiful women in particular, are drawn to men who remain aloof from them, or wipe their shoes on them ...

Norval returned to the table with a dangling cigarette in his mouth and two drinks in one hand. "There should be a pound where you can leave people like that. With anaesthetists. And cages."

Noel wasn't listening. He was brooding over the same things he was brooding over when he arrived at the bar. Samira. Her love for Norval. Her attempts to understand him. Norval's feelings for her. Norval's capacity for love. He described the sentiment in his novel, realistically, poignantly. And Dowson's "Cynara," he had confessed, was on his Top Ten list. But how to approach all this? He took a sip of the beer that Norval had placed in front of him.

"I don't understand you," he said finally.

"In general, or with reference to some particular?"

"When you say you've never been in love."

Norval took a gulp of his Irish whiskey. "Which word escapes your understanding?"

"I don't understand the concept. I'm convinced you're lying. Are you?"

"Never felt less inclined to. Love exists for only one reason—to spread the genes of the person doing the loving. It may boil down to a chemical called oxytocin. Do you know it?"

"Well ... yes."

"I am thus unable to love one woman. But quite able—compelled, in fact—to love hundreds."

"When you say 'love,' you mean 'have sex with.' But why hundreds? Why so many?"

"Because the best moments of a relationship occur at the *beginning*, when you're deluded by infinite possibilities. The middle and end is a lemming-walk."

"But have you ever even reached the middle?"

Norval waved the question away with his cigarette, obscuring it in a cloud of smoke. "And because there comes a time in everyone's life when some serious arithmetic has to be done—comparing the sum of pleasures life has left to offer versus the sum of pain. And this comparison leads, at a certain age, for those that have the guts, to suicide. So before I get there I'll do the one thing that gives pleasure, while I still can."

Noel shook his head. He'd heard this sophistry before. "But it must be so ... unsatisfying. Not to get to that final stage. To commitment, marriage, a happy ending ..."

"Happy ending? Have you been paying attention? It's happy for me when the beginning and end are rolled up in the first encounter."

"... and the whole thrilling process of falling in love. Which is the closest most of us will come to glimpsing utopia."

"Oh, please. Sex and drugs give much better glimpses. Noel, you're a spectacularly easy faller-in-love, and what good has it done you? Let's put this romantic crap to bed. The world is not like *Romeo and Juliet*, with random arrows flung by Cupid. Romantic love is a Darwinian trick that blinds us to each other's flaws. Falling in love. Falling implies that you were once at a stable position, at a higher point than before. I prefer the stabler, higher position."

"But didn't you say—at JJ's party—that you enjoyed falling? 'Savouring the aesthetics of descent' and all that?"

Norval arched an eyebrow while tapping redundantly on his cigarette. He was unused to logical ambush and surprised by its incidence. "I was ... we're talking about two different metaphors."

Noel smiled. "Maybe you've just been unlucky, Nor, the right dart hasn't hit you. Cupid shoots darts of lead and gold, remember, for false and true love. You've been getting lead, that's all. Don't give up hope."

Norval rolled his eyes. "Another hope fiend. The hope of true love is haunted by mortality."

"Children help you get around that."

"Children? Children are instruments of torture. I share Byron's view: 'No virtue yet, except starvation, could stop that worst of vices—propagation.'"

Noel had tuned out completely; he was thinking of Samira, of what it would be like to have a child with her ...

"Have you flown recently?" Norval continued. "Babies should not be allowed on board. Can't they be Fed-Exed? Or doped and put in cages with the pets? Noel? Are you with me?"

Noel was not. "Yes, I ... I was just thinking." The idea of fathering Samira's child was not the only thing that held his thoughts; he had a burning question for Norval, one that he'd been planning to ask since he first sat down. How best to phrase it? He had asked the same question

221

of JJ, who had answered no; he had asked a similar question of Sam, who had also answered no. How would Norval respond? Seconds passed before his lips stopped moving. "Norval, what letter ... are you ... in love with Samira?" At least this was what he intended to say, more or less. The first part of the question was faint and garbled, the last spoken at quadruple speed. Sweat surged from all pores and red fire burned on his cheeks.

"Was that English? Are you all right, Noel? In violent fevers, I'm told, people have been known to talk in ancient tongues."

"Are you in love with Samira?"

Norval held a freshly lit cigarette over an ashtray, seemed to examine the bent butts left by his predecessors. He then noticed his friend's expression and for a second softened. "No, I'm not."

Noel heard the words over the thundering of his heart. And yet felt not an ounce of relief! What difference does it make whether he is or not? What difference does it make to *me*? A pawn in love with a queen. Tin in love with Iridium. She probably has enough suitors to fill an iPod. "But what I don't ... you know, understand is ... It's just that everybody ... or almost everybody ..."

"Spit it out, Noel."

Noel drew a huge breath into his lungs, unsure of where he was going with this and why. "It's just that everybody has at least one love in their life ... or a memory of one. Samira has one, JJ has one, my mother has one, and I—"

"Well *I* don't."

"But ... but no one could write *Unmotivated Steps* without having felt mad, blind love."

"I was barely out of my teens when I wrote that drivel. And besides, it was a romantic parody."

"The critics didn't see it that way."

"The *critics*? The critics praised the weakest parts of the weakest chapters, and were obtuse to everything else."

Noel scratched at his beer label, recalling something he and Samira had talked about. "We ... I have a theory about you—would you like to hear it?"

"No."

"It's not really a theory. It's more like a feeling or hunch—it's not a fully thought-out position—"

"Get on with it for Christ's sake."

"Your life has been ... well, martyred to a single memory. Because of what happened to you as a child—when your mother cheated on your dad, when she left him for that rich old man—"

"My father was rich too."

"You've been looking ever since for an antidote in affairs, an antidote to the pain of ... well, losing your mother that day. But since you're unconsciously seeking a mother rather than a mistress, all women disappoint you."

Norval nodded. "Noel, something is impairing your reason, and I think I know what it is: sexual deprivation. A semen backlog is blockading your brain."

"And because your mother was vulgar and faithless, you fear you've got a similar defect. You fear you've been genetically stained."

"*Genetically stained?* Give your head a shake."

"And so you're incapable of refusing any woman whose attentions confirm that you're ... attractive and lovable."

Norval nodded again, as if in agreement, as if finally seeing the light. "Interesting theory, Noel. Really interesting. It suffers from just one small drawback: it's complete rubbish."

"Hence your blend of snobbery and rebellion and your low opinion of women—which is due, at least in part, to your lifelong, unresolved quarrels with your mother."

"Are you finished, Herr Doktor? Are you? Because if you are, I would like to interject here and thank you, from the bottom of my heart, for having clarified my entire life."

"Sometimes a little psychiatry—"

"*Psychiatry?* Psychiatry is the most spectacular error of twentieth-century thought. It should be consigned, if it hasn't been already, to history's great intellectual shitpile. The twenty-first century will lump psychiatrists in with astrologers and witchdoctors. Do you want to know why? Because brain disorders are *chemical*. Our brain is just a piece of meat with chemicals and electrical charges and switches. Feeling and thinking and imagining—they're just forms of information processing. Every aspect of our mental lives depends entirely on *physiological* events in the tissues of the brain. Personality? It can be defined by *the spaces between the brain cells*—the synapses, which are distinct for each individual."

"Then why do you work with Dr. Vorta, a trained psychiatrist?"

"Because he feeds me mind-altering drugs. And then pays me to feed him an endless stream of lies on which he bases an endless stream of articles which are endlessly dismissed."[49]

"Come on, Norval, they're hardly dismissed. He's quoted all the time. And one of his books was a best-seller."

"Which?"

"*Smart Drugs.*"

"You've *got* to be kidding. Halcyon bought 75,000 copies of that ... fable, and distributed them to doctors and pharmacists around the world. You want to know why? Because Vorta *strongly* recommended one of their drugs. Which is now one of their blockbuster drugs."

"How do you know all this?"

"And he only recommended it because they offered him shares in one of their affiliates. A drug-investment house called Helvetia Capital Management."

"How do you know all this?"

"Because I'm writing an article, an exposé, on the mad doctor. I'm blowing the proverbial whistle."

"Come on, Nor, be fair—"

"The man's lost it, his circuitry's fried. He'll be checked in any day now, mark my words."

"He's a brilliant researcher, highly regarded around the world! A man who studied under Dr. Penfield, for Christ's sake! Who's sacrificed most of his life working on memory disorders, on cures for—"

"We need a cure for men like him. For doctors who misdiagnose and murder in the name of research and academic advancement. Why do you defend him? Why so loyal? Why can't you see through the bastard? It doesn't take X-ray vision."

Noel sighed. "Because he was my father's closest friend and because—"

"He was a *business acquaintance*, who bought drugs from him. And didn't charge for his sessions with you, because he was *exploiting* you for his experiments. Yes, he got you a job in the lab—so he could use your research and ideas to write articles under his name. You shouldn't be prostituting your genius to a thieving little midget like him."

"He ... he guided my research, structured the articles, got them published. And he also got me jobs in two other labs, don't forget—when no one else would hire me, when I didn't have any experience or credentials. And he wasn't exploiting me. He was interested in me. He has a sincere love of science—and of the arts too, just like my father. He's devoted his entire life to helping mankind."

"Any nurse with a bedpan has done more for mankind. Volta's patients are valuable to him only as subjects for some new fundable experiment, some new scientific paper. He wouldn't hesitate for a nanosecond to sacrifice human life—animal life goes without saying—for the sake of adding one more particle, one more article, to the great dunghill of fudged research and published irrelevancies."

"What are you ... I can't believe you said that. About sacrificing human life. How can you possibly think that? I just ... don't understand what you have against him. Why can't you leave him alone? He's an old man, getting frailer and frailer—"

"So are Nazi war criminals."

"*Nazi war criminals?* Norval, you are a master of hyperbole, of shock-art. What has he done that could remotely compare?"

"At Buchenwald they experimented on living human beings—to study the effects of artificially induced diseases."

"I repeat: what has he done that could remotely compare? Where do you get all this ... rot?"

Norval paused before speaking, something he rarely did. Was he about to betray a secret? Surely there was no truth to any of this. Noel's breathing stopped as he waited for an answer.

"From his wife and daughter," said Norval.

Noel closed his eyes. "*His wife and daughter?* Be real. His wife has an agenda, and a divorce lawyer. And his daughter despises him because he stopped her from seeing you!"

"Among other reasons."

"So what did they say? What'd they accuse him of?"

"The first controlled induction of Alzheimer's disease in laboratory animals."

Noel bit his lip, scratched the side of his thumb. "It was done for a reason."

"And then in a test group of humans he deliberately induced the disease."

Noel jumped. "Look, Norval, I've heard that ... those stupid rumours before. Do you know who started them? A colleague—a jealous, possibly disturbed archrival—who was fired last month by the university, and not by Vorta. It's a preposterous accusation, which has never been substantiated in any way."

"Do you want to know something about the so-called 'archrival'? This archrival—Charles Ravenscroft—had some astonishing results in clinical trials of an early-onset AD drug he developed. PYY-16. Which became SB-666."

"SB-666? Vorta discovered that on his own."

"Ravenscroft kept his results secret just before publishing them. But Volta got an early peek, because he was on a panel reviewing his grant application."

"Norval, for as long as I've known you you've had this ... this violent prejudice against him. And his name's not 'Volta.' Where do you dig up all this ... dirt?"

"I tripped over it. He's swept everything under the carpet for years and now there's a huge bulge."

"He's a world-famous neurologist, for God's sake! An *authority* on memory. And dreams. History will lump him in with two other famous doctors from Montreal—Wilder Penfield and William Osler!"

"William Osler? Isn't he the one who thought the best method of diagnosis was one finger in the throat and one in the rectum? From what I've heard, that's Volta's preferred method for his memory tests."

Noel closed his eyes. "If that's supposed to be—"

"And if he's such a hot-shot neurologist, why isn't he working for the Montreal Neurological Institute, as Penfield did, instead of some fourth-rate lab for rejects run by the Health Minister's cross-eyed wife? Who he's been swording for years."[50]

"I'm not going to discuss these ... these inventions from divorce lawyers and jealous colleagues. It has nothing to do with what we were talking about."

"Which was ..."

Noel paused, took a deep breath, tried to block out Norval's wild accusations. His mind began turning, bleeding colours like a washing machine. There was no truth to any of this, surely. "Childhood trauma," he said finally, in a near-whisper. "And true love."

Norval stared at his friend, whose eyes were averted. "Any last words on either subject, so we can bury them forever?"

"Yes. I predict that one day, in some fabulous future, you'll find closure for what's happened in the past—you'll find the right chemistry with someone and fall madly in love."

"I want you to promise never to use that word again in my hearing."

"Which word? *Chemistry? Love?*"

"Closure."

"Closure, closure, closure ..."

"And this would be a reversion to ... age five?"

"I'm simply making a prediction, that's all."

"What is this, a career move? You're now a soothsayer?"

Noel remained silent. Norval, he knew, was concealing something. He'd known it from the beginning of their relationship. He had an intuition, a gut feeling, even though he'd never had an accurate one in his life. He paused before trying another tack. "What happened to your father?"

"My father?"

"He went mad, right?"

"He drank himself to death."

"Because your mother betrayed him?"

"He drank to forget."

"And so now, in revenge, you're fucking over as many women as you can, treating them as numbers. Or rather letters. Demeaning and debasing them for the sake of childhood wounds."

"Don't be a stooge. Things will be less foggy when you catch up on your sleep. Or go to a brothel."

"You have two half-sisters, right? And you made love to them both?"

"Correct."

"Is that the dark secret you're hiding?"

"How many times do I have to tell you there's no darkness, no secrecy? I don't give the episodes a backward thought, haven't a scintilla of remorse. Nor do they."

"Does your love for one of them, or for your first true love, prevent you from committing yourself to another?"

Norval broke into laughter. "Are you auditioning? Is this stand-up?"

"Then why don't you commit to anyone?"

"It's not something I want on my résumé."

"What about that Spanish woman we ran into the other day? From Barcelona. She said she was an old flame of yours."

"A spark, a mere cinder."

"How about ... Kayleigh? The one you lost to that performance artist, Scott Free."

"I didn't lose her so much as wipe her off my shoe."

"OK, what about that beautiful French-Canadian? Who left for Belgium. Didn't that break your heart?"

"Which beautiful French-Canadian? They grow like weeds in this town."

"The one you picked up at Ex–Centris. Chantal."

"Chantal? The journalist? You'd need a fork-lift to pick her up."

"Not that Chantal. The other one, the dancer."

"She was a C. Nothing more. Taken on the sperm of the moment."

"But she was ... *beautiful.*"

"Show me a beautiful woman, says the Hindu proverb, and I'll show you a man who's tired of fucking her."

"What about Lise, the acrobat with Cirque du Soleil?"

"She's not an acrobat, as it turns out. At least not for the circus. She's a professional fluffer."

"A *fluffer?* What the hell's that?"

"Her job is to keep porn stars aroused between scenes."

"Right ... But didn't you say she was an ex?"

"More like a why. She was a fling, an amourette. She was three months gone at our first passade."

Noel shook his head. He couldn't *imagine* what it would be like to have women like this in his gravitational field. To be in Norval's position, just for one day. Sometimes he thought he'd do almost anything to trade places: light a fire in an orphanage, push the Pope off a cliff ... But the feeling would pass. Because he was looking for something more romantic, longer-lived, something found in fairy and technicolor tales. Does this sort of thing exist in the real world? It would certainly never exist for him. With the curse of his memory, and now his mother's memory, it was pointless to pursue love or marriage. These things were about as possible as making a wedding ring out of mercury, or honeymooning in Atlantis. He stared at Norval, in simmering silence. "How exactly did we become friends, Nor? It seems that in every single way we—"

"As soon as you told me your name. You had Byron's adopted first name, and Bonaparte's initials. And mine."

The flip answer, despite Noel's resistance, pulled him headlong into the past, into his childhood lab with its laminated Periodic Table. Memory particles fell on him like snow.

Norval recognised his friend's dead-eyed stare. "What are you seeing, Noel? Noel?"

"Just ... memory flakes, nothing important."

"Tell me."

"Not this time, Norval, I don't want to play, I'm not in the mood."

"Come on, lighten up for Christ's sake."

"No. I don't feel like it."

"One more time. Play the bloody game."

Noel sighed. All right, for the last time. "I was thinking of Nb. Niobium. Group Vb of the Periodic Table."

"Physical appearance?"

Noel closed his eyes. "Like steel, except it's soft and ductile. When polished, it looks like platinum."

"Rare?"

The servant entered, carrying a large mahogany chest of chemicals, with a coil of platinum and two lead clamps ... Noel opened his eyes, bleaching lurid images from *Dorian Gray*. "No, it's more plentiful than lead."

"Principal uses?"

Noel reclosed his eyes, waited for the right map to sharpen, like a print under emulsion. "Tools and dies, superconductive magnets. Claddings for nuclear reactor cores—either alone or alloyed with zirconium—since it's compatible with uranium and resistant to corrosion by molten alkali-metal coolants ..."

Norval erupted into laughter.

"... and has a low thermal-neutron cross section."

"Of course, mustn't forget the thermal-neutron cross section. Atomic number and weight?"

"Forty-one and 92.906."

"Proceed."

"Melting point 2,468 degrees C, boiling point 4,927."

"In Fahrenheit?"

"4,474 and 8,901."

"In Kelvin?"

"I don't know, you idiot."

"Go on."

"Specific gravity 8.57, electronic configuration $(Kr)4d^45s^1$."

"Derivation of name?"

"After Niobe, the daughter of Tantalus."

"The mythical king? Who was condemned to stand in water that receded when he tried to drink? Or was it with fruit that receded when he tried to grab it?"

"Both."

"But what's that got to do with Niobium?"

"Because the two elements, Tantalum and Niobium, are always found together."[51]

"Noel, do you see now why I hang with you? Because you're a fucking marvel—with possibly the largest cranial junkyard in the world. But maybe I should write this all down, make sure you're not making it up."

"I wish I was, believe me."

"So what were we talking about? I've completely forgotten."

"So have I."

"Liar."

"We were talking about ..." Noel let out a sigh, not his first of the day. "... the psychology of love. We then moved on to all the women you've loved and lost."

"Right, the null set." Norval looked at his chained watch. "I vote we change the subject."

"I'll be right back."

Noel rose and walked quickly to the men's room, where a tottering man was using both urinals, and the wall between them. So he stepped inside the only stall. I'll try one last approach, he thought, I'll ask him about Cynara. After another drink. He zipped up his fly but did not flush, as the bowl was blocked by a light bulb and a waterlogged roll of paper towels.

At the bar he had to shout to be heard, something he never liked doing. "The toilet! It should not be flushed under any circumstances! And there's a man lying face down in his own urine!"

"What can I get you?"

Noel paused. What does Norval say? "Irish single, two-storey. And a Blanche de Chambly." *Much* cooler when he says it. With an attempt at Norvalian nonchalance, he glanced at a blonde woman with tweezed eyebrows on a barstool beside him, then at the table, now empty, where the man with the laptop had been sitting, then at a "Culture Board" with posters advertising *Helium Induced Orgasms: The Musical* and *Who Put the "KY" in FUNKY ASS?*

Norval, meanwhile, was conversing with two gentlemen: one was the guy in motorcycle leathers who had blocked his path earlier; the other was tall and stringy and metallic with a tiny hairless head, like a Giacometti man.

"My girlfriend says you're a hotshot writer," said the leather man, with the inflection and warmth of a dial tone. "Before I kill you, I want you to read my bro's script." He nodded towards his slender companion, whose blinky grey eyes were cautious, constantly on the watch.

Norval looked calmly from one man to the other, and then at an attractive redhead at the next table. "What's it about? The Pope's visit to Canada?"

"You're a dead man," said the Giacometti man, displaying teeth like black pumpkin seeds. "You cease to exist."

"It's called *The Phyllis Killers*," said the leather man, a toothpick shifting from one corner of his mouth to the other. "It's about two guys who rape and kill women—but only bitches named Phyllis."

Norval nodded. "A sentimental comedy? Have you tried Disney?"

"Ain't no fuckin' comedy, dead man," said the Giacometti man.

"No? Is it based on your doctoral work in Greek tragedy?"

"You know where fuck-heads like you end up, don't you."

"Riding motorcycles?"

"At the bottom of the Saint Lawrence, you little fucker. We know where you live, dead man. Next time we'll get the right house. You get my drift, you frog faggot?"

"Let me put it another way," said the leather man. "You go near my girlfriend again and I'll send her your fried pecker in a Fed-Ex box ..."

🪔

On his way back from the bar, Noel watched as the two bikers clomped towards the door. They had been replaced at the table, he noticed, by a crimson-headed woman. Noel ducked behind a wooden column with shelves for potted plants, and set the drinks down on a table. I'll wait till she leaves, he decided. I'll just make a fool of myself. He peered round the column. Maybe I'll pick up some pointers. Focus focus, hocus-pocus, don't let the colour-wheel spin ...

"Let me get this straight," said the woman in French. "I tell you my name, and because it's the *right* name, I have the honour of going back to your place."

"Correct. You qualify."

"I qualify." The woman nodded, chomped on her gum. "Tell you what. *You* qualify if you've got a million bucks, are built like a gymnast and hung like a horse."

Norval slowly exhaled smoke from his cigarette, squinted at her through the cloud. "The first two conditions I can satisfy," he replied, "but I'll be damned if I get a penis reduction for any woman."

Through fleshy green leaves Noel saw the woman's electric-red hair fly back, heard her high-pitched detonation of laughter. *Yes*, thought Noel, you have to make women laugh, something I never seem able to ...

The woman, shimmying her spandexed hips, was being escorted away by someone with a boyfriend's authority. But she'd had time, Noel remarked as he approached the table, to leave a white slip of paper. A business card? Was she an *S* or a *T*? Noel craned his neck to see. Candy colours: wild cherry, menthol, blueberry, white chocolate, green apple, peppermint. *Simone?*

"You get everything? Or do you want me to read out the bits you may've missed?"

"What? No, sorry, I just ..." Noel set down the drinks, pulled out a chair. "So who were those two guys? They looked pretty rough."

"Nullities. Expendables. Toilet flushings."

"Right."

"Unless you've more questions, I'll think I'll fuck off." With a flick of the wrist, Norval tossed back his drink.

"Well, actually, I did have one more ... but, you know, you don't have to answer it."

Norval looked down at his suede thigh, at a streak of fallen ash. "Glad to hear it."

Noel took two great gulps of beer. "Who's Terry?"

Norval looked up quickly, then just as quickly inhaled the last of his cigarette. So, Samira did some snooping around, he deduced. "You tell me."

Noel took a blind stab at it. "The person you once loved. Who you call Bess in your novel."

Norval crushed out his cigarette. "*Je vais aller pisser.* I may or may not be back."

Noel sat and waited, repeating the name Terry over and over, watching the letters change chromatophorically into *Cynara*. Yes! The truth about Norval is in that poem. That was his confession! He closed his eyes, conjured up the last stanza. When he reopened them, Norval was sitting across from him, slumped in his chair. Seconds passed before he looked up. Noel searched his friend closely, trying to read the truth in his eyes. Should he continue to bluff his way through this?

"You *did* love Terry. Because the relationship was doomed, because he or she was sick, because like Cynara—and Bess—Terry was dying, am I right?"

"Piss off."

"Tell me what happened. Was it like in your novel?"

Norval paused. "No." The word was spoken in a humbler key and with a look that Noel hadn't seen before. It wasn't anger. It was more like bone-weary, world-weary sadness. His mask had slipped. For the first time since the two friends had met, Norval's expression was the same as Noel's.

Chapter 18
Norval's "Diary" [52]

O n an unremittingly monochrome day in the fall of 1989, at the end of a tree-lined cul-de-sac near Nottingham, Norval rapped on Mrs. Pettybone's front door. He unhooked his leather knapsack, turned round to examine the front yard: walkways swept and reswept, hedges clipped with Euclidean precision, garden ruthlessly weeded, leaves dusted, gnomes groomed.

He clapped the polished knocker again, harder, and was answered by the rattle of a chain, the sound of bolts being drawn back and a key turning in the deadlock. Like a mastiff bitch peeping out of a doghouse, a woman's face emerged—tense, hurried, hostile. She examined Norval top to bottom and didn't seem to like what she saw. "What do you want?" she growled.

"A room."

"And what makes you think I'd have a room?"

"Because it says B & B on the sign."

"Oh, is that still up?"

"And it says 'Welcome' on the mat."

Mrs. Pettybone eyed Norval's unshaven face and riotous hair, his mud-spattered greatcoat and high boots, like relics from an ancient war. "Well you're not welcome. I'm full up." She closed the door with force.

"Gally gave me your address!" Norval shouted, with irritation, at the oaken wood. He had come a long way, on foot, in mud.

Inch by inch, creakingly, the door reopened. Mrs. Pettybone, her face now drained of colour, seemed to be struggling against tears. "Come on in, then, and sharp about it. And take those boots off."

Inside, it was clean—mercilessly, tyrannically clean—with the stench of disinfectants warring with the scent of air fresheners. A pink carnation motif on the curtains and wallpaper, fake daffodils on the mantelpiece, funereal furniture waxed and polished to a frenzy.

234

They stood, without words or motion, sizing each other up. A half-century-old volcano, Norval decided, dyed red hair, smouldering eyes, churning and foaming inside, and yet attractive in a way … A bone-lazy young hooligan, Mrs. Pettybone decided, handsome enough if you scraped through the layers of dirt, but a hooligan all the same. "What you need is a good scrub," she said.

"Does that come with the room?"

"Don't be impudent. How many days, Mister …?

"Blaquière."

"How many days do you intend to stay, Mr. … Black whatever. Mr. Frenchman with the Oxbridge accent."

Norval glanced at the burnished floors and unblemished walls. *Starry Night*, with Van Gogh's name in large letters along the top, hung on one of them, and on the floor beneath it stood a padded mallet, oriental looking. "Just the one."

"Are you married?"

Norval gave a quarter-smile, shook his head. *Où est le rapport?* "Hardly. Why do you ask?"

"Because I have a daughter—whom I shall thank you to steer clear of. There shall be no carnal commerce in my house, do we understand each other? You're all alike, you men. And I don't want you wagging your thingy at me as one of our guests did, the late Reverend Hickenby."

Norval nodded. "You know, Mrs. Pettybone, now that I think of it, it may be more convenient for me to get a room in town—"

"Come this way," she said. And for some reason he obeyed, penetrating deeper into the maze of the house, ascending a back staircase, steep and narrow, perhaps for servants, at the top of which Mrs. Pettybone pushed open an unlocked door. She stood before a renovated en suite bathroom. "Do you know what a bidet is for, Mr. Black? Are you aware of its function? Last year, I had an American boy who defecated in it. I'll have none of that in my house, do we understand each other? No Yankee gangsterism in my house."

"I'm French, Mrs. Pettybone. We invented the bidet."

"There's the shower, there's the soap." She pointed to translucent anti-bacterial bars on dishes and racks. "Use them." On this congenial note she left, closing the door behind her, giving it a click on the other side, as if locking him in.

Like walking into a spider's parlour, Norval thought as he looked around the room. Tapestried four-poster bed with a picture of the Holy Child over

235

top, plastic pink roses in a vase on the bed table, curtains with the red flounce put in coffins, milky iridescent wallpaper with bunches of pinkish lilies cascading in each corner. The same pink lilies, Norval noted, on the white ceramic of the toilet, sink and shower. The bathroom, like the rest of the house, was as cold as a crypt.

Norval shed his clothes and opened the sink cupboard, searching for shampoo. It contained nothing but cans, aerosol cans, lined up in groups of three: Alpine Rose, Cinnamon Apple, Citrus Fresh; Country Air, Country Breeze, Country Cornucopia; Hawaiian Breeze, Island Breeze, Jasmine Utopia; Lavender Meadow, Lavender Mist, Minty Jamboree; Mountain Berry, Mulberry, Oceanside Breeze; Ocean Spray, Passion Fruit, Spicy Potpourri; Spring Rain, Summer Rain, Wintergreen Bouquet ...

"This can *not* be happening," Norval muttered in the shower, while lathering his hair with anti-bacterial soap. "Alphabetical order, for Christ's sake. The woman's a burning lunatic. This is a must-flee situation."

❖ ❖ ❖

When Norval opened his eyes the next morning, a fierce ray of sun blinded him. Mrs. Pettybone had hoisted the hospital-white blinds and was now securing the draw string. Wearing a red jogging suit, white apron and red garden gloves, she began plucking articles off the floor. A look of disgust warped her features as she dropped each article of clothing into a large white sack. "Breakfast at seven," she barked while striding out of the room. "Sharp," she added from the hallway, hauling away the sack like an anti-Santa. "And no smoking!"

Norval squinted at the alarm clock. Six thirty. He shook his head, rubbed his eyes, threw the bedclothes back, swore, swore again, turned over and instantly fell back to sleep.

Fifteen minutes later his body was vibrating from a loud, hollow noise, repeated at regular intervals. It was the sound of a gong.

"Mr. Black!" a voice shouted, as if from under the bedsprings. A few seconds later Mrs. Pettybone reappeared in the doorway, releasing vapour from a violet can.

Norval watched, one eye glued shut. "What's the fragrance of the day, Mrs. Pettybone? Guest Neutraliser? Norvalicide?"

"His lordship's breakfast is served."

And so it was. Plates so full that Norval wondered if a party of stevedores would be down any minute. Fried eggs, rashers, sausages heaped on one plate, mounds of fried potatoes and tomatoes on another, stacks of toasted brown bread dripping margarine on yet another. Jars of marmalade and honey, two miniature boxes of Corn Flakes, a pitcher of milk, a pitcher of orange juice, and something grey and viscous that looked like a pot of glue.

"You're late, Mr. Black. I believe in the three *p*'s: punctuality, propriety, cleanliness."

Norval arched an eyebrow, but let it pass. Mrs. Pettybone, in trainers and tracksuit, was bobbing and fidgeting like a runner in a relay, waiting for the baton. She made several adjustments to the items on the table, all unnecessary. "Eat," she commanded, before racing back to the kitchen.

Norval did as he was told, gratefully, ravenously, while glancing at a *Nottingham Post* folded neatly beside his plate. Not a bad woman, actually. Must bring up the subject of money. And Gally. As he bit into an oil-popping sausage he thought he heard footsteps from above, in the vicinity of his room.

Mrs. Pettybone returned with a stainless-steel pot. "Will you have milk first or last in your coffee, Mr. Black? I'm not offering tea because frogs don't drink it." She said these words with the speed of an auctioneer, as if she'd just consumed a pot or two herself.

"I don't take milk," Norval replied. "So listen, Gally mentioned that—"

"I suppose you've no money to pay for your room, am I right, Mr. Black? I do not care for economic cripples. Least of all French ones."

Norval nodded. "Yes, well, as a matter of fact, Mrs. Pettybone, I am a bit undercapitalised. My accountant, I'm afraid, has buried my wealth in impenetrable shell companies and offshore accounts. Very difficult to get at."

Mrs. Pettybone's eyes narrowed. "Very funny," she replied. "If I wanted a clown, I wouldn't have divorced my husband." She began pouring milk into Norval's coffee. "So what do you do for a living, Mr. Black? What is your trade?"

Norval hesitated, wondering how best to answer this. "I'm a professional actor."

Mrs. Pettybone recoiled, as if he'd said he was a professional leper, take my arm for this dance.

"In fact," Norval continued, "that's why I'm here in England. But there's been a few foul-ups … Gally thought that—"

"That I'm a soft touch. We'll discuss the matter later." Mrs. Pettybone, now wearing orange rubber gloves, removed his plate, as well as a fork from his hand. "I'll just do the washing up," she said. "And don't even think about lighting up that cigarette!"

By the time Norval finished his newspaper, lingered over his coffee and returned to his room, his clothes were washed, dried and ironed. Impossible, he calculated. Surely a record of some sort. Must call Guinness. Even his socks and underwear were ironed. He put on his chlorinated, fabric-softened clothes, butted his cigarette, then hitchhiked into Nottingham in search of a job.

❖ ❖ ❖

This pattern, unbroken, continued for the next seven days. Norval, the only guest in the house, awoke to blading sunlight or a flicking lightswitch, then reawoke to a gong; he ate like a swine at breakfast to obviate lunch and dinner, went out looking for work, came back after dinner without work. Why did he stay? Because he was penniless, because Mrs. Pettybone no longer mentioned money, because he was starting to like the woman. The way she doted on him, the way she darned the darns on his socks, sewed buttons on his shirts, polished and repolished his boots, appointed them with Odour Eaters. True, he could do without the ironed underwear and crease down his jeans. True, the woman was insane. But you can't have everything. Besides, there were mysteries to solve. Who exactly was Gally? And where was the inviolable innkeeper's daughter?

On his eighth day Norval got a job: playing an eighteen-year-old Rimbaud in a film based on the poet's life in London in the 1870s. He couldn't believe his luck. I dazzled the director, he thought, I was made for this role …

Returning to the house well after midnight, with celebratory beer on his breath and a script under his arm, he got lost in the manor's dark labyrinths. He tiptoed right, left, up one corridor and down another. His memory had completely fogged. He climbed what he thought was his staircase but arriving at the top realised it went nowhere. It just stopped four or five feet from the ceiling. He walked back down, shaking his head, worse for drink than he thought. On the landing a door opened.

A figure in a man's white dress-shirt, torn tights and unlaced boots stepped out of the shadow. "*Monsieur Blaquière, je présume?*"

Norval scrutinized her pale, makeup-less features, radically short hair and tattered clothes. *She was in utter disarray*, he said to himself, the words floating back from his audition. *Rattlings of death and rings of muted music made her goddess-like body rise, expand, tremble like a ghost …*

"I'm Teresa, Mrs. Pettybone's daughter. Are you … hearing-impaired?"

"No, sorry, I'm just a bit … lost. Well, more than a bit. Wholly. I went up those steps, you see, and …"

"Unmotivated steps."

" … and then I … I'm sorry?"

"They're called unmotivated steps—they lead nowhere. My grandfather liked them for some reason, liked the irrationality of it all. So do I, for that matter."

The hall light began to flash on and off. "Teresa?" a high voice clucked from below. Mrs. Pettybone's. "Are you all right, dear? Is that boy violating you? He's from the theatre!"

"I'm fine, Mother!"

"And he's French!"

"You can go back to sleep, Mother!" To Norval, *sotto voce*, she said, "We'd better talk in here. Can I offer you a drink?" She smelled the beer on his breath. "A coffee?"

Norval glanced at the neckline of her shirt, which had slipped to reveal the lace of a white bra. "Well, yes, fine …"

"It's just that … I haven't talked to anyone in a while, apart from my mother. And doctor. I'm sort of in quarantine."

"You're in quarantine? For …?"

"You name it, it's a long list. I think I managed to thoroughly scare my doctor—he said if I was a building I'd be condemned."

"That's … some bedside manner."

"He probably thought I was going to disintegrate right there in his office. But enough of that, I must sound like some doddering hypochondriac. Come."

Ignoring an amber light inside him, and the strictures of Mrs. Pettybone, Norval entered Teresa's bedroom. It was a sty, looking and smelling of sickness, a tornado aftermath of laundry and magazines and empty mugs and medicine bottles and half-filled crossword puzzles and pages ripped from sketch books and bordelloish antiques like brass oil lamps and pewter candle snuffers … A series of candles illuminated two De Chiricos on the wall—deserted piazzas, illogical shadows, dark arcades, hidden danger—as well as paintings of her own showing shuttered summerhouses, neglected parks, marble steps overrun with weeds, paths strewn with dead leaves. Two small charcoal drawings lay on the floor: one of her mother, decades younger, and one of herself, with long wavy tresses to the waist.

After closely examining the latter, Norval sat down in a teetering wicker chair. Teresa plugged in a kettle. Under the flickering candlelight he got a better look at her: early twenties, fair and frail, sickly pale, eyes so preternaturally blue as to be from another species or universe. It was while looking into these eyes that Norval had a shocking premonition: her future, however short, would be entwined with his.

"How in God's name did you end up here?" Teresa asked with a faint smile. She had full, naturally crimson lips and teeth as white as toothpaste. "We haven't had guests for ages."

"Gally gave me the address."

"Gally Santlal? Are you serious? And you told my mother?"

"It's the only reason she opened the door." Norval rooted around in his pockets and pulled out an empty cigarette pack. "Do you smoke, by any chance?"

"The doctor asked me the same question. I said no and he said, 'Well, you might as well.'" Teresa took two cigarettes out of a jar and tapped them on the back of her hand. One match lit both. "So how is Gally these days? What's he up to?"

Norval shrugged. "I don't know that much about him. He's a glazier … as I guess you know." He took the offered cigarette, drew on it as though it were his last. "He'd just finished replacing windows in some church. Which were smashed or stolen. In Hucknall? Let's see … oh, his wife died, which is why he could join me for—"

"His wife died? You're kidding. I didn't know that. Recently?"

"No idea. But he didn't seem all that shaken."

Teresa poured tepid water into a mug, emptied a packet of instant coffee into it. "So how … where did you meet him?"

"Newstead Abbey." Norval took a sip of the coffee and winced. "At the restaurant, I forget what it's called. The one with the doilies and vomit-green rug and squawking peacocks outside …"

Teresa laughed. "The Buttery."

"Where I was abysmally drunk by three in the afternoon, much more than now, and semi-suicidal amidst the peacocks. Did I mention the peacocks?"

"Semi-suicidal?"

"I'm an actor, in a manner of speaking. A very loose manner. I was supposed to be in a play that was cancelled."

"In Nottingham? At the Playhouse? Theatre Royal?"

"No, at a library that someone burned down a few days before we arrived. Wish they'd told us. Wish they'd paid us."

Teresa laughed again, showing her beautiful white teeth. "I'm sorry, I suppose it's not very funny. Which play were you doing?"

"*Tartuffe.*"

"Molière?"

Norval nodded. "In French too—a harebrained government project that wouldn't have drawn more than four people, including the ushers and janitor. Anyway, as I'm having a ..." Here Norval reached into his coat pocket and pulled out a cardboard beer mat. "... a 'Worthington Cream-flow Bitter,' Gally sticks his head through the window and scares the living shit out of me."

Teresa grinned. "Why would he do that? Oh, I see, he was replacing it."

"There was no glass in the window but I hadn't even noticed. So we start chatting. And then he offers me another ..." Norval's hands patted all pockets.

"Worthington Creamflow Bitter," said Teresa.

"Correct. Anyway, as he leaves he gives me your mom's address. Along with his card and the name of a film company he used to work for. Where, by some miracle, I got a job today." Norval held up his script. "Well, not a miracle exactly. The guy who originally got the part is now at Queen's."

"The hospital?"

"After doing some *very* strong drugs, he did a perfect jackknife into an empty swimming pool."

Teresa winced, then crawled back into bed with her boots on. "Congrat-ulations," she said before washing down a handful of pills with liquid from an amber bottle. "I guess." Awkward seconds ticked by. Norval sipped his Maxwell House, glanced at her hair. Was it razed in the name of fashion, he wondered, or because of something more sinister? He began leafing through his script. *Scarlet and black wounds burst on the proud flesh. Life's own colours darken, dance and divide ...*

"Who is Gally exactly?" he asked suddenly. "I mean, what's his connection with your mom?"

Teresa took a long haul on her cigarette. "He wanted to marry her—until, that is, he found out she was pregnant. With me. Then he changed his mind. At least that's Mom's version. I have another."

"Which is?"

"Well, Gally is ... Trinidadian, East Asian. At the time, for my mother—and her family in particular—that was a problem. Anyway, they haven't spoken to each other since his own wedding day over twenty years ago. My mom's never gotten over it—it's been like a canker, eating away at her daily."

"Because she was in love with him?"

Teresa nodded, tapped ash into a mug filled with cigarettes. "She was seeing two men at the time—Gally and my dad—but she loved only one. Gally. But my dad was a persuasive character, shall we say, and somehow made love to her without ... you know, protection. She's never gotten over the shame or guilt. So after divorcing my dad she turned the place into a B & B. And she's been cleaning ever since—spraying, airing things out, condomising the place."

Norval tried to smile but no smile came, a strange sadness raining down on him. He looked around the squalorous room. "I take it she's not allowed in here."

Teresa laughed. "I rebelled long ago. But she's doing it—the war on germs, I mean—for my sake too. I've been sick for a long time. It's funny, it's like the boy who cried wolf. When I was young she always insisted I was sick, taking me to the doctor's and to hospitals when nothing was wrong with me. And now ... Anyway, you must think she's mad as a hatter,[53] not to mention a redneck, but she's all right, really. Generous, thoughtful, do anything for me."

"She's done a lot for me too, I don't quite know why."

"It is a bit surprising, I have to admit. She's not usually open to ... well, you know, foreigners. Although you certainly don't sound French."

Norval nodded. "I was thinking of giving her something. I mean, besides money for the room. Does she have any hobbies? Does she read?"

Teresa stubbed her cigarette out on the side of her bottle. "She used to read—about astronomy mostly. She had this telescope, this really cool telescope that Gally gave her years ago. She was absolutely mad about it, she could gaze at the sky for hours. It was her prize possession—until one day she smashed it to pieces."

❖ ❖ ❖

The film was being shot in London, with rehearsals taking place in a church basement in Harlesden. Owing to production delays and winter rain it took longer than expected: Norval was gone for over four months. At first he had no intention of returning to the house, but as the days turned over he found he couldn't get either Mrs. Pettybone or Teresa out of his mind. After his first month away, he sent Mrs. Pettybone a postal order and a present; after his second, he sent Teresa a letter, with *x*'s at the end, and instructions regarding the present. Remembering a parting kiss with parted lips, he also posted these lines from Rimbaud:

Fists in torn pockets I departed.
And I listened, sitting by the road
In soft September, where the dewdrops
Were strong wine on my forehead;

And in fantastical shadows rhyming,
I plucked like lyres the laces
Of my ruined boots,
One foot against my heart.

Have I lost my mind? Norval wondered, the moment the letter dropped into the box. He put his fingers into the slot, peered in. Should I try to retrieve it?

Two weeks later he received a response, slipped under his door at the Staunton Hotel in Bloomsbury. It was a thin blue envelope with a postcard inside. On the front was a black-and-white photograph of the church in Hucknall, in whose cemetery they had drunk a bottle of wine and kissed for the first time. On the back of the card, in the address square, was one line: *Come back, you madman.* On the message side was a pastel sketch of Norval himself, in Byronic attitude:

On the last day of shooting Norval bolted from the set to catch an express train to Nottingham. He decided to pass on the wrap party, and on interesting propositions from two actresses and a make-up artist. Measured by watch hands, the train journey was brief, but to Norval it felt like a ride on the Trans-Siberian. After switching to the Robin Hood Line, he found himself sprinting across a muddy field by a cow pond, in twilight rain. "I've lost my mind," he concluded, not unhappily. He was gasping like a marathoner as he approached Mrs. Pettybone's B & B.

It was unrecognisable. An unfamiliar van sat in the driveway; the garden had grown wild; drainpipes and gutters were clogged. Inside, dust accumulated, dishes were unwashed, odours unchecked. Mrs. Pettybone no longer rushed about, no longer wore a jogging suit, no longer rose at dawn. The gong was gone. During the day she could be found lounging on a daybed, reading or singing or raving about Ganymede or Maxwell Montes or the Bay of Rainbows; at night she mysteriously disappeared, climbing up the creaking back stairway, sitting atop the unmotivated steps for hours.

To all appearances, Mrs. Pettybone was finally over the edge, finally bereft of her scant remaining faculties. Or perhaps, thought the neighbours, she'd given up the war on germs because her daughter had died. But the neighbours were wrong: about the war and about Teresa too.

While Norval was away in London, on a day when Mrs. Pettybone did her errands in town, Galahad Santlal arrived at her house for the first time in twenty-two years—with putty knife, lead hammer, glass pliers, glazing sprigs, beam compass, glass cutter. With Teresa supervising from below, Gally climbed the unmotivated steps, cut a round hole in the ceiling and installed a pivoting skylight. As well as a chair, a tripod supporting Norval's gift, and a shelf for two books on the galaxies, from his own collection. He then waited for Mrs. Pettybone's return.

꧁

Minutes ticked by as Noel fidgeted and Norval drank. "OK, so don't tell me the story," said Noel. "Whatever happened, I'm sure you behaved like a bastard—an unromantic, unsentimental, unthoughtful bastard."

Norval's head was bowed, uncharacteristically. He was on to his fourth double Irish. "Dead on."

"Were you in love with Terry? Did she leave you? Is that why you were in love with her? Because nobody else has ever dumped you, ever broken your heart?"

Norval swirled the dregs of his Connemara. "I am not my father. I decamped, *point final*. I thought about what I was doing, then boarded the first plane to Canada."

"But why? I mean if you—"

"I was at an age—not that I've outgrown it—when I couldn't deal with being in ... never mind."

"Being in what? In love? Is that what you were going to say?"

"It's like measles—I had it once and now I'm immune."

I *knew* it! Noel exclaimed, to himself. "But is it ... too late? Can't you go back and—"

"It's too late."

"Why? Is she married? Did she die? Tell me the story."

"No." He glared at Noel with drunken hostility. "You'll never hear it." He rose from the table unsteadily. From his back pocket he extracted a crumpled note of massive denomination and flung it on the table. "At least not from me."

Norval stayed two months at Mrs. Pettybone's B & B. The proprietor assigned him the finest room in the house, which happened to be across the hall from her daughter's. Gally had also been assigned a room, on the ground floor, next to Mrs. Pettybone. But Gally stayed longer than Norval; in fact, he never left. A week after installing the skylight and telescope he proposed to Mrs. Pettybone, for the second time in twenty-two years, and this time was accepted. The wedding was to be held in the spring, a civil wedding at The Orangery at Newstead Abbey.

A double wedding? thought Norval. The idea was so preposterous, so antithetical to everything that he—the very symbol of bachelorhood—believed in that he suggested it to Teresa. It had the right touch of the absurd, the anachronistic, the harebrained. She hasn't long to live, a few years maybe (and who knows how long *I've* got?), so why not seize the Christly day, do something shockingly, uncharacteristically unselfish? But that's not even the right word, he thought. It *is* selfish—I want to spend every last second with her. And maybe they'll find a cure ...

Teresa, after realising Norval wasn't kidding about the proposal, said no. "Don't be mad. It's just ... not done anymore."

"Must I arrange it with your mother? A forced union? And what if you're pregnant? Gally will come after me with a shotgun. Or putty knife."

Teresa laughed. "A marriage *would* make my mother happy, deliriously happy. But a double wedding? Not in a million years. I wouldn't want to steal her thunder, and I don't want to deal with old relatives and friends. But ... if you're absolutely sure about this, Norval, if you're not doing it out of some Florence Nightingale motive or to obtain a Boy Scout badge, then I *will* elope. Anywhere you like, any time."

For Norval, it was the first time he'd been happy since the age of nine. He was in his first relationship that lasted more than a week, a place he never thought he'd be. He could scarcely believe what was happening—he was *falling in love*, for Christ's sake, something he thought was impossible, an emotional state he had ridiculed his entire life. But that was pre-Teresa ...

They arranged to marry in London, in Camden, partly because Norval had to be there to reshoot the ending of *Rimbaud in London*. The two left on the train together but Teresa, who had been feeling ill all morning, complained of double vision. Norval had noticed that one of her eyes wandered, and that she seemed to be tilting her head to the right. So she got off the train to see her doctor in Nottingham, insisting that Norval ride on without her. They would meet up the next day, she promised, on the steps of the Camden Town Hall.

The following day, an hour before they were scheduled to meet, Norval was there waiting, worried, his back against the wall of the building, sheltered from the pouring rain. He waited two hours, checking his watch every five minutes, peering out from behind a rain-battered column. I had a feeling she wouldn't come. How could I think she would come? She's changed her mind, can't go through with it. Or is there someone else? Her ex? Craig Slandon, beer-guzzling imbecile, aged twenty-one? Another hour passed, maybe more, before he phoned Mrs. Pettybone's B & B. No, she wasn't there. We thought she was with you in London. Oh dear.

Norval took the first express train north, to Nottingham, then a taxi to Queen's Hospital. Yes, a receptionist informed him, Teresa spent the night here, but went home this morning ... He flew out the door to hail another cab. At the train station, a tree down at Newstead kept him waiting for another murderous hour. After standing the entire way, chain-smoking between carriages, he jumped off the moving train at Hucknall, and ran with bursting lungs through fields of decaying vegetation and stagnant pools of water, to Mrs. Pettybone's B & B.

Teresa was not there. Norval raced up and down steps, opened up doors and closets of rooms that hadn't been used in years, madly, rampageously, even climbing up to the attics. "Teresa!" he shouted repeatedly. "Terry!" The three of them—Mrs. Pettybone, Gally and Norval—scoured her bedroom for a sign, a farewell message, a suicide note. Nothing. She had vanished and clearly did not want to be found.[54]

Chapter 19
Norval & Company

Liszt's *Symphonic Poem No. 2* was starting as Noel placed a fake log on the fire. Lounging in Mr. Burun's La-Z-Boy, his right cheek and sandwashed Nepalese silk shirt uncharacteristically smudged with black, Norval observed his new environment while cracking nuts and inhaling Armagnac.

"Fish rule in effect," said Norval.

"Fish rule?"

"An old Danish proverb: 'Fish, like guests, begin to stink after three days.' On second thought, I'll get a hotel." In his head Norval began to rewind the evening, scarcely able to believe he was sitting where he was. He had taken a taxi home from the bar less than an hour before, seen something there that sobered him up at once, took another cab to Noel's. Where for the first time in his life he was admitted—by Mrs. Burun.

"You can stay here," said Noel, "as long as you want—especially after what you've just been through."

Norval paused to listen to the cellos and double bass evoke the spirit of Byron's Tasso. "Got any cigarettes? Where's JJ and Sam, by the way? Upstairs shagging? Oh, hello Mrs. Burun."

Mrs. Burun had returned from the bathroom. "Call me Stella," she said, while reaching for a cigarette case on the mantel. "Noel, I think this gentleman will be a bad influence on you."

"Everyone needs a bad influence from time to time, wouldn't you agree, Stella?"

"That's how I fell in love with my husband."

Norval laughed. "Shall I pour you one of these?"

"Yes, why not? Would you like one of these?" She opened up the silver and cloisonné enamel box, a birthday gift to her husband.

"You're too kind. Say when."

"Mom, I'm not sure if ..." Noel paused, distracted by a coppery head that popped through the doorway then withdrew behind a wall, like a tortoise into its shell. "*Salut*, Jean-Jacques."

JJ gradually materialised, squinting in the direction of Norval. He was wearing shiny pyjamas of interstellar blue, covered with planets and stars and smiling moons. A cell phone protruded from his pocket. "Nor? Is that you?" He rubbed his eyes, like a bad actor seeing a miracle. "A-yo, dude! What brings you here at one in the morning?"

Norval reached over for a toss cushion on the sofa, examined its running wave border. "It's two in the morning."

"Norval's place was torched," said Noel. "He's going to be staying here for a while. For three days."

"Not another arson! Jesus Cockadoodle Christ! This is getting scary. This time we've got to report it, I'm sorry." JJ pulled out his cell and punched in zero. "Hello, operator? Get me the number for 911. I mean the number—"

"JJ, put your phone away," said Norval, with an indulgent half-smile. "Everything's been taken care of."

"Everything's been taken of, operator," JJ repeated into the line. "Sorry." He snapped his phone shut, all atwitter, then fumbled it onto the floor. "Do you know who did it, Nor? Is everything OK? Are you OK?"

"Everything's fine. We'll talk about it in the morning, all right?"

"Any damage? Do you know who could've done it? You sure we shouldn't report it? I really think—"

Here Norval got up and walked towards him, carrying the toss cushion. To Noel's surprise, instead of stuffing it in JJ's mouth, he tossed it back onto the sofa and stooped to pick up the cell phone. He slipped it into JJ's breast pocket, put his hand on JJ's shoulder. "I appreciate your concern, JJ. I'm just going to the bathroom now and then to bed. I'm dead. I'll fill in the blanks tomorrow."

"I'll show you where the bathroom is," said Mrs. Burun. "Then I'm off to bed myself."

"Good night, guys!" said JJ as the two disappeared down the hall. "Oh, Noel, I almost forgot. The sun is square to Saturn. Mars and Jupiter in your fourth house. Buy no new footwear."

"Got it," said Noel.

Noel fixed his eyes on the multicoloured flames, which fluttered like a school of tropical fish. Orpiment, nacarat, aurora, cinnabar, ultramarine ... He sipped his cranberry juice, not tasting a thing, wondering what he had just done. Norval and Sam here, together? *My mother and Norval?* Not good combinations, not good at all ...

Norval settled back into his chair, reached for the Boingnères Folle Blanche 1994. "Nice bathroom, Noel." He poured out the biggest glass of brandy Noel had ever seen or heard of. "Just what I always wanted when taking a crap—an instruction manual."

"Yeah ... it's ... I'm going to take all that stuff down ... soon."

"Why didn't you tell me?"

"About what?"

"About your mother."

"Because ... JJ already told you."

"Why didn't *you* tell me?"

Noel sighed, took another sip of juice. "Because ... because you would've ridiculed the whole situation, said I was running a 'mommy daycare' or something, suggested I put her in a home, that I was wasting my time."

"Yes, I would have. And you are."

"Some things are private."

"So that explains why you look so dug-up lately. And why your house is falling apart, like some decaying mansion out of Poe."

"Should've seen it before Sam and JJ arrived."

"And yet your mother seems ... fine. I mean, in the few exchanges we've had."

"She's getting better."

"Was it ... is it Alzheimer's?"

Noel nodded.

"At fifty-six? Shit. Wasn't that the age that Claude—"[55]

"Yes."

"So you feared ... what? You thought that since I couldn't stand my mother I wouldn't understand your ... your devotion to yours? Your martyrdom, sacrifices?"

"Martyrdom? Sacrifices? What am I sacrificing? I've nothing else. She spent practically her entire life caring for me. She used to drive thirty miles out of her way, *daily*, so I could go to a special school. And after Dad died it got even harder for her, to say the least. And she didn't go out with other men—she didn't have time, she said ..." Here Noel flashed to a colleague of hers in the history department who was mad about her, whom he had stupidly objected to one evening, for no valid reason, whom she immediately stopped seeing. "So why wouldn't I care for her? Helping her, on a small scale, as she helped me?"

Norval was surprised by this sudden outpouring. He was moved as well, on a small scale, but made sure not to show it. He undid a smoked-pearl button on his shirt before covering his face with the brandy snifter. An intoxicating perfume of almonds, vanilla and poached pears.

Noel watched him, almost enviously. He would never be able to knock back an amount like that, not without retch and spasm.

Norval savoured the long spicy (clove and pepper?) finish. "I hear you're working with JJ," he said evenly, feeling a pleasant internal flush. "Down in the dungeon."

"Correct."

Norval gave a slight nod. "That sounds promising. To save time, why don't you just tie a millstone around your neck and jump in the Saint Lawrence?"

"No, you really don't know him—"

"What's that, that clusterfuck over there?" Norval pointed to a side-board with a marble top and brass rail at the back, on which mounds of faded papers and airmail envelopes were scattered.

"Samira and JJ found them. They're my grandmother's stuff, her documents. She was a witch. Who cast spells."

"Your grandmother cast spells."

"Correct. She also had a great memory. Probably a synaesthete too, although I can't find any references to it. She ended up in an institution."

"So you'll end up in the same place?"

"Very likely."

"So what are you going to do with it? Put it in a recycling bin?"

"Well, Samira and JJ suggested I throw a bit of mysticism and spirituality and irrationality into my ... research."

"You're going to cast spells."

"In a nutshell."

"Great. Now all you have to do is trade a cow for some magic beans."

"We're already starting to get results. Samira's already cured her insomnia with an insomnia spell."

"I'm afraid to ask what that involves. Eye of newt and toe of frog? Six pinches of powdered orangutan nuts?"

"Look, it's right here: 'Hot milk, turkey, nutmeg and oregano.' Lactose is a sedative—that's the scientific part—and milk is 'sacred to the Mother

Goddess, containing the spiritual power to comfort, soothe and nurture.' Turkey contains tryptophan, an amino acid that causes drowsiness. Nutmeg has medicinal and magical properties similar to those of opiates or peyote. And then you just repeat this chant—"

"Jesus Christ, Noel. Has JJ bit you on the leg? Is this what you three Cuisinartists have been up to? Staving off the inevitable with *spells*?"

"There's nothing 'inevitable' about my mother's condition. You'll see."

◆

The television was echoing in the cathedral-ceilinged family room when Norval stumbled down the steps the next day at noon, unkempt, unshaven and underdressed. He made his way into the kitchen as if sleepwalking, a smouldering filter in his mouth. Half-moons under his eyes matched the dark stains on his smoker's fingers.

At a table heaped with the wreckage of breakfast, Noel was absent-mindedly filling in the squares of a cryptic crossword. "What can I get you, Nor?"

Norval looked briefly for an ashtray before tossing his cigarette butt into the sink, which sizzled like an electrical short. "I don't know," he said with a gravelly voice. "What do you Scots have for breakfast? Haggis? Arbroath smokies with stovies? Soor plooms and chittery bite—"

"There's coffee behind you."

In the family room Samira was arranging blue irises in two vases on a side-table made of split-bamboo. Red-gold sunlight lay in bright puddles on the rush-matting beneath her bare feet. Behind her, on an overstuffed sofa, JJ and Stella sat side by side, watching soccer on an arcane sports channel.

"*OK, Brian, it's time for the second half of our feature match, Holland versus Saudi Arabia, which is shaping—*"

"Saudi Arabia?" Norval said from the doorway, coffee mug in one hand, cigarette in the other. "The Saudis couldn't score in a brothel."

Samira turned. "Well, well, well, a breath of French air."

"Nor!" said JJ, looking as bright and alert as a squirrel. "Join the party! Have a seat." He wiggled closer to Mrs. Burun, patted the seat beside him. "Here."

Norval remained standing, took a gulp of coffee.

"Hey Nor, why did the coach give lighters to his players?"

"Careful now. You wouldn't want me to spit out my coffee."

"Because they lost all their matches."

251

"You hit the hilarity motherlode with that one, JJ. Let's all take five minutes to slap our thighs, shall we?"

A belated burst of laughter came from the sofa. From Mrs. Burun. Looking her way, JJ dissolved in a jelly of giggles, which started Samira up.

"Hey Mrs. B," said JJ, "why do golfers wear two pairs of pants? In case they get a hole in one."

Another detonation from Mrs. Burun, followed by one from Samira. Norval's face remained blank as the two women screeched.

"A guy in a restaurant, Nor."

"JJ ..."

"'Waiter, there's a giraffe in my omelette—'"

"JJ ..."

"Yes?"

"Sod off."

"Right."

"... *Saudi Arabia on the attack. We're two minutes into the second half and it's six-nil Holland* ..."

"I vote we switch channels," said Norval.

"How about Fashion TV?" JJ offered, wiping tears from his face. "Maybe Mrs. B would like that." He pushed a number on the remote.

"Fashion TV," said Norval, "can be watched only one way."

"Really? How's that?"

"Muted."

"Are there any sports you like, Norval?" asked Samira, as JJ muted. "Besides swimming and archery?"

"Certain moments. My favourite is watching a bullfighter get gored by the bull. Or a horse trampling its rider."

With one hand over his mouth, JJ switched channels with the other, to a Quebec show called *Ayoye!*

"Must we listen to that language?" said Norval.

"*That* language?" said Samira, a crease of irritation appearing between her eyes. "It's your mother tongue. And JJ's."

"Look, it's about time everybody stopped being politically correct about this. The so-called French spoken in this province is bilge—mongrelised, pidginised gibberish. The premier knows it, the education minister knows it, and anybody listening to Canada's Prime Minister knows it. But nobody has the guts to say it. Not only do most people in this province have a vocabulary of less than a hundred, but the accent is the vilest and vulgarest on the planet."

"Why you don't tell us what you really think?" said Samira. "Don't be shy."

"It's the Emperor's New French."

Samira nodded. "Do you ever actually think, or do you just spit out words like a wired doll? Prejudices, sweeping statements, generalisations—you never seem to get beyond that."

"Sweeping statements are the only kind worth listening to. Balanced opinions are for bores and third-rate minds."

"*Must* you always talk in aphorisms and faux profundities? Who are you trying to be? La Rochefoucauld? *Every* language on earth has people who use it poorly. This province no more than any other. Vile? Vulgar? Those are subjective terms. I happen to think the accent is lovely. And who made you the grand arbiter of taste and beauty? Who gave you that title? Why do you despise people who are different from you?"

"I despise people who are like me as well."

"You hate everything and everybody. You're nothing but an embittered, middle-aged cynic."

"Middle-aged? I was a cynic in kindergarten."

"A bellyacher and a bleater."

Norval exhaled a long jet of smoke while squinting at Samira. "Let's switch to the weather channel, JJ. I heard the forecast last night, but no one said anything about a shitstorm."

"Hey!" said JJ. "Where's the love? Friends are us."

Norval glared at JJ and was about to say something but decided instead to butt his cigarette in the earth of a potted geranium.

"Friends and relatives are supposed to have a calming influence," JJ continued. "They reduce stress and heart attacks and increase longevity. Even make you less susceptible to the common cold!"

"Really," said Norval. "What about the friends and relatives who lie and betray? Who drive you to depression and suicide?"

"Married men live longer than single men. That's a fact."

Norval took a gulp of his *café au lait*. "They don't actually live longer. It just *seems* longer."

JJ let out a high-pitched tweet of a laugh. "How did you ever get to be such a pessimist?"

"By listening to you optimists."

Identical laugh. "Good one. So how do you like my *café au lait*?"

Norval felt something fiery and amphetamine racing through his blood. "Has a bit of a bite, I have to admit. What's in it?"

"It's triple-caffeinated with roasted guarana and the soymilk contains a natural homologue of Benzedrine."

Norval emptied his mug. "Got any more?"

"No, but I also made some tea. An old Algonquin recipe. Young twigs of mountain-ash with old twigs of white spruce, leaves of wintergreen and flowers of Canada elderberry. A real pick-me-up."

"Great. Then I'll paint my face, put on a war bonnet."

JJ pursed his lips, as if about to whistle a song.

"Why don't you make your announcements now, JJ," said Samira, as Noel entered from the kitchen with a hesitant and unbelonging manner.

"Right you are. Hey, it's the Noelmeister! Join the party, dawg. I'm about to make some announcements. Four in total. All good. Let me just turn this off. Right. Number one: we're forming a club, with us five as members, with our headquarters here at Mrs. B's. This will qualify us for some very sweet municipal grants. The Alzheimer Alchemists is the name I propose for our club. All those in favour, say—"

"JJ," said Norval.

"Yes?"

"Get on with it."

"Number two: federal and provincial grants all lined up—for mortgage payments for our new clubhouse, lab equipment, medications, and for generally easing any ... financial embarrassment. On one of the grant applications, by the way, I had to say we're making a feature-length documentary. Which will bring the private sector on board to fill our coffers—because with my film experience I'm going to handle the PR and funding! And you know what? I'm going to sue the companies that stole my film tagline—for general, punitive and aggravated damages—with all proceeds going to the club. We're going to reach an amount that only astronomers can make sense of!" Here JJ stood up and raised his arms, as if trying to start a wave.

A few seconds of puzzled silence followed, which Samira filled with an "All right! Good for you, JJ!"

"And the good news," said JJ, "keeps coming! Number three: CBC4, the satellite channel, is auditioning contestants for a quiz show. In May. I'm sure you've all seen it: *Tip of Your Tongue!*" He looked directly at Noel. "But it gets even better. Guess what the subject is for the month of May."

"The subject doesn't matter," said Norval. "Noel will memorise everything ever written on whatever it is. Right, Noel?"

254

"No, that's not right," said Noel. "I'm not going on television. That would ... not be possible."

"What's the subject, JJ?" Samira asked.

"Are you ready for this? The subject is ... poetry. *Poetry*, can you believe it? It's destiny! Opportunity rocks!"

"What's the top prize worth?"

"If you go all the way, fifty g's! And Norval has a plan, a real humdinger. *Totally* foolproof."

"Foolproof depends on the size of the fool," said Norval.

"Veux-tu continuer, boss?"

"A few years ago a British army major won the million-pound jackpot on the British version of *Who Wants to Be a Millionaire*. It turns out he was helped by an audience member, who used a system of coughs to help him answer correctly. You must have heard about it. Well, if Noel refuses and I have to go on—assuming I qualify—then we're going to do something along the same lines. Not with coughs, that's hare-brained, but with a supersonic hearing device. Any questions I can't answer will be answered by Noel, who will give me signals with a dog whistle."

"And Norval will be wearing my watch-transponder!" said JJ. "Is that brilliant, Noel?"

But Noel was preoccupied; he was juggling coloured letters in his head, anagrammatizing *supersonic* into *percussion*.

"To proceed," said Norval, "Noel will tell me if the answer is *a*, *b*, *c* or *d* by one, two, three or four blasts of the whistle. Very simple. So, unless there's anything else, I move we adjourn."

"Not so fast," said JJ gruffly, letting seconds tick by for dramatic effect. "One last topic. Number five. Arson."

"God, I almost forgot about that," said Samira. "Was there much damage, Nor?"

"Some furniture, a few paintings singed—I was getting tired of them anyway. All insured—with enough to cover JJ's place."

"Who do you think did it?" asked Samira. "The same person that set the other one?"

"This is what we're about to find out," said JJ. Norval's insurance offer had no effect on his expression, which remained detectival. "My gut tells me ... that somebody in this room is responsible for both fires. And nobody's leaving until we find out who."

The room fell silent. Samira nodded, struck by the inherent logic of the assertion. Could it have been Noel? Tracked down by one of his lunatic

255

research patients? Or Stella, when wandering, unaware of what she was doing? How many times has she set off smoke alarms? But that's impossible. No, it must be Norval ...

Stella looked anxiously from face to face, feeling something sinister in the air. Which one of these people lights fires? Because it's not me, and certainly not my son. It can't be him, he's much too sweet a boy. Or her, she's too sweet a girl. It must be him, the handsome one ...

Noel fidgeted. Yes, he thought, JJ may be right. *It's one of us* ... He looked around the room, dismissing each candidate in turn, until he got to Norval, whose face was buried in his hands. He must be behind this. Was he about to confess? Everyone in the room was now staring at Norval, waiting.

Norval's foot began to tap slowly. He raised his head, guilt seemingly etched on his face. "JJ, I'm struggling to put a positive construction on this. Until now, I have treated your herbally-warped ideas with benign contempt. But now I feel awe: even by your own high standards, you have outstripped yourself in pointlessness. Every day with you is like a trip to Pointless Island."

"But I saw this murder mystery on TV about an insurance scam and—"

"Then your TV needs to be childproofed. The guy who set both fires was out to get me, a settling of accounts. He caught me *in flagrante delicto* with his girlfriend, Rainbaux. And then I caught him in my loft with a canister bomb. But there's nothing to worry about. He won't be setting any more fires for a while."

JJ was in a tizzy. "Really? You caught him? What'd you do? You held him until the cops arrived, right?"

"Something like that."

Chapter 20
Norval & Stella

Arrow removed from man's head

Presse canadienne

MONTREAL, QUE.—A 28-year-old man is expected to be released from hospital today after doctors removed an arrow from his head.

The arrow hit the upper part of the man's left eye socket, missing the eye, and lodged in a sinus cavity, narrowly missing the brain. The man's name was not made public.

The victim, who is well known to police for drug-related activities, is being held as a suspect in an arson case on rue de la Commune in Old Montreal. The man claimed to be leaving a friend's loft when an arrow, shot by an unknown assailant, lodged 10 centimetres in his head. The arrow is currently being examined for clues.

The following day Norval was reading a newspaper, comfortably asprawl a Murphy bed in his chosen quarters, a secret and sacred lair that a younger Noel had cunningly carved out of the attic. A knock on the door distracted him from an article of interest.

"Enter," Norval commanded. He was facing away from the door, and did not turn round to see who entered.

"Norval, I was wondering if you ... if you'd like a drink."

"I would, yes. Just set it on the table."

"I mean, downstairs, with my mom. I was wondering if you could ... you know, keep her company for a while. Until JJ and Samira get back. She's all alone and I've got some things brewing in the basement ..."

Norval had still not turned his head toward his visitor. A cigarette smouldered from the fingers that also turned the page of his newspaper. He now stopped to listen, not to what his friend was saying, but to

Herman's Hermits' "Mrs. Brown You've Got A Lovely Daughter," which was wafting from Mrs. Burun's room below.

"Not too many people know this," said Norval, "but Herman recorded another version of that song. A gay version."

Noel listened. "He did? What was it called?"

"'Mr. Brown You've Got a Lovely Pecker.'"

Noel paused, then straight-faced began to sing the rising echo-line, "Love-ly pe-cker ..."

Norval laughed, uncharacteristically.

"So what are you reading?" Noel asked. He walked closer to the bed, the sprung floorboards undulating under his feet, and peered over Norval's shoulder.

Norval frowned, put the paper down. "Noel, I can't stand people reading over my shoulder. Especially during sex, because that means I'm getting buggered."

"I'm not reading over your shoulder. I'm trying to see the cover of that book beside you." Noel craned his neck to read the title: *In Praise of Older Women*. A fuse began to crackle inside his brain, lit by a letter from the word *Praise*, a writhing scarlet *S*. "Norval, surely you're not planning on ... you know ..."

"Spit it out, Noel. On seducing your mother? Not in the least. But I *am* fond of older women ..."

You can't *still* be on *S*, thought Noel. What happened to red-haired Simone?

"... and in fact I've adopted Byron as my model. He had sex with the Countess of Benzoni of Verona when she was sixty-one."

"She was from Venice."

"He then upped the ante with Lady Melbourne, who was sixty-two, and a few days later seduced Lady Oxford's daughter, who was eleven."

"He raped her and was caught in the act by her mother. With whom he was having an affair."

"Really? I did something similar with a mother-daughter duo. The age gap, though, wasn't as great, and it was a consensual three-way."

"Is this one of your fabrications for Dr. Vorta?"

"Hardly. It involved his wife and daughter."[56]

"High-end port you have here, Burun. How *odd* that you should serve it in a claret glass." Norval held the crystal up to the light.

"Screw off."

"I noticed a pipe on the mantelpiece. A Comoy's, I believe. You wouldn't have any tobacco for it, would you?"

"Yes, I've got some Latakia."

"Don't know it. What's it like?"

"Middle Eastern, dark and aromatic."

"Perfect."

"But I'm not giving it to you. Or the pipe. Smoking a used pipe is like wearing another man's underwear, my father used to say."

"Quite rightly. Noel, your mother needs a refill. So do I, for that matter. Is there a bell I can pull?"

"My mother's already had a glass. I think that's enough."

Mrs. Burun was sitting calmly in her favourite blue armchair, silently observing the two men.

"Of course it's not enough," said Norval. "You're not up on the latest research. Alcohol is good for Alzheimer's. It breaks up, or frees up ... well, doesn't matter what. Something that needs breaking and freeing up."

"It breaks up blood platelets. And frees up acetylcholine in the hippocampus."

"Exactly. Which is good for learning and memory, *n'est-ce pas?*"

"Yes. Aromatic alcohols with intact phenolic groups act as neuro-protectants, guarding against oxidative damage and cell death."

"I rest my case."

"But other research suggests that it's not alcohol, but the red grape. And the same research indicates that too much alcohol leads straight to dementia. Which, judging by the amount you've had since break-fast, is where you're headed."

Norval inspected his nails. "Noel, does that sort of thing pass for wit back in Scotland?"

"And why is my mother chewing gum?"

"JJ gave it to her. He says studies at Northumbria University—"

"Suggest that it improves the memory."

"Well, yes. Thirty-five per cent improvement, in fact. JJ will tell you all about this, and more, if you're not careful."

"And you've got my mother smoking again, I see. She hasn't smoked in twenty-five years. Those cigarettes are for guests."

"She asked for one, said she always liked a good smoke. Didn't you, Stella. And besides, tobacco's good for the memory.[57] And especially Alzheimer's."

"It more than doubles the risk of getting it."

"Rubbish. My grandfather's ninety-three. Smokes like a bonfire. And clear as a mountain stream. Who's the oldest living North American? A tobaccoholic named John McMorran, who's 113. And besides, I'm putting my foot down. I'm limiting your mum to a pack a day."

"I don't want her smoking."

"Let her have some fun, for God's sake. Let her eat, drink and remarry."

"No. Alcohol doesn't interact well with the new compounds I'm giving her. Nor does nicotine."

"Let's drink and be jolly and drown melancholy," said Stella, lifting her glass in a Scottish toast. Tipsily, thought Noel. "*Slàinte mhath!*"

"There you go," said Norval. "You can't disobey your own mother."

"You heard me," said Noel.

"What is it with everybody around here? I'm surrounded by pleasure police. Sam's a prissy-ass vegetarian, JJ's a homeopathic e-quack, and you're a ... factualist. Blinded by science. 'Wisdom, ever on the watch to rob Joy of its alchemy ...'[58] What is it with today's society?"

Noel looked at his watch. This, he knew, was the preamble to a long lecture. "Look, Norval, I've got to go down—"

"Today's healthism fanatics, nutrition cheerleaders, lifestyle correctors—they're ruling people's lives the way the Church used to. They want us all in a perennial state of Lent. Instead of conspicuous consumption, they want conspicuous self-denial. If it's pleasurable, let's do some studies and find something wrong with it. Let's get everybody believing that if they eat the food we tell them to, they'll be leading the 'good life', will live forever, be beautiful forever, paragons of morality. And anybody who smokes or drinks, anybody who eats a hamburger or a fried onion ring, will be excommunicated, cast off as undesirables, untouchables."

Norval was speaking slowly, to give the impression this was unscripted, an old trick of his.

"OK, Norval, you've made your point, so now—"

"The world has become *afraid*. Worriers and hypochondriacs. Candy-asses and bores, the bland leading the bland. Parents are the worst. 'Put your helmet on, Bobby, you're opening a can of Coke.' Where'd you say the liquor cabinet was?"

"I just finished saying that I don't want you—"

"Keep everyone afraid and they'll consume—it's the new corporate motto. The drug companies in particular—they're the real fear factories, the scaremongers, along with the doctors of course, who can cram more patients into their schedules by prescribing the drug-of-the-month. But do we need all this shit? There are fifteen thousand new drugs a year. We don't have enough diseases to go around. So what do the drug companies do? They hire psychiatrists to invent more. What was it Oliver Wendell Holmes said? You with me, Noel?"

"Said about what? He said a lot of things."

"Well, what are we talking about? Drugs."

Noel heaved a tired sigh. "That if the world's entire pharmacopoeia were thrown into the sea, it would be better for mankind, but worse for the fish."

"Exactly."

"But he said that in the nineteenth century."

"And do you know what old people say—*really* old people—when they're asked about the secret of longevity?"

"Yes, because I'm the one who told you."

"'Stay away from doctors, never take any medicines.' They all say the same thing."

"But in my mom's case—"

"The French Revolution," Mrs. Burun interrupted, but let the words hang in the air.

An awkward patch of silence followed. Noel held his breath. Mrs. Burun took a long drag on her cigarette.

"What about the French Revolution, Stella?" said Norval.

"Norval, please leave her—"

"Changes in health philosophy," Mrs. Burun replied, dropping her cigarette butt into her glass and watching it sizzle.

"Really? What kind of changes?"

A look of doubt began to creep into Stella's face. Is this relevant? Or have we moved on? What was the last topic? Coercive health, or over-medication? "Nothing," she said. "I think I ... I think we've moved on ... we're talking about something different ..."

"We were talking about health philosophy. What happened during the French Revolution?"

"Norval," said Noel under his breath. "I suggest we—"

"Changes," said Stella, "based on the idea that proper diet and lifestyle were the best ways to make people obedient, compliant ... And in

Germany, around the same time, the merchant and upper classes got more or less the same idea. That the best way to keep things running smoothly, to prevent unrest or change, was to make sure that workers were healthy, fit."

"Like feeding the galley slaves to keep the boat moving," said Norval.

"They even had terms like 'medicine police' and 'health police'. And then of course the eugenics movement came along, suggesting that only the 'superior' variety of people should propagate."

"Not a bad idea, actually ..."

"So then poor health, which was previously seen as unavoidable, as bad luck, was seen to be the result of bad habits, or bad lifestyles. And from there it was a short leap to a new theory—that control of breeding and lifestyles was the legitimate business of governments."

"The philosophy of the Third Reich," said Norval.

"Exactly," said Stella.

Norval reached over, clinked glasses with Stella. "Noel, we *need* bad habits, for Christ's sake. We need risky lifestyles, dangerous lifestyles. You know why? Because with all the boomers going into retirement, the state is not going to be able to pay these people to hang around doing bugger-all—apart from pumping iron and prancing around in gyms. Soon we'll need fleets of vans that cruise around all day picking up joggers and taking them home—they'll be in great shape but won't remember where they live. So the healthists have got it all backwards. Smokers and alcoholics should be thanked, saluted, for selflessly chopping years off their life. Binge-hogs who scarf down Big Whoppers and fries sitting on their whopping asses, knocking back beer in front of the box, should be canonized for cashing in early."

Stella laughed, a deep belly laugh, one Noel hadn't heard in a while. "My mother used to feel the same way," she said. "She had every bad habit in the book—and told her doctors to go to the devil."

Noel was now smiling, delighted at his mother's new coherency—and the latest drug responsible for it. "All right, Mom, I give in. If cigarettes and alcohol are a pleasure, go for it." He could hardly wait to tell JJ—it must be the A-1001. He should make more. "Listen, I've got some things to do in the lab, and a couple ideas I want to work out. You two'll be all right? Got everything you need?"

Norval gave a slight nod, then waited for the basement door to close. "Let me light that, Stella."

As she leaned over the match Norval caught a glimpse of the cleft of her breasts and black lace bra. When she resumed her position, he studied her swept-back salt-and-pepper hair, her patrician face, her upper lip the shape of an archery bow. More like Lauren Hutton, he decided, than Catherine Deneuve. About the same age and with that seductive incisor gap that a tongue might just slide its way through. And that luscious Scottish accent ...

"Stella, in the interests of art, I was wondering if you'd help me out with this project I'm working on ..."

Chapter 21
Stella's Diary (II)

20 April 2002. The quick brown fox jumps over the lazy dog. The quick brown fox jumps over the lazy dog. The quick brown fox jumps over the lazy dog. Jackdaws love my big sphinx of quartz.

Well, that feels better. My fingers feel better, my mind feels better. I'm not all the way there but I feel like I can finish sentences now. And I can remember what I had for breakfast this morning.

If the sword of Damocles fell, it missed.

21 April. Touch wood. I remembered something else today. When Noel reads to me at bedtime -- as I read to him aeons ago -- he often mumbles something before starting, almost like a prayer. Which sometimes makes me cry. But no matter how hard I tried, I could never remember what it was, until today: 'To you mother I will read these lines, for love of unforgotten times.'

24 April. Finally met Noel's best friend, a Frenchman named Norval Blaquière. He's what my students would have called 'hot'. I never thought I'd use that word. He's handsome (almost looks like a Burun!) and his clothes -- tailor-made by the look of them -- are exquisite: white muslin shirt with metal snaps, leather jacket of the deepest green, black wool trousers with grosgrain trim ... But all on the well-worn, genteel-shabby side, as if picked up at an aristocrat's jumble sale.

And he can be quite charming, despite his air of self-satisfied superiority in all matters of taste and intellect, and this cold, cutting tone he has (he wears his hatchet on his sleeve). Still, he makes me laugh -- even more than JJ. The strangest part of it all is that, from the way he looks at me so piercingly, I almost think he's attracted to me, that he's 'making love to me' (in the old-fashioned sense). Is that a figment of my imagination? Wishful thinking? A faded beauty's yearning for attention? But I did feel something -- unless, like so many other things, my woman's intuition is failing me.

25 April. After my husband died my relationship with men seemed to die as well -- apart from two or three unhappy skirmishes. The chemistry was never quite right. Or perhaps it was the past that got in the way. I've often thought about Shelley's wife in this respect, his first wife, whose name escapes me. She drowned herself in the Serpentine, leaving her husband 'a prey to the reproaches of memory'. For years this is what I felt, and it must have affected my interactions with men. I may be wrong. In any case, I had enough trouble making a living, bringing up a son -- romantic turmoil was all I needed! Teaching and Noel (in reverse order) -- those were my passions. But when Noel moved out, and seemed to be doing well, I started thinking about men again, about relationships. I was very fond of a colleague in the history department, who shall remain nameless, and he seemed to be fond of me. He asked me out several times over the years, but I always declined, for one reason or another. And then, just when I had changed my mind, just when I was about to ask him out, well, that's when I began to lose my memory!

Harriet Westbrook. (Thank you, Noel.)

26 April. I scarcely know where to begin. I thought this sort of thing was over for me. Norval, this friend of my son's ... modesty forbids me to finish the sentence. Suffice it to say that I was right -- Norval was attracted to me. Will

265

wonders never cease! It was an 'art project' of some sort -- I
have to admit I can't remember all the details (an alcoholic
mist, nothing more) and I couldn't tell whether he was
kidding or not -- but who cares? It was incredible. And
shocking. Doubts, inhibitions, fears somehow disappeared,
and for the first time I didn't go back in time, into
heaviness, I just stayed in the present, in lightness.

I know this won't happen again, and that's perhaps for the
best. Norval's heart belongs to another, although he didn't
actually come out and say it -- but I could tell by the way he
didn't actually come out and say it.

Probably not a good idea to tell Noel, we both agreed. At
least for now.

27 April. One last thing about yesterday. In the morning,
as my head gradually cleared, I asked Norval why he chose
me and not another S, someone younger, more beautiful ...
like Samira, for instance. 'It takes two to tango,' he replied,
with no shilly-shallying, no false compliments. 'When I was
interested she wasn't, and when she was interested I wasn't.'
'And why weren't you ... interested?' I asked. 'None of your
business,' he answered, his words riding a stream of smoke.
'With all due respect.' I nodded, watching a wobbly ring
dissolve, knowing the answer. Because of Noel.

Sunday, 28 April 2002. I know what day it is today. And the
year. All week long I've known. I'm not quite there, but
almost. (ALZ well that ends well, as Norval says. Let's hope
he's right.) On Monday I see a neuropharmacologist or
neuropathologist (I've forgotten her name but I only heard it
once!) who's apparently working with AD compounds similar
to the ones Noel is using with me or that target similar
brain functions, I'm not sure which. I do hope all this leads
somewhere, not only for me but for the whole world. Could
this get me back to teaching? Could I go back to Scotland one
more time! Assuming I survive the tests and treatments ...

Norval came over this evening. With a bouquet of flowers, which he handed to me not sheepishly, not secretly, but matter-of-factly -- right in front of Noel! 'Here. These are for you, Stella,' he said.

'How lovely!' I exclaimed. 'Yellow roses -- that means something, doesn't it, Noel? Friendship?'

Noel gazed at the petals, with a bit of a scowl. 'Yellow symbolises jealousy,' he replied. 'Or it can mean guilt or treason or depraved passions ...'

'It means,' said Norval, 'that they didn't have any red ones.'

1 May. Very clearheaded with fewer and fewer fuzzy areas -- a miracle? Is it possible that I never had AD? Noel, JJ assures me, is becoming a brilliant neuropharmacologist. Or is Émile behind all this? Noel's last concoction, in any case, seems to have worked wonders. But it has side-effects, unbelievable side-effects! I felt like I was floating near the ceiling, looking down on my own body, like a soul freed of its earthly bonds! Or maybe I was near death and this was a dress rehearsal ...

11 May. Noel is in love with Samira, and I hardly needed Norval to plant that seed in my mind. Although I should probably stay out of it, I'm going to try to bring them together, if I can.

14 May. Hope I'm not being a drama queen or nag, but for the past couple of weeks I've been asking (pestering?) Noel about his health. He says he's just lost a bit of weight, but he doesn't look at all well to me. I've asked Norval to talk to him about it.

15 May. Strange coincidence. A few days ago we talked about trying to get on this quiz show (which Noel hates) and this afternoon JJ and I watched an episode of The Honeymooners, the one where Ralph goes on a TV show called The $99,000 Answer. He chooses the category Popular Songs. We were laughing like lunatics, but I have to admit I find it

painful to watch when Ralph, who knows the category backwards, can't name the composer of 'Swanee River' in the very first question. I know it's silly but I'm getting so nervous about Norval's appearance. It's in two days! Fingers crossed.

Chapter 22
The Arabian Nightmare
(Noel's Diary III)

May 17. The applause sign flashed and a handful of people obeyed it, including a frenetic JJ on one side and the fumbling ghostwriter on the other, who was trying to balance a clipboard and a Memorex CD-R on his lap at the same time. My mother and Samira were smiling at each other as they clapped; I was frozen with nervousness but understood every word, or almost.

"Welcome to CBC4's Tip of Your Tongue! Brought to you by ... Memorex! And now, please welcome your master of ceremonies, Jack Lafontaine!"

From the entrance of the studio, Jack Lafontaine came trotting down the aisle, high-fiving people who weren't high-fiving back, waving to a crowd that seemed unsure of who he was.

"Cut!" said the director, a fuzzy-haired boy with a pre-pubescent voice. "We need more noise than that, people. When the applause sign flashes, please, everybody—"

"We can juice it later," offered the soundman, sniffing badly from a cold, or line of cocaine.

"I don't want to juice it up later. We've been criticised for that—how are we going to sell this show to the States if it sounds like a home video? And for the audience shot, can we get that dog out of the aisle? Yes, that dog. How many dogs are there in the studio? What are we doing, 101 Dalmatians? Let's take it from the top, after the intro. Three, two, one ..."

Jack came running down the aisle again, with dyed black wind-resistant hair that seemed to have been glued on, and a tight tuxedo that made his movements slightly penguinish. He hopped up the stairs to the makeshift stage. The applause was only marginally louder.

"Thank you, ladies and gentlemen, for that warm welcome. Glad to have you aboard for Tip of Your Tongue! Let me just catch my breath. All right, tonight's theme is ... poetry! This is show number seventy-seven and so far no

one has gone all the way to the top. Let's hope the double sevens will be lucky for someone tonight! So without further ado, let's meet a new group of contestants in search of ... fifty thousand dollars!"

APPLAUSE sign.

"Tonight's questions have been prepared by Dr. Émile Vorta, the distinguished neurologist from the University of Quebec—and a poet in his own right!—who will also be acting as tonight's referee. Thank you, Dr. Vorta, it's an honour to have you here. All right contestants, are we ready to roll? It's time to put on your thinking caps—because here comes the quick-digit query. Using the buttons in front of you, I want you to put the following poems in chronological order, according to year of publication:

(1) *In Memoriam—Lord Tennyson*
(2) *Remember—Christina Rossetti*
(3) *Much madness is divinest sense—Emily Dickinson*
(4) *I Remember, I Remember—Thomas Hood*
(5) *The Old Fools—Philip Larkin*

"Time's up. The correct answer is 4, 2, 1, 3, 5. Let's see who got it right. Sylvie Viau and Ronald Sheldrake. Sylvie's time was 8.7 seconds and Ronald's ... 9.3! Good for you, Ronald, I mean Sylvie. Step up here, please! No, not you, Ronald."

Norval, his finger still resting on one of the buttons, looked stunned. JJ slumped in his chair. Samira and my mother exchanged glum looks. I was distracted by the odd colour form, but understood the question when I saw the screen, saw the numbers. Should I say something? I turned and whispered into Samira's ear.

"Are you sure?" she said. She then whispered into JJ's ear; he leaned over to look at me and I nodded.

"Congratulations, Sylvie—"

"Hold on!" a voice came from the audience. JJ's. "There's been a mistake!"

"Cut!" said the fuzzy-haired boy.

Dr. Vorta, in an agitated state, lifted his beard from a reference book. "Yes, I fear there has been an error. The 1 and 2 should be reversed."

"You sure, Doc?" said the fuzzy-haired boy. "Positive? OK, Pierre, can you change the graphic? Jack, we'll start again at 'The correct order is ...' Ready? 3-2-1 ..."

"And the correct order is 4, 1, 2, 3, 5. Let's see who had the right answer ... Two people again. I mean two people. And the one with the fastest time is ... Norval Blaquière! Norval, come on up here please!"

This time the ovation was thunderous, mostly because JJ was rabid, out of control. With his patented smirk Norval walked casually onto the stage, and sat down with his arms folded across his chest.

"Well done, sir. So how does it feel, Norval, to be in the hot seat?"

"It's cold plastic, Jack."

"Good one! I see we've got a livewire tonight! A lit disturber! All right. So, my friend, it says here you're a writer and a teacher. Where do you teach?"

"I see no reason to embarrass the school, Jack—I'm about to be sacked for unethical conduct."

"Shall we get started? You know the rules—you'll be asked a series of questions of increasing difficulty. Let me remind you: you may stop at any point and take the money and run. Otherwise, if you answer incorrectly, you will leave with zero. Take a deep breath. Ready?"

Norval rolled his eyes.

"Let's play ... Tip of Your Tongue! These sealed envelopes I'm holding in my hand are secured each week in a bank vault at the Laurentian Bank headquarters until just before show time. Which reminds me—check out their new mortgage rates! Shall we get started? First question, for a hundred dollars: What is an abecadarius? Is it (a) an acrostic, the initial letters of whose successive lines form the alphabet; (b) a verse arranged in such a way as to spell names or phrases; (c) a notebook which lists the rudiments of a subject; or (d) a lover's diary in which conquests are listed alphabetically?"

"A."

"Just won a hundred bucks! A two-parter coming up. Which type of poem is the following, and what is the metre? Check it out on the monitor ..."

> A lesbian bride and her groom
> Asked a gay man up to their room.
> They spent the whole night
> In a hell of a fight
> Over who should do what, and to whom.

"Is this (a) a sonnet; (b) a villanelle, (c) a—"

"Limerick."

"Uh ... right you are. Second part. Is the meter (a) iambic; (b) ionic; (c) trochaic; or (d) anapaestic?"

"Anapaestic."

"Ultimate, untakebackable answer? You sure? Glad to hear it, because you've just won five hundred bucks! Let's give it up for Norval Blaquière!"

APPLAUSE sign.

"So, Norval, it says on your résumé that you've worked as a film actor ..."

"That was a fabrication I used to get on the show."

Jack burst out laughing. "Don't tell anyone, but that's how I got on the show too! OK, third hurdle for a thousand dollars. Have I got the right question? Here we go. Another two-parter. A certain lover of Lord Byron's, who in a fit of jealousy bit through her glass at dinner when she saw the poet leaning towards another woman, later sent him a lock of her hair, asking for his in return. For one thousand dollars, who was this lover and what was the poet's response?"

"Caroline Lamb. Byron sent her another woman's hair—the Countess of Oxford's pubic hair."

Jack paused before looking up from his card. "Could someone get me a fire extinguisher? Because Norval's brain is on fire! All right baby! Three in a row! Are you loving this, audience?"

APPLAUSE sign.

"Have you thought about what you'll do with your money, Norval?"

"Yes Jack, I have. It'll go towards providing a university education for my twelve foster children in Africa."

"All right baby! Maybe we'll see one of them on the show one day! OK, it's time for the five-question lightning round. You must get at least three of five correct to move on. Are you ready? You've got twenty seconds to tell me the author of these lines on the monitor."

(1) He is crazed with the spell of far Arabia,
    They have stolen his wits away.

(2) Ah tell me not that memory
    Sheds gladness o'er the past;
    What is recalled by faded flowers
    Save that they did not last?

(3) Forgetfulness has made its country your red
    Mouth, and the flowing of Lethe is in your kiss.

(4) A dream before the ledger flitted,
    A dream before the brain;
    Ah, yet the toil is unremitted,
    The journeying is vain!
    The train the city never quitted,
    'Twas but a phantom train!

272

5)   *The Clock! Sinister, demonic god that makes us tremble,*
     With threatening finger tells us: "Remember!"

In no apparent hurry, Norval scanned the audience with impervious calm.
Was he looking at me? No, at Samira. "One. Walter de la Mare. Two. Letitia
Elizabeth Landon. Three. Baudelaire. Four. May Kendall. Five. Baudelaire."
   Jack bit his lip, slowly nodded his head. "Amazing. Absolutely freaking
AMAZING! All five correct for five thousand dollars! Let's hear it for our
resident genius, Norval Blaquière—who may be going where no other
contestant has gone before!"
   APPLAUSE sign.
   Following JJ's lead, Samira jumped to her feet, clapping wildly. Would she
ever do that for me? I wondered, as I clapped along. Of course not. Why would
she?
   "All right, let's pause here to catch our breath. When we return, Norval will
be going for ... ten thousand dollars!"
   APPLAUSE sign.
   "Back in the early seventies the image of Ella Fitzgerald's recorded voice
shattering a wine glass was seen and remembered by millions. And the
accompanying theme line, 'Is it live or is it Memorex?' was quickly adopted
around the world. To continue this tradition of excellence, we are now
introducing our Pocket Memory CD-R. At three inches, Pocket Memory goes
where no recorder has ever gone before ..."

*   *   *

"All right, we've got Norval Blaquière on the hot seat. Or should I say, cold
seat? So far Norval has won ... five thousand dollars! Do you have any kids, my
pal?"
   "No."
   "For ten thousand dollars, another two-parter. First part: what does
Liebestod signify? L-i-e-b-e-s-t-o-d. A German word, isn't that right, Dr. Vorta?
Is it (a) death as a result of unhappy love; (b) mutual love in which both
lovers prefer union in death to separation in life; (c) a utopian state in which
marriage does not exist; (d) a poem by Dorothy Parker?"
   "B. And D."
   "Right you are! But you're not out of the woods yet. Second part: in which
of the following Elizabethan poems—"
   "Hero and Leander. Christopher Marlowe."

"Uh ... sure you don't want me to finish? No? Glad to hear it, my man, because you've just won ten thousand clams!"

APPLAUSE sign.

"I'm jazzed, and I know our audience is too! Are you jazzed, audience? Are you amped? I can't hear you! All right, we're now approaching the game's final stage. It's time to narrow your field. Which language is it going to be: (a) French, (b) German, (c) Spanish, (d) Italian or (e) Arabic?"

"E."

"Really? Are you serious? Excellent stuff. Now, you know things are going to get trickier—no more multiple choice! Are you ready to rumble?"

"No, I'd like to use one of my lifelines at this point. I'd like my friend Noel Burun to trade places with me. Because my memory has suddenly gone blank."

The studio went silent. "But ... we don't have lifelines on this show," Jack said, with a puzzled expression. "What's that, Dr. Vorta? We can bend the rules? We put it to the audience? OK, what do you say, audience? It's in your hands. Should we go with the flow?"

APPLAUSE sign.

Jack shielded his eyes with his hand, surveyed the crowd, counted raised hands. "No question about it—the audience has spoken. Is Noel Burun in the audience? OK, when we come back, we'll meet Norval's tag-team partner for the final round! We're what? We're out of time? All right, ladies and gentlemen, I'm afraid you'll have to tune in next week to see what happens on ... Tip of Your Tongue!"

APPLAUSE sign.

"Fifteen-minute break," said the fuzzy-haired boy. "Then we'll wrap this up."

*　　*　　*

The fuzzy-haired boy stood in front of me, smiling, waiting for an answer. He reeked of stale sweat and his voice had almost no colour, no inflection.

My mouth was dry, a sandbox. "I can't do it," I croaked, petrified at the thought of going on TV. "I have ... problems. Stage fright."

"Can't you try, Noel?" Samira asked. Her voice was velvety, haloed. "For your mom? And me?"

I could feel my teeth grinding, my bottom lip being bitten, the side of my thumb being scratched till it bled. I looked at my mother, who smiled at me.

She'd never forced me to do anything before, and wouldn't now. "That's all right, Noel," she said softly, reassuringly. "I understand ..."

A jolt, like an electrical surge, made the house lights flicker and I was suddenly backstage, in claustrophobic corridors, all of them colourless, all of them blind.

*　　*　　*

"Welcome to Tip of Your Tongue! Brought to you by Memorex and a brand-new co-sponsor ... Maxwell House coffee! One hundred per cent pure Arabica. Now in resealable canisters. Take it away, Dr. Volta."

"Vorta."

"Take it away, Dr. Vorta!"

"Maxwell House coffee, according to our researchers, was named after the Maxwell House Hotel in Nashville, Tennessee, where Joel Cheek's blend became the house coffee in 1892. Legend has it that on a visit to Nashville in 1907, President Teddy Roosevelt declared that Maxwell House coffee was 'good to the last drop.' One hundred years later, that familiar slogan remains the brand's promise to its customers. Good to the last drop!"

"Thank you, Dr. Volta. Let's hope our viewers could cut through that thick Swiss accent! All right, at the end of last week's show, Norval Blaquière, a thirty-three-year-old bachelor from Montreal, earned a total of ten thousand dollars before narrowing his subject to ... Arabic literature! And then decided to pass the torch on to his best friend. So now it's time to meet Norval's torchbearer. How about a warm hand for Noel Burun!"

APPLAUSE sign.

"Welcome to the show, Noel. How do you feel about coming into pinch-hit for your best buddy? A little nervous with all that money on the line? Noel?"

My insides were twisted, my bones molten. I cupped my hand to my ear, as if I couldn't hear.

"I asked how the old nerves were. Noel? Should we cut here, Pierre?"

"We'll edit. Keep it rolling ..."

"As you know, you can either try for the top prize of fifty thousand dollars, or with one wrong answer fall to zero—an Arabic word, isn't that right, Dr. Volta? Yes? What would you like to do, Noel?"

Inside my head, round and round as if caught in a sandstorm, feather-edged aubergine beads reeled with centripetal force. I closed my eyes, let my head sway gently to and fro, slowed my brain to the brink of vegetabledom.

"Noel? I said what would you like to do? Noel? Are you all right? Nerves getting to you?"

The voice was small, like the sound from someone else's walkman. "No, I … I'd like to continue please, Mr. Lafontaine." My own voice had a quaver—I could hear it myself. "Thank you."

"Excellent stuff. All right, on the subject of Arabic literature, we are now ready for the first of three sealed questions. I've been assured by Dr. Émile Volta, the world-famous neurologist, that he's concocted some real ball-busters … shit."

"Cut!" said the fuzzy-haired boy. "Start again from 'I've been assured.'"

"I've been assured by Dr. Émile Volta, the world-famous neurologist, that he's concocted some real brain-busters this week, so we'll find out in the next few minutes if Noel's brain can be busted. Are you ready, sir?"

I nodded, wiped my face with a Kleenex. I felt so hot I thought I could smell burning flesh. Off camera, I'd just chewed on some betel leaves with lime, which JJ had given me. Voices were now much bigger in my ear, as if I were wearing headphones.

"All right, here's your first question! Omar Khayyam, the eleventh-century poet-astronomer from Persia, is best known for a collection of epigrammatic quatrains, one hundred and one in all, called the Rubáiyát. For twenty-five thousand dollars, recite the 74th quatrain."

A murmur went through the audience as I squeezed my eyes shut, tried to block everything out while trawling my memory. I saw my mother's face—so much younger!—then heard her voice …

"Noel? Are you with me? Shall I repeat the question?"

"'Yesterday this day's Madness did prepare; / To-morrow's Silence, Triumph, or Despair: / Drink! For you know not whence you came, nor why: / Drink! For you know not why you go, nor where.'"

Jack pored over his card, raised his head, and with grave disappointment said, "Noel, I'm sorry but … I'm a very slow reader. I've now read every word on my card and have to inform you that … you're wrro … right! You're absolutely right! Are you loving this, audience? Were human beings meant to be this entertained?"

APPLAUSE sign.

"All right. Moving up the ladder. Second question, for thirty-five thousand dollars. In The Arabian Nights, also known as The One Thousand and One Nights, there's a story entitled 'The Tale of the Hashish Eater,' in which a man makes a bit of a spectacle of himself. For thirty-five grand, can you recite the relevant passage?"

276

I closed my eyes again. This one was easy. JJ had shown it to me the night before. "'They were pointing out to each other his naked zabb, which stood up in the air as far as was humanly possible, as great as that of an ass or an elephant. Some of them poured pitchers of cold water over this column.'"

Jack Lafontaine looked down at his card, up at the audience, then sideways at Dr. Vorta. "I don't know about the ass, but Noel certainly has the memory of an elephant!"

APPLAUSE sign.

"All right, excellent ... Oh, do you hear that drum roll? It can mean only one thing. The final question. Will Noel be able to stave off execution once more, like Scheherazade? Did I pronounce that right, Doctor? How are the nerves now, Noel?"

"To tell you the truth, Mr. Lafontaine, I'm nervous. But the shades of your voice are quite comforting—they're soft and silvery-white, like potassium."

"They ... are? Well, thank you for that, Noel, that's very kind. Am I blushing? I hope our producer is listening—you hear that? He likes the silvery-white shades of my voice! All right, enough of that. I don't know if you can feel the tension at home, but in the studio you can cut it with a knife—or should I say, a scimitar! We've arrived at the moment of truth. Are you ready, Noel? Again, in The One Thousand and One Nights, *in a tale called 'Al-Rashid and the Fart,' a very peculiar cure is recommended to a traveller. For fifty thousand dollars, name the ingredients of this cure."*

This rang no bells, none whatsoever. Did JJ show me that passage, when I wasn't listening? Did my mom ever read me that story? I waited for the words and colours to unsilt themselves ...

"Ahem. Uh, Noel? Are you with us? Time's running out ..."

I tried to focus, but on what? I could feel my head getting hotter and hotter, my alpha waves crashing into each other, my search engine overheating ... I looked down, distracted by something moving—my shaking hands. I couldn't even bring them together to wring them. Around my wrist, I noticed for the first time, was JJ's canine transponder. Was the answer there? Was Norval signalling me? I looked closer. The display was blank.

"I'm going to need an answer in the next ten seconds, my friend, or you leave with zero. Fifty thousand loons on the line ..."

A hailstorm of numbers struck me as time extracted the seconds: $10 \times 1/31{,}556{,}925.9747$ of the tropical year; $10 \times 9{,}192{,}631{,}770$ cycles of radiation in the spectral transition of cesium-133 ...

"Noel, I'm afraid we'll have to ..."

Cesium. *Soft white metal; symbol Cs; atomic number 55, atomic weight 132.91 ...* A fierce light hit me hard, but from behind, like a rabbit punch. I squinted out at the audience, but couldn't see a thing! And the voice I just heard—it was in black-and-white ... I turned to the quizmaster, but it was like looking through night-vision goggles: his face had a milky grey glow and his eyes were missing.

"... acht, sieben, sechs ..."

Is that Dr. Vorta? In a countdown? I turned to the audience again, and this time saw the blurred image of my mother, as if through tears, the way I saw her when my father died. Head bent, eyes shut, fists clenched. I can't let her down!

"... drei, zwei ..."

Someone from the audience was walking towards the stage ... Heliodora Locke!

Words filled the air, and I suddenly realised they came from my lips: "'Take three ounces of the breath of the wind, three ounces of the rays of the sun and three of the rays of the moon ...'"

"Continue."

"'Mix them carefully in a bottomless mortar and expose them to the air for three months. For a further three months pound the mixture, then pour it into a shallow bowl with holes in the bottom.'"

Dr. Vorta looked down at his card. Was he nodding or shaking his head?

"What is Youssef Islam's former name?"

"What?" I must have misheard—that's got nothing to do with the subject. Do I win the money or not?

"What is Youssef Islam's former name?"

My brain was splitting, my mouth empty of saliva, I couldn't form words. I looked around for water. My glass was empty. "Cat Stevens," I rasped.

"Which of the following words are not of Arabic descent: alchemy, assassin, alcohol, scarlet, checkmate, zenith?"

"But ... they all are."

"What is the etymology of the second word mentioned?"

"I ... I don't understand. 'Assassin' comes from an Arabic word for a consumer of hashish."

"Who wrote the novel Zabibah and the King?"

A light was now shining in my face. My mother's hunter's lamp. Held by Dr. Vorta. "Saddam Hussein."

"Who wrote The Village is the Village, the Land is the Land, the Suicide of the Spaceman and Other Stories?"

"Colonel Muammar Qaddafi."

"Who is the father of Arab chemistry? And where and when did he die?"

"Jabir ibn Hayyan. Kufah, Iraq. 815."

"Who is Persia's 'Prince of Physicians' and what was his legacy?"

"Avicenna. His Canon of Medicine is the most famous single book in the history of medicine, in both East and West."

"How many synapses are in the brain?"

"But what's that got to do with—"

"How many synapses are in the brain?"

I once asked my dad this same question. What was his answer? "There are as many synapses in the brain as there are stars in the sky."

"Correct. The inventor of the television—please put your answer in the form of a question."

I lowered my head, put my hand over my eyes. "Who is Vladimir Zworykin?"

"The goddess of memory, and mother of the Muses."

"Who is Mnemosyne?"

"An audio question coming up. I want you to tell me the name of the composer and piece."

I listened to the first two bars. Key of D. "Stephen Foster. 'Swanee River.'"

"Do you have, or have you ever had, sexual fantasies with regard to your mother?"

"No."

"Correct. Have you had with Samira Darwish?"

"Yes."

APPLAUSE sign.

"When you were one and a half, what was the colour of your bib? Was it (a) green; (b) white; (c) yellow; or (d) red?"

"It was none of those colours."

"Correct."

"Dr. Vorta, why are you asking me these questions? They have nothing to do with—"

"We're going to keep going until you miss one."

"But ... why? You're going to ask an impossible question, an unanswerable question ..."

"Using the Nato alphabet, spell and then define 'olibanum.'"

"What? This isn't a spelling bee."

"You were the Quebec champion in '79, were you not?"

"Yes, but ... we were never asked to define the word."

"Spell and define 'oh-LIB-anum.'"

"Olibanum: Oscar, Lima, India, Bravo, Alpha, November, Uniform, Mike. It was used in Arabia as an embalming agent. It's also called frankincense."

"Correct. Do you know who committed the two acts of arson?"

"No."

"Do you think it was me?"

"No."

"Do you think it was your mother?"

"No."

"She has lit fires before."

"It wasn't her, all right?"

"Then who was it?"

"I don't know. I don't know the answer. So that means the game's over, am I right?"

"Which game?"

"This game of ... interrogation. The pumping, grilling, harassing that's gone on for twenty-five—"

"Have you found a cure for Alzheimer's?"

"Yes."

"Do you believe that I intentionally gave your mother the disease?"

"No."

"Is Norval a liar?"

"He exaggerates, but he does not lie."

"Do you believe that his memory disorder has anything to do with my experiments?"

"What? What memory disorder?"

"Do you think I'm responsible for his suicide?"

"What suicide—"

"Do you think I'm responsible for your father's suicide?"

"Of course not."

"Are you in love with the Bath Lady?"

"No."

"Are you in love with Samira?"

I hesitated, bit my lip, felt my face filling with blood. I glanced towards Samira, who was giving off these emanations—incandescent double, triple, quadruple outlines flowing around her—that dazzled my brain like flashes of the sun, leaving thousands of gold coins and dancing spangles within my eyes. I looked away, towards Dr. Vorta, whose sequinned face was changing into someone else's. I covered my eyes. "Yes."

"Yes?" asked Jack Lafontaine. "Are you sure? Do you want to reconsider? You can take the money and run. I'll just pretend we never asked that question ... No? Are you sure? Absolutely positive? Well, guess what. I have something to tell you. You've just won FIFTY GRAND! Let's go insane for Noel Burun!"

APPLAUSE sign.

"All right, let's pause to catch our breath. Wow! I hope you've enjoyed this ... electrifying, one-of-a-kind performance, I know I have! Will there be another? Now that we've given away all our money, will there be another show?" Jack paused to hold up an oversized cheque. "Here you go, Noel. It's all yours. Is that your girlfriend by the stage, waiting for you? Excellent stuff. Well, I'm sure she'll find a way to spend this if you can't! All right folks, when we come back we'll welcome some new contestants, and a brand-new category. Whew! Don't go away!"

Noel's eyes opened slowly as Dr. Vorta unfastened the wires and removed the bonnet of what he facetiously called "the hair dryer." When he heard the doctor's voice, a cold jagged sensation traversed his body. It was like someone had thrown a switch and disconnected him. For the first time in his life, he saw no colours.[59]

MR. JEAN-JACQUES YELLE
AND COMPANION ARE CORDIALLY
INVITED TO

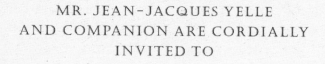

The Filler
Blue-Chip Awards

The Canada Science Council will present the FBC Awards
at a dinner and ceremony commencing at 6 p.m. on
November 21, 2002 at the Hôtel Bonaparte in
Victoriaville, Quebec.

Promotion of the FBC Awards is sponsored by
Helvetia Capital Management
through support for the awards dinner and celebratory
announcements in newspapers across Canada.

Montreal Neurologist Honoured

Nouvelles Télé-Radio

VICTORIAVILLE, QUE. – Montreal neurologist Dr. Émile Vorta received the Best Science Book Prize at last night's Filler Blue-Chip Awards, held at the Hôtel Bonaparte in Victoriaville. *Comme si j'avais mille ans,* a book on synaesthesia ("coloured hearing") published by Memento Vivere, was hailed for its groundbreaking insights and rigorous research.

"Émile Vorta is Canada's Columbus, a neurological explorer, a man in quest of new lands and unknown territory," declared the head of the jury, Professor Antoine Blorenge of the Université du Québec, who also lauded the poems inaugurating each chapter.

In his acceptance speech, which lasted close to an hour, Dr. Vorta said that "good research is like a good novel. Everyone can understand it; everyone can relate to it." After praising his "roving mind and driving ambition" Vorta promised to donate a portion of his $10,000 prize money to the Alzheimer Society of Canada.

Alzheimer Conference Opens Amidst Major Scientific Advances

Alzheimer's Association Presents Lifetime Achievement Award

Agence Suisse

Basel, Switzerland – The world's largest Alzheimer's disease research conference opened in Basel today amidst scientific breakthroughs in the treatment of a disease that will strike millions more people as the world population ages and world life expectancy increases.

In the opening ceremonies, the Association presented Émile Vorta, PhD, professor of neurology, University of Quebec, Canada, with the Friedrich Caflisch Award for Lifetime Achievement. The Caflisch Award, the highest honour bestowed by the Association, recognises an individual whose extraordinary accomplishments provide ongoing inspiration to the international neuroscience community.

Last week in The Hague, Dr Vorta was inducted as a Companion in the Order of the Dutch Lion, an honour bestowed by Her Royal Highness Queen Beatrix of the Netherlands.

See ALZHEIMER'S CONFERENCE, P. A2

(January 21/03)

The Gazette

Showbiz chez nous

Film Lawsuit Tossed Out

A Quebec court judge has thrown out a lawsuit brought by a Montreal film promotion copywriter.

The legal action was brought against a group of American entertainment companies by Jean-Jacques Yelle, who claimed his tagline formula "A film about blank, blank and other blanks" had been used without permission.

But Judge Anne Dupré dismissed the suit before it was set to go to trial on February 15.

"We are extremely pleased with the court's ruling," Warner Bros said in a statement. "The plaintiff's theory that our corporation required his permission to use a common syntactical form profoundly threatens free speech."

MGM called the dismissal "a victory for all writers, who may continue to find inspiration in rhythmic models and catch phrases without having their creative visions censored or compromised."

(February 14/03)

Date-Rape Drug Bust

Agence Québec Presse

MONTREAL, QUE. – The RCMP said yesterday it has helped dismantle a drug ring that sold chemicals used to manufacture the so-called date-rape drug or "Forget Pill."

Police received a tip from unnamed sources and arrested two people in the Montreal borough of Lachine on Wednesday. In a sweep following their arrest, a total of 32 people were apprehended in 12 cities across North America.

Alleged ringleader Pietro Debeurme was indicted yesterday in Albany, New York, for several offences including importation and distribution of GBL. He has pleaded not guilty.

His brother Marc Debeurme was named in a separate US indictment. He was recently released from Montreal's Hôtel Dieu Hospital after being hit in the head with an arrow.

The two Quebeckers are accused of operating a website that allegedly shipped about 5,000 orders for GHB "kits" containing chemicals to make the date-rape drug, including GBL and BD. Police seized more than $160 million worth of GBL, which is legal in Canada but outlawed in the United States.

GHB is a potentially fatal nervous-system depressant that can cause drowsiness, dizziness, nausea and loss of inhibition. There are numerous documented cases of GHB being used to sedate and rape women across North America and Europe.

The Link, Concordia University

Memory, spirit stay alive in Alzheimer's art show

Monday, May 5, 2003
By Daphne Dubois, Link Staff Writer

Stella Burun didn't pick up a paintbrush until she was 56 years old,
but that didn't stop her from exhibiting her first works when she
was 57.

Works by Burun and three other Alzheimer's patients will be
displayed in "Off By Heart," an art show in the lobby of the
Hall Building organised by the Art Therapy Department of the
University of Quebec and the Montreal Chapter of the Canadian
Alzheimer Association.

"After an Alzheimer's diagnosis, most of us would say that life—
or at least the quality of life—is over," remarked art therapy
student Samira Darwish, who helped curate the exhibit. "But there
is life after AD, and there is art. We hope this show will make people
realize that there's a spirit in these people that transcends the
disease, that is undying."

In addition to six watercolours by Burun, there will be tapes-
tries, sculptures and other works by Montreal-area AD patients
Esther Goldbloom, François Hogue and Maria Calderón, who
recently passed away.

Darwish hopes the show will be an eye-opener. "Alzheimer's
doesn't have to be all doom and gloom. We're celebrating the spirit
of these people. Their lives have enriched their families, their com-
munities—and even the world."

*For further information, call the Montreal Alzheimer Foundation at
(514) 319-0800.*

(November 11/03)

Breakthrough in battle vs. dementia

REUTERS

Montreal, November 11, 2003 – A new, potentially revolutionary "memory pill," some of whose ingredients were thought to be used by mediaeval Arabian apothecaries, appears to halt memory loss and physical decline in Alzheimer's patients, according to a study of what could be the first effective treatment for all stages of the mind-robbing ailment.

There is no cure or known prevention for Alzheimer's, which affects nearly 250,000 Canadians, and for which the only approved medications treat earlier stages of the disease.

But a six-month test of the drug A-1001 in patients with moderate to severe Alzheimer's showed it halted deterioration from the disease, researchers report in this month's *Journal de médecine de Québec*. The compound is derived in part from alpha-ketamine, Hyperzine A (club moss), and amaranth. The latter two ingredients are mentioned in *The Arabian Nights*.

"*C'est un miracle, rien de moins – à la fois pour les soignants et pour les patients*," said Dr Émile Vorta of the School of Neurology of the University of Quebec, who led the study.

A renegade member of the research team, Noel Burun, who is rumoured to have come up with the final formula, declined to be interviewed.

A-1001 attacks amyloid deposits and blocks excess amounts of the brain chemical glutamate, which can lead to nerve cell damage.

(November 13/03)

Scandal at U of Q
Incriminating video found in psychology lab

Journal de Montréal

MONTREAL – MUC Police said yesterday it has made arrests in a date-rape drug crime dating back to January of 2002.

Police received a tip from unnamed sources and arrested two people in the Montreal borough of Westmount on Wednesday.

An incriminating video was found at the Experimental Psychology Department of the University of Quebec. The video, barely two minutes long, showed the unconscious victim of the crime, Samira Darwish of Montreal, being examined by two individuals in lab coats. Both wore surgical masks.

The names of the pair, whose voices were identified by a former lab technician, were not made public.

(December 1/03)

TOP HONOURS FOR MONTREAL SCIENTIST

APQ

OSLO, NORWAY – Émile S. Vorta, Professor of Neurology at the University of Quebec, has been named the 2003 Edvard-N. Scientific Award laureate for his contributions in the field of Alzheimer's disease research.

The "Edvard-N." prize is awarded each year by the Norwegian Institute, a world-renowned scientific think tank based in Oslo.

The Swiss-born Vorta supervised the research that led to the discovery of A-1001, which has made it possible to intervene at the stage of mild cognitive impairment that precedes full-blown Alzheimer's, altering or halting the course of the disease; it has also proved effective in reversing mid- and late-onset AD to mild cognitive impairment.

For the first time ever, the announcement of the Edvard-N. laureate provoked a storm of controversy, as three American newspapers have recently published articles questioning Dr Vorta's role in the discovery of A-1001.

The Edvard-N. prize is valued at 2 million kroner, the equivalent of nearly $400,000 CDN. The award is named for its benefactor, a Norwegian investor.

(August 24/04)

THE NEW YORK DAILY TIMES

ÉMILE VORTA 1930-2004

Neuroscience pioneer provided foundation for treating Alzheimer's

MONTREAL – Dr. Émile S. Vorta, a former professor of neurology at the University of Quebec and publisher of Memento Vivere whose research in the field of memory led to perhaps the greatest neuropharmaceutical discovery of the last quarter-century, the so-called A-1001 "memory pill," died yesterday at the Philippe Pinel Institute in Montreal. He was 74.

Vorta retired from research and publishing in 2003 after a 42-year career studded with international honours. "Émile Vorta was one of the most distinguished neuroscientists of his generation," said Patrick L. Lavigne, president of the Université du Québec.

The Swiss-born neurologist was one of the first researchers to chart the frontal lobe of the brain, once regarded as inaccessible and unchartable. He employed various techniques – electric impulses, neuro-pharmaceuticals, hallucinogenic drugs, behavioural responses and other unique methods – to explore and describe its structure, particularly as they related to memory tasks.

He was also a pioneer in his investigations of synaesthesia and hypermnesia, for which he developed a modified transcranial magnetic stimulator named after him (VTMS).

Vorta received numerous scientific awards, held hundreds of patents, and published over 500 articles in scientific journals throughout the world. His long and distinguished career was not without controversy, however.

See VORTA, P. 2.

Chapter 24
Noel's Diary (IV)

January 5, 2004. How does it go again? "The world has achieved brilliance without conscience. Ours is a world of nuclear giants and ethical infants." I can't remember who said that—it'll come to me—but he or she was right. It goes back to what JJ said about intelligence of the brain vs. intelligence of the heart ...

And it goes back to what my father said about poets freeing those feelings we keep locked in the heart. I was never really sure, to be honest, what feelings he was referring to. Which ones have to be set free, and why? My mother gave me an answer: what we're all really seeking is the freedom to give ourselves away. To stop maniacally holding on to ourselves, to escape from the jail of living solely and vainly for our own sake. This is the treasure, I think, buried in the pent heart.

Omar Bradley. (I just asked my mom.)

January 6. Large snowflakes swirl. "They're plucking geese in heaven," my mother told me when I was four, outside our bay window in Babylon. She zipped up my woollen coat of double blue, which she herself had knitted, and set me down in the snow with a small shovel. "Your grandmother used to say that," she added, her hair of rich reddish-gold grazing my cheek as she wound my scarf tight. That memory is solid, but almost all others are delicate and fugitive, like the white flakes that now vanish as they kiss the glass.

This will be my final entry.

My mother has turned back into the person she once was, worth more to me than winning the world's praise, more than winning a million lotteries.

She said I was welcome to stay with her, but I think it's time to move on. There is someone new in her life, and there is someone new in mine. "Ask her to marry you," my mother whispered at the airport.

I never wanted wealth or fame, never sought either. Like the ancient Greeks I simply combined, in a novel way, work that others had done before me. I saw previously overlooked patterns, made "irrational" connections, saw beauty, nothing more. And this would never have happened without the compass and charts of my father, the witchery of my grandmother, the flighty optimism of JJ and grounding pessimism of Norval. Without Samira, my muse and mind's balm, who proved that darts of gold can come of chemistry; without my mother, whose love for me—and need—lifted me to a higher plane of existence, turning me into a knight, a magician, a fool, unblinding me to the miracle.

Chapter 25

Ghostwriter's Epilogue

T he documentation and anecdotal information runs out here.[60] Regrettably, we have neither Henry Burun's lab notes from 1978 nor his son's from 2002, which contain key details regarding the evolution and synthesis of the "memory pill." These notes were thought to be in the possession of Dr. Vorta, who was attempting to secure drug patents before he died. These documents have never been found.

Dr. Vorta was undeniably a brilliant neuroscientist; he was not, as Norval Blaquière contended, a jealous mentor trying to undercut a brighter protégé. Nor was he a "quack." With the exception of A-1001, all his discoveries were verifiably his own. All his awards, save those for A-1001, were earned. Over the course of his career, however, Dr. Vorta made several enemies—his wife among them—who were determined to discredit him. The last decade of his life was spent trying to ward off a series of accusations, including medical malpractice, criminal negligence and insider trading.

In the early 1990s, for example, Dr. Vorta developed a promising drug for treating early-onset Alzheimer's, but Food and Drug Canada (FDC) withheld approval from the company he was working with (Memoria Drugs) because of shortcomings in its clinical trials. It later emerged that he sold his shares in this firm just before the FDC's decision was published. Dr. Vorta was subpoenaed for insider trading but not charged.

In the mid-1990s, charges that Vorta put pressure on the Chief Scientist at the FDC to greenlight or fast-track drug approval were dropped for lack of evidence.

In the late 1990s, Dr. Vorta was accused in the press of receiving kickbacks from corporations sponsoring psychomnemonic research, as well as excessive fees to refer patients to clinical trials; a money trail allegedly led back to two European drug companies, an instant-coffee manufacturer and an investment firm, Helvetia Capital Management.

In 2002, following allegations from an anonymous "whistleblower" that Dr. Vorta's students wrote many of his articles, the Experimental Psychology Department of the University of Quebec conducted "a full investigation." The unanimous conclusion, announced on November 4, 2002: "total exoneration."

In 2003, a number of scientists, including Dr. Hyalmar Tjarnqvist of Sweden's Karolinska Institute, challenged some of Dr. Vorta's discoveries, in particular his claim to have placed an artificial memory in Noel Burun's hippocampus. Yolande Foisy, the Administrative Director of the Experimental Psychology Department and wife of Quebec's former Health Minister, oversaw two investigations. The unanimous conclusion from the ad hoc panel: "complete endorsement and corroboration" of Dr. Vorta's discoveries. His lab displayed "scientific rigour and exemplary laboratory practices" and "allegations to the contrary are unfounded."

In December of that same year, after Dr. Vorta received his lifetime achievement award in Oslo, a University of Quebec colleague, Dr. Charles Ravenscroft, accused him of administering a substance ("Vortagon") that induced Alzheimer's disease in at least two patients: Stella Burun and Norval Blaquière. No proof of this accusation has yet been found.

That same month, with regard to the so-called "date-rape video" shot at the Experimental Psychology Laboratory, Dr. Vorta was charged with administering a noxious substance to commit an indictable offence. But not with rape or sexual assault, as there was no evidence to support either charge. At a disciplinary hearing of the Collège des médecins du Québec, Dr. Vorta denied any involvement, but could not explain away the DNA evidence linking him to the crime. At a pre-trial criminal hearing, he was found not guilty by reason of insanity, and was committed to the Philippe Pinel Institute in February of 2004.

A subsequent investigation by the Association des neurologues du Québec absolved him. Norval Blaquière, who had shot the video with a hidden camera for his "private investigation" of Dr. Vorta, demonstrated that the two individuals in lab coats, one wearing Vorta's coat, were actually Drs. Charles Ravenscroft and Isabelle Rhéaume. Their voices, in a barely audible exchange involving the words "excess" and "palace of wisdom," were identified by Noel Burun.

A preliminary hearing revealed that the couple was attempting to avenge "past injustices"—including Dr. Ravenscroft's dismissal—by planting false evidence. Before driving Samira Darwish to the police and then home, they evidently decided—impulsively, and at the husband's instigation—to take her to Dr. Vorta's lab to plant incriminating DNA evidence and microscopic fibres. As their attorney pointed out, however, the couple did not administer the date-rape drug (the offender has yet to be found), and they did rescue Samira from a potentially more serious crime. In a plea bargain, they each received 18 months of probation, a $5,000 fine and 150 hours of community service at two assisted-living facilities on the island of Montreal.

Stella Burun, who was destined for one of these facilities, made a full recovery and has returned to the classroom, teaching history at a Montreal Cégep. She is currently dating a younger colleague in the department who has been in love with her for years: a widower with a ten-year-old daughter. The couple plan to get married in Aberdeen, Scotland in the summer of 2006.

JJ Yelle's retreat into boyhood ended when he met his ex-girlfriend at Montreal's Greek Independence Day Parade. An ageing prostitute, she had just come out of detox—"as if waking up from a nightmare after hibernating in hell," he remarked in an audio interview. They lived together for nine months but did not marry. After JJ helped her get back on her feet, financially and emotionally, she decided to go back to her biker boyfriend. Which did not unduly upset JJ, because he was then free to propose to Sancha Ribeiro, the Bath Lady. The couple now live on a hothouse farm in northern Vermont, where they are experimenting with a genetically modified hybrid of skunk cabbage and Oriental sassafras, a healthy replacement for tobacco. Projected income in 2006, including patent earnings and seed money from R.J. Reynolds: $6.2 million. JJ is currently negotiating to purchase Mount Royal Cemetery.

Norval Blaquière never got to Z, never got beyond *S*. Nor did he get beyond the first round of *Tip of Your Tongue*. After completing his twenty-six Sunday school classes at the university chapel, and releasing his "exposé" on Dr. Vorta, Norval was hospitalised in early 2004 for short-term memory loss and brain-tumour-like symptoms, thought to be the result of ingesting experimental psychotropic drugs over an extended period—among them methaqualone (which produces excessive dreaming and amnesia), chloral hydrate and Vortagon, an applicationless drug suspected of triggering Alzheimer's disease. Norval's memory lapses were first noted by Noel Burun in a journal entry from October 24, 2003:

"What the Christ are you talking about?" said Norval. And I could see by the look in his eye—I'd seen the same in my mother's—that he really couldn't remember. "What alphabet?"

After checking himself out of the Hôpital Hôtel-Dieu in the spring of 2004, Norval journeyed to Hucknall in Nottinghamshire, where he stayed briefly at Mrs. Pettybone's B & B. On a cloudless Saturday in mid-April, his body was found on the north shore of Byron's lake at Newstead Abbey, where Teresa had drowned herself twelve years before.

Since November 2005, when Amaranthine-1001 received FDA approval, Noel Burun has declined all interviews, public honours and scientific awards. He has also declined credit for the compound, attributing its discovery to a research team composed of Henry Burun (now deceased), Norval Blaquière (now deceased), Jean-Jacques Yelle and Samira Darwish. Patent and other monies are therefore to be split four ways, with the estate portions going to Norval's mother and Henry Burun's widow.

With regard to Noel Burun's synaesthesia, it was not eradicated by Dr. Vorta but rather reduced to a hyper-mild form, one that no longer warps his communications with strangers. His memory, accordingly, was reduced to a fraction of its former potency. Despite suffering acute—vein-openingly acute—despair over his looted inner world, he has come to accept this disease of ordinariness as a trade-off.

While Noel Burun and Samira Darwish have jealously guarded their privacy, there are unconfirmed reports that the couple lived briefly on the southwest coast of Long Island, and in the fabled city of al-Hillah, where Samira did the groundwork for a community/arts centre. There are also unconfirmed reports that their baby girl is a synaesthete.

Notes

1 This entry from NB's adult diary (05/05/91) first appeared in my *Curiosités mnémoniques* (Montréal: Memento Vivere, 1993, p. 27). Seemingly sunk without a trace, the book, thanks to discerning praise from several scientists, slowly grew to a recognition it has never forfeited. Reproduced below, from the book's twelfth impression, is NB's colour chart.

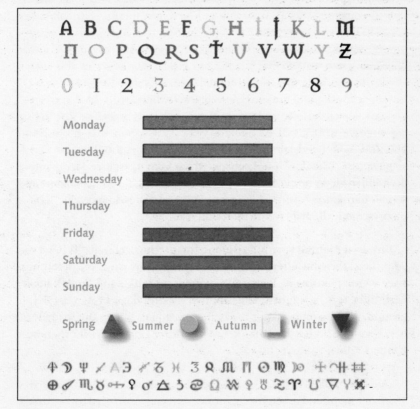

2 Synaesthesia (following definitions by Fleurnoy 1895, Vernon 1930, Marks 1975, Cytowic 1989, Vorta 1990) is a condition in which one type of sensory stimulation evokes the sensation of another. In NB's type, sound triggers the perception of vivid colour; like Vladimir Nabokov and many others, NB also perceives written letters in colours. In North America, female synaesthetes predominate in a ratio of 5:1 and left-handed synaesthetes (like NB) at 4:1. Synaesthesia is also reported by those who have used hallucinogenic drugs, such as lysergic acid diethylamide or mescaline, as we shall see.

3 I have never used chimpanzees in my research.

4 There is no evidence to suggest that Proust was a synaesthete, nor do I recall ever mentioning him (possibly a misread word in NB's diary). Be that as it may, we can add two painters to the list, Kandinsky and Hockney, as well as French composer Olivier Messiaen and (perhaps) the Russian filmmaker Sergei Eistenstein and Japanese poet Bashō. No two synaesthetes, of course, see the same sound colours: to Rimsky-Korsakov the key of F# major appeared green, to Scriabin it appeared violet. (The score of the latter's *Prometheus* incorporates multicoloured lights.) Rimbaud's synaesthesia ("I invented the colours of the vowels!—*A* black, *E* white, *I* red, *O* blue, *U* green— I made rules for the form and movement of each consonant," he says in *Une saison en enfer*, "Délires II: Alchimie du Verbe") was enhanced by hashish and absinthe. As for Baudelaire, he alludes to his synaesthesia in the poem *Correspondances*: "Like drawn-out echoes, which from a distance/Merge into a deep and shadowy unity/As vast as night, as vast as light,/Scents, colours and sounds harmonize." And in *Flowers of Evil* he declares, immortally: "I have more memories than if I were a thousand years old."

5 Physicist Richard Feynman among them, who declared: "When I see equations, I see the letters in colors — I don't know why. As I'm talking, I see vague pictures of Bessel functions from Jahke and Emde's book, with light tan *j*'s, slightly violet-bluish *n*'s and dark brown *x*'s flying around. And I wonder what the hell it must look like to the students." R.P. Feynman, *What Do You Care What Other People Think?* (London: HarperCollins, 1988), p. 59.

6 Audio recording, September 12, 1977. As I have stated elsewhere, NB's "memory map" and mnemonic gymnastics recall those used by the Greek

poet Simonides (c. 556–468 BC), the so-called "inventor of the art of memory." At a banquet at the court of Scopas, King of Thessaly, Simonides was once commissioned to chant a lyric poem in honour of his host. This he did, but he also included the gods Castor and Pollux in his praise. His vanity offended, Scopas informed the poet that he would pay him only half the sum agreed upon, adding that "Castor and Pollux will doubtless compensate you for the other half." Amidst the brays of laughter from the king's courtiers and sycophants, a message was brought in to Simonides that two young men on horseback were anxious to see him outside. The poet hastened to the door, but looked in vain for the men. Suddenly, the roof of the banquet hall collapsed with a thunderous crash, burying Scopas and all his guests. The corpses were so badly mangled beneath the rubble that the relatives who came to take them away for burial were unable to identify them. Simonides, however, remembered the exact place where each guest had been sitting at the table and was able to indicate to the relatives their respective dead. For the poet, the main principle of the art of memory was *orderly arrangement*. According to Cicero, "Simonides inferred that persons wishing to train this faculty [of memory] must select places and form mental images of the things they wish to remember and store these images in the places, so that the order of the places will preserve the order of the things, and the images of the things will denote the things themselves, and the places and images will be employed respectively as a writing tablet and letters" (*De oratore*, II, xxxvi, 351–4). Most synaesthetes have above-average spatial memories, and typically recall large blocks of conversation, prose, movie dialogue, and so on.

7 Among the many articles that quote me at length are Vernon McQueen's "Extra-Sense Perception" in the Babylon *Beacon* (15.12.1977), Monika Binder's "Eine Verabedung um grün Uhr" in *Wormser Zeitung* (28.02.1978), and Felicia Brawne's "Mommy! I Hear Colours!" in *The National Enquirer* (09.03.1978). If my skin were thinner, I would take umbrage at Ms. Brawne's description of my accent as "thick as dry porridge [...] in screaming need of subtitles." In the same article is a photograph, purportedly of me: the gentleman depicted has a vigorous white beard and bald head, whereas my crinal configuration is the exact opposite. He is also substantially older than I.

8 As impressive as these numbers may appear, they do not come close to the world records (34.03 seconds, 22.5 decks, 400 and 1,820 digit

numbers, respectively). The female world memory champion, incidentally, is Svetta Nemcova, a vivacious Czech and the so-called "third party" evoked (baselessly) in certain tabloids with regard to my much-publicised divorce.

9 The confabulations and fantastications of NXB, often seen in alcoholic Korsakoff cases, are described in my "Confessions of a Pathological Liar" (*Frontier Science*, May 2001). The "free drugs," principally LSD, mescaline and psilocin (especially *Psilocybe mexicana* and *Stropharia cubensis*), refer to NXB's participation in my pilot studies of drug-induced synaesthesia.

10 Heinrich Kluver, a forgotten scientist until I rescued his work from oblivion, identified four basic hallucinatory form constants in 1930: (a) spirals; (b) tunnels and cones; (c) cobwebs; and (d) gratings and honeycombs. The colour forms of NB's idiopathic synaesthesia generally fall into one of these four categories, particularly the first. NXB's drug-induced synaesthetic forms include these four, along with twenty-three others: lazy tongs (extensible frameworks with scissor-like hands), swastikas, scutiforms (shield shapes), galeiforms (helmet shapes), rowlock arches, lumbriciforms (like earthworms), cochlears (like snail shells), quadrants (quarters of a circle), doughnut shapes, amygdaloids (almond shapes), anchor shapes, botryoidals (like a bunch of grapes), clothoids (tear shapes), ensiforms (sword shapes), infundibuliforms (funnel shapes), moniliforms (string of beads), pinnate shapes (feathers), sagittates (arrowheads), unciforms (hook shapes), villiforms (resembling bristles or velvet pile), virgates (shaped like a rod or wand), scroll shapes, and sigmoids (curved in two directions, like the letter *S*).

NXB's remark about my being "cuckolded" (see note 9 above) continues to rankle. With respect to my much-publicised divorce, the pump of scandal was primed by insinuations and fabrications of that sort—the stock-in-trade of newspapers specialising in lurid crimes and juicy sexual irregularities. For a more factual account of the divorce, see *Le Devoir* of April 2, 2001 (page-one feature beginning "In the world of brain sciences, Dr. Vorta is a star of high wattage ...").

11 NB may be referring to this passage from Shelley's *Prometheus Unbound*, a favourite poem of his father's:

Prometheus saw, and waked the legion hopes
Which sleep within folded Elysian flowers,
Nepenthe, Moly, Amaranth, fadeless blooms;
That they might hide with thin and rainbow wings
The shape of Death ... (II, iv, 59–65)

12 "You wake up one morning and find you are old" (literally "the fleeting years glide by"). Alas, how I identify with Stella in this respect! I devoted my life to science, and it cost me the love of my wife and daughter. There was a moment, in the late eighties, when I realised what I was losing, and what I had to do to regain it. And still I chose another path: sixteen-hour days, drinking Maxwell House coffee to keep me awake, driving my career forward with no concessions to age or family. True scientists, like true artists, make bad husbands.

13 The provincial motto "I Remember"—as I was informed by a former Quebec Premier, who urged me to run in a by-election with a view to becoming Minister of Health—derives from an anonymous poem beginning "*Je me souviens / que né sous le lys / Je croîs sous la rose*" ("I remember / that born under the [French] lily / I grow under the [English] rose"). It is perhaps my sovereignist convictions that deterred me, subconsciously at least, from improving my spoken English. See note 7, second sentence, which continues to grate.

14 Quebec filmmaker Claude Jutras was a friend and collaborator of François Truffaut, Bernardo Bertolucci and Jean Rouch, and admired by Cassavetes, Cocteau and Jean Renoir. (In April of 1972, on our first anniversary, my wife and I saw Jutras' *Mon Oncle Antoine* in Geneva.) He studied medicine at the Université de Montréal and worked for a time as an intern, which is when I met him. I learned later he was the son of a prominent radiologist and descended from a line of physicians. Jutras was a Renaissance man, for he went on to work as an actor, writer, painter and, of course, film director. After being diagnosed with AD, Jutras left his home one day in November of 1986, never to return. Did he lose his way, forget who he was? The mystery was not solved until several months later, when his badly decomposed body was found floating amidst the ice of the Saint Lawrence River. He was identified by a scrawled note in his pocket: "I am Claude Jutras."

15 Who said the Swiss have produced nothing besides the cuckoo clock? This towering sixteenth-century physician and alchemist—who was born in my native village of Einsideln—established the role of chemistry in medicine and sowed the seeds of homeopathy. He published *Der grossen Wundartzney* ("Great Surgery Book") in 1536 and a clinical description of syphilis in 1530.

16 I have never "chemically whitened" my beard.
   As for the rest, read on.

17 NXB, as usual, is wildly overstating. Humans remember approximately two bits per second. Over a lifetime, this rate of memorisation would produce some 10^9 bits, or only a few hundred megabytes. The analogy, in any case, is flimsy: a computer is a serial processor, whereas our brain is parallel. See "Dracula, Let Me Count the Bytes" in the *Journal of Cognitive Science* 12, 1998, pp. 244–65, written by a student under my supervision.

18 See note 15, first sentence.

19 In an article entitled "Oedipus Anorex" (*Scottish Journal of Art and Cognitive Neuropsychology*, April 1991), I compare Lord Byron's incessant dieting and his equation of starvation with self-mastery with the practices of today's young anorexics. His revulsion at the sight of women eating was obviously related to both his compulsive dieting and his mother's obesity. As for Noel Burun's being occasionally "fat and mad," Noel's weight consistently fell within the norms for his age and height, and he is no madder than I.
   By now the reader will have noted my interest in the arts. My publishing house, although specialising in scientific texts, also publishes poetry, novels and short stories dealing with scientific themes. For one of the chief purposes of art lies in its cognitive function: as a means to acquiring truth. NB's father, Henry Burun, went farther: he considered art the avenue to the highest knowledge available to man, to a kind of knowledge impossible to attain by any other means.

20 The jest may call for a gloss: it is a reference to Prince Philip's (in)famous remark, which contains—let's be honest—a kernel of truth. In 1996, I hired a Paki who designed a laboratory electrical system not unlike JJY's.

21 Émile Nelligan (1879–1941) is generally regarded as Quebec's national poet (despite the fact that his father was from Dublin). After "burning out" creatively at the age of nineteen, Nelligan spent the rest of his life in insane asylums. See my "La schizophrénie et la poésie" in *Art et neuropathologie* (Memento Vivere, 1988).

I should point out to the reader that I am not only an art theorist, but a practitioner as well: as my readers well know, it is my custom to "set the tone" for my research articles, or chapters of longer works, with an epi-grammatic poem or "intermezzo" of my own composition. (In my canton, I was once the semi-official *Mundartdichter*, or local poet.) Indeed I am mistaken if a single one of these poems fails to preserve at least some faint thrill of the emotion through which it had to pass before the Muse's lips let it fall. One of them, entitled *Der Regenbogen* ("The Rainbow"), elicited the following critical response: "Each phrase is so meticulously calibrated that we feel the concluding line as an emotional thunderclap" (*Neue Zürcher Zeitung*, 09/08/99).

22 JJY, far from being "crazed," periodically or otherwise, is a generally well-adjusted individual with an above-average IQ (in the 120–125 range). Because of a history of minor behaviour disturbances as a child, including enuresis, soiling, somniloquy and bruxism, JJY's family physician referred him to a psychiatrist, who in turn referred him to a neurologist in our department, Dr. Charles Ravenscroft. After several tests, Dr. Ravenscroft discovered a deficiency of large nerve cells called Purkinje cells and an excess of serotonin, and thereby concluded that JJY had a mild form of autism, of which there is a familial genetic component. Because I suspected careless procedure and analytical irregularities, I personally repeated all tests and scans and reached my own conclusion: that Dr. Ravenscroft had made yet another misdiagnosis.

JJY's memory skills are also above average: on testing he had an excel-lent memory for pictures, recalling 10 out of 12 objects after a 40-minute delay, and perfectly reproducing the Weschler designs after a similar delay. His memory for verbal material was not as good, but still within the average range of the Weschler Logical Memory Scale. Psychiatric profile: displaying a number of paedomorphic traits, JJY is more or less delayed at the second stage of pyschosexual development. With the loss of his mother and father, and the loss of his girlfriend to another, JJY has sought refuge in an idealised, nostalgicised youth: in the rampant "Peterpande-monium" (a term I coined back in 1992) that characterises his generation.

See my "Peterpandemonium" in *Zeitschrift für die Gesamte Neurologie und Psychiatrie*, LX, pp. 399–419.

By now, my interest in the story's protagonists should be obvious. But for the slow-witted, here is the research pentagram: (1) NB—synaesthesia/hypermnesia (idiopathic); (2) SB—amnesia (Alzheimer's); (3) NXB—synaesthesia (drug-induced); (4) SD—amnesia (short-term, antidotal); (5) JJY—nostalgesis/creativity (TMS-induced).

23 See note 15. Ulrich Boner was a fourteenth-century Swiss writer whose collection of fables in verse was the first book to be printed in the German language (1461). It was called *Der Edelstein* ("The Precious Stone") because precious stones were said to cast a spell and Boner hoped his tales would do the same.

The French writer mentioned before him, Antoine Galland, published *The One Thousand and One Nights*, the first translation into any Western language of these ancient Persian-Arabic tales, between 1704 and 1717. One of them, "The Sleeper and the Awakener," would prove to be an inspirational wellspring for NB.

24 My researchers assure me this is nowhere near a record. A British writer named John Creasey, over a period of seven years, wrote numerous novels for which, by the time he got his first book published in 1925, he had received 743 rejection slips. Two of these books, he claimed, were written in a week, with half-days spent playing cricket.

25 I considered it my moral duty.

26 In psychiatric terms, NXB suffers from satyriasis, or Don Juanism: an excessive preoccupation with sexual gratification or conquest, a chronic pursuit of high-risk behaviour, leading to persistently transient and exploitative relationships. He steadfastly resisted my efforts to refer him to a psychosexologist.

27
> *The feverish room and that white bed,*
> *The tumbled skirts upon a chair,*
> *The novel flung half-open where*
> *Hat, hair-pins, puffs, and paints, are spread;*
>
> *The mirror that has sucked your face*
> *Into its secret deep of deeps,*

And there mysteriously keeps
Forgotten memories of grace;

And you, half dressed and half awake,
Your slant eyes strangely watching me,
And I, who watch you drowsily,
With eyes that, having slept not, ache;

This (need one dread? nay, dare one hope?)
Will rise, a ghost of memory, if
Ever again my handkerchief
Is scented with White Heliotrope.

—Arthur Symons, "White Heliotrope" (1895)

28 NB, as usual, is correct: sea lions have the best memory of all non-human creatures. Although many other mammals, including the macaque monkey and chimpanzee, have impressive long-term memories, the sea lion outperforms them all. In 2000, a California sea lioness named Rio broke animal memory records by remembering a complicated trick involving letters and numbers—*ten years* after first learning it. Marine biologists (Kastak and Schusterman, 2001), employing a mnemonic model strangely resembling one I designed for rhesus monkeys in the mid-eighties (Vorta and Rhéaume, 1986), taught sea lions to relate specific gestural signals to objects (e.g. bats, balls, rings), modifiers (e.g. large, small, black, white), and actions (e.g. fetch, tail-touch, flipper-touch). For example, in the simplest "single object" instruction, the presentation of the signs SMALL/BLACK/ RING/ TAIL-TOUCH would result in the sea lion touching the small black ring with its tail, while ignoring the other objects in the pool. Years ago, when I took my ten-year-old daughter to MarineLand in Niagara Falls, she remarked how "cool" these animals were, and suggested we move to Ontario to study them. Given my current problems in Quebec, I should have listened to her!

29 To finish JJY's sentence, what I gave him was a memory "escalator" (essentially balm of Gilead and sage) that he himself exhibited at the 2000 *Cultiver sa mémoire* symposium in Montreal. It improved his memory not one iota.

30 In Muslim legend /Arabian demonology, a *jinnī* is one of the sprites or spirits able to assume human or animal form and exercise supernatural

influence over people. It brings to mind a comment made in 1989 by a Genevan television critic regarding the inspiration for one of my epigrammatic poems (see note 21): "The lines seem to be whispered by a *jinnī*, communicated by a dream, or revealed by an angel from on high ..."

31 Henry Burun was bi-polar, what we used to call "manic depressive"— as were numerous artists, including poets Robert Lowell and Sylvia Plath, painters Vincent Van Gogh and Georgia O'Keeffe, jazz pianist Charles Mingus, etc. Had he had access to today's new generation of antidepressants, Henry would have been able to "hold the dragon at bay," as he described it, and still be alive today.

32 In his classic *The Mind of a Mnemonist*, the Russian neuroscientist Aleksandr Luria recorded the case of "S" (Solomon Shereshevski), a man who appears to have forgotten nothing. S was also a synaesthete; after meeting the legendary filmmaker Sergei Eisenstein in the 1930s, he described his voice as "a flame with protruding fibres." Although possessing a greater eidetic memory than NB, S had similar difficulties in understanding and adapting to the everyday world around him (*die alltägliche Umwelt*). Neither one, to say the least, can be considered a typical synaesthete.

33 NB's mistake here was crediting information supplied by NXB. I am not using chloral or chloral hydrate in any of my studies, either for amnesia or brain cancer. And although the drug was clearly from my lab, I am not the one who ordered it. It may have been part of NXB's "literary studies," as the highly addictive—and dangerous—drug was prescribed for insomnia in the nineteenth century. It hastened the mental collapse of Friedrich Nietzsche, gave paranoid hallucinations to Dante Rossetti and Evelyn Waugh, and destroyed André Gide's memory.

34 Coincidentally, Alois Alzheimer, who practised in Germany in the 1890s, took an interest in his own country's "Decadents," particularly Jakob Wassermann, Frank Wedekind and Hanns Heinz Ewers. He makes only passing reference, however, to the earlier French *Décadents* Baudelaire, Verlaine, Rimbaud, Mallarmé and Huysmans; and none at all to the English Decadents of the "Yellow Nineties": Arthur Symons, Oscar Wilde, Ernest Dowson and Lionel Johnson.

35 Emily Dickinson, "Wild Nights," in *Poems* (1890).

36 Art therapy is based on the premise that words can act as a barrier, preventing people from expressing what is on their minds, and that creating art can allow people to describe their feelings without words. Through creating art and talking about the process of art-making with an art therapist, patients can "increase awareness of self, cope with symptoms, stress, and traumatic experiences, enhance cognitive abilities, and enjoy the life-affirming pleasures of artistic creativity." I'm quoting from an Art Therapy of America pamphlet belonging to my wife, who took (expensive) courses in it. Some of this stuff is flaky at best, and most of it unproven.

Far more interesting are my experiments in transcranial magnetic stimulation, which will have applications for cognition, creativity and well-being. Using my own modified stimulator (VTMS©) on research subject JJY, I enhanced his visual and spatial memory, along with his creative skills and pleasure quotient. I targeted an island of tissue in the human gyrus, near the left ear, which serves as a kind of booster rocket for creativity. Below are the results of an experiment in which I asked JJY to draw a picture of a cat four times, at different stages of his exposure to VTMS©:

| 1. Practice | 2. Before | 3. During | 4. After |

I then asked him to rewrite a line from his novel *The Right Chemistry*:

Her blouse was a really loud red colour.	*Her blouse was scarlet, like the scream of someone falling through a skylight.*
1. Before	2. After

At the final stages of each of these tests, JJY had a broad grin on his face. Like sex and eating, creating and experiencing art are pleasurable acts. Since the brain reinforces creative acts by rewarding brain cells with the neurotransmitter dopamine, creativity has an obvious role to play in our health and survival. Creative expression, in fact, may be the brain's natural method of protecting itself from disease. I play the xylophone, for instance, as a means of preventing neurodegeneration: compared to the general population, a much lower percentage of musicians get Alzheimer's disease. See my "Art Therapy and Alzheimer's: Why Researchers Have Been Wrong Until Now" in *Psychology Tomorrow*, winter 2001.

37 Cf. Ralph Waldo Emerson's line "The surest poison is time" in "Old Age," *Society and Solitude* (1870). Memoryless and demented, Emerson died of Alzheimer's disease twelve years later.

38 It is not always possible to control the ambitions of one's subalterns, who clearly flirted with unprofessionalism in this regard. One of the experiments that NB refers to was conducted to see whether memory impairment occurred in synaesthetes after electrical stimulation, as it normally does with non-synaesthetes. Another was inspired by experiments conducted by the Montreal neurologist Dr. Wilder Penfield (who was once called "the greatest living Canadian," even though he was born and educated in the US). Penfield found that by stimulating the temporal lobes he could evoke memories incorporating sound, movement and colour, which were much more vivid than usual memory, and often about things unremembered under ordinary circumstances. In short, he made his patients relive the past as if it were the present. As Cytowic (1989) memorably describes it, "This was Proust on the operating table, an electrical *recherche du temps perdu*." Patients were shocked (pardon the pun) to re-experience long-forgotten conversations, a kindergarten classroom, a certain song, the view from a childhood window. They were convinced that what they experienced was real, even though they also knew they were on an operating table in Montreal. Now, the obvious next step is to open up the cranium of a synaesthete, stimulate the visual cortex and see whether the resulting experience resembles their experience of synaesthesia. Treading on thin deontological ice, you're thinking? Perhaps, but not with transcranial magnetic stimulation, which is what we used on NB. This gentler method of stimulating the cortex generates a magnetic impulse that passes through the skull and causes nerve cells in the brain to "fire." In non-synaesthetes I have been able to elicit colour percepts, or chromatophenes, by stimulating the occipital lobes. My next step is to stimulate the same regions in a synaesthete, and compare the two

"optical" events. Should they prove to be similar we might, all of us, experience the rainbow world of a synaesthete!

39 *Speak, Memory* by name, wherein Nabokov—who spent the last eighteen years of his life in Switzerland—describes his synaesthesia:

> I present a fine case of coloured hearing. Perhaps "hearing" is not quite accurate, since the colour sensation seems to be produced by the very act of my orally forming a given letter while I imagine its outline. The long *a* of the English alphabet has for me the tint of weathered wood, but a French *a* evokes polished ebony. This black group also includes hard *g* (vulcanised rubber) and *r* (a sooty rag being ripped). Oatmeal *n*, noodle-limp, and the ivory-backed hand mirror of *o* take care of the whites.
>
> (*Speak, Memory*, Weidenfeld & Nicolson, 1967).

Nabokov's parents, wife and son, interestingly enough, were all synaesthetes.

40 My preliminary research points to three ways in which caffeine can protect against or reverse dementia-related changes in the brain: (1) it can stimulate brain cells to take in choline, needed to make acetylcholine, which is reduced in dementia; (2) it can interfere with another neurotransmitter called adenosine, a knock-on effect that may disrupt AD mechanisms; (3) it seems to tone down the activity of "housekeeping" cells called glia, which, although important in ridding the brain of dead and injured cells, can sometimes be overzealous and damage contiguous areas. My department is currently engaged in double-blind studies involving caffeinated and decaffeinated Maxwell House coffee.

41 See note 15.

42 Overleaf is KL's synaesthetic alphanumeric character set (this colour chart, and the one in note 1, account for this book being slightly more expensive than most):

Letter/Number	Label
A	Boy (smart)
B	Girl
C	Girl
D	Girl (vain)
E	Boy (nerdy)
F	Boy (sleazy)
G	Tomboy
H	Both
I	Boy
J	Boy (cool)
K	Tomboy
L	Girl (free spirit)
M	Boy
N	Boy (geek)
O	Girl (fun)
P	Girl
Q	Girl (has issues)
R	Girl
S	Girl (pretty)
T	Girl (confident
U	Boy
V	Girl (psycho-bitch)
W	Girl (drama-queen)
X	Boy (neurot)
Y	Girl
Z	Boy (suave)
0	Girl (dull)
1	Both
2	Boy
3	Girl (bubbly)
4	Boy
5	Tomboy
6	Boy (dorky)
7	Boy
8	Boy
9	Girl (blends in)

43   In essence, this was "it" as it turned out: the pharmaceutical Cinderella, the magic bullet, the Viagra for the Mind. I should perhaps take the time here to clarify my role in its discovery. (1) At least two of its ingredients (federally unapproved at that time) I personally obtained for NB, at considerable risk to my career and reputation, and at least one other was spagyrically tinctured by JJY, who was then working under my direction. (2) It is no secret that Henry Burun's notes served as a compass for his son's research. In the context of our professional relationship, Henry and I often discussed psychopharmacological issues relating to mnemonics and nootropics, as his lab books clearly indicate. (3) The Nepenthe-Amaranth-56 "memory pill" (later modified and named Amaranthine–1001) has its roots in a discovery made by a former teacher of mine, the Montreal neuroscientist Wilder Penfield, who published a paper in 1955 that described the strange effects of applying electrical currents to the brain, including hallucinations, memory loss and, in one case, a woman who said she felt as if she had just left her body. The crude instruments of the era were unable to determine the specific area of the brain involved or to replicate the out-of-body effect, but in 2002 Swiss scientists identified the part of the

brain involved: the *right angular gyrus*, which sits about an inch above and behind the right ear. Although my genius was not, strictly speaking, of the same titan calibre as Dr. Penfield's, as a student-technician working under him I strongly suspected that this was the area involved, and I must have discussed this idea years later with Henry Burun. A disruption at the right angular gyrus—involved in processing information from the visual system, the balance system and the somatosensory system—creates an illusion of floating in which one's own body feels and looks distant. The phenomenon has inspired talk of a spiritual self that can roam free of the body and, after many accounts of patients "watching" themselves before pulling back from the verge of death, has been seen as evidence of an afterlife. I myself became interested in the topic when, as a student at the University of Basel, during an indescribable parlour game in which someone with scissors made an "animal sculpture" out of my beard, I underwent an intense out-of-body experience, visiting Renoir's house at Cagne-sur-mer on the Côte d'Azur. To verify whether I had actually left my body, the following day I went up to the roof to see whether it bore the convex terracotta tiles I had seen while floating over my dorm. Shockingly, it did. But I digress. A-1001 is a benzoquinone-naphthoquinone-methaqualone-based compound with a dual mechanism of action: (a) it activates the right angular gyrus and hippocampus, improving brain metabolism and protecting the cell membranes against lipid peroxidation and dysregulated calcium; (b) it inhibits an enzyme that breaks down the chemical messenger acetylcholine, while acting on key receptors in the brain, which leads to the release of more acetylcholine. It is rooted in an important discovery: the "missing link" between plaques, tangles, and the death of acetylcholine-producing neurons. The connection between these three processes has eluded scientists for years. As sometimes happens in science, its discovery was a fluke; I searched independently for the link for years, methodically and pertinaciously, and finally the sorcerer's apprentice, NB, found it more or less by accident. (His conception was right, but he was a haphazard experimenter.) On which more in a future article.

44 Rossetti's "Without Her" (1881) begins:

> *What of her glass without her? The blank grey*
> *There where the pool is blind of the moon's face.*
> *Her dress without her? The tossed empty space*
> *Of cloud-rack whence the moon has passed away ...*
> *Her pillowed place without her?*

> *Tears, ah me! for love's good grace*
> *And cold forgetfulness of night or day ...*

Ernest Dowson's over-quoted 1891 poem "Non Sum Qualis Eram Bonae Sub Regno Cynarae" ("I am not what I was under the reign of good Cynara") ends:

> *I have forgot much, Cynara! gone with the wind,*
> *Flung roses, roses riotously with the throng,*
> *Dancing, to put thy pale, lost lilies out of mind;*
> *But I was desolate and sick of an old passion,*
> * Yea, all the time, because the dance was long:*
> *I have been faithful to thee, Cynara! in my fashion.*
>
> *I cried for madder music and stronger wine,*
> *But when the feast is finished and the lamps expire,*
> *Then falls thy shadow, Cynara! the night is thine;*
> *And I am desolate and sick of an old passion,*
> * Yea hungry for the lips of my desire:*
> *I have been faithful to thee, Cynara! in my fashion.*

45 See note 15.

46 I am pleased to see that my mock-romantic "lampoon," a parody of the Greek poet Anacreon, hit its mark.

47 Can 5' 8½" be considered "dwarfish"?

48 There was only one other writer involved, who was dismissed not because he told the truth, but because his translations did not convey the tenor of my endnotes. The workmanship, in other words, fell short of the material. Regarding NXB's other insinuations (product-placement, miserliness, quackery, etc.), see note 9.

As for the "chapter of Norval's novel" alluded to earlier, it is reproduced in Chapter 18 below. Norval may have refused permission, but his publishing house did not. My industry connections and name had something to do with that. See note 52.

The reader may wonder at this point why I run my own house (which NXB described, through ignorance, as a "vanity press"). The answer is quite simple: people are often blind to new ideas. Especially scientists. I have not always managed to get my complex research understood or appreciated by some of the more "famous" scientific journals and publishers. And I am far from being the only genius, in the annals of science, to have had this problem! Although I attempted, repeatedly, to explain this to my wife, and to account for the many long evenings devoted to publishing matters, she remained unyieldingly sceptical, portraying me in one English newspaper as a "vain, condescending, name-dropping, spotlight-seeking, philandering monomaniac." Because her English is unfluent, I can only assume these epithets came from her feminist attorney.

49 See note 9.

50 See note 9. For the record, our department director, a supremely skilled administrator, is not "cross-eyed." She has a glass eye.

51 Niobe has a special resonance in my own life. In Greek mythology she is the prototype of the bereaved mother, weeping for the loss of her children. She was turned into a rock on Mount Sipylus, which continues to weep when the snow melts above it. Her story conjures up memories of a holiday my wife and I took to Turkey in 1996. It was to be our last. We hiked to the top of the legendary mountain (Yamanlar Dag, northeast of Izmir), and saw Niobe in stone. "*Du hast mich betrogen,*" my wife said calmly in the failing light. I remember I was wearing Tyrollean lederhosen and an alpine hat with bersaglieri feathers. When we arrived back in Montreal, my wife and daughter moved out of our nineteenth-century (and now echoingly empty) mountainside home, never to return.

Yes, I was unfaithful—I will admit it here for the first time. I am a man of vigour, I won't deny it. Women in the lab threw themselves at me, knelt before me. With a wife who deprived me of what are considered conjugal rights, and with my ongoing studies of Viagra (of the blue-green colour blindness associated with the drug), who can blame me for the odd indiscretion? Does this signify, to quote a Montreal tabloid, that I am "suffering from satyriasis"? Do I deserve to be bracketed with a swine like NXB? (See note 26.)

52 This chapter, except for the last two sections, is taken directly from Norval Blaquière's autobiographical novel *Unmotivated Steps* (London: Faber, 1992), with one modification: real names have been substituted for the fictional.

53 Florence Crandall obviously suffers from mysophobia, a dread of dirt or contamination. More famous mysophobes include Jonathan Swift, Louis-Ferdinand Céline, George S. Kaufman, Alexander Scriabin and Charles Baudelaire. (The Goncourt brothers described Baudelaire's hands as "washed, scoured, cared for like the hands of a woman"; Rimsky-Korsakov described Scriabin, who perpetually wore gloves, as "half out of his mind"; Kaufman washed his hands forty times a day.) For an exhaustive account of the condition as it relates to literature, see Chapter 7 of my *Art et Neuropathologie* (op. cit.).

54 From here the novel descends into bathetic implausibility and stock literary referentiality: the lovers find each other again, and eventually walk hand in hand into Byron's lake at Newstead Abbey in an act of *liebestod*! A modern-day Hero and Leander! Or Tristan and Isolde or Rosmer and Rebecca! (Or, in real life, Heinrich Kleist and Henriette Vogel, Stefan Zweig and his wife Lotte, Arthur Koestler and his wife Cynthia, et al.)

Here is what I suspect occurred, based on NXB's second recurring dream, various drug-induced hallucinations, and medical records from Queen's Hospital in Nottingham. When Miss Teresa Crandall was nineteen, doctors found a marble-sized lump in her breast, which a biopsy showed was cancerous. Subsequent tests revealed that the cancer had spread to her spine and liver, which meant that surgery could not fully remove it. She was referred to Dr. Evelyn Nichols at Queen's for chemotherapy. Tests on the tumour showed that it was insensitive to hormones—which ruled out the blocker Tamoxifen. A scan showed that three tumorous deposits had spread from the breast to the bones in the neck, and four to the liver. With aggressive chemotherapy, it was possible to shrink these metastatic deposits, but no amount of radiation would destroy every cancer cell in her body. The prognosis was dire, in other words. The treatment would be palliative; at most, she had two years to live.

NXB's second recurring dream, and several of his hallucinations, contain a powerful sequence of him running away from a building, sometimes a church, sometimes a town hall. During one hallucination, induced by phencyclidine, the once-lionised actor and author scrawled the following words on the laboratory floor:

Mr. and Mrs. Galahad Santlal
are obliged to recall their invitation
to the marriage of their daughter
Teresa Crandall
to
Norval Blaquière
as the latter is a vile, black-hearted bastard

According to my researchers, the Registrar of Camden Town Hall is certain that NXB did not show up for the wedding ceremony, and equally certain that Miss Crandall did. After her tests at the hospital, she boarded the train to London as promised. NXB was doubtless hiding in a bar, or brothel. He cravenly backed out of his own wedding, in other words. And when he reconsidered, and returned to Hucknall unannounced a year later, it was too late. A week before he arrived, Teresa Crandall took her own life.

NXB's inability to commit is thus not related to his mother's betrayal, as NB conjectures, or to a girlfriend's, as SD believes. It relates to his own betrayal.

55 NXB was about to say "Claude Jutras" (see note 14). By a grim coincidence, Alois Alzheimer discovered the disease exactly one century ago, after performing an autopsy on the brain of the once-fair "Augusta D," a woman in her fifty-sixth year from Frankfurt.

56 See note 9. As indicated in the Foreword, I am leaving this and other instances of calumny intact, as they enrich the psychological portrait of NXB. With regard to his earlier comments on Lord Byron, I should point out that NXB suffers from "created dramatic identity syndrome," a form of schizophrenia, modelling his behaviour on, or assuming the identity of, certain historical or fictional figures. He has moved, for example, from Astérix, Baudelaire and Poe in his childhood to fin-de-siècle Decadents in his twenties, to Regency rakes in his thirties. See my *Le Double psychologique en art: de Cervantes à Cocteau* (Memento Vivere, 2000), in which, en passant, I compare NXB with Rameau's nephew, whom Diderot describes as "... [quelqu'un] composé de hauteur et de bassesse, de bon sens et de déraison."

This may be a good time to point out the extent to which NXB's over-rated novel *Unmotivated Steps* ransacks Proust's *Remembrance of Things*

Past. Compare, for instance, the following passages from Proust and Blaquière respectively:

(1) *Memory nourishes the heart, and grief abates:* Memory feeds the heart, and starves sorrow.

(2) *Our memory is like a dispensary or chemical laboratory in which chance steers our hand to a soothing drug, or dangerous poison:* Love is a drugstore, where hazard guides our hand to a painkiller or poison.

(3) *Memories are enclosed, as it were, in a thousand sealed jars, each filled with things of an absolutely different colour, odour and temperature:* Memories are stored in a million vessels, each with a different scent, colour, texture, and each in a different state of decomposition.

This may also be a good time to mention an incident that occurred recently at a federal penitentiary in Donnacona, a maximum-security facility west of Quebec City. It appears that someone has been shooting drug-filled arrows into the prison's recreational yard from a nearby forest. The drugs, including certain hallucinogens, were packed into straws and then squeezed into the hollow shafts of the arrows. Why do I mention this? Because I happen to know that NXB made at least two trips to Quebec City around that time. Coincidence? Perhaps.

57 NXB should know: he twice volunteered for double-blind, placebo-controlled studies involving nicotine, which indicated that smoking a cigarette immediately before presentation of a fifty-word list improves recall after intervals of ten and forty-five minutes. Higher-nicotine brands are more effective than low. There are many good reasons for not smoking, but memory loss is not one of them: under laboratory conditions, I have demonstrated that nicotine can enhance factual recall.

Regarding alcohol and memory, my studies have shown that alcoholics like NXB, when sober, have trouble finding things they have hidden while intoxicated; when they drink again, the memory tasks become much easier. See my "Understanding the Rise of Memory Loss: Two Factors that Explain It and Ten that Don't" in *Scientific Canadian*, 83, pp. 104–17.

As for cigarettes and Alzheimer's, NXB hasn't the faintest idea of what he is talking about.

58 Byron, *Don Juan*, II, cciii.

59 NB recorded this quiz-show episode in his diary as a dream, or rather a hyperrealist "nightmare" (May 14, 2002), but it was neither, because he was not asleep. As is well known by now, it stems from an experiment I conducted with a modified transcranial magnetic stimulator (VTMS©), in which I altered NB's cortex by electromagnetic pulse, neuropharmaceuticals and verbal cues, generating this complex "memory" of an event that never occurred. I call it a "memory" as it was stored in NB's hippocampus, amidst genuine memories. The implications of this experiment boggle the mind. On which more in a future article.

60 The above note was Dr. Vorta's last. After being anaesthetized for routine eye surgery, he lapsed into a coma from which he never awoke. His wife Anna Sautter-Vorta requested that the story be published by another press, unaltered, save for three concluding chapters and this final endnote.

Acknowledgements

I'd like to thank Helen and Laura for their encouragement and faith, and Seán for his advice, some of which was followed properly. For my research on synaesthesia, the following works were treasure troves: John Harrison's *Synaesthesia: The Strangest Thing*; A. R. Luria's *The Mind of a Mnemonist*; Richard E. Cytowic's *Synesthesia: A Union of the Senses* and *The Man Who Tasted Shapes*. The chemical magic was inspired by both Oliver Sacks and my father—a chemist, drug salesman and child at heart who helped me make nitrogen iodide and other dangerous things. Information on Alzheimer's was gathered from various sources, including the Canadian Alzheimer's Society, the New York Memory & Healthy Aging Services, The American Journal of Alzheimer's Care & Related Disorders, and my parents Robert and Barbara Moore, both of whom were victims of the disease.